DIARY *of a* GALWAY GIRL

KEVIN KELLY

KEVIN KELLY PRODUCTIONS

Cover design by Shamrock Graphics.

Published by KK Productions, Sydney, Australia.

Diary of a Galway Girl / Kevin Kelly

ISBN 978-0-6486335-0-1

Printed in Australia.

Chapter One

WAXIES

Blonde locks swirled with the wind. The hem of my red dress twirled around with the stormy Galway gusts. My lashes fluttered constantly in an attempt to stop the loose strands of hair from obscuring my vision. I couldn't decide whether to tame my skirt or catch the blinding curtain of hair; at some point, I gave up on both. I must've sworn, "Feckin' wind," a thousand times in my head as it did its best to blow me sideways.

We could have chosen any city bar, but no, Rosie had her mind set on dragging us to a popular new venue that'd just opened. Apparently, it offered great live music, hot guys and two-for-one classic margaritas during happy hour.

Truth be told, the thought of fresh, crisp margaritas excited me. That was before my new heels had turned into torture weapons, and my once-impeccable look had been torn apart by the outlandish weather. "It's feckin' freezing, girls!" I complained.

Suddenly I recalled the monotone voice of the RTE newsreader that morning: "Tonight, a Status Red wind warning has been issued by Met

Éireann for Galway and Clare. Storm George is set to bring about gusts of up to 120 kilometres per hour." Recalling his foreboding words, I screamed, "Girls, where is this place? My heels are feckin' killing me!"

From behind me, I heard Rosie's high-pitched voice rise above the beeping cars and whooshing branches. "Come on, Bridget and Laura! Get a move on; the bar's just around the next corner, and it's not going to drink itself!"

"She said that ten minutes ago!" Laura shouted from beside me, wrapping her leather jacket tighter around her. Unlike mine, her jet-black hair remained perfectly in place, cascading down her back in a sleek high ponytail. Laura always looked immaculate, even in a storm.

"Stop whingeing, girls. I can hear you," Rosie retorted. Then she screamed excitedly, "Ladies, there it is!"

Facing into the wind blew aside all the loose strands of hair, and I could finally see properly. Rosie was right; we'd made it. The bar was to our left, its new fluorescent "Waxies" sign proudly displayed above the entrance. The light show hosted within, blazed out through the bar's large Georgian-style sash windows. The bar was huge, far bigger than I'd imagined, and it was packed to the rafters with the in-crowd. Right away, I could see it was as good as the rumours had said. The music was loud; the sound of a live band boomed from inside, intensifying whenever the large door next to the ripped doorman swung open.

"How are you stormy ladies tonight?" teased the doorman as we hurried up the slippery cobblestone path towards the entrance.

He was a big burly bear of a man dressed in black, and his muscles bulged underneath his dark polo shirt. He made for an imposing presence, but when he flashed us girls a smile, it was warm and welcoming. He opened the door for us, and my excitement started to build as the flashing lights from the stage illuminated our faces. The other girls' loud and constant clacking of heels melted into the music's beat. My companions didn't spare me a single glance as they bounced ahead, their eyes twinkling with excitement. It was safe to say our long walk and the freezing winds had already been forgotten.

"Wait for me, girls!" I shouted, picking up the pace, just as eager to escape the brewing storm.

I caught up with them just inside the door, and we headed to the ladies' to resurrect our storm-damaged appearances. When we emerged into the main club, Waxies was even more sophisticated than I'd imagined. It felt wild yet chic, filled with a young and fashion-conscious crowd. From the stage, a crazy light show flashed across the dancefloor, timed in perfection with a thumping sound system. Bands were busy setting up their gear while a young DJ packed the dancefloor in between sets. The well-dressed crowd seemed to be having a lot of fun. I couldn't see a single person sitting still; everyone was swaying with the music, getting right into happy hour. The atmosphere was infectious; the sounds of clinking glasses, laughter, and cheers echoed distinctly through the sounds of an Avicii track.

I turned on my heel, searching for the girls. Of course, they were already at the bar and struggling to carry cocktails. Laura's gaze searched intensely through the rows of tables for an empty one. Finally, she pointed towards a table in the back, jumping slightly in excitement. Balancing drinks, she sprinted through the dancing crowd, only stopping beside me for a split second to say, "Bridget, we've got the margies; you get the shots in. Okay?"

I meant to object, to say that a double round of margaritas was enough to kick off the night, but she was already halfway to the table, her hips swaying to the music, leaving me alone to silently concede to her whims, like always.

With a deep sigh, I turned towards the bar. I noticed some fit musicians side-stage, talking excitedly amongst themselves whilst tuning their guitars. I presumed they were the next band to go on. Sadly, the guys onstage had just announced their last song of the night. I liked their music and would have loved to have danced to at least one of their songs, but then again, I was curious about this next band too.

"What can I get you?" asked the barman.

My mind was in a world of its own, and I didn't even hear him. Feeling embarrassed, I nodded and ordered three tequilas.

"Let the young lady think, will you?" another voice intruded. "Excuse Mick. He's having a rough night behind the bar."

Slightly startled, I turned around to see who'd spoken. Rarely am I speechless, but I was then, as I found myself staring into piercing blue eyes, like the bluest oceans I had ever seen.

My heart raced; nervous butterflies circled in the pit of my stomach. They fumbled in the darkness; their tiny little voices had nothing to say.

"Yes. Sorry, what did you say?" I enquired once I was drawn back to reality. "My mind was miles away."

"Daydreaming?" he asked. I noticed him staring into my eyes. He didn't look away. In the flashing lights of Waxies, his eyes sparkled as they looked down at me. Their blueness was intoxicating, like whirlpools that pulled me into them.

"Something like that." I stared towards the stage, not wanting to make it so obvious I thought he was gorgeous. My heart raced, and I was pretty sure it had nothing to do with the booming bass of the music.

He noticed me staring at the next band setting up on the stage and laughed. A few seconds later, I got a better glimpse of him. The dark shade of his hair, the shadows his curls cast on his brow. Against the bright blueness of his eyes, these features gave him an alluring, almost otherworldly look. I took in his broad shoulders and the way his white shirt outlined a lean, muscular body.

"Have you seen the next band play before?" he asked with a cheeky grin.

"No. It's my first time coming here." The loud background music gave me an excuse to talk into his ear and inhale his cologne. It was an intoxicating smell, oaky and rich, with a hint of spice. I breathed in deeply. Hints of bergamot and lavender emerged as well, and these elegant scents flooded my senses with their raw sensuality.

"They play a mix of electro dance and traditional Irish fusion. It's a bit of a weird combo, but I promise it's good." He laughed out loud and held up both hands in defence.

"I've heard of bands like Afro Celt doing that kind of mix. I think it really gets the crowds revved up." I gave a playful shrug and sent a wink his way.

Looking back, I have to admit, it was funny how easy he was to talk to. He gave me a sense of familiarity, like when you meet an old friend.

Also, I'm not one to make small talk or easily bond with any man whose name I didn't even know. Rosie and Laura were my witnesses to this over the years.

With him, it was different. I didn't have to search for the right words or even think of an answer. It came naturally. Maybe it was the intensity with which he looked at me, as if he really wanted to hear my thoughts. Whatever it was, the flirtatious undertones of our conversation made my heart race with desire.

"Well, I hope you'll still be interested by the end of the performance," he said, smiling as he stepped back from the bar. His eyes scanned me for a few seconds, and he then turned towards the barman.

"Mick, whatever this girl orders, it's on me!" I was about to protest, and then he spoke again. "I'm Conor."

"Bridget," I got out in between nervous laughter.

"I'll come by after the show. I hope my performance doesn't make you run for the hills."

A few moments later, I realised what his playful words and gaze meant.

Conor walked on stage, strumming his guitar. "Hello, Waxies. We are Ocrás."

Grabbing the mic, he introduced their first song as the cheering crowd filled the dance floor.

Chapter Two

Innocent Stalker

Sighing, I sank deeper into my green couch, my thumb aimlessly scrolling down the list of names I'd already searched for multiple times on Instagram. Conor and his mysterious band were nowhere to be seen. Even checking Waxies' Instagram and Facebook produced zero results. Whoever managed their social media affairs needed to be shot at dawn. Feeling frustrated, I started imagining the firing squad. I'd been stalking him now for hours—in fact, ever since my earlier-than-anticipated exit from Waxies—no matter how many times I searched, it was impossible to find him anywhere online. Only knowing his first name didn't help matters, either.

Bridget, are you going completely crazy? My questioning mind enquired. Why are you stalking this guy? Are you turning into some kind of groupie? Does he charm all the girls with those piercing blue eyes? It was perfectly possible. I wouldn't be surprised if many of the women who frequented Waxies were after him.

There were no answers to these questions. To this day, I'll never know why I was so determined to find him. I wasn't even sure what I would do if I did.

True, my stalking skills were rather poor, but it wasn't like I went looking for a stranger's social media account every day. Why was I being so obsessive? We'd barely spoken; I hadn't even seen his full performance. We'd left early, thanks to Laura's unexpected fall. She'd slipped and twisted her ankle carrying another round of cocktails.

What was it about this musician that aroused such interest? These strange feelings I couldn't explain. Also, the ease with which we talked. The skips my heart made when he smiled were far too memorable to ignore. Something told me I had to at least try and find out more. *Curiosity killed the cat, but satisfaction brought it back*, I thought.

In the background, I could hear Laura whining about her sprained ankle. Between moans and dramatic cries, she apologised profusely for ruining our night out. She'd really nothing to apologise for; those damn heels of hers decided to betray us and maybe a few too many cocktails. However, I'd be lying if I said I wasn't disappointed, having to abandon ship so early. Plus losing the chance to talk to Conor again after his show was playing on my mind.

My apartment was small but snug, with an open-plan kitchen and sitting area that I had filled with plants and some of my own sketches and watercolours. The kitchen had a new, marble-effect laminate countertop, upon which I'd decorated with modern appliances, including a sleek chrome coffee machine. It gave the room a chic yet cosy aesthetic. The sitting room had two leather loveseats, one of which Laura was stretched out upon, her sprained ankle elevated and resting on the coffee table. On the mantle over the fireplace were pictures of the three of us on various nights out in Galway. By the door, where my jackets were hung, the girls sometimes left their own coats. They visited so often that the place felt as much theirs as mine. I'd even loaned them my extra sets of keys.

"Earth to Bridget." Rosie started waving her hand sarcastically in front of my face.

Crashing back to reality, I nearly jumped out of my skin, dropping my phone on the carpet. Until then, I wasn't aware of how deep I'd fallen into another world. Rosie snatched the phone without warning, her eyes now fixed on its Instagram search results. Frowning, she looked in my direction. My cheeks were suddenly on fire. I knew what was coming; the teasing, the questioning and the Spanish Inquisition.

Now fully in retrieval mode, I tried to rescue my phone as if I could possibly avoid the grilling that was about to unfold. Rosie then pounced like a cheetah, landing on the yellow armchair where Laura was sitting. The girls squeezed together, staring at its screen, both with curious and excited grins. Their eyes met mine, then fell back onto the phone, and playful smirks appeared on their pouting lips. Embarrassed, I started sinking deeper into the green sofa, ready to accept their anticipated interrogation.

"Well, well, well…" Laura began. "Who's Conor?"

"Who have you been hiding from us, Miss Bridget Kennedy?" Rosie teased, raising a brow.

I contemplated my next words carefully, so I didn't sound like a complete stalker. They were going to scold me either way for keeping last night's brief encounter a secret. Sighing, I squeezed in between the two girls, excited to reveal details of the mysterious Conor.

"I met him last night standing at the bar in Waxies. He was the one who bought the shots for us at the start of the night. I can't find any trace of him, and it's driving me insane."

Both girls gasped. Teasing laughter filled the air with loud excited clapping. Laura cautiously stood up, then fell down beside me, winking as she handed back my phone, her wide green eyes ushering me to continue. "Well, where did he go, and why didn't he join us?"

"He was playing on stage. I was kind of expecting him to talk to me after the show, but well…" I took a deep breath, pointing towards Laura's bandaged ankle.

"He's the singer!"

"Was he the fit singer? That's right, I remember you grinning at him like a Cheshire cat."

I nodded.

"Wow, BK, a real-life man? And here I was starting to think you'd written off the lot of them."

"Ah, sure, lay off her. It's a good thing she has such high standards. She's waiting for her Prince Charming."

I blushed even deeper, unsure of what to say. How could I explain to the girls how Conor made me feel? It sounded silly to say out loud. We'd only just met, but he fuelled something in me that I'd never felt before.

"Don't be dramatic! He's not Prince Charming, is he?" She noticed me blushing and shrieked with laughter. "Oh, girl, you're *smitten!* Our Bridget, speechless over a man. I never thought I'd see the day."

I shook my head, but it was true. My usually calm and collected self had gone AWOL since meeting Conor. I couldn't think straight or concentrate on anything.

"BK, you're such a silly moose. You should have told us! You could have gone back into Waxies on your own!" Laura scolded with annoyance, her loud voice nearly piercing my eardrum.

"That would have been crazy. I'm not a groupie."

"We're going there again!" Rosie finally declared. Despite being clearly excited about Rosie's proposal, I was about to protest. Just before I got to say another word, my phone started ringing. The ringtone blasted through the room, making everyone jump. It was a withheld number. I fumbled with the device before I eventually managed to answer.

"Hello?"

"Is that Bridget?" an unfamiliar voice spoke.

For the next couple of minutes, I listened carefully to the voice on the other end of the phone. I beamed with happiness. The excitement I felt about last night's encounter was now enhanced with good news.

Rosie and Laura watched as I nodded into the phone. I paced around the room, every once in a while, making notes while leaning on the small shelf behind the green couch. By the time I'd finished the call, both Rosie and Laura were behind me, staring over my shoulder at the scrap of paper I'd written a time and an address on.

"Girls! Do you remember the festival job I applied for a few weeks ago?" I squealed, turning around and raising both hands over my head. "Well, I've just been offered the gig!"

A few seconds later, the girls engulfed me with deep hugs. Two pairs of arms started literally squeezing the life out of me.

"Congratulations, BK!" their excitement and squeals echoed around my living room.

"Calm down, ladies, please move aside. They want to meet in a couple of hours. I need to get ready."

Chapter Three

SERENDIPITY

Taking a deep breath, I smoothed out the wrinkles on my favourite red dress. I wanted to put more effort into my appearance, but unfortunately, the clock was against me. After trying on several shoe and jacket combinations, I finally made up my mind on a less formal, casual festival look. I decided on my red strappy sandals and a much-loved black leather jacket. The jacket still looked great. Rosie and Laura insisted on curling my hair and picked out a pair of gold amethyst earrings, also adding black eyeliner and mascara to my lashes. Rosie finished off the look with nude lipstick that she said made me seem serious and professional but still sexy. So, thanks to the girls, my plain outfit had some kind of sparkle to it. It wasn't anything too grandiose or fancy. I thought this outfit looked the part to make a good first impression at the festival meeting.

Leaving my apartment, I quickly checked the address and worked out it was going to take twenty minutes to walk to William Street, the location of the festival office.

In defiance of last night's tempestuous weather, the sun shone high in the sky, beaming from beyond the few clouds that roamed above the damp pavement. The brightness of the day added to my feeling of optimism. The smell of soil and rain lingered heavily around the streets, along with the chilling air that was born from Storm George. A light breeze played against my jacket and lifted the curls of my hair from the back of my neck. It was crisp, light and refreshing.

On the street outside my apartment, I couldn't believe what I was seeing. My favourite oak tree had fallen victim to last night's storm. Her final resting place was tightly cordoned off with orange netting. Men in high-vis yellow jackets stood around her. Talking. Preparing their chainsaws. I felt sad witnessing her final resting place and seeing her broken branches and leaves scattered throughout the street. A few weeks ago, I sketched her beauty from my balcony. I estimated her age to be over a hundred. I'd watched children joyfully climb her lower branches. I took one last look and said goodbye.

Carefully, I checked the street signs ahead and double checked my phone's map app. I was heading in the right direction ahead of schedule. Even so, my heart fluttered in anticipation, and my palms felt clammy. Saying I was nervous was an understatement.

The upcoming Galway360 Festival was generating a lot of buzz amongst the events industry, with many of my contacts eagerly anticipating its arrival. Located just a short fifteen-minute drive outside the city the festival promised to be a massive event. Many of my contacts in the events industry had been talking about it. My first interview was with the artistic director, a guy called Declan. I'd been informed on the phone earlier that he was moving overseas and I now would be required to take on some of his role.

My heart began beating faster with every step. Despite my experience in event planning, this would be my first music festival. Though confident in my extensive knowledge of music genres and artists, I couldn't shake off the nerves.

The competition had been fierce, and just a few weeks ago, I never thought I stood a chance. But here I was, only fifteen minutes away from meeting the festival owner and her crew. With each step my nerves and excitement grew.

I wasn't sure what to say when I met the festival owner Ciara Breen. I'd just have to play it by ear. I had already rehearsed several scenarios. *Fake it 'til you make it, Miss Kennedy*, I thought.

Thinking about music and bands made me think of Conor. The girls' proposal of returning to Waxies certainly sounded more appealing. For now, I had other pressing matters on my mind. I blessed myself, sent up a little prayer to Himself, and pushed my way through the two glass doors of the festival office.

The atrium that I stepped into was modern and chic, with large glass windows that bathed the space in natural light. It was cavernous and echoey, and my heels clattered as I stepped across the polished floor.

The building looked huge. There must have been at least six floors to its modern glass facade. The interior appeared to be an endless maze of offices and desks scattered throughout. I was certain that I'd get lost, given my bad sense of direction. The friendly receptionist was a rather large lady called Mary, who escorted me to the lifts. She then gave me directions to the boardroom on the top floor.

I arrived a few minutes early. Inside the meeting room sat a well dressed middle aged woman working on her laptop. She was sitting at the head of a long chrome-based glass table.

I entered, and she stood up, her lips curling into a kind smile.

"Hello, I'm Ciara."

"Bridget!" I responded, my voice a little too high, betraying the emotions I was trying to hide.

"Thanks for coming. I know it's such short notice, but some of the crew and I have to leave for a few days, so we're short on time."

"No! It's totally fine." I smiled nervously. "Are all the bands going to join us?"

"Well, not all of the members, just their agents and some of the stage crew. I wanted you to meet the team before you started, so moving forward, you'll have an idea of the festival line-up, the crew and what to expect."

The meeting room started filling up mostly with sound, lighting and operations crew. They were a burly bunch of bearded men and had a real festival look about them. They wore flannel shirts, the sleeves of which were rolled up to reveal tanned forearms from days spent outside. Two music agents arrived who'd be representing several acts, including three international artists. Both men were well-spoken, wearing navy suits and were polished in their appearance. A well-dressed guy in his forties sat to my left. Ciara introduced him as Festival Frank. He would be running festival safety protocols.

A jovial atmosphere filled the meeting room. Tea, coffee and biscuits arrived after ten minutes, brought in by Mary, the receptionist. Everyone seemed to know each other. They chatted amongst themselves, exchanged pleasantries, asked about kids, and joked about whether or not we'd get rained out this year. Apparently, it had happened at other festivals. Everyone seemed excited about the new 360 Festival. Just as I was starting to feel comfortable and a little less nervous, a familiar voice spoke from the doorway:

"Sorry, thank God I'm not too late!"

In a heartbeat, I turned around; my eyes wide open, already knowing who it was. My muscles froze, and my heart stopped for a second. Life has a funny way of presenting coincidences. Nothing ever happens by accident, I thought to myself.

"Conor! You're just in time. There's still a few chocolate biscuits left," Ciara teased sarcastically, her joke creating an echo of laughter throughout the meeting room. "Anyway." She continued, gesturing to him to grab a seat. "Everyone, I'd like to introduce you to Bridget

Kennedy. Bridget will be the events manager in charge of programming, marketing and social media." Everyone in the room sent a polite acknowledgement in my direction.

I tried my best not to look directly at Conor. However, I noticed a familiar smile that crept slowly onto his lips. His eyes shone with the same intensity I'd seen the night before in Waxies. He looked even more handsome in the daylight, I thought to myself. The sunlight made Conor's eyes even bluer, like the summer sky on a clear day. They reminded me of stretching out on warm grass to gaze up into the heavens. His sky-blue eyes invited me to fall into them.

After forty-five minutes of presentations, the meeting successfully came to a close. Leaving the boardroom, Ciara politely stopped me.

"Bridget, I'd like to introduce you to Conor O'Neill. You should see this one on stage. He may be a little flaky when it comes to timekeeping, but he certainly knows how to rock the crowd."

Smiling, Conor extended his hand. I shook it firmly, letting myself savour his touch. His fingers were rough, calloused from years of playing guitar. The feel of them sent a tingling sensation through my body. It felt like I was frozen for a moment, too nervous to move and obviously too scared to speak. He took my breath away.

His eyes creased with a smile. "Nice to meet you, Miss Kennedy."

Chapter Four

WHERE ARE WE GOING, MISTER?

Waxies was familiar now. Its lively atmosphere and in-crowd felt like a breath of fresh air. Other people might find the hot crush of bodies and loud music overwhelming, to me, it felt like home.

This time, myself and the girls made it in record timing, given we were spared from gale-force winds and knew its exact location. One thing that hadn't changed was my excitement, walking through the main doors.

After the festival meeting, Conor and I exchanged numbers and from there, we began texting endlessly. Conor's messages and playful flirting had me charmed.

It was refreshing, for once, not to play games with a man. Other men I'd matched with—on the various dating apps I downloaded and then deleted with growing urgency—liked to play it cool, aloof. Not Conor. He was direct in his compliments and clear in his wants, even if they still felt too good to be true. That Friday, he invited myself and the girls back to Waxies to see Ocrás perform.

As I entered the main bar, my eyes quickly scanned the room, I spotted him and the lads onstage.

Conor's band Ocrás sounded exhilarating; their layered fusion and deep bass rhythms rushed through my body just like the first time I watched them. The sound of Ocrás filled the room. As I looked towards the main stage it was clear that the crowd were having a great time.

Their music felt raw, like it was meant to scrape deep into your gut and pull out your most hidden desires. Music that could make you forget all your fears and let go.

Conor was a passionate performer - his lyrics flowed effortlessly through the microphone,

When he sang, his face was a canvas of emotion, his eyes shut tight in concentration. Was he the one who could make me forget my fears and insecurities about love?

His captivating presence on stage drew me in, and I couldn't help but notice how effortlessly he charmed his audience. It was infectious. Anyone could see how much he loved performing. He felt the lyrics as he sang them. Women all around me stared up at him, their faces rapt and their mouths echoing back the words. Watching him, I was impressed with how he interacted with his band members on stage, projecting their energy and elevating their audience. He was a true artist in the zone.

I understood that space. Often, I got lost there with my own art. A space where time stands still. Hours feel like minutes. A peaceful place where no one can judge you. It had been a long time since I'd shown anyone my paintings.

Slowly, I turned around, looking for the girls. Rosie was standing behind me, helping Laura keep her balance. Even a sprained ankle couldn't keep Laura away from the dance floor and meeting the mysterious Conor. The three of us got quite close to the stage.

"Hang on to that one!" Rosie yelled in my ear.

Almost as if Conor had heard Rosie, he turned and pointed in our direction. His eyes and lips mimicked thoughts meant especially for me. He smiled, winked and blew me a kiss. My heart somersaulted, and a deep blush burned my cheeks. In a text, he said he'd do this if I came right up close to the edge of the stage. God, he was bold. And oh, how I wanted those lips. Imagining kissing them sent fireworks erupting through every inch of my skin.

"Wow! He's a hottie, BK! You'll have to fight the girls off for that one," joked Laura, making me laugh out loud.

"Stop teasing Laura. How's your ankle holding up," I shouted as I waved back at Conor.

"It's feckin' killing me! Now that I've seen his majesty perform, can we please grab a seat? I need at least two cocktails to numb the pain," protested Laura.

To be honest, I would have been happy staying right there watching Conor's band, but Laura always got her own way.

A few minutes later, we were sitting in one of the cosy booths near the bar. Rosie and Laura were arguing about cocktails, deciding which combinations would get them both hammered the quickest. Laura was resting her ankle on a red cushion, looking like the Queen of Sheba. Their conversation was going in one ear and out the other. The girls often talked over the top of each other. Neither of them listened.

Knowing Conor would join us after his set made me feel nervous. He said he had a surprise for me in one of his messages earlier. I tried to keep a calm composure.

Our booth had table service, so after the cocktails arrived, I tried to chill out, forget about Conor's surprise and focus on the girl's new conversation about the best length of beards for men. They even figured out how to score them from one to ten based on length, fluffiness and presentation. The girls really cracked me up laughing sometimes. However, no matter how much I fought the urge, I found myself staring towards the stage. It was safe to say I was smitten. I was bewitched by Conor's energy onstage. I'd always thought myself immune to this dazzling energy that musicians exuded. I was usually the type to go for moody, pretentious artists whose work I liked more than their personalities. But not Conor. He was brash and open and full of life. Watching his performance made me yearn for his touch and feel the same intensity that he exuded on stage.

"I guess that was their last song, BK," alerted Rosie as she sculled back her second margarita. We watched the band members put aside their instruments. Conor was now heading in our direction.

As Conor approached our booth, my nerves started to build. I took a moment to collect myself and reached for my cocktail, grateful for the coolness that washed over me as I took a sip. I had been too preoccupied to enjoy it fully, though. The thought of introducing Conor to Rosie and Laura filled me with anxiety – they were unpredictable at best. I reminded myself that Conor seemed to have a thick skin and an easygoing nature. Nonetheless, the nerves lingered, and I felt a sense of apprehension in the pit of my stomach.

"Here comes Prince Charming!" Laura announced sarcastically, hiding her wide grin behind her Long Island iced tea.

Conor's smile was warm and open as he approached the table. "How's it going, ladies? Are you enjoying Waxies?"

Conor kissed me flirtatiously just below my ear as he sat down. His flirtatious gesture sent shivers down my spine and I couldn't help but get lost in the moment. His cologne, a musky and masculine scent, was intoxicating, and it conjured up lustful images in my mind. While his touch made the hairs on the back of my neck stand up, I tried my best to remain composed. As our knees brushed against each other, my heart started to race. The electric connection between us was undeniable as we locked eyes, and I couldn't resist daydreaming about NSFW scenarios. However, Conor's smile kept me grounded and reminded me to hide my true feelings.

"Conor, this is Rosie and Laura!" I said as the girls shook his hand.

"Lovely to meet you both," he said. "Can I steal your friend for a few moments?"

He'd only sat down, and this was such a cliché line to come out with; I must have heard it a million times around bars and clubs over the years. But this time, when he said them, the words made butterflies fly in the pit of my stomach, and I felt myself blush. It didn't feel like a line. It felt like he was actually stealing me away.

The DJ's new set kicked in, booming loudly as we escaped the booth. Both girls teased us leaving, but we couldn't make out their exact words. The music was so loud. Conor held my left hand, guiding me through the dancing crowd while his right gently rested on my lower back. Folks on the dance floor recognised him and stared as we passed through. I felt like the cat that got the cream.

"Where are we going, mister?" I shouted suspiciously, knowing he had no intention of staying around the main bar.

"To the rooftop, missy!" he shouted back as we headed towards a spiralling staircase behind the bar.

My choice of skirt was rather short. I felt relieved when Conor decided to lead the way. His teasing words about my outfit made me blush as we weaved up through the staircase.

From the rooftop of Waxies, we were treated to a breathtaking view that stretched beyond the city. In the distance, the shimmering waters of Galway Bay were visible, while the damp cobblestones reflected the bright green glow of Waxies' neon sign. In the streets below, jovial crowds sang and chanted between pubs, filling the air with popular Irish songs. As the full moon emerged from behind the clouds, it cast a magical shimmer across the historic rooftops and slates of the city's old buildings, completing the scene in a truly unforgettable way. Beyond, we noticed the distant lights of fishing boats heading out to sea.

A white awning stretched across the balcony. Beneath it were several wicker chairs. Each had bright purple cushions. Vividly-coloured bean bags lay scattered around. The place looked cosy. Glistening fairy lights were wrapped around a modern glass balcony. A small stage area lay towards the back wall; I guessed the place was designed for band practices or private functions. We had the place to ourselves.

"Wow, this place is amazing," I said.

"I'm glad you like it. It's your surprise." He smiled at me. "It's nothing too fancy, but I thought it would be quieter than downstairs," he said as he walked me towards the awning. A few seconds later, he handed me a crystal glass. "Would you like some French wine, Miss Kennedy? I hid a bottle up here earlier, hoping we could enjoy a glass or two together in private."

Conor smiled as he poured some pinot noir. As he handed me the glass, I raised an eyebrow. "French? I thought musicians were supposed to be poor."

"It was a gift. Perks of being in the band."

I smirked. "From one of your groupies?"

Conor waved a hand. "I'm not good enough for those."

He was good enough for groupies, and we both knew it.

I flashed him my most sceptical look. "Don't be humble. It's not as charming as you think it is."

"Yes, it is."

He moved a step closer to me, his boyish grin illuminated by the soft glow of the fairy lights. These, and the moonlight, made his skin look soft and tanned, his eyes alight with mischief. I thought of him again, how he'd looked downstairs while engrossed in his music, the stage lights shimmering on his face and lips. My heart began to hammer, and I clutched my wine glass more tightly.

"Don't break that," he observed, ruining the moment.

I laughed and tasted the wine, savouring its earthy flavours. It was very good. *Damn. His groupies must really want him.*

It was cold outside. My jacket was in the cloakroom downstairs, and I'd chosen to wear a white blouse that, by now, was maybe too revealing considering the chill. He noticed and immediately placed his glass on the high table beside him and took off his jacket.

"No, I'm fine," I protested, but his warm jacket was already draping over my shoulders. On anyone else, I might have suspected that the gallantry was an act. On him, it felt natural. As he slipped the jacket over my shoulders, his fingers grazed my skin. As they did, a shiver went through me that had nothing to do with the chilly Galway night.

"Come on, let's find a cosy spot to sit." His voice was gentle. His eyes, I noticed, stared into mine.

As we sat down, Conor slowly moved closer towards me. Our lips touched for the first time; our tongues swam in unison like playful dolphins do, two spirits swimming in an ocean of blue. His tongue was soft and warm, and as I parted my lips, I let out a soft moan. Instinctively, my mouth opened wider, and he cupped my head with his hands, drawing me closer. "I wanted to kiss you like this down there, in front of everyone," he whispered into my ear.

"Don't tell me that now." I laughed, twisting a finger into his hair. "That's every girl's dream."

"Next time."

Between kisses, we teased each other, finished our wine and got to know each other more. We then danced slowly without music to our own magical rhythm. Only the sound of the breeze off the Atlantic accompanied us as we circled slowly on the spot, his lips pressed to my forehead. Each time he ran his fingers through my hair that night, it felt like an overdose of love.

Chapter Five

STONE CIRCLE

The festival's location was four kilometres on the outskirts of Galway, about an hour's walk from my apartment. Unfortunately, the main wooden gates to the site were locked on my arrival. So, I decided to climb over them. Thanks to a hidden rusty nail that caught my skirt, I got well and truly stuck. After a few moments of struggle, my tug of war failed, and I fell, landing square on my backside. Luckily for me, there were no spectators to witness my epic Houdini moment, followed by my grand circus finale.

Once I regained my composure, I checked for any injuries, dusted off my bruised ego, and headed to my planned vantage point. This was at the top of the next hill that overlooked the meadow and Drumderg stone circle.

Feeling inspired, I paused for a moment, then curled my fingers lightly around my pencil. Its thin grey tip hovered over the sketch pad. I imagined the festival's layout, with all of its stage lights in full glory. Lost in my own world, I began to sketch. As I did so, the scene came to life before my eyes: I started to imagine the sounds and atmosphere of the festival. In my mind, I could hear the cheering crowds and their applause echoing throughout the location's natural amphitheatre. Alone on the hillside, the only sounds were the gentle swish of the wind through the grass and the scratch of my pencil on the paper. But in my head, the fans were screaming with excitement as Conor's voice rang out through the night, "We are Ocrás!" Drawing transported me, as it always had.

My skin tingled as I felt the chilled air whisper past. My eyes were wide open, yet I was lost in my own thoughts as I imagined the festival. As the sunlight faded, I took in the natural beauty of the surrounding hills, and the colourful changes of the trees and their intricate patterns in the meadow below. As the sun set, it left behind a beautiful tapestry of orange, gold and violet colours that stretched for miles. All around, tall trees cast their shadows, almost like trails from snails leaving their shells behind for the night.

Few people frequented the festival location, especially at night. I enjoyed the silence and solitude it offered.

As I breathed in deeply, I watched the full moon rise slowly to the highest point of the meadow, above the ancient stone circle. The fading light still reflected off of the stones, painting them orange and red as the sun slowly descended below the horizon. The magnificence and mystery of the thirteen standing stones were the main reason the location was chosen for the festival. I'd read earlier that morning that stone circles were aligned with the sun and moon and formed complex prehistoric calendars. The ancient people who built them certainly had significant knowledge of astronomy, engineering, and what was needed to complete these early observatories. It was awe-inspiring to be around. These stones had markings etched upon them, spirals, moons and other strange shapes. The symbols had once meant something to the ancient Irish. As I looked at them, I wondered what indecipherable secrets they kept.

When it came to the festival's marketing campaign, there were many ideas playing on my mind. I wanted to transpose these thoughts and ideas into catchy social posts. Then, create ads that would inspire, and light up marketing campaigns that would attract a big following. After the initial meeting with the festival team, I had my first vision of the socials and what they should look like. Each group and solo artist should have their own identity yet blend their different styles into a central running theme.

I closed my eyes again and imagined myself walking through the festival grounds, listening to each of the bands. I chatted with people in the audience and felt their excitement. I then walked between stages, sampling the amazing tastes and flavours the food vendors had on offer. The sweet fragrance of Belgian waffles and crepes filled the air, followed by the smoky rich flavours of barbecue meats. These smells and images blended together; the shapes and figures slowly transformed into a beautiful vision. My hand moved freely over the paper's smooth surface, turning my thoughts into art as if by another force.

I was so caught up in my own thoughts I failed to notice that a dark shadow had appeared behind me. I shuddered nervously as the hair on the back of my neck stood up. The shadow lingered only a few seconds; it felt like an eternity in my mind. Eyes watched me.

A voice suddenly spoke out, "Bridget, is that you?"

Startled, I turned around. My sketch pad and pencils fell into the long grass. It took a few seconds for my eyes to adjust to the poor light. I then made out the outline of the masculine shape I'd become so familiar with. His eyes stared into mine; his lips slowly curled into a smile. I was speechless for a few seconds, shocked by his sudden appearance.

We'd exchanged messages all day, but neither of us had mentioned visiting the festival site. It was in moments like these that made me think that other forces were at work, throwing us together. I'd experienced many coincidences since we'd met. Followed by strong rushes of emotions each time afterwards. These feelings felt alien to me. They rushed through me every time I laid eyes on him. It felt exciting followed by a sense of melancholy that made my heart sink. Why was I experiencing these emotions?

"Conor!" I screamed.

"What the hell are you doing here?"

Slowly, I stood up.

"Bridget, it's okay. I can't believe it's you. I sometimes come here to watch the full moon rise over the stone circle. I've been doing this for years. Tonight it's my first time visiting in ages. This meadow feels peaceful. It's a great place to think and chill. Call me a weirdo, but I'm as freaked out seeing you here as you are seeing me..." Conor shrugged his shoulders, and we both laughed.

"Why are you here?" His eyes suddenly shifted to the abandoned sketchpad on the grass.

"Now it's my turn for you to think I'm the weirdo," I said as I reached down to retrieve the sketchpad.

"I came here to check out and visualise the festival site. I know it sounds crazy, but I need to imagine what an event looks like before I start planning media posts, advertising and promotions."

"What's with the sketchpad?" Conor enquired as he lowered himself down beside me.

Nervously, I contemplated whether or not to show him my drawings. Also, it was now quite dark, so I had the perfect excuse.

A few years ago, I was accustomed to people seeing my art, but after much negativity towards it, and a classmate called Stella, who destroyed one of my favourite paintings at a school exhibition, I decided to throw in the towel towards any public scrutiny or commentary.

My confidence had been shattered, and I was no longer comfortable with anyone critiquing my drawings.

Conor suddenly reached for the sketch pad.

"Sure, you could be the next Picasso! Do you mind if I take a peek?

"Trust me, I'd rather if you didn't..."

It was too late. Conor shone the light from his phone over my drawings.

As he looked over them, he lowered his gaze to the page. My art had been hidden in darkness for years, but now, it was finally returning to the spotlight, both literally and metaphorically. He whispered words I couldn't quite make out.

Nervously, I stared at his expression. Conor was the first person to see my drawings in years. Plus, I felt nervous as he was directly involved with the festival. I couldn't make out his reaction due to the fading light. I waited anxiously. I could tell he looked shocked more than anything else. But what was going through his mind?

"I know they look muddled up, but they're just my initial ideas and concepts. I—"

"Bridget, these look amazing!" He interrupted me.

"You don't need to be nice." I smiled. "I know they're quite abstract."

"Nonsense," he fought back, pointing towards the sketchpad. His eyes were shining with admiration. As I looked into them, I could tell he was being sincere. "When I look at these drawings, I see the bands on stage and the crowds swaying. It's like you've brought the festival to life. The details are incredible, Bridget. You're quite the artist. I'm impressed. Really. I'd love to see more, especially in daylight."

I was so flustered yet pleased by his compliments that I wasn't sure what to say. Thankfully, he spared me from speaking with another question.

"What's with the circular stage?" he quizzed as he waved my sketchbook in the air.

I grabbed the sketchpad back, shook my head and laughed. "If I tell you, I'll have to shoot you." Conor laughed out loud and then pretended to be wounded.

"The festival organisers are planning to have a 360-degree stage that revolves. The concept is that the audience can stand all around the entire stage, just like the ancients would have done around the stone circle." I then pointed towards the stones. Behind them, the full moon had started to rise.

"It needs to get the green light from Ciara—it hasn't been fully signed off yet. Mr O'Neill, you're not supposed to know anything about this. Okay?"

"Don't worry, it's our secret. I do love the idea of a 360-degree rotating stage." He smiled. "Seriously now, where did you learn to draw like that?"

"Well, my mum's an art teacher. I used to draw and paint with her lots when I was growing up."

"One thing's for sure, you've got talent. Can I see more of your work sometime?"

"Let me think about it. I'd say yes to a lift back into town, though."

"Okay! On one condition. Can I buy you fish and chips on the way home?" Conor asked.

"Only if you kiss me first!"

Chapter Six

Bobbing Obama

I took a step back, tilted my head to the side to admire my work, and then smiled, delighted with how the painting had turned out.

I'd spent my entire morning dusting my old brushes and canvases. I'd even cleaned the mahogany easel my mum gave me for my twenty-first birthday. All that was missing were a few extra colours in acrylics and oils. I promised myself that I'd stock up on my next trip into town.

For some miraculous reason, I felt motivated to paint again. This urge surfaced as soon as I woke up. I'd have been crazy to ignore this rare impulse.

I was painting the full moon rising over the stone circle as it would have looked in ancient times. It rose with spectacular beauty upon a clear and star-filled night, golden light touching the tops of each of the standing stones as if opening up a tunnel into another world.

These images were fresh in my mind from last night. The canvas had practically painted itself.

I felt exhausted; my morning coffee hadn't kicked in. I'd spent the entire night chatting with Conor on the phone. He'd called me about half an hour after he dropped me home. If anyone had asked me what we'd talked about, I wouldn't have had a clue what to say. However, I would say one thing: Conor O'Neill was flirting with me all night. We talked about anything and everything at the same time. The ease of our conversations scared me a little. It flowed in a way that made time stand still. It felt like talking to my reflection.

"So, now, are you going to bless us with those abstract paintings again?"

I had almost forgotten about Laura. She was sprawled on my couch, snoozing since the early hours of the morning like a stray cat. She'd let herself in using the spare key I'd given her. She came bearing two chocolate croissants and two cappuccinos, so I couldn't have been happier for her early visit.

"Not really. I just got inspired and felt like setting up my old easel. Something tells me they won't be abstract anymore."

"Let me have a wild guess where this sudden urge has come from," teased Laura.

There was no doubt that hanging out with Conor and seeing his performances on stage inspired me. I'd forgotten how great it felt to express all my thoughts and emotions on canvas. On stage, he looked so free, happy, and energetic. I longed to be in that creative zone again through painting. My soul now yearned for more freedom through art. I was still unsure how to achieve this liberty—my creativity and confidence remained shattered by the haters at grammar school—but hopefully, it would return soon.

Laura stood up, guzzled the remains of her cappuccino, and then threw herself back onto the couch. She was such a drama queen. I hadn't touched my coffee or taken a single bite out of my croissant. Laura's, on the other hand, was completely devoured. The only evidence left was the trail of crumbs she'd left on her jumper and throughout her long dark hair.

"So, what's the craic with the mysterious Conor?" she asked as she flaked the last of the crumbs from her hair onto the living room carpet. "Have you talked to Prince Charming since Waxies?"

As I looked at Laura's crumbs, I fell into a daze, then recalled the trail of kisses the night before as we left the festival grounds. We couldn't keep our hands off each other. His hands seemed to instinctively know where I wanted them to go. It was as if he already knew the parts of my body that most yearned for his touch. Even getting back over the locked gate with his help was a breeze. But by the time we reached the car, I was wobbly with desire, so much so that he had to open the door for me. Inside the car was no better, as we kissed so passionately that the windows began to fog. This was followed by the most flirtatious chip takeaway I'd ever experienced. I fed him like a little bird. In between bites, he would lean across the car and kiss me, the gear stick poking into his side. The discomfort was nothing compared to the pleasure of my kisses. I never thought salty lips could taste so sexy.

I suddenly snapped back into reality. "We did. Last night, I went to the festival site to check the place out and get some ideas; he just happened to be there too. We talked for hours," I said with starry eyes. "We got chips on the way home. He then called me after he dropped me off, and we ended up talking until 3 a.m."

"Wow, you talk about it so casually, but your eyes tell me you're completely besotted. He sounds like a stalker if you ask me, just turning up like that out of the blue," Laura teased, her hands raised in surrender as she catapulted herself off the sofa.

I wanted to object to her allegations and deny my obsession, but my facial expressions had already let the cat out of the bag. I certainly wasn't the type to fall for a guy so quickly, if at all. I was a much harder nut to crack. Well, that's what I'd been told. Several times.

In fact, over the years, many men had accused me of being a cold-hearted bitch, even a snow queen, just because I didn't swoon at their corny compliments or cheesy advances. But Conor was different. There was no way I could ever explain how I was feeling. The emotions were beyond words. Our attraction was magnetic.

I'd known Conor for only a few days, but inside, I felt we'd known each other for a lifetime. It was the way his skin felt. The way we talked like old friends do. The way he kissed me like I'd always wanted to be kissed. Also, the way my heart raced at the very mention of his name.

"Give me a bucket, for God's sake. Bridget, your face gives it away. I've never been one for romance, so there's no way I could understand your Titanic love affair. I fell in love once with a Long Island iced tea, then finished the night off with a Screaming Orgasm." Laura laughed out loud and then fell backwards onto the couch to retrieve her purse.

Wow. That girl certainly knew her drinks. "Are you still going to meet Michael tonight?"

Magic Mike, or Manhattan Mike as I affectionately called him, had been my bestie for years. I'd known him since kindergarten and throughout grammar school. Even though he'd moved to New York, we still messaged on a regular basis and met up once or twice a year when he came back home to visit his folks in Galway.

This time, he swore he was leaving New York City for good. He always made out that he hated Manhattan, and one day he'd settle back in Galway. He'd announced this saga a million times, but I didn't believe a word of it... Anyway, I was excited about his return and looked forward to catching up.

Every time Mike came back home, we'd go shopping, go on pub crawls and spend entire days together, catching up on lost time. It was like hanging out with one of the girls. I thought he was secretly gay but had never come out. Well, not in Ireland, anyway. Maybe he led a more elusive life in New York and dressed like the fashion icon Iris Apfel.

Michael always returned with a scandal or two, plus cheesy American souvenirs purchased from the tourist stores and airports.

Bobbing Obama was the funniest. It sat on my car's dashboard, and its head bobbed around every time I hit a bump. Michael's gifts were hilarious, and so was he.

"Yep, I'm meeting Michael tonight. Would you like to join us for dinner and drinks?"

Rosie was away visiting her parents in Donegal, so I'd hoped Laura would be up for a night out on the town.

By the way she shook her head, I knew I had little chance of convincing her.

"I'm washing my hair tonight!" she exclaimed as she flicked the remaining crumbs from her jet-black locks onto my living room carpet.

"But I have to say, Conor has some stiff competition now that the Manhattan Cowboy is back in town," she said teasingly.

The real reason for not joining us was Laura was still embarrassed by Michael turning her flirtatious drunken advances down six months ago. I rolled my eyes and threw her a glare.

"There's about as much chance of me hooking up with Michael as you vacuuming the crumbs off my feckin' living room floor!"

"Nope. None whatsoever!" Laura exclaimed in a high-pitched voice.

We both laughed out loud. Laura's facial expression and vocal impression mimicked that Michael wanted absolutely nothing to do with the female race.

My ringtone suddenly blared across the room, making us both jump.

"Which Prince Charming will this be?" joked Laura.

Chapter Seven

Magic Mike

"Oh, my God! Bewley's hasn't changed in years!" Michael declared excitedly as we walked with the waiter towards a table set elegantly with a white linen tablecloth, silver cutlery, and crystal wine glasses.

Between the place settings, a taper candle flickered in a ceramic holder, casting a warm and cosy glow over the hardwood floors. Michael then sat down nervously in front of me; his fingers fidgeted as he tapped each of the wine glasses. With a running commentary, he slid his blue framed glasses down to the tip of his nose, then critiqued the restaurant.

"It's nice," he conceded, "but old-fashioned. The trend in New York is away from tablecloths and waiters in penguin suits. Minimalism is all the rage these days. Chefs who dress like lumberjacks and waiters who look like Brooklyn hipsters, you know?" I didn't know, but he didn't wait for me to respond. He picked up and examined the wine list. "And these wines... they're expensive, but they're the same ones we've been drinking for the past five years. They should bring in a sommelier, someone who can introduce them to winemakers doing cutting-edge things with grapes. The other day, I had a Stellenbosch shiraz at this little hole-in-the-wall in Soho that was just..." I stopped listening. Michael could be such a typically opinionated New Yorker sometimes!

I smiled and nodded to our immaculately dressed waiter as he approached. Contrary to Michael's unfair assessment, he wasn't wearing a tuxedo, but he looked sharp in a crisply ironed white shirt, blue sports coat, black dress pants, and Oxfords. Less Brooklyn hipster and more Irish lad in his Sunday best. I preferred that, but I could see why Michael thought the place was a bit antiquated. It hadn't changed at all, in the many years we'd been coming here. But that was also part of its charm; it was an establishment. Just like on our last visit about a year ago, the round tables were neatly arranged to one side, leaving enough floor space for guests to dance to live music throughout the evening. The ambience in the room had an air of sophistication. Bewley's certainly was more chilled in comparison to the thumping atmosphere and mayhem of Waxies.

On a small stage sat a pianist who played Irish classics. Impeccably dressed, he was wearing a black dinner jacket with a white tuxedo shirt and silver cufflinks. His red velvet slippers stood out as they tapped against the brass piano pedals. He blended each song beautifully with the soft chatter and clicking of silver cutlery that filled the room. Bewley's was certainly a sophisticated joint, no matter what Michael said.

We knew exactly what we wanted without even so much as a glance at the menu: Bewley's claim to fame was their speciality seafood dish, renowned for being the best in Ireland.

STEAMED MUSSELS WITH
GARLIC AND PARSLEY
*Butter, shallots, garlic, red
pepper flakes, wine, mussels,
lemon juice, and parsley).
Steamed in a sea of white wine
and garlic, creamy and rich in
a thick rustic chowder.*

We'd both ordered this dish on Michael's last visit home, along with a popular fruity Sauvignon Blanc.

Just after the waitress had finished pouring our wine, which Michael declared adequate after a rather exaggerated tasting, I asked, "So, Michael, how long are you staying this time?"

"Oh no, darling!" Michael then exhaled dramatically as he placed both hands over his heart. "Have you tired of me already, Bridget?"

My eyes rolled up to the heavens. I then took a rather large drink of wine. I savoured its bouquet. "For God's sake, Michael, you're such a drama queen. Of course not."

"I'm just staying for a couple of days." Michael then sighed out loud. "I have some paperwork to sign. My grandmother has given me a small plot of land. She also demands that I return home, settle down with a local girl and build a house in her back field before she kicks the bucket."

"Only two days? There was a rumour you'd finally decided to move back for good," I said jokingly.

"How could I deprive all those lovely ladies in New York City?" Michael then rolled his eyes and winked as he sarcastically pointed to a facial expression that mimicked an orgasm. "Speaking of orgasms"—he then leaned across the table towards me and said—"is there anyone special in your life, Miss Kennedy?"

I felt myself blushing. My mind suddenly pictured Conor. I tried to hide my starry-eyed look, but Michael picked up on it straight away..

"Oh, there is? And you've been keeping him a secret all this time, you sneaky stop out?" He laughed out loud, then leaned back on his chair as he sent me another wink.

"Well, it happened suddenly. I met him a few weeks ago at a new bar called Waxies. He was performing with his band."

"So, he's a charming singer? Oh my goodness BK, that's so cool. Sounds like I've got some stiff competition here," he joked, as his hand gestured for me to continue.

"That's about it." I clammed up, then shrugged my shoulders. "There isn't much more to tell. But when there is, you'll be the first one to know." I winked, then sent Michael a cheeky grin.

Michael didn't seem convinced by my lack of details.

"I know when you're hiding things from me, Miss Kennedy. After that epic cliffhanger, I'm going to visit the little boy's room. I'll be back in a few minutes."

I was left alone to ponder my thoughts, but not for long. After only a few minutes, a hand tapped me on the shoulder. Expecting Michael, I turned around in my seat and said, "Back already?" These words died on my lips when I saw a familiar pair of blue eyes staring at me.

Conor stood behind me with an excited grin on his face and a mischievous look in his eyes, then gently grabbed my hand.

"I know you're here with someone, but I can't help but ask for a sneaky kiss and a dance since you're all alone."

Yet again, Conor had appeared out of thin air. My mind started to run wild, and I was in shock. Maybe Laura was right, and Conor really was a stalker—but I was still happy to see him and felt excitement beyond words. I wanted to accept but felt guilty. After all, I was there with Michael.

Oh, feck it, Michael will understand! My inner voice yelled from deep within.

"Just one dance," I warned with a smile, my hand already cradled in his.

As we walked towards the dance floor, I saw Michael return to our table. He frowned and pointed towards Conor with a thumbs up, mimicking funny gestures like, *is he the one? He's hot.*

I rolled my eyes and thanked the heavens that Conor hadn't noticed Michael's charades.

"So, what brings you here?" I asked as soon as we began to slow dance with other couples in front of the pianist. I'd hoped that some small talk would distract me from the electrifying feeling erupting from below my navel. This pulsing desire spread like wildfire from between my legs to the rest of my body, making it difficult to move in time with the music.

"We're having a band meeting upstairs with our manager. The guys are still up there; I've just sneaked away for a few minutes to see you." His voice was low as his hand pressed against my lower back, bringing me closer. Our bodies were now pressed against each other, like lips locked in a tight embrace. The feeling made my head spin. His voice grew even more tender. "By the way, you look gorgeous tonight." He whispered these words into my left ear as he pulled me even closer into him. He then kissed my earlobe and nibbled it a little. Arousal flooded my senses, and I tried not to gasp as his tongue traced the outline of my ear. I felt goosebumps rush over me as my body heated up. His physique moulded perfectly into me as we slowly danced. 'A Rainy Night in Soho,' was being played and sung beautifully by the pianist. Our steps matched perfectly, just like our breathing, as we swayed to the song's chorus. Being so close felt intoxicating, like being close to a volcano ready to erupt. The smell of his cologne made me giddy, drunk on the rich notes of bergamot and cardamom that I had come to associate with him, and I felt my heart beat nervously in my chest.

"Should I be worried about your date?" he whispered into my ear.

"He's just a friend," I breathed, unsure how I was managing to speak when my mind was so clouded with desire.

Conor smiled. "I'm glad to hear that, Miss Kennedy."

We then kissed slowly to the music. Our tongues brushed over each other in soft, sensitive strokes. Our kiss felt pure and innocent, but it made my heart race. It was short but intense enough to leave me breathless. I smiled against his lips, my hands still on his chest. His heart thumped wildly. I knew he felt the same throbbing need that possessed every inch of me. As the song slowly ended, we pulled away from each other.

My heart still cantered with desire.

I wanted more.

Chapter Eight

THE PICNIC

We returned to the standing stones together and on a mutually arranged date. Conor surprised me by bringing a brown cane-woven picnic hamper. I'd never been spoiled by a man like this before, and the thoughtfulness of the gesture made my heart ache. He'd arranged everything like a true gentleman. He claimed the basket was filled with French wine, a selection of fine aromatic cheeses, a baguette, smoked salmon, cured meats rubbed with black peppercorns, decadent dark chocolate truffles filled with caramel and sea salt, and a few other delights. This time, the main gates were open on arrival, so I was spared from any acrobatics. *Thank goodness Conor didn't see me in such a dishevelled state*, I thought as I walked by.

The girls liked to tease me that Conor was Prince Charming, and as we strolled through the grass, the sunlight felt warm and luxurious on my skin, the fresh scent of grass thick in the air, I knew that they were right. Conor knew how to pamper a woman. I was used to being the responsible one in my relationships. With Rosie and Laura, for instance, I always had to be the grown-up. But now, I was the one being taken care of. Conor treated me like a princess, and the thought sent bubbles of happiness through my body.

He unfolded a tartan picnic blanket and began to lay out the meal he had prepared for us. I recognised some of the cheeses as Roquefort and Epoisses. As I breathed in, I could smell the intense creamy, tangy, and earthy flavours of these delicacies on my palate. I realised he'd spared no expense, and its romanticism made me feel like I was floating.

I had time to watch him as he cut the baguette into slices and unwrapped the cheeses from their filmy wax papers. He was wearing a sage green shirt that was loose but fitted, with a slight scoop neck that allowed me to glimpse his collarbones. Around his neck, he wore a tasteful leather necklace, which he tucked into the front of the shirt. But it was his body that held my attention. Conor had smooth, toned arms that looked as if they were sculpted from marble and large, strong hands. As he uncorked the wine, I watched his arms flex and bulge. Veins protruded from his forearms and biceps, and my heart fluttered at his strength and virility. He was backlit by the sun, and the amber illuminated his dark hair and broad shoulders. When he turned to reach for a knife, his shirt hugged his back muscles. I longed to slip my hands under the soft fabric and feel the tautness of his skin. I wanted to run my fingers over the ridges of his ribcage, press my palms into his hard stomach, and lay my ear against his heart.

Looking around us, I was taken in by the beauty and peacefulness that surrounded the festival site. A single cloud towered above the ancient stone circle. Its fluffy white outline and sheer size floated aimlessly against an endless, jewel-blue sky. It moved peacefully, almost as if to admire the natural beauty of the emerald-green valley below. The hillside where we sat was lush and verdant, while the smell of the air was fragrant and earthy. It made me feel at one with the world. I reached out and ran my fingers through the grass, taking in its softness. The day was warm and languid, and the low hum of insects added to the feeling of tranquillity. I imagined how I would paint this masterpiece using a selection of watercolours as I watched the cloud slowly float away.

Wildflowers flaunted their many shades of red, yellow and blue as far as the eye could see. They shimmered and sparkled, wearing the crisp morning dew amongst cobwebs and grass. Their colourful beauty spoke to me through floral scents carried by the wind that circled the valley. Insects chittered as squeaking swallows chased flies all around us in a dance of life and death.

Conor poured two glasses of Pinot Grigio as a light breeze gently blew the flowers around our picnic blanket. I picked up a buttercup, kissed it and placed it gently under Conor's chin.

"Conor, do you like butter? When I was a little girl, we played this game. Folklore says if there's a yellow reflection under your chin, you like butter," I explained.

Conor laughed at my childhood tale. He then picked another buttercup and said, "If this glows yellow under your chin, Bridget Kennedy, it means you're ticklish, and I'm going to smother you with kisses." Conor kept to his word and tickled me half to death. We rolled around the picnic blanket, then amongst the long grass in laughter for several minutes until we both fell back, exhausted.

We watched two blackbirds playfully swoop between the standing stones as we both enjoyed a selection of French Brie. We applauded as they performed a dance through the air to a perfectly choreographed melody. They clearly enjoyed themselves as much as their appreciative audience. They were courting, I realised, just like us. My fingers slowly intertwined with Conor's, and the heat of his touch seeped through my skin. The sensation sent a wave of longing through my body, as forceful and shocking as diving into the ocean. He held my hand gently yet firmly in a way that made me feel delicate and protected. I felt safe and fulfilled. His skin felt warm and rough. The grass underneath us tickled my back while the sun stroked my skin softly. I breathed in.

The air was filled with the scent of flowers blooming. Everything was perfect.

The sun sat high as it evaporated the last drops of the morning dew, giving us some brightness and warmth for the first time in months. I closed my eyes as my fingers played with the soft blades of grass I'd gathered unconsciously. In a daze, I imagined the future. I decided we would come here often, every year on our anniversary, and tell stories of our first date. We would no longer be new and scared, but familiar and safe. I yearned for that day.

After ten minutes, we stood up as if drawn towards the tallest of the stones. It towered above us by at least twelve feet. The space it commanded provoked an uninterrupted silence. Its magnetic presence made me feel grounded and alive. It was untouched, unbowed, by the centuries that had passed since it was erected here. We humans lived such short lives, full of pain and doubt. Our existences ended before they had really even begun. But this stone, how many people had it outlived? How many generations had come to worship at it, to connect to the heavens or the earth below? In its presence, I felt connected to those people too. We had all stood on this spot, in the shadow of this monument, and hoped to find something more.

Conor and my hands intertwined as they traced across its timeworn surface. It felt cold and rough to the touch, which sent shivers down my spine.

As my fingers grazed the stone, the scene seemed to change before my eyes. Days played backwards, suns rising in the west and setting in the east, stars traversing the sky in the wrong direction, as time took me backwards, back to the beginning of the circle. All around me, grass grew long and then short, trees grew tall and then died, and summer became spring, winter became autumn, again and again, until I reached the stone's origin. Thousands of years had passed since strong hands from this ancient time had positioned this monolith into place. I felt connected to their souls as voices whispered to me from the past.

I couldn't make out any distinct words, just murmurs borne towards me in the winds of time. I closed my eyes and breathed in, letting myself drink in the message they were trying to impart. It was more of a feeling than a sound that I could hear inside my head. I opened my eyes again and gazed at the stone. Or was it? They were calling to me, reaching out through the stone, as if beckoning me to step back into the past.

"I've heard stories of this place before," said Conor, bringing me back to reality. "Of the magic it holds. I'd never have believed it until now, standing here for myself. I can feel every hair on the back of my neck standing up. There's a sticky atmosphere around these stones, just like before a thunderstorm. It also feels like people are watching us, yet we're alone. I know this sounds weird. I feel a sense of joy and sadness running through my veins, like an electrical current."

"I feel the same way," I said, although I hadn't realised it until he'd voiced the thought. "As if I'm grieving something I haven't yet lost. I want to feel only happiness, standing here with you, and yet I also want to cry."

Our lips collided before we even realised it. They moulded into a smooth kiss, both timeless and passionate. Our tongues traced each other while pulling our bodies as tightly as possible. As his tongue explored mine, electric and delicious, I felt the heat rise in my cheeks. Kissing Conor was like nothing I'd ever experienced. It was like falling from a cliff, like getting swallowed by the unknown abyss. It was odd and beautiful, filling my blood with adrenaline and lust.

Slowly, I pulled away and met his eyes once more.

There was no doubt that this place had a certain magnetic pull. The stones seemed to speak to my soul, to invite me to dance to a song I'd never heard but whose steps I instinctively knew. It was both spiritual and mysterious. No earthly words could describe how I felt as I kissed this man among the stones. Who was he?

While my imagination was captivated, Conor positioned himself behind me and wrapped his arms around me. The smell of his cologne was addictive and made my heart race.

I smiled, then relaxed into him, welcoming his presence and his body's warmth. My head fit perfectly on his shoulder as if it had been designed for me to rest there. We folded into each other easily, like pieces in a puzzle coming together.

"Did you know that the stones align with the setting sun of the midwinter solstice?" Conor suddenly said, breaking the silence. "Apparently, in ancient times, this period represented a time of rebirth and renewal."

I'd heard these stories before, but I didn't stop Conor from talking. I loved the softness and tone of his voice.

"They say druids made sacrifices here. They'd use enchantments and songs to accompany their offering. Some were animals, maybe others were human. Who knows?"

I imagined druids standing amongst the stones in ceremony, wearing long crimson robes looking mythical and majestic. Their faces were painted blue, and their eyes were wild, the excitement of the night and, perhaps, Ireland's native magic mushrooms coursing through their veins. Ancient chants accompanied Bodhrán drumming as they carried their chosen one towards an altar, offering them up to whatever god they believed in. At the altar, a priestess stood, her breasts bare and milk-white in the moonlight, her dark hair long and matted. The *banfhile*, or wise woman, who represented the fertility Goddess, accepted the sacrifice on her behalf. As the chosen one was lifted onto the altar, the *banfhile* raised her arms, and her throaty call filled the night. It sent goosebumps down the spines of all within the stone circle. Her breasts shook as she began to dance, and the druids responded to her call. The air was filled with the strangeness of their voices. Under a full moon they chanted and worshipped the gods and goddesses whose names have since faded from memory.

Conor nibbled the crook of my neck; his breath fanned my exposed skin, making a chill run to the base of my spine. His touch brought me back to the world of the living, and I snuggled closer.

"I wonder what it must have been like, living back then," I said suddenly, the words leaving my lips before I even acknowledged them.

"Well, it certainly would have been a time full of loyalty and honour. Back then, a man would have preferred to die rather than lose his honour," Conor said, his voice sounding melancholy. "People lived much closer to nature and the seasons. They were much more connected to the natural world and its spirits. They considered trees sacred, especially the oak. Back then, I imagine they would have been much more content and happier with their lives than people today."

His words resonated with me, and I couldn't help but think he was right. Ancient times certainly had their own tragedies. But so did our present. In all honesty, I would trade the peacefulness of the past for the chaos of modern life any day. I thought back to the scene of the druids that I'd imagined. It was a chilling ritual to envision, but also strangely alluring. I had never been as attuned to nature as those ancient people.

"Conor, if you'd lived back then, you'd have been privileged to be here with me," I teased, then suddenly spun around to face him.

"Mmhm..." he responded with a flying kiss and winked at me.

I laughed, shook my head, and then slapped him playfully on the backside. "I'm joking. I would have gone through hell or high water just to spend a few moments like this with you."

Conor's eyes were more serious now, his pupils dilated as he looked straight into mine. "You know, Bridget Kennedy, this is more than nice. I've never believed people when they said that when you meet someone, sometimes it feels like you've known them for a lifetime. But I'm not too sure now!" he confessed. My heart fluttered with his every word. "I know it's crazy." He laughed as he tucked a strand of hair behind my ear.

Maybe they were crazy. Maybe the feelings were too strong for anyone's mental health. They were too cliché to be real and too intense to be called sane. But this was different; I knew exactly what he meant because I felt the same. But if he was crazy, so was I. I wanted to return the words, but I couldn't express what I really felt. So, I did the second-best thing. Swiftly, I turned within the circle of his arms. My hands wrapped around his neck as I pulled him closer. Then I rose on my tiptoes to kiss him again. He responded immediately, lifting me off my feet and pressing his lips passionately against mine. I wrapped my legs around him and gave in to his caresses, letting out soft moans as his gentle kisses left my skin tingling. Eventually, he lowered me onto the grass and pressed himself down upon me. His weight was heavy and reassuring. My body was alive with desire, and every touch sent a shudder through me. Around us, the clouds passed lazily, the wind rustled the grass, and the stones sang out their otherworldly song. In the magic of the afternoon, we lost all track of time.

Chapter Nine

WILD ATLANTIC WAY

As we left the festival site, we decided to take a long drive south of Galway and follow the notorious Wild Atlantic Way. The verdant landscape unfolded around us, rolling hills giving way to sheer cliffs and frothing seas. Neither of us noticed how far we'd travelled. We were in our own little world. The coastal drive felt hypnotic and mysterious, the roads narrow and winding. The powerful Atlantic ocean stretched to the west on one side, while wild rocky landscapes towered to the east. The views were breathtaking. Seagulls circled above the cliffs, their wings pearly white against the black rocks. A lighthouse was situated on one particularly jagged promontory. The picturesque setting resembled a captivating Irish landscape painting, with the rugged cliffs below bearing witness to the ceaseless onslaught of crashing waves. These foaming tides relentlessly battled against the forceful western gusts sweeping in from the vast expanse of the Atlantic. To the east, we saw endless fields of green. They were interrupted only by low stone walls and intermittent flocks of sheep. The sheep looked up and bleated as we passed. It was as if they were saying hello. I rested my head on the window and watched them. I felt blissful and content. The world's beauty matched my own sense of joy and satisfaction. Far behind us, a mist was curling in off the sea. The thick tendrils of white were like gauze against the rugged coastline. In this state of reverie, we lost all track of time.

Occasionally, in between conversations, Conor would bring the car to a halt so we could breathe in the ocean and take in the natural beauty of the Irish coastline. At each of these stops, the salty spray would fill our noses with the sharp, fishy scents of brine and kelp. The spray was cool and refreshing on my bare arms, but soon I began to grow cold. Conor saw me shivering and wrapped his jacket and arms around me. He pressed me firmly into his chest so that I was encompassed by his warmth and musky scent. His arms were strong and snug. We stood together, his chin resting on my head, and gazed out across the vast Atlantic ocean. The soft tones in Conor's voice and the way he held me close to him filled my heart with joy. I felt protected and safe with him. Nothing could harm me when he had his arms around me. It was like being snuggled in a blanket on my mum's couch on Christmas morning, except even better. I'd had many Christmas mornings, but never before had a man held me like this.

Conor pulled into another scenic viewpoint on the outskirts of a small coastal town called Ballyscullion. This time we watched the sunset as red velvet colours blanketed the sky and crowned an already perfect day. As we pulled over, the engine of the car growled to a halt, and the gravel underneath the tyres crunched loudly. We'd been off sealed roads for a while. The sides of the car were caked in dust and mud from the dirt of the narrow country lanes. But this seclusion gave us the best views of the sunset, which painted the sky like a tapestry. As the last of the golden light faded, Conor suggested instead of driving back to Galway in the dark, we should stay somewhere local. I had no objections to this plan. In fact, at the suggestion, I felt butterflies flutter in my stomach. This time I was ready to invite them into my heart. I knew what getting a hotel with Conor meant. I was strangely nervous. Even though I wanted him with every fibre of my being, I'd never been intimate with a man I liked this much. What if I got in my head and wasn't able to relax? What if I somehow disappointed him in bed? However, as soon as I looked up into his eyes, I realised that this worry was unfounded. Conor liked me no matter what.

Much to our relief, after trying several options, we found O'Malley's, a small hotel in the centre of town, that still had its vacant neon sign switched on. The town of Ballyscullion was a quaint Irish coastal town. The main street was lined with pubs, all painted in different colours and sporting names like Keogh's, O'Neill's, and *Tigh Cóilí*, all written in that classic, curling Celtic font. The streets were narrow and cobblestoned. They were lit by tall street lights that culminated in vintage lanterns. These looked like they could have been from the 18th century, except that they were lit with electric lights, not oil lamps. Here and there, elderly couples walked arm-in-arm, bundled up in Aran sweaters against the cold. Many of the men sported tweed flat caps. It felt like we had gone back half a century in time.

"You're lucky we've just had a cancellation. It's the last room in town," reported Tilly, probably the oldest receptionist I'd ever checked in with.

She sat behind an old wooden desk as we walked in. From the nicks in the wood, I knew it had seen better days. The lobby had low ceilings and tartan carpeting. It smelled slightly of old wool. Behind the counter, an intricately carved grandfather clock kept the time. In the far room, a television blared too loudly. During our brief conversation, Tilly informed us she was originally from Cobh, County Cork. She had come to Ballyscullion with her late husband in the sixties. After he died, she continued to run the Inn. She didn't look sad when she told us this, but my heart nevertheless ached. I hated to think of her working here all alone. But she reassured me that her children helped out. Tilly was definitely in her eighties and had kind eyes. They were bright and clear, despite being encased in folds of wrinkles. They twinkled playfully as I wondered how many young lovers she had booked in throughout the years. Clearly, enough to know what we were up to, for a knowing smile creased her lips as she took in our clasped hands and eager expressions.

"Oh, to be footloose and fancy-free again. If you kids are having breakfast, it's from 7:30 a.m. and finishes at 9:30 a.m. sharp." She smiled, winked at Conor, and then handed me the keys that were attached to a miniature hurling stick. Her hands were paper-thin and splotched with discolouration. They shook slightly as I took the key from her. They reminded me of my grandmother's hands. Grandma used to sit in a rocking chair in our sitting room, knitting us sweaters and socks. As a kid, I liked to lay at her feet, drawing in colouring books and listening to her stories of Irish myths and legends.

The room we were in was small. Nearly all it contained was a medium-sized bed, a bedside table and a boxy television that looked like it hadn't been used since the eighties. In fact, it was so old we didn't even try to turn it on. Instead, we joked that it might go up in flames or one of us would get electrocuted.

The room was warm and cosy. It was simple but comfortable, with nautical art set in thick gold frames and a throw blanket that appeared to be hand-knitted.

We basked in each other's company as we sat on the edge of the bed, drinking the remainder of our picnic wine and enjoying the last of the cheese and dark chocolate truffles. We took swigs directly from the bottle and kissed each other between them, our lips stained red and our laughter giddy. We had no interest in going out looking for a restaurant in town. Everything we needed was right here.

"What do you mean; you don't know how to ride a bike?" Conor suddenly questioned as his eyes widened at the confession I'd just made.

"Well, believe it or not, when I was a kid, I was really chubby. My dad bought me a bike for my eighth birthday. On that same day, I lost control going down a steep hill. I crashed so hard into a ditch it completely broke the frame into three pieces!"

I couldn't help going bright red as I recalled the incident. The memories of my buckled wheel and the shattered frame and confidence were still vivid in my mind. I didn't like admitting my insecurities to Conor, who was confident enough to get up on a stage and perform for large audiences. But it also felt good to be vulnerable in front of him.

"My dad, bless him, tried to weld it back together, but I never rode it again."

"That's it! Next weekend, I'm teaching you how to ride a bike," declared Conor as he drank the last of his wine.

"I'm afraid that the train has left the station. You can ask Laura and Rosie. I'm a lost cause," I protested.

"Well, I'm not Laura or Rosie," replied Conor. "I hate to boast, but I am a pretty good teacher."

A cocky grin appeared on his lips, accompanied by a playful wink. In that moment, my stomach flipped, much like it would on a thrilling roller coaster ride. Conor had a way of making me a nervous Nellie.

"Is this the moment when I tell you you'll have to teach me how to swim as well?" I admitted shyly.

I already knew the reaction coming my way. Almost everyone thought I was lying when I told them about the multitude of normal things that I didn't know or couldn't do. But, in my defence, I'd already admitted my rather chubby childhood, so clearly, sports hadn't exactly been my thing.

"I changed my mind. You are a lost cause," Conor declared as he placed the empty wine bottle on the bedside table.

"Conor, stop teasing me!" I lunged forward to slap him on the backside. Conor saw the slap coming, dodged it, and then jumped off the bed before I could get a grip of him. I fell to my knees, slightly unbalanced on the soft mattress. He then burst into a fit of laughter, clearly amused by my failed attack.

"Where are you going, mister? Huh?" I asked, just before I lost my balance again and nearly fell off of the bed.

Conor escaped in laughter to the corner beside the old tv, ready to pounce. I slid across the bed towards him. Conor stared at me with a mischievous smile.

"So, you wanna fight? Shall we find out if you're ticklish?"

With wide eyes, I shook my head and backed away so that the backs of my knees were pressing against the edge of the bed. Conor seemed pleased with my reaction. He lunged towards me, now confident, and grabbed onto my waist, his fingers tickling my ribs. I giggled loudly and fell back onto the mattress with Conor's body hovering over me.

"Do you give up, Missy?" He then paused for a moment and waited for my answer.

But he didn't move away. He stayed leaning over me, his face close to mine, the fresh smell of his cologne as intoxicating as ever. His blue eyes bored into mine, probing their depths, and the air between us seemed to sizzle.

My hands were on his chest, and my fingers gripped the soft material of his shirt. Eagerly, I pulled him in closer.

Our lips brushed over one another. Unlike previous times, this time, there was nothing sweet and innocent about it. Our kiss was rough and full of passion and desire. I immediately felt myself grow slick between my thighs as if my body were welcoming his touch. The strong emotions we'd been feeling since the moment we met erupted into action. I couldn't hold myself back anymore, and neither, it seemed, could he. He nibbled at my lower lip, his tongue brushing the surface, asking for permission. I welcomed his tongue into my mouth. While our tongues indulged in an exotic and sensual dance, our hands had a mind of their own. Mine roamed over his chest, needing to feel every inch of him, and then moved lower to fidget with the hem of his shirt. I struggled to take it off, but eventually, I managed. The piece of fabric was cast away the next second. My fingertips eagerly traced the curves of his chest. I felt the strength of his muscles and the rhythm of his heartbeat. I had been dreaming of touching him like this, and the reality was even better than I could have imagined. His smooth yet sculpted skin was warm and soft. I needed to be as close to it as possible. Touch wasn't enough. I needed to taste him. I needed our bodies to melt into one.

His mouth had left mine and was now slowly trailing down my neck, leaving behind a trail of burning fire. I gasped and shivered with every kiss, my mind delirious with desire. While his hands stroked the bare skin of my neck, I quickly took care of my own shirt, unable to resist the urges piling up below my navel. My stomach felt tight, almost sick with longing, and between my legs, the fire was beginning to rage. Every inch of me yearned for him.

That night began with an electric spark and continued for hours, as waves of intense emotion swept over both of us. Even now, I can confidently say that I have never encountered anything as powerful as that first night with Conor. There was no room for nerves or uncertainty; everything felt beautifully and effortlessly right. As our bodies intertwined and merged into one, an enchanting sense of magic filled the air, echoing the whispers from the standing stones.

Beneath him, I discovered colours that existed solely within me, bursting forth with every stroke of his touch. The sparks behind my closed eyelids ignited by his gentle caresses. In his presence, I awakened like never before. A primal instinct stirred within me, guiding my movements with ease and confidence. There was no shame, no fear of inadequacy; only a profound sense of perfection and beauty when intertwined with Conor.

That night, pure magic enveloped us. It may sound unbelievable, but being with him made me feel complete once more. It was as if a missing piece of myself had returned, unbeknownst to me. I could only hope that Conor felt the same deep connection.

Chapter Ten

Festival Frank

Two weeks out from the festival, some of the main stage and marquees were starting to take shape. Construction crews wearing orange safety vests were busy mapping out the festival zones with multiple flags; they allocated different coloured flags for food areas, bar areas, and backstage areas and cordoned off larger zones where other marquees were soon to be built. The festival site had a real buzz about it. Men in hard hats could be heard shouting instructions and taking the piss out of each other while the usual sounds of hammers and drills filled in the background noise. It gave the whole site the feeling of anticipation. I spotted safety Frank and headed in his direction with my camera.

"Hey Frank, there ye are! What's the craic?"

"Ah, Bridget, it's yourself. Sure it's going grand. I think if I was any happier, I'd turn into a beautiful butterfly, flap my wings a few times and fly away."

"Frank, you're feckin' hilarious. What time did you get here?"

"I've been here since 6 a.m. keeping an eye on these feckers." Frank's laughter was infectious.

"Frank, the 360-degree stage looks amazing. Can I get some publicity shots with the standing stones in the background? I just need you to get one of your boys to move that truck."

"Consider it done! You work away, Miss Kennedy!"

"I'm planning to use a few sneak preview photos for some of our social posts. I've heard there are other smaller stages being built for dancers. When do you think they'll be ...?"

"Sorry, Bridget," Frank cut me off mid-sentence to answer his phone in his usual jovial manner. Thirty seconds later, he'd finished the call with, "Yip, got that boss, consider it done. See you when you get up here." He turned back to me and grinned.

"Yes, Bridget, you were asking about the dance podium stages. We're just getting the skeleton structures up today and tomorrow. The final bump-in starts next week."

"You sound flat out, Frank! Is there anything you need help with?" I asked in between his noisy radio chatter.

"There is, actually! I need someone to help organise some nice ambient lighting for the musician's green room. Maybe some coloured fairy lights or flood lights to give it a cool muso vibe. We've already got funky rugs and a few sofas. Choosing a few lights would help me immensely. You're an angel! And I know you've got good taste."

This man could charm the birds from the trees—or at least make them laugh so much they'd fall off their branches.

Immediately my mind filled with images of elegantly draped bistro lights and vintage lamps salvaged from charity shops. "Frank, I'd love to help with that." I laughed, then snapped a sneaky picture of him.

"Jaysus, girl, you'll feckin' break that camera." Frank laughed out loud, then hurried off as another voice called out his name across the radio.

I paused for a moment between pictures to imagine what the bands would look like. I could see them as they played in full flow, surrounded by an energetic crowd that danced around the 360 stage in every direction. I then imagined Conor's band Ocrás as he teased the audience, sending them into a wild frenzy. It was easy to picture their excitement as he got them immersed in their performance. The thought filled me with giddiness. It was still somewhat surreal to believe that Conor had actually chosen me to be his girlfriend.

The standing stones aligned perfectly in the shots. I smiled as I recalled the picnic we'd had a few weeks back and the connection we'd shared amongst the stones. The spot felt like our secret place now

The layout of the festival was starting to take shape. Plus, ticket sales were already past eighty per cent. It was going to be an unforgettable festival, the kind university students would be raving about for years to come. The field where I stood stretched out several acres until it gave way to rolling hills dotted with oak trees. The trees looked ancient. Their twisted trunks looked as if they'd been intricately carved. Jutting out from these trunks were branches resembling antlers, adorned with lush dark green leaves that gently rustled in the breeze. Against this backdrop, the solemn and sombre standing stones cast a mesmerising spell over the festival site.

When Ciara Breen arrived on site, everyone seemed to step it up a gear. As she passed by teams of workers, I could see the way that they stood up a little straighter and ceased their idle chatter. Ciara seemed to know most people by name. It was impressive. She nodded and called out greetings as she passed by. She made for a powerful presence as she strode towards me, her hands in the pockets of her pantsuit and her look purposeful. From my vantage point, I overheard some of her conversation with Frank and his crew.

"I also want to create a spacious environment. People can watch our 360 stage from every direction as it revolves. Without considering the appropriate flow, the main festival area could become congested and hinder the overall experience."

Ciara had been running major festivals for over twenty years and certainly knew the business. Everyone on our crew loved her, but was also a little scared of her. I had also been told she wasn't a woman to get on the wrong side of. It was surprising but refreshing that there was never a hint of annoyance in the way they said this. Everyone seemed to respect her and the fact that she was fair but firm.

"I was thinking there should be two main bar areas at opposite ends of the 360 with dozens of high-standing tables," Ciara said as she pointed to the southern end of the site near the main entrance.

"That's a great idea. It would free up much more space for the food trucks," agreed Frank.

"From my experience, I think it would be wise to also consult some of our main food vendors and get their input. That'll keep everyone happy."

Her words made me think. She was right—it was always best to keep people well informed, well fed, well watered and well entertained. I was learning from her already. The thought made me excited. She was like a mentor to me.

"That's true," Frank agreed. "I know some of them were asking me about access to water. There doesn't seem to be enough hook-ups for everyone."

"I'll double-check that, but the Galway City Council has assured me that we will have enough. In the meantime, we should check the exact dimensions of the food trucks so that there are no last-minute surprises."

She paused and looked down at the ground, then firmly pushed her foot against the grass as if checking its firmness. "Do you know when the TerraGuard Flooring is arriving? I want to make sure we get that down as soon as possible. Someone could get hurt if it rains and gets too muddy during the installation. We are liable for injuries, after all."

"It'll be here the day after next," Frank reassured her.

"Okay, perfect. The grass needs time to penetrate and establish a firm bond with the matting before the festival opens, and we have hundreds of people walking around."

"There should be plenty of time. But I'll let the vendors know that it's coming and to save their heavy load-ins for after it's set up."

Ciara looked in my direction and then smiled as she approached the 360 stage with Frank and two of his crew.

"Bridget! There you are. How are the final couple of weeks of the campaign going?"

Ciara and I had been meeting weekly for me to go over the social media strategy and for her to sign off on my work. She'd given me a lot of independence. It made me feel trusted and valued. I had worked from home the past few weeks. My work included editing videos for Facebook and creating Instagram posts with Canva. Ciara liked the posts I made, even if she didn't understand all the memes!

"Ciara, it's going great. We've been getting an amazing response, and I can feel the excitement building."

"That's music to my ears Bridget," she replied.

"I've also been putting up behind-the-scenes footage of our favourite bands rehearsing, being interviewed and answering questions from their fans. We're getting the most views on TikTok of all places. I think it's reaching a lot of younger fans."

Ciara smiled and then came closer as she nodded her head. "Good, good. If we're going to compete with Electric Picnic, we need to ensure we're reaching the under-25 demographic."

I agreed and added, "The running schedules are now available across all our platforms, and all social posts that you've approved are on track."

She nodded, pleased. "How're your photos going today?" Ciara asked as she tilted her head towards my camera.

"Going great. The light's perfect."

"Keep up the good work, Bridget." I beamed at her, pride surging through me. I wanted the festival to be perfect. It meant a lot to me that Ciara was impressed.

Ciara, Frank and the rest of his entourage then headed towards a large white marquee that would be one of the main bars.

Just as they walked down the stage steps, my phone buzzed. It was a message from Conor.

Morning, BK. How're the photos going? Could you round up the girls for a special dinner Monday night? The band has a bit of a surprise announcement. We're celebrating. Meet you at 7 p.m. at the downstairs bar at Waxies xxx

I frowned as I read the message. I really hated surprises. Being such a curious person, surprises always made me feel anxious. Any form of secrecy or anticipation would always wind me up like an alarm clock.

I started to wonder what Conor's big band secret was going to be. My thoughts were running wild. Part of me was tempted to text him back and ask what the surprise was. I could just explain that surprises caused me anxiety, and he would understand. But Conor was still discovering this annoying part of my personality. While I wanted to introduce it to him immediately, I decided to let the poor guy enjoy his moment. In the past, other men had found it irritating, especially when they were trying to do something nice for me.

"Bridget Kennedy, just go with the flow, for feck's sake!" I said to myself. I imagined the excitement in Conor's eyes. That helped. I wanted to make him happy, after all.

I'll give the girls a shout. I think they should be grand to join us, I texted back.

PS, I'll only go if you come shopping with me!

I grinned to myself just as I pressed send, knowing all too well he would panic at the thought of going shopping.

Okay?

Relax. It's only to buy some lights and festival props for the musician's green room. It'll be more fun if you come along xx

What is it about shopping that drives men crazy? Turning them into huffy sulky puppies. Is it really that torturous? You would think a man I was dating would like watching me try on cute outfits and modelling for him. I'd certainly like it if *he* did that for *me*. I'd feel like he cared about looking good for me. It was always shocking to me that most men didn't put much effort into their clothes. If they did, they'd certainly have a lot more luck with women. Conor was an exception; he had good fashion sense. But even with him, I got the impression that he'd be sitting on a chair in the corner ten minutes into shopping, bored, scrolling through his phone and barely looking up as I asked his opinion on different ensembles.

Still, he agreed to it. This made me feel super excited.

Chapter Eleven

First Shot On Us

The girls and I arrived at Waxies at 7 p.m. sharp. As we walked through the main doors, I spotted Conor waiting for us at the downstairs bar. I'd never seen Waxies so empty. There were only a few people seated at tables in the back. In the corner, a DJ played soft indie rock that wouldn't get anyone dancing. However, it was a Monday night, and we'd only experienced it packed to the rafters at the weekend.

Earlier, when we were getting ready at my place, Rosie and Laura had teased me relentlessly that Prince Charming was about to propose. They ran through multiple scenarios of what the mysterious announcement could be. These ranged from Ocrás winning the lottery, being offered a major record deal, being invited on the Late Late Show with James Corden, or wanting us girls as dancers in their next music video. I found their suggestions hilarious, especially the marriage proposal. I told the girls to wind their necks in and instead concentrate on applying their lipstick and mascara. We spent ages getting ready. Rosie even taught me how to do wings. I'd never been able to apply the liquid eyeliner by myself without getting it all over my eyelids. Rosie had the patience of a saint as she drew the thick black lines above my eyelids. Her own make-up was flawless, as per usual. Laura looked fabulous as well in red lipstick, a bold wine-red blush and smoky eyes. Tonight they were going to meet the rest of the band, so I warned them to be on their best behaviour. Especially Laura. The last thing I needed was her joking about a proposal in front of Conor. Nothing scared a guy off faster than acting like you wanted to marry him after only a few weeks.

As we approached the bar, Conor's face lit up. This was followed by a wave.

"Ladies, thanks for coming. You're all looking stunning tonight!"

He exuded an excited demeanour and, from the tone of his voice, was obviously buzzing about his surprise announcement.

"Go on, Conor, give us girls a clue. What's the surprise announcement?" quizzed Laura.

I could have feckin' killed her for being so cheeky.

Conor laughed out loud, then in a calm and composed voice, answered, "Don't worry, Laura, you'll find out soon enough. Let's head upstairs, and we'll grab a couple of drinks. Ladies, please follow me."

He took charge and led us behind the bar towards a familiar spiral staircase.

As we climbed the stairs, memories of our magical first date on the rooftop came rushing back. I could still remember every detail, still feel Conor's lips on mine. With a hidden gaze I admired his physique as he climbed the stairs in front of me. The sight of his fitted blue denim shirt clinging to his muscular back and tight jeans sent a charge of desire through me. Also, memories of our night of passion in the hotel came flooding back, overpowering my thoughts.

The clatter of our heels echoed around the stairwell. The girls joked and giggled as we spiralled our way up towards the rooftop. They clung dramatically to the railing and let Conor give them his hand and help them off at the top without making fun of him. They really had heeded my advice and decided to be sweet tonight.

"We'll never get down these stairs after a few drinks," joked Rosie.

"I'm definitely not feckin' carrying you," retorted Laura.

"Don't worry, the boys and I are strong," Conor said chivalrously.

The girls froze in their tracks as their eyes took in the rooftop patio. Rosie even gasped. The transformation that greeted us at the top was impressive. For me, it was an even bigger surprise.

Conor had told me on our first date that Ocrás used this space to rehearse for shows and try out new material. It had a small covered stage area and also an indoor rehearsal space near the top of the spiral staircase where they stored their gear.

I could never have imagined the sight that greeted us as we arrived on the rooftop. The girls also couldn't hold in their admiration; it was magical. They oohed and awed, and Laura even took a picture on her phone.

Conor and the boys had strung up multiple fairy lights, which crisscrossed the patio, casting a beautiful white glow over a long dinner table that was dressed in a crisp white tablecloth. On the table were six place settings. Each had a glass that contained a miniature bottle of Jameson Irish Whiskey with a note that said: 'First shot on us,' OCRÁS XX.

There were woven rattan placemats, metallic silverware and blue-and-white ceramic dinnerware at each place setting. Above, softly-lit Edison bulbs draped luxuriously. They added to the dreaminess of this relaxed outdoor table setting.

Dozens of old wine bottles filled with mini LED lights made a dazzling display. They were carefully placed along the centre of the long table. Others were scattered around the balcony. The bottles were unusual. They came in different shapes, both squat and slender. They had been placed in multiple positions along the railing, in the corners, on the small stage and at the entrance to the spiral staircase. The golden lights were carefully chosen. They winked and sparkled from within the glass. They would be an enchanting talking point before dinner.

Conor then introduced us to the boys from Ocrás, James and Donal.

"Well, if the band doesn't work out, you can always become interior decorators," joked Laura.

Honestly, at that point, I wanted to string Laura up with the lights.

James laughed out loud at Laura's joke and handed her a glass of sparkling. He then pointed up at the decorations.

"I disagree. I nearly broke my neck earlier stringing those feckin' lights up. Playing in a band is a much safer option. I'm James, by the way! Nice to meet you."

"Cheers, nice to meet you. I'm Laura." She clinked glasses with James and then went uncharacteristically quiet for the first time in hours.

James had a certain swagger about him. He came across as the reserved and sultry musician type. He had intriguing deep green eyes and was slightly taller than Conor. He dressed fashionably in Doc Martens and a long black trench coat. Maybe that's what made Laura go so quiet?

Conor had told me the story of the first time he'd heard James play.

Conor was on a day trip to Belfast to check out new guitars, when they first crossed paths. James was busking outside Queen's University, captivating the surrounding crowd with his mesmerising guitar skills.

"Jaysus, he could really play," Conor had told me, "and had a spellbinding swagger about him that stopped everyone in their tracks, especially the ladies. He sent them into a hypnotic musical trance. Somehow his undernourished look and hollowed out cheek bones made him even more alluring, almost angelic. A bunch of women were standing around staring at him, listening to every note. I think they convinced themselves that he needed to be saved, and if they opened their purses, they could take him home with them, wash him, feed him, trim his hair and beard a little, then keep him like a pet poodle primed for a private house concert."

"And did they?" I'd asked.

"Yes! Women had taken him home and then regularly booked him for private house concerts!"

Conor told me he took a closer look, and James's guitar case was full of gold coins and a few notes—well, fivers, anyway. Conor then spun a pound coin strategically into the case at the end of an instrumental, ready to initiate a conversation. The gold coin spun perfectly and made a nice crisp clink sound as it hit other coins in the guitar case.

"Nice playing. Do you sing?" he asked James.

"Nah, I leave that up to the Gallagher brothers. I'm a strings man, mostly rhythm guitar, bass and some keys. What about yourself?"

The one thing James had in common with the Gallagher brothers was Liam's hairstyle and swagger. "Me? Sure, I dabble."

Conor told me he'd already made up his mind the moment the coin started spinning through the air. There was an undeniable enchantment radiating from James. He thought this guy was perfect for Ocrás, and wanted him as his rhythm guitarist. A few weeks later, Conor convinced James into moving to Galway to join the band.

We were all introduced to Donal, the band's drummer. He was tall and slender and had long brown hair and a long brown fluffy beard. He looked like he was from ABBA. He came across as a gentleman. Conor had told me he was a man of few words but was the type that would give you the shirt off his back. He was truly loyal. Meanwhile, Rosie was bending his ear.

Two members of Waxies' staff arrived with starters and placed them on the table; they then topped up our glasses with more sparkling wine. It was Cava, I noticed, and had a bready, almost nut-like taste to it, like brioche or a toasted almond croissant. It was delicious.

A lot of thought had gone into the evening, its aesthetics and menu. Conor had gone all-out to impress my friends. He wanted to spoil us girls and ensure we had a good time. To say Rosie and Laura were impressed was an understatement. Conor really knew how to wow his audience, both on and off the stage.

It had rained earlier. That brought with it a slight damp chill on the breeze. I didn't mind, as I had a warm jacket. The girls, on the other hand, had short skirts, bare legs and light cardigans. They were starting to look a little chilly. You'd think that they'd know how to dress for Galway weather after all this time living here, but no. Laura and Rosie didn't mind the cold and were distracted by the drinks and the cosy setting. Besides, they'd rather be wined, dined and dolled up than sitting at home in their pyjamas on a Monday night.

Almost as if he'd read my mind, Mick, the barman from downstairs appeared, as he wheeled out a large gas mushroom heater from a rooftop storeroom. He placed it at the top of the table, then lit the gas. It ignited with a loud thud. He winked at Conor and said, "Horse, gimme a shout if you need anything."

Jaysus, this man has some pull around here, I thought to myself.

Conor pulled out a seat for me at the table. He promptly took his place beside me, then intertwined his fingers with mine underneath the table.

Everyone else sat down. I didn't pay much attention to them, I was lost in the magical ambience Conor and the lads had created on the rooftop. My eyes travelled to and from the lights. I also admired the flowers that dotted the centre of the table. White and red roses intermingled in rose-gold round glass vases set in delicate brass stands. It was breathtaking. It felt like we were at a chic rooftop restaurant in Barcelona, not on the rooftop of a club in Galway.

"Cheers, everyone! First drink is on Ocrás, so let's all do a shot of Jameson's to kick off the night," Conor said as he turned towards me and kissed me.

As we hoisted our glasses into the air, I took a mental snapshot of everyone's facial expressions. All six of us glowed under the lights. I felt truly grounded. As best I could, I tried to savour the moment. I wanted to remember this forever. On Conor's lead, we toasted "To Ocrás!" and all six of us downed the whiskey.

I listened to the conversations that flowed around the table. Laura was in front of me, trying to teach James the best cocktail combinations she'd learned on a recent trip to London. Rosie was next to Donal, laughing and giggling. She tried to explain how she and Laura graded beards from one to ten. Also, the rules associated with judging them. Donal seemed to find this hilarious and was eager to get his rating.

After a few minutes of whispering, they decided to give Donal's beard an eight out of ten, and James's score was a seven. James laughed generously at this, although I thought I saw him eyeing Donal's beard, as if wondering what it had that he didn't. Everyone was having great craic and laughing with each other as we each enjoyed the roasted stuffed mushroom starter.

"What's the most important instrument in the band, Conor?" Laura asked mischievously.

He took his time, looking around the table at all his band members before returning his gaze to Laura, who was wickedly waiting for his response.

"You can't say everyone is important, by the way," Rosie chimed in. Conor laughed.

"I think the most important instrument in the band is its soul," he answered as he poured everyone more wine.

"You aren't getting away so easily, champ. Explain that." Laura chuckled.

"If you take away the guitar, drums and vocals, you are left with the humans, the guys who wield the instrument. The collective soul is the most important instrument. It is what we string up each time we want to make music. It is the life force of our music that connects us to the audience," Conor replied.

"Aw," Rose cooed. James nodded in agreement, as did Donal.

"Deep Conor, very deep, but not a bad answer at all. No wonder BK likes you. Let's all drink to that!" Laura replied as she raised her glass high in the air.

Rosie drifted off towards the balcony with Donal. They sat off to the corner after their main course, talking and giggling like school children. Laura was at the other side, staring out into the street below while chatting animatedly with James. Everyone seemed to be having a great time.

Conor held me close to his chest. No words passed between us then. We just savoured the beauty of the evening and the lights. I could not quite reconcile all the feelings that surged through my pulsing heart as I watched a star on the distant horizon. On the one hand, I was happier than I had ever been in my life. On the other, I couldn't shake the feeling that something was about to go wrong. A sense of dread lingered in the back of my mind, persistently nagging at me. Everything was going well. *Too* well. Conor was handsome, thoughtful, good with my friends and the lead singer in a band I loved. We didn't fight. In fact, it was so easy to talk to him and be around him that I felt as if I had known him forever. But in my experience, if something seems too good to be true, it usually is.

As these thoughts played through my mind, I was quiet. I simply tried to enjoy the atmosphere. My head was resting on Conor's shoulder, my hand wrapped around his, my eyes scanning the scene before me. The happiness I felt when I saw my friends get along with the guys in the band was beyond words.

It was refreshing to see the girls accepting Conor. They disliked previous boyfriends I dated or showed any interest in. With Conor, it was different. They'd warmed to him almost immediately—not that they had any reason not to. It seemed like my heart and mind weren't just playing tricks on me. Conor was indeed as perfect as I imagined him to be. But there it was again: the feeling of dread. Conor did indeed seem perfect. That made me afraid. No one was perfect. So when was this bubble going to burst?

When Laura finished her story, Conor smiled and gave his band members a meaningful glance. Then he started to tap his glass to get everyone's attention. They seemed to understand him immediately and fell silent. Conor stood up beside me, but he still held my hand. They came trickling back, smiles on their faces. It was then that I recalled the night wasn't over yet. He still had the surprise announcement.

"Ladies, we are so glad you could all join us this evening. Good news isn't as exciting if it's not celebrated and shared with friends."

I stared at his face as he spoke, the words falling from his mouth the same way his songs did: smoothly, layered with beauty as he picked his words one after the other. He paused, a nervous smile playing across his face.

Even though Conor was about to reveal the surprise, I felt anxious. Curiosity rushed through me like a nervous wave. I felt my heart beat. Laura and Rosie couldn't be right, could they? There was no way he was going to propose to me... right?

"We are very pleased that you honoured us with your company tonight. As you know, we've got some great news," he said with a big grin. Laura gave a hoot.

Rose yelled, "Hear, hear!" and I smiled, returning my gaze towards Conor.

"I don't really know how to give speeches, so I will just come out and say it. We have been invited to play in Sydney, Australia, to perform at a huge festival in Hyde Park sponsored by Jameson's Irish Whiskey. Hence the shots of whiskey earlier."

Elation rushed through me. Immediately, I jumped out of my seat and hugged Conor. I threw my arms around his neck and kissed him. Laura and Rosie yelped happily and hugged the boys, congratulating them. Ocrás really deserved this opportunity. Their music needed to be heard, and the world deserved to see them on bigger stages.

"I am so happy for you, Conor," I whispered in his ear, feeling the tears well up inside me and trying my best to hold them back. It wasn't just elation that I felt, although I didn't want him to know that. It was also a selfish sadness at the thought of him going so far away from me.

"Thank you, Bridget." I could hear the emotion in his voice, my arms still wrapped around his neck, my head buried now into his chest.

"That's enough, you two!" Laura shouted. We broke it off with some laughter, turning to face the others. With short hugs, I passed my congratulations to the band and turned to face Conor.

"When is the festival?" I asked.

"This weekend," he replied.

"Wait, what? How is that possible? Festivals book their performers months in advance," I said.

"We got the call only a few days ago. They had originally booked a band from Dublin, but they couldn't make it. Something happened internally, and they've had to pull out. So then we got the call. I actually think Ciara Breen had something to do with it. I've been dying to tell you, but we decided it was such good news we should celebrate. So that's why we're all here tonight. Jameson's have agreed to sponsor our flights and accommodation."

"Oh, sad news for the other band, their loss, your gain. I am so happy for you!" I said again, hugging him once more. "When are you getting back?"

"We fly from Dublin on Wednesday morning. We're playing at the festival on Saturday night, then leaving Sydney Sunday night. So we've plenty of time to get back for Galway360."

"That's a relief. Ciara Breen and I would throttle you guys if you pulled out at the last-minute."

I really was so happy for Conor. He had earned this. Anything could happen now to make his dreams come true. Maybe a producer would hear them play in Sydney and sign them to a record company. The thought made me simultaneously ecstatic and sick to my stomach. Conor, a famous musician on the world stage, with thousands of women throwing themselves at him every day...

"You two better not start kissing again," Laura teased, then grabbed James and pulled him towards the balcony to show him her favourite bars in Galway.

Just after midnight, Conor held my hand affectionately as we walked through Eyre Square towards my apartment. University students were out and about, drinking on benches and huddled together on the grass, surreptitiously passing joints. It was cool but not cold, one of those perfect Galway summer nights when the whole town was abuzz. A queue of drunk lads had formed outside O'Connell's. They were laughing loudly amongst themselves while the smell of pizza wafted across to us from Dough Bros.

Just before midnight, James and Donal had helped get the girls down the spiral staircase after some hilarious moments and Laura losing both shoes. Then Laura and Rosie jumped in a cab waiting outside Waxies.

"Can we stay out a bit longer?" I asked.

"What do you have in mind?"

"Let's have a walk around Eyre Square?" I suggested.

The sky was dotted with stars. All the constellations were out tonight. Conor pointed towards the Big Dipper while I sought Sirius, the brightest star in the sky.

Conor felt like my Sirius now.

"Did I ever tell you about my first gig?" he asked.

"No, tell me."

"I sang in a tiny bar with about five people, including myself and the barman. I didn't mind. I just wanted to get some experience."

I turned to look at him as his voice grew wistful.

"The pay was zero. A few pints, but I didn't mind. All I wanted to do was sing. I went there every Monday night and sang my heart out."

"Now you will be singing to thousands of people," I said.

He nodded. Above us, I thought I saw Sirius blink. My hand stretched out and found Conor's hand. We sat in that silence, staring up into the sky. It struck me then that where he was going, when he looked up into the night sky, he wouldn't see the same stars that I did. Not even Sirius, guiding him back to me.

"I'm going to miss you, Conor O'Neill."

"Me too, missy."

Chapter Twelve

Bon Voyage

I've always dreaded airports. No matter who I'm dropping off or where I'm heading, old chapters in life I'm leaving behind or new beginnings. For me, airports always evoke feelings of pain, loss or nostalgia. These feelings can make you realise how temporary life is. Everyone becomes a memory. Even lovers who have spent an entire lifetime together. When one of them dies, the other is left with only a recollection. It frightened me to think that everyone I loved, including Conor, would one day die. Someday, he would turn to dust and become just a memory.

Goodbyes are tricky, even at the best of times. They can be emotionally draining and painful, especially in public settings. Or they're anti-climactic, and you're left feeling as if you wasted your last moments with that person. But when Conor and the boys needed a lift to Dublin Airport, I volunteered to drive them. I knew it would be difficult to say goodbye to Conor in front of everyone at the airport. However, this small gesture made me feel part of their Australian trip. Anyway, it was the least I could do to help them out.

We left Galway around 7:30 a.m. James and Donal were still half-asleep, curled up in the backseat. Conor was wide awake and sat in the front with me. It started to rain as we left, but the wet weather was behind us when we reached Athlone. A dark cloud hovered above the west ominously. We passed endless fields of sheep and estates of terraced stone houses as Conor played me songs he thought I'd like. After a while, I asked what other bands would be on the programme at the Australian festival. He played me some of their music as well. We had a great laugh about the bands we liked and bands that didn't appeal. Conor also speculated about the musicians he thought he'd get along with. I felt a hard knot of despair in my heart between the laughter. I desperately wanted to be in Sydney with Conor when he met the other bands. The thought of us being apart from each other was unbearable.

All too soon, the drive was drawing to a close. I saw the signs for Dublin Airport like they were warrants for my own arrest.

We arrived at Dublin Airport's Terminal One shortly after 9am. Their flight was leaving around midday, so they had plenty of time to check in their instruments and luggage. Conor asked me to park the car and come in with him. As the guys unloaded the last of their luggage and music gear out of my car, I stood off to the side with Conor and tried to memorise as many of his features as possible. I thought to myself these mental images would be all I had to keep me company until his return. He looked so cute with his guitar on his back, like someone who was about to busk his way across Europe. Each image sent an agonising stab of love through my heart. How had I been lucky enough to meet this man? Out of everyone, he had chosen me.

Conor stood confidently at the check-in desk, his passport in one hand and his other holding tightly onto mine. Even though he was only leaving for less than a week, it still felt painful to say goodbye. As the seconds ticked closer to when he would leave, I found myself growing even more anxious and depressed. The tears pricked at my eyes with fearful urgency. I was determined not to let Conor see me cry, but this was becoming harder and harder. It was taking a great deal of effort to hold the tears in. Anger even sprouted from me, unbidden, when the woman behind the check-in desk smiled sweetly at Conor. I wasn't really jealous of her. But it was easier to be angry than it was to be sad.

Meanwhile, my insides were churning wildly. I thought I might be sick. My stomach felt like it had tied itself into a knot, and my heart ached. I'd heard the term "heartache" before, but never in my life had I felt it. It was exactly what it sounded like. The left side of my chest hurt so badly that I thought my internal organ was going to split in two. These feelings felt bizarre to me, and I knew it was because Conor was leaving.

I read recently in a magazine that loving someone can feel great, almost like a high. But, when a relationship goes astray or when someone is leaving, those feel-good chemicals take a nosedive and wreak havoc on your love-high body. It's like a love hangover, or more aptly, love withdrawal. As my legs began to shake and my heart hammered with anxiety, I knew I was experiencing the symptoms of love withdrawal.

I looked at Conor fondly as he checked in, not wanting to let go of his hand. Since the first festival meeting, we'd talked and messaged each other non-stop. This familiarity, once so foreign to me, was now the most comforting part of my life.

Over the last few weeks, it felt like Conor was always next to me. We talked all the time, in person, through messages or on the phone. It felt like he was never far away. Now he would be on the other side of the world. This filled me with anxiety. My mum had always talked about the anxiety she felt when her children were far from her. However, I had never understood it until this moment. If anything were to happen to Conor, it would take me at least a day to get to him—and that was if I could afford a last-minute flight to Australia, which I probably couldn't. Even though I knew nothing would happen, my mind seemed to want to find the worst-case scenario.

Instead, I tried to focus on how important this trip was for him and the future of the band.

Ocrás deserved success. The gig in Sydney could be a taste of things to come. A stepping stone. Sometimes new opportunities are waiting just around the next corner. When preparation meets opportunity. Conor was prepared. Hopefully, this trip would open more doors and lead to new and exciting adventures for Ocrás. I wasn't going to ruin that by voicing my anxieties and fears.

I looked at him through a strand of hair as my right thumb nervously drew patterns on the back of his hand. These touches would soon be over. I'd have to wait a whole week to feel his skin under mine again. Every moment I touched him now felt precious and all too short. I wanted to remember every detail of his skin, memorise every inch of his body. I had certainly gotten busy memorising the more secret parts of him the night before.

James and Donal had already checked in. As they passed by us, Donal yelled excitedly, "Conor, we'll see you in the bar near the departure lounge!"

James then smiled at me and said, "Bridget, thanks a million for driving us reprobates to the airport. Trust us, you aren't going to lose him for long. We'll bring him back to you in one piece. If anything, we are doing you a favour by taking this big eejit off your hands for a few days!"

Even though my heart felt heavy, I couldn't help but laugh. James has the best sense of humour. I shook my head at his fun banter and gave both lads a huge hug. When they had disappeared behind the glass doors of the departure terminal, I turned to look into Conor's eyes. My hand was in my pocket now, fidgeting with the Claddagh bracelet I'd bought along. I was hesitant, unsure whether he would find my intention silly. I didn't want to come off as stupid and make a scene when he was only leaving for a few days.

While my heart battled with my head, Conor noticed I had something in my pocket. His eyes travelled between my gaze and my fidgeting hand, both brows raised in question. Conor made a curious smirk that became a full-blown smile. It was infectious, causing me to smile with him.

"What have you got there, missy?"

"I – I know it's kind of lame and corny, but..." I trailed off as I opened my palm, revealing the leather Claddagh bracelet. "I saw this about a week ago in town, and I bought it for you. I didn't know when to give it to you, but when you announced you were flying halfway around the world... I thought it could keep you safe and maybe bring you some luck."

Conor looked down at the bracelet, curiosity sparkling through his dilated pupils. To my intense relief, he didn't seem to find it corny. In fact, he looked touched.

I wasn't used to talking like that. I had never been a person full of emotions and gentle gestures. No guy ever made me want to do such cheesy yet thoughtful things. Maybe, I'd changed!

"I... I don't know what to say!" he whispered, his eyes meeting mine once more. He was looking at me softly, even reverently. Then he held out his hand.

I smiled, then grabbed his wrist with both hands. "You don't have to say anything. Just make sure you tell every Aussie girl that this is from your Irish girlfriend," I joked as I slipped it onto his wrist.

The bracelet was made of braided leather strips of different shades of brown that came to meet behind a silver Claddagh metallic band. It wasn't anything expensive or fancy, but it was something that, I believed, suited him.

"So, the bracelet isn't just to protect me?" he teased as he lowered his lips onto mine.

"It will protect you and bring you luck!" I said in defence.

"I'm only going away for a few days, you know?' he whispered softly in my ear.

"I know I'm being a sad puss, but you'll be miles away from me."

"I feel our hearts are closer than ever, just like that Claddagh bracelet," he said, placing my hand on his chest. I'd never felt more connected to him than in that moment. We gazed longingly into each other's eyes. I was sure that my heart would burst from the effort of containing everything that I felt.

"I'll miss those lovely hands," he winked mischievously.

"You're so cheeky, Mr Musician," I said. He always knew how to lighten the mood and make me laugh when I was sad.

I grabbed his hands, holding them tight as we stared into each other's eyes. I was not usually one to be possessive or anything, but everything felt different with Conor. He aroused feelings inside of me that I never knew existed. The thought that he might prefer another woman over me had rarely entered my mind before this trip. On the odd occasions it had, I had brushed it aside. The intensity of our connection was too sacred to allow such profane musings. But now, as he stood on the verge of a journey that I couldn't make with him, jealousy stole into my heart. I felt its black slither, and I hated it. It polluted our love.

Jealousy twisted its way around my thoughts as I gazed up into his blue eyes. How long does the memory of love last? Does a man forget his beloved when she is far from him? Conor was trustworthy, but no one on earth could love someone forever, could they? Surely, if we lived two hundred years, five hundred, or even a thousand, we would not be monogamous. The intensity of love could not be sustained over such a length of time. And, no matter how much we might admire and care for each other, we would, eventually, seek the burning fire of new love again.

I blinked, suddenly scared that Conor could read the dark thoughts that were hidden behind my eyes. I was being silly. Conor was only leaving for a few days. And yet...

My blood called to me. It urged me to throw myself at his feet, to beg him to love me forever. Where were these strange emotions coming from?

Conor bent down and planted a long kiss on my lips, then another on my forehead, before turning to walk towards departures. The place where his lips had touched me was like a talisman. I wanted to press my fingers to it and feel the wetness of his kiss as if it would help me hold onto the person.

"I gotta go."

"Wait!" I said. I didn't know what I wanted him to do. He couldn't stay. Prolonging the goodbye was only making it hurt more. Maybe I wanted some kind of reassurance. Maybe I wanted him to tell me that I had nothing to fear.

Conor didn't say anything. He just grabbed me and kissed me again, then pulled me closer to him inside his long coat.

His breath fanned my face, and my entire body burned with desire. I wilted against him, awaiting his final touch before departure. But it never came.

"I'll see you soon." He gently kissed my cheek. Then he turned and walked away.

I watched him disappear behind the glass doors of the departure terminal.

Tears welled up inside me. I didn't know how I was going to drive back across Ireland in this state. The pain in my chest was so acute that if I hadn't known it was sadness, I would have thought something was seriously medically wrong with me. I stared at where Conor had disappeared. A small, selfish part of me hoped that he would emerge from it and tell me that he had changed his mind and couldn't leave me. But I didn't want that, not really. I wanted this opportunity for him and Orcás. Still, I couldn't help but feel like my heart was breaking in two. It didn't matter if what I was feeling was disproportionate to the brevity of his absence. I was gripped by a horrible feeling, as if I would never see Conor again. It was irrational, but it was potent. Every inch of me felt sick with dread.

The sadness I felt at that moment was beyond words.

I just couldn't understand why.

Chapter Thirteen

THE EMERALD RING

A ray of pure sunlight pierced through the white clouds above. Its light cascaded upon swaying blades of grass below like a thousand twinkling opals. Golden light caressed the standing stones all around me, almost like a scene from an enchanted tale. I smiled and reached towards the tallest stone, my fingers stretched across its rough, mossy surface.

All around me, sycamore seeds fell gently, the amber seeds glinting in the golden sunlight. They swirled through the air like a million tiny ballerinas pirouetting and sashaying across a stage, like soft flakes of gold streaming through the crisp, clean morning air.

The clothes I was wearing felt peculiar at first, a close fit to my body. I looked down and was surprised to see that I was wearing a full-length dress. The gown was an earthy, dark brown colour and flared out around my ankles. It was unlike anything I'd worn before. My hands slipped over the material, feeling the thickness of the fabric. Everything I was wearing was so different, and yet I felt so at home in them.

The under-tunic was made of white linen, and over it, a long ankle-reaching tunic.

My long brown gown felt feminine and warm, with its bodice tailored to fit and embrace every curve of my body. I enjoyed the feminine feeling of the full woollen skirts as they swished around my ankles. Each skirt was stitched with golden threads that swirled across the front in beautiful embroidery. An elaborate design was embroidered into the front of the bodice. My fingers traced it, and I realised that it was a harp.

My hair was styled differently, too. My curls were drawn toward the back of my head, and although I couldn't see it, I felt a butterfly-shaped hair clip holding them in place. The touch of its smooth metal felt foreign against my skin. The craftsmanship was delicate and deliberate. I could tell that it had taken a long time to fashion.

Suddenly, the loud hollow croak of a raven made me jump. I turned quickly in its direction. Through the mist that clung to the spindly tree branches, I saw a tall oak tree. Its trunk was as wide as several men, and its bark was wrinkled with knotted grooves. The mist appeared to be coming from the tree, although I knew this was impossible. It lay like a cloak along its branches and slipped between its leaves like a fine silk cloak through the fingers.

In the hollow of the tree was a raven.

His feathers were striking, jet-black yet full of life, with an iridescent sheen that danced over his body as he moved. He was more beautiful than any bird I had ever seen. He rustled his wings, and its long feathers fanned the surrounding leaves.

The raven seemed to be looking towards me then, at something far beyond its reach. His deep rasping call spoke of all its desires and the places he had yet to see. His eyes were yellow and flickered as if a flame was nestled within them, as if ancient wisdom was buried deep behind the irises. This creature, I somehow knew, was there to guide me. Smiling, I approached him, unaware I had stepped outside the stone circle.

The grass blades poked at my bare feet, tickling my senses and grounding me closer to the natural beauty of the emerald-green valley that surrounded me. With each step, my feet sank into the earth. It had rained recently, and the dirt was still soft and damp. The mud squelched between my toes. The soft, after-rain dew was cool and refreshing. The air, too, smelled cleaner than I had ever noticed before. I breathed in deeply. It was like drinking the freshest water I'd ever tasted.

I came close to the raven, but not close enough. It was staring at me with a beady expression. I had a funny feeling that we had met before. Cautiously, I reached out my hand. The raven cawed as if from deep within its chest. I froze, my fingers outstretched. The bird hopped forward onto a branch, coming closer to me. I held my breath as I took another inch forward. The tips of my fingers were mere centimetres from the raven's shiny, black feathers.

Before I could touch it, the raven took flight. The empty branch bounced, fluttering its layers of leaves in its wake. The rustling sound of leaves echoed around me, competing with that of the air waves generated by the bird's wings. The leaves fell around me like leafy snowflakes cascading down in a shower of green light. They landed in my hair, and I brushed them away.

"Don't be sad. The raven is too loyal to stay, but it may return another day."

I turned instantly towards a familiar voice.

"At least we got a brief glimpse of it."

The man who had spoken was sitting quietly behind me on a rock beside some bushes. He was holding a small liar harp in his hand. It was the same kind that was embroidered on my bodice. My heart quickened at once as I laid eyes on him.

Just like me, the man was wearing an old style of clothes. His long tunic shirt was hanging over the waist of his tight stirrup pants. The brown leather boots he was wearing were finely hand-made, with some stitches perfectly sewn in the front.

"Where did you come from?" I asked as I approached him with a newly found spring in my step.

"A few moments ago, I enjoyed watching you walk amongst the stone circle." He smiled at me through kind blue eyes as his long hair fell against his cheek.

"Are you making a habit out of sneaking up on me?" I asked him as I sat down beside him. My dress gathered in a pool of material beneath me.

"I did not sneak up on you. You asked to meet me here."

"I did, but you should have called out my name when you arrived!" I exclaimed. "Instead, you watched me."

"I was admiring your beauty while I was resting here! I have a long journey ahead of me. It may be some time before I return from the King's service."

"Of course you were watching me." I nodded sarcastically, rolling my eyes.

Our laughs seemed to echo around us, followed by a long moment of silence.

The bard began to play a slow, melancholy song on his harp. The song didn't have any lyrics, but the melody was sweet and harmonic. It filled the space where we sat with an enchanting sound, like crystal chimes caught in summer rain. I tried to imagine its meaning. It was a song of heartbreak, I guessed. I'd heard him play this piece many times before, and each time was heart-rending. He always seemed to make the harp weep with his fingers. I knew it was because he caressed the strings with the same loving embrace with which he touched me. This time was no different. The tune he played was one of yearning. Somehow, I knew it was for me that he yearned.

He finished playing and looked at me. His eyes were full of sadness.

"What will your mother say when she finds out we are now betrothed?" he asked as he leaned towards me, a smile tugging at the corners of his lips.

"She won't be pleased," I replied, thinking of how much my mother disapproved of my love. He might have the King's blessing, but he was still a bard without land or wealth. "But, after you've won great honours on the battlefield, you can come again in your finest attire with a bunch of wild flowers to ask for my hand." I smiled and looked him in the eye playfully.

He pretended to contemplate, rubbing one finger over his chin and squinting at nothing in particular. "As long as she doesn't feed the flowers to the animals again!" he finally exclaimed.

Although I knew he was just teasing, I couldn't help but respond sternly. I stared at him with daggers, showing how disappointed I was. He should think of ways to win over my mother, not make jokes. Of course, my reaction did nothing more than amuse him. He placed the harp to the side and reached towards my face, cupping my cheeks in his hands.

"Maybe the King will honour your loyal service with land of your own," I said after a moment. "Surely my mother could not deny you then."

"Nothing will stop me from claiming you," he said defiantly. "Not your mother's disapproval, not this war, not even God Himself could prevent me."

"Do not speak so! Do not anger Him before the battle."

"No matter what, I will return and ask for your hand!" he said more seriously. "If I were to die and be reborn a thousand times, I would always try to make you mine."

His hand traced my cheek, and his eyes bore into mine. The intensity in them made my heart pound relentlessly, like a war drum.

"Mo cuishle," he murmured, calling me by the name that he only used when we were alone. "I swear to you, when I return from battle, I will marry you before God and my King."

My heart ached at his words. I felt a lump form in my throat.

We'd pledged ourselves to each other many times, but I never tired of hearing him say it.

"Even if my mother killed you all those thousand times?" I asked with half a smile.

"Even then." He took my hand in his and kissed it fondly. All around us, the sycamore seeds slowly spiralled towards the ground. Thoughtfully, he contemplated them. Then he caught one and placed it gently in my palm.

"It's like us two lovers falling together," he murmured.

I touched it. "And like our love, it will only grow stronger and more beautiful."

"I don't want you to leave me."

His eyes shone with love.

"I have a gift for you," he said at last, "before my journey. Please close your eyes. This gift was given to me by our King Brian Boru for ten years of loyal service." I closed my eyes and felt him slip something onto my finger. Slowly, I opened my eyes. There, upon my left ring finger, was a heavy gold ring set with a large, glittering emerald. The ring was beautiful. The gold band glinted as it caught the sunlight. The emerald that was set deep into it was lustrous *and radiant. Green colours danced in the air and on my skin, like sunshine streaming in through a canopy of leaves.*

He took both my hands and walked me towards the tallest of the stones. We stood before them, holding hands, ready to perform a hand-fasting ceremony. This was not our formal marriage, but a private one between the two of us. He looked down at me, and in his eyes, I saw a devotion that felt deeper than any ocean. Next to us, the stones looked on in silence. They seemed to watch over us and bless our union. They were our witnesses and our priests. I could feel their energy flowing within the circle. It matched the same magical energy in the emerald ring I'd just been given. Just like the emerald in the ring, these stones were as old as the earth herself. And just like its band, the stones were set in a circle. The circle bound us together. There was no end to a circle, just as there would be no end to our love. It would go on and on forever. It would outlive us.

Solemnly, he said, "Today, I give this emerald ring to my beloved in the hopes of supporting a strong, unwavering love and commitment for the rest of our lives together. I ask for peace, and longevity in our soon-to-be marriage."

Startled, I sat bolt upright in bed. For a moment, I had no idea where I was. The darkness of the room pressed against my eyelids. I looked wildly around, expecting to see the stone circle and the shaded glen. They were gone, replaced with my small bedroom. Energy coursed through my body with an electric current. My heart raced with the feverish abandon of dance. My senses were registering that I was back in my bed, back in the twenty-first century, but my heart told me Conor was the bard in the stone circle. I took a deep breath, and my heart rate began to slow.

It was just a dream, just a dream... I told myself.

But why did I feel as if my life had just changed forever?

The Bard's last words rang in my ears long after I woke up. Staring at the shadows playing against the wall, I replayed the conversation in my mind time and again. I couldn't help but feel that it had been more than just a dream. My heart recognised Conor's words as real, not just some random conjuring of my imagination.

The dream aroused an emotion that I couldn't quite put my finger on; it was definitely a happy one. But it also left me with an ache of sadness that settled over my bones like a winter chill. No matter what I did to reassure myself, I knew I could not dispel this cold.

Was it really a dream? Why did it feel so real? For one thing, I could remember it with perfect clarity. Dreams weren't like that. I forgot my dreams as soon as I woke up. But I could remember this in detail. For another, there were things in this dream that I shouldn't have known but which I somehow did. As I retraced the scene, I realised, with a jolt, that Conor and I had been speaking to each other in Irish— and despite having taken Irish in school, I couldn't remember it well enough to carry on a conversation in it.

What did this mean?

Surely, it couldn't have been a... memory?

I stared down at my arms, which had just erupted in goosebumps. It *couldn't* be a memory. That defied all logic. All reason. And yet... it felt right.

Hope flared suddenly in my chest. If the "dream" was a memory, then that meant I had met Conor before. The thought of having met Conor in a past life was beyond magical.

I wasn't the first person to consider the possibility of past lives, but no one I knew believed in them. We were all raised Catholic, and while all of us lapsed now, we maintained a healthy scepticism of anything non-papal approved. I could only imagine what Laura and Rosie would say if they could overhear my thoughts. How Laura would scold me! And Conor... he would probably think I was completely off my rocker.

Speaking of Conor... I wasn't sure if he would be awake yet, but I took my chances and reached for the phone. I wasn't going to tell him everything, but I knew that he'd like to hear I was dreaming about him.

Chapter Fourteen

GIRLS, GIRLS, GIRLS

My hands ran softly over the shiny red satin dress. It hugged my shape beautifully, lifting my spirit like a carefree breeze. The dress was beautiful, with a sweeping cowl neck and a low back, but it certainly wasn't what I had envisioned. It made me feel strong and feminine. The fabric was slinky against my skin, and the short skirt made my legs look long and elegant. It was the kind of dress that would turn heads, although there was only one head I cared about turning.

On the other hand, Laura had tried on half the dresses in Galway. So far, none had met our approval. Her birthday was in a few days' time, but somehow, the responsibility to make sure she looked fabulous rested on our shoulders. With my phone in hand, I fell backwards into the large wicker chair that sat in the corner of the changing rooms. The dressing room was nice and cool, at least. A noisy air-con in the far corner churned an icy breeze into the small area, making my skin shiver. This was probably to prevent customers from sweating in the clothes and ruining them, but I liked it. The coolness felt refreshing after a long day of shopping.

I had never been inside this boutique before. Tucked down an alley off of Dominick Street, it was usually out of my price range. I preferred to look in the windows every time I passed and imagine myself being able to afford it. But for her birthday, Laura had insisted we splurge and try it out. The interior was beautiful, with large bay windows, exposed brick walls and a crystal chandelier. The aloof woman behind the counter had told me it was salvaged from an old hotel in Dublin that was being demolished. Even the dressing rooms were fancy. They were set with dusty pink settees, hardwood floors that creaked under our feet and full length velvet curtains. The mirrors weren't mounted on the walls like in department stores, either. Instead, each changing room was outfitted with a full-length, gold-rimmed standing mirror. Their intricate gold frames and gently curved tops took my breath away. I'd never been somewhere so posh. I'd even sent a text to Conor joking that the snooty woman behind the counter was going to kick me out for being an imposter.

A beautiful woman like you? Over my dead body, he'd texted back. *More likely to ask you to be their model. Just you wait and see.*

Despite the nice choice, Laura had been struggling to find a dress that suited her. So far, I had already turned my nose up to most dresses she had tried on. It was a battle of wills. Still, I knew she wanted my approval and that she wouldn't buy a dress until she got it.

It helped that Rosie hadn't approved of the dresses either. Otherwise, Laura would have thrown me out of the boutique's changing room for going against popular consensus.

Admittedly, I had been miles away, staring into my phone like a smitten kitten. Conor's next text could arrive at any moment, and I didn't want to miss it.

He had only messaged me once in the past three hours, which was starting to make me anxious. Conor's last message was a voice note to say he would be tied up for the next few hours. There was lots of shouting going on in the background, and then the message stopped. So I knew that I shouldn't expect anything from him. And yet, I couldn't keep myself from checking my phone every few minutes, just in case. It was getting me in trouble with Laura. I'd been caught more than once checking for text messages when I was supposed to be paying attention to her outfit changes.

I turned to look at the girls in the long, three-panelled mirror at the end of the changing room. I watched them for a few moments in a daze as they struggled to zip Laura's dress. I waited in anticipation to see whether or not she would faint. The dress was tighter than anything I'd ever seen her squeeze into. There was barely any room for her lungs to breathe. It was strapless and made from a rigid, lime-green material that hugged her all the way to the ankles. Hideous, if you asked me.

"Bridget, are you here to help us or are you here to stare into that stupid phone of yours?" snapped Laura.

"What makes the phone stupid?" I snapped back.

"Well, either the phone is stupid, or the owner is," she retorted, then stepped back into the changing room.

"That dress has to be the tightest you've tried so far," I called after her in a petty reprisal. "It looks painted on."

"Well, we can't all lose a stone and a half in a few days like you!" her voice shouted out from behind the curtain.

I looked at Rosie, who raised her eyebrows.

"Have I really lost that much weight in a few days?" I asked, aghast.

"You've barely eaten since Conor left," Rosie said fairly.

"Don't tell us you've become anorexic over some boy!" Laura called out from inside the dressing room, her voice icy.

"You look like a praying mantis in that dress," I shot back, which shut her up.

Sighing, I dropped my phone onto a fluffy cushion and relaxed further into the wicker chair. Maybe they were right. My anxiety about him being gone was starting to affect me in unhealthy ways. Perhaps paying more attention to Laura would distract me. However, she was annoying me so much that I didn't want to be too nice. Feeling brave, I was ready to tease Laura some more as she emerged in the next dress.

However, she came out of the dressing room looking fabulous. The sarcastic comment I had planned died on my lips. My mouth was open, but I couldn't find the words to describe the dress.

"Wow!" Rosie exclaimed for all of us.

She ran over to Laura and made her twirl in the dress, displaying all the best angles. The dress was dark red. It was like a second skin on her body, hugging her near-hourglass figure firmly until about mid-calf. It had a sweetheart neckline and thin straps and was made from a mesh-like material that flowed down her body like water. She stood admiring herself in the mirror.

"If you match this dress with a stunning pair of heels, you'll be the talk of the town," said Rosie.

"What do you think, Bridget?" she asked, turning to find me glued to my phone.

"Bridget? Are you still here?" Hastily, I stuffed my phone back into my purse and looked back up at Laura. I'd gotten a Facebook notification that Conor had arrived in Australia. I already knew that, so he must have just updated his location. Rosie laughed at my sudden awe as I returned to reality. Laura, however, stared at me angrily. I could tell she wasn't pleased that I'd ignored her moment of glory.

"It's magnificent! I haven't seen a dress that's suited you as much as this one," I said, overcompensating a bit for my inattentiveness. "It's perfect. You're perfect in it. You have to get it," I insisted. "And then we can feckin' get out of this boutique," I muttered under my breath.

My phone suddenly chimed, interrupting our conversation. I quickly escaped to take the call.

"What's with the phone obsession?" I heard Laura ask Rosie.

"Conor, of course. Who else?"

"Oh please, give me a bucket and help me zip up this dress," she snapped to Rose.

I heard Conor's voice crackling on the other end of the line. It sounded distant and very far away.

"Hello? Hello?" he shouted.

"Conor? I can hear you! Are you there?"

"Hello? Bridget? Can you hear me?"

"I can hear you—Conor?"

The call got cut off almost immediately. The line went dead, and I was left staring at the phone, longing to hear Conor's voice once again. He'd said he didn't have much cell service where he was, but how was that possible? Australia wasn't exactly a third-world country. There was nothing I could do, so I sighed heavily and returned to the changing rooms.

"Are you sure you won't die in that?" I asked sceptically, pointing towards the tight, corset-like back of the garment. My good mood was gone, and I felt annoyed and resentful for how long Laura had kept us shopping. My feet hurt, I was hungry, and I wanted to get home and call Conor back.

"Well, I'm not sure," Rosie answered for Laura as she pretended to wipe some sweat off her forehead.

"I'm sure I'll die! But..." Laura trailed off as she struggled to turn to get a reflection of herself from the side in the mirror. "Can't I at least die happy and looking this hot?" We all giggled together, which cleared the air instantly.

It was true; she looked like a goddess in that dress. The colour suited her features to perfection, and the structure of the dress accentuated her curves in all the right places. If I were a guy—leave that, even a girl would stop and stare. But, no matter how hot she looked, as her friend, I had to make sure she would feel comfortable and beautiful at the same time. I would rather have her enjoy her own party than gasp for air the entire time. Also, I knew that if she was uncomfortable all night, she would end up taking it out on Rosie and me. Luckily, I had been friends with Laura for long enough to know the secret to making her change her mind.

"You do know you won't be able to dance in that, right?" I pointed out.

If there was anything Laura loved more than looking hot, it was dancing. She was one of the few people I knew that actually went to parties to dance. Not just to get wasted. And she was a pretty good dancer. She'd never had any classes, but she moved naturally and unselfconsciously on the dance floor. She really loved dancing which was much to my advantage in this situation. Truthfully, my motivations weren't purely selfless. My own dress would clash with the one she was wearing. After all, it was a similar shade of red. And I wanted to stand out for Conor.

Rosie seemed to notice what I was doing. From where she stood behind Laura, she sent her excited thumbs up silently.

"Then what should I wear?!" Laura exclaimed, fidgeting with the hems of the red dress. She was starting to sound hysterical.

"Why don't you try that blue one we saw?" Rosie shrugged.

"You think?"

"Just go and try it on. Bridget and I will be here."

I was about to nod and support Rosie, but was stopped before I even opened my mouth by the ding of a phone notification from the chair behind me. I jumped to retrieve the device without another thought about the dresses.

"Where is she going in such a hurry?" Laura asked from behind me.

"It's Conor. She made a custom notification alert to ensure she won't miss a text."

"Oh, I've heard it all," replied Laura. Then she clicked her fingers and headed back into the fitting room.

I knew that I was being rude by ignoring the girls, but I didn't care. We'd gone shopping together in Galway countless times. And each time, Laura spent forever trying to find the right outfit. She would change her mind, ask us our opinions endlessly and even buy multiple ensembles that she would end up returning. But I'd never had a relationship like this before. Laura would survive without me. I spent the next few minutes chatting with Conor. I could hear him a little better this time. He said he'd moved outside where there was better service, but he'd only just begun to tell me about band practice before he was cut off again, and I returned to join the girls.

"When are you due back? Will you make it to Laura's birthday party on Thursday night?" I texted.

"Yes. We hope to be back in time for the party. The phone signal is rubbish here. Should I be expecting any surprises?" he replied.

I acted innocent. But already I had a surprise dress planned for him. The red satin dress I was about to pay the cashier for. The red dress would have his eyes popping out of their sockets. If I paired it with some stiletto heels I already owned, it would make his jaw hit the floor. Or maybe this was an excuse to buy new shoes...

No. I was starting to sound like Laura.

I had no interest in impressing anyone else but Conor with the way I dressed. I was only interested in one man.

"What kind of surprises?" I texted coyly.

"What do you have in mind?" He texted back.

"Come on, Bridget, what are you sneaking around outside for? Are you in Galway or Sydney?" Laura bellowed. Rolling my eyes, I quickly texted the last message and ran back in to join the ladies again.

Laura was being very demanding for her birthday. She wanted something special to wear and her ladies-in-waiting to choose for her.

She looked beautiful in the blue dress as well. It was a dark blue velvet wrap dress with a pencil skirt that came to her mid-thigh. While it hugged her curves like the red one, the material had a lot more give and would be easy to dance in. Its spaghetti straps meant that she wouldn't overheat on the dance floor, either.

"You've got to get that dress," I said as I stepped out of my texting haven with a giant smile on my face.

"I know, right?" Laura beamed, turning around to show how snug the dress looked. But then her eyes narrowed. "You've said that about all the dresses so far. Are you just teasing me?"

"No," I said quickly. "This one looks as good as the red one, but it's less binding in the bodice and skirt. You'll be able to dance in it."

"Okay, you're right," Laura said, looking back at herself in the mirror.

"It really is fab, Laura," Rosie chimed in, sending a secretive eye roll my way.

Rosie was simply glad that this aspect of the party had been sorted out, and her face showed her relief. I smiled at her. I understood how shopping for clothes with Laura could be; demanding at the best of times. Now, if we could find her the perfect shoes, all the fashion boxes would be ticked.

Conor's name popped up; my eyes lowered towards the phone. I struggled to unlock the screen. There were dozens of love heart emojis, one after the other.

You better be dreaming about me again, Miss Kennedy!

I rolled my eyes as I read the words, my mind immediately conjuring up Conor's sarcastic face. If only he knew exactly *what* kind of dream I'd had about him—he would think I was crazy!

It's four in the afternoon here, and I'm shopping with the girls! Why would I even be sleeping?

Late nap? I wish we were in bed together now!

A smile spread across my face as we texted back and forth. I couldn't help but smile, amused both by our lame jokes and by how happy these messages made me feel.

No reply? Is this where I should remove the bracelet?

Don't you even dare, buster!

"Earth to Bridget!" Laura's voice brought me back to reality so abruptly that I almost dropped the phone. "Rosie, did you see that smile? I think we've truly lost our friend to a kangaroo."

Rosie nodded dramatically, pretending to wipe a tear away.

"Oh, be quiet, girls!" I exclaimed as I put my phone away.

"Rosie, I *saw* who you were texting as well earlier! You were down under too!" I accused Rosie, referring to the few texts I'd seen between her and James.

Rosie's face went pink at once, and she opened her mouth to defend herself, but Laura cut her off.

"Okay, enough about that. Let's focus on more important matters," Laura announced, turning to look in the mirror again. I suspected she didn't like that both Rosie and I were texting men when she wasn't. "We still need to find shoes. Where should we go? Schuh?"

#

As we finalised our purchases—the snooty cashier informed us that all sales were final and that we couldn't return our dresses if we decided we couldn't afford them—I smiled at her sarcastically as we left the store.

We then turned our attention to the shoe hunt. We had visited three stores before finding a shoe that Laura even remotely liked. She had very long legs, legs that some people may consider a gift from God. However, she had inherited her father's large feet. Tricky to find heels for.

A silver wedge hugged her feet tightly as the criss-cross leather straps sat freely on her feet. She took them off and stared at them with a smile.

"They're a maybe."

"I don't think they go with the dress," I said critically.

"Silver goes with everything!" she retorted.

"Yeah, at Mardi Gras! But this is your birthday. Anyway, wedges are so early noughties. You should go for something more elegant."

"Always with the elegant," Laura mimicked, annoyed. "Sometimes I just want to have fun, BK. And wedges are easy to dance in."

"What about a block heel?" Rosie suggested. "Those are in right now."

It was obvious Laura didn't want to leave them behind, but our words seemed to have left her in doubt. Rosie grabbed her by the arm and began to lead her away, the two of them bickering about block heels versus wedges. I suggested that we try a charity shop for something vintage, but Laura shot that down immediately.

"I want something *new* for my birthday," she exclaimed. It took us another hour to find shoes that fit. Finally, she made up her mind at a small boutique on Middle Street that we almost passed by. In the end, she decided to go with a pair of silver and gold pointed stilettos that were encrusted with rhinestones. They wouldn't be the easiest to dance in, but she was going to practise before the party, and they looked great with the dress. She also bought a pair of delicate gold drop earrings to match.

After all the shopping, we headed to Bewley's for a well-deserved treat. Shopping for Laura required some form of treat to reclaim our spirits after a punishing experience.

"We should petition your maker, Laura. Your shoes should be custom-made all the damn time!" Rosie said, laughing at Laura's funny expression.

"You know we like shopping with you, babe," I enthused.

"Your favourite part is when we're eating ice cream," Laura said, rolling her eyes at us. Laura was right. Laughing, we all agreed unanimously. Maybe we'd have time to sneak in a few cocktails.

Chapter Fifteen

FRIENDS, ALWAYS

Laura's birthday bash was only a few hours away. Every time I checked my phone, I felt my heart sink. Every second that passed by brought home the fact that Conor and his band weren't going to make it to the party. They'd missed their connecting flight out of London Heathrow by a few minutes. Their next flight wouldn't leave for a couple of hours. Conor's recent message read that their late arrival into London was due to bad weather and severe turbulence.

Lost in thought, I let out a heavy sigh as I smoothed my hands over the vibrant red fabric of the dress that held me tight like a second skin. All the curves I wanted to display for Conor were on show, and boy, that was a first for me. I was never into vanity, ever. But I couldn't help feeling disappointed he wouldn't get to see me so elegantly dressed. I stood still as I looked at myself in the mirror. My make-up was perfect, thanks to some great instructions on YouTube on how to do those wonderful smoky eyes to match my blonde locks that fell softly around my face. These eyes had taken me almost twenty minutes to do, but the end result was flawless, and I had to admit it made me look intelligent as well as alluring—the effect I wanted. I decided to splurge and invest in a quality foundation for my makeup routine, opting for a contoured blusher that I typically overlooked. To top off the look, I'd painted my lips with deep red lipstick—not too bright, but a great match to my dress and the overall look. I couldn't help but admire myself in the mirror. I looked absolutely stunning - and I could say that with complete confidence! My makeup was flawless, radiating a youthful glow. And the dress I wore was beautiful in a way that was entirely unique and unexpected. *What a waste of a great dress and make-up*, I thought to myself. I knew I had to lift my spirits and be there for Laura. After all, it was her birthday, and I needed to put on a brave face and be a good friend.

As I left the bedroom, my phone rang. The first few bars of "What's New Pussycat?" told me the call was from Conor. He'd thought it was hilarious when he added his own personal ringtone before he left on his trip down under. The sound made my stomach swoop with excitement. Surely, he would only be calling with the good news that he'd been able to get on an earlier flight!

"Hey, Bridget," his voice sounded full of remorse and regret. Immediately, my hopes were dashed. I knew he felt as awful about missing the connecting flight as I did.

"Will you be able to make the next flight?" I asked, resigned.

"Yes. But it will take another hour before they start boarding. There is no way we can make it to the party. I'm really sorry." My spirits sank even lower.

There is something about disappointing news, even when you know it's inevitable. You still hold a flickering candle in the hope of last-minute reprieve.

"Bridget, are you still there?" His voice mirrored the emotions we both felt.

"I'm still here. We're about to leave for the party. I might not be able to talk later. Have a safe trip," I said, trying to conceal my disappointment.

I thought, *it's only a birthday party and a dress. I can wear the dress for him another night.* There would be other parties. I knew that. But the disappointment still felt heavy in my chest. I'd never had a boyfriend like this before, and I'd been looking forward to introducing Conor to all our friends. This was going to be our debut as a couple.

"Will you be okay?" he asked. As he spoke, I heard the sound of moving cars and then a car honk. *Didn't he say they were at the airport?*

"What's that sound?" I asked.

"A car. I stepped out of the lounge to take this call, away from the boys." *How is that possible?* I thought to myself. *If he left the airport, he'd have to go back through security.*

"They already think I'm completely under the thumb," he said, making a comical whipping sound. The way it flew out of his mouth was so smooth, it had me in stitches.

"Wait, is James leading this circus?" I asked.

"He's the head honcho," Conor replied.

"Well, give him a playful slap from me, will ya?"

"Consider it done. I gotta run now. Have a blast at the party," he pleaded.

"I'll give it my best shot. No guarantees though."

Before I could even finish my sentence, the call abruptly ended. The conversation felt strange. It wasn't like Conor to hang up quickly or to not spend longer reassuring and comforting me. I felt even more disappointed. I'd been hoping that he'd offer to take me to another party sometime soon, maybe one in Dublin with some of his musician friends. I knew I was being silly. Conor did so much for me already. But I still felt a little let down.

My buzzer went, and I headed downstairs to grab the girls. They'd forgotten their spare key. They were all dressed to impress. Laura looked like a queen in her blue dress. Her hair was slicked back into a tight bun, and she was wearing a dark bronzer that made her cheekbones look high and sharp. Her lipstick was a bold dark brown.

All in all, she looked like a model about to hit the red carpet. Rosie was similarly breathtaking in a long black dress. It had pockets and a deep V-neck, which she'd complemented with a flashy silver spiral pendant necklace. She had curled her hair, and it fell down her back in flowing waves. Both girls shrieked with delight when they saw me. They immediately began to exclaim over my appearance and how good I looked. I couldn't help but feel flattered.

The venue Laura had booked was a small boutique bar called Annie's not very far from my apartment. It had a great vibe, delicious cocktails and an inviting dance floor. Laura had picked the best venue for her birthday. For a party like this, all we needed was the perfect balance of alcohol and a spacious dance floor. And this venue? It exceeded those expectations and then some. It's not like I was a complete stranger to getting all dolled up and having a night out on the town. Memories of our late-night adventures at Trinity flooded back, and I couldn't help but smile. They were a staple of my times as a student. But as for the party girl persona I once had? Well, she had been dormant for quite some time now. But I was ready to bring back the party girl in order to celebrate Laura's birthday. If anything could bring out my wild side, it was my best friends. Laura deserved to have the biggest and best night of her life, even if I was missing Conor.

When I saw how excited the girls were, I decided I wasn't going to put a damper on Laura's big night out.

"Are you girls ready to party or what?" Laura screamed. Rosie grinned like a Cheshire cat. I couldn't help but smile. Laura's excitement was infectious. I grabbed both girls and gave them an enormous hug.

"Let's do this!" I shouted enthusiastically.

"One for the road?" Laura announced, pulling out a silver hip flask from her handbag.

"Go on, ye mad thing." I laughed.

Laura took a swig, made a face, and then passed the flask to Rosie. In turn, she passed it to me, and I drank. It was a cheap tequila that burned my throat, but the warmth spread throughout my body immediately and pleasantly. I looked up at the girls happily, only to see that Laura's eyes had filled with tears.

"Look at us," she said, her voice thick with emotion. "We've been friends for such a long time, even through all the dramas of boys and careers. I'll always love you two. Thanks for putting up with me."

"Happy birthday, babe," Rosie said, giving her a long hug.

"We love you, too, Laura," I agreed, grinning. "Now let's go party!"

Laura threw her hands up and cheered, and Rosie and I joined her.

I really did love these girls. We'd been through so much together. Even if Conor wouldn't be there tonight, I was glad to be with my best friends.

After making a final fashion check, we grabbed our coats and ventured out into the night.

Arriving at the venue, the vibrant sounds of laughter and music filled the air, energising me further. The moment I stepped foot into the party, familiar faces greeted us with excitement and warmth. It was as if time had stood still, and we were transported back to our carefree days as students. The tequila shots were clearly starting to kick in. The three of us looked super hot.

The reserved area was teeming with activity as Laura's thirty guests poured in, including her cousins who had made the journey from Dublin and found accommodation in a nearby hotel. Many familiar faces filled the space - friends and acquaintances I had come to know over the years of our enduring friendship with Laura.

I'd met most of her work colleagues, and of course, we had some mutual friends in attendance. Everyone loved being part of Laura's birthday celebrations.

"Why are musical instruments set up here?" I asked Laura as I looked towards the small stage.

"I'd hoped Conor and his band would have shown up tonight. Too bad they've chosen to disappoint me." She pouted, dismissing the band issue with a wave of the hand. I felt myself heating up.

"I'm sorry it didn't work out," I said, feeling embarrassed and the need to apologise on Conor's behalf.

"Don't you worry about it, girl. DJ Moonshine knows his music. I am sure we're in good hands," she replied.

As if on cue, the DJ played a favourite of Laura's. The three of us were on the dance floor in a flash, movin' and groovin' to the music. I watched her dancing, happy that her night was getting off to a good start. As we swayed our hips on the dance floor, memories of our college years flooded my mind. Back then, Laura was always the life of the party, never shying away from the opportunity to dance all night long.

When the song finished, she ran back to where I was standing at the bar, grinning like a Cheshire cat, then skulled another Long Island iced tea.

"How'd I do on the dance floor?" she asked as we both leaned on the bar. Her face was flushed, and I could tell she was having a great birthday.

"Pretty good," I replied, laughing. "But you know that already."

"Sounds even better when you hear it from your best friend." She giggled. "Why is your hand behind your back, Bridget? New posture?"

"This is for you, Laura. Happy birthday!" I said, revealing the package I'd been hiding as she approached.

"Oh my God, you shouldn't have, BK. You have given me the best birthday gift anyone could have asked for, birthday after birthday after birthday, same gift, same effect!" She teared up again, and to my surprise, I found myself getting emotional too.

"What gift is that, Laura?"

"Our friendship. I wouldn't trade it for anything in the world," she said as she threw her arms around me in a tight hug. As she held me close, my heart swelled. Laura could be difficult, and we'd had our fair share of arguments over the years, but she was loyal 'til the end. She loved me unconditionally, as I did her. We were lifelong friends.

"I wouldn't trade that for anything either. I just wanted to get you something else too, something you will like. Promise me you won't open it without me," I said, smiling. She held out her pinkie finger and wagged it in front of my face, reminding me of our childhood ritual.

"Pinkies?" She asked. I intertwined my pinkie finger with hers as we twisted them so that the fingers slipped out to conclude the childish promise.

"This song is going out to someone special. Someone close to our hearts."

As soon as I heard the voice over the PA system, my heart jumped with excitement. It was a voice I knew all too well, and it never failed to bring a smile to my face.

Perplexed, I turned to Laura and questioned, "Did Conor send you a heartfelt message to compensate for their absence?" Laura's mischievous grin widened as she playfully seized my shoulder, swiftly swirling me around. And there, to my astonishment, stood Conor, accompanied by James and Donal, on the intimate stage.

Goosebumps immediately erupted on my arms as tears filled my eyes. Conor was here, standing on the stage in front of me. It was as if he had walked out of my imagination and into the room. I was shocked and elated. I thought my heart might stop from surprise or burst with joy.

Conor looked excited and more than a little pleased with himself. He was scanning the room eagerly, as if looking for someone. The moment his eyes settled on mine, my heart skipped a beat. He grinned broadly, then winked.

Conor moved closer to the microphone. As he did, James struck the first note on his guitar. The sound sent a shiver down my spine. Silence fell immediately through the venue. A spotlight came up on Conor and the boys, washing them in a cool, electric blue. Conor gripped the microphone with his right hand, his arms flexing and exposing the toned muscles in his forearms and biceps. He held the microphone close to his lips as if he might kiss it. All of him was taut, like a diver about to jump from the diving board. It was as if his need to sing had overtaken him. Donal came in next on the drums. The music began to build. Conor rocked back on his heels. He was *feeling* the music as he waited for his cue. Then, with a look from James, he leaned forward, gripped the microphone tighter and parted his lips to sing.

As he started to sing, our eyes connected, and in that fleeting moment, something happened. My breath caught in my throat, and my legs felt weak. Desperate to remain steady, I clung onto Laura for support. And then, like a switch the entire room exploded into motion, the infectious beats of Ocrás pulling everyone onto the dance floor.

The song was a reinterpretation of a classic Irish love song. Ocrás had turned its lilting melody into something more upbeat. Combined with Conor's deep voice, it possessed an aching passion that brought tears to my eyes. Suddenly I understood the look he'd sent me. He'd been telling me that this song was for me. He wasn't singing to the audience; he was singing to me.

As I closed my eyes I allowed myself to be carried away by the music. It transported me back in time, all the way to the moment when Conor serenaded me amidst the stone circle, as sycamore seeds slowly descended from above.

A nudge in my side brought me back to reality. I opened my eyes to see Laura looking excitedly at me.

"Were you surprised?" she yelled over the music, grinning.

"Very!" I laughed.

She smirked. "Well, you're welcome!"

"How did they get here?" I shouted, staring up at them again to check I wasn't dreaming.

"Conor wanted to surprise you, and I'd also booked the band to play on my birthday!" she replied.

I threw my arms around her shoulders and hugged her close. Laura had always been there for me, but this was above and beyond. She'd been annoyed at me since Conor left for Australia, and with good reason. I'd been self-absorbed and thoughtless the past few days. I'd even spoiled her shopping spree. Nevertheless, she'd put aside her frustrations and organised a huge surprise for me. On her birthday! I loved her so much I thought my heart would burst. She had shown me the true meaning of friendship.

Chapter Sixteen

SYCAMORE SEEDS

I was still in shock from Conor's surprise appearance at Laura's party. Any lingering disappointment vanished as I caught sight of his mischievous smile.

As the party began to wind down, I eagerly suggested that we politely say our goodbyes and leave. We navigated the cobblestone streets back to my apartment, consumed with desire. Like two infatuated teenagers, we exchanged kisses on every corner, unable to keep our hands off each other. The rain started pouring, but it didn't matter to us. As if straight out of a scene from a romantic movie, the passing cars illuminated the raindrops with their headlights, enveloping us in a beautiful silhouette of light as we kissed on the corners.

My head nestled perfectly on Conor's shoulder as we ascended the steps to my apartment. Once inside, I reluctantly tore myself away from him to remove my party dress, but our connection remained strong. Without wasting a moment, we hurriedly kicked off our shoes before collapsing onto my bed, united in our love and desire.

"You look so beautiful in that dress. I love it!"

He smiled as he pulled me towards him, giving me a gentle kiss on the lips that melted my heart.

Conor then began to slowly undo my red dress. As he leaned forward, his lips gently met the nape of my neck, this sent shivers down my spine. As the zip went lower, his kisses traced a path down my back, blending with the drops of rain that ran down my skin. With a gentle brush, he licked the raindrops to savour the taste of me. Soon, the dress was fully unzipped. He asked me to raise my arms so he could quickly slip it off. Turning around, I met his intense gaze as it roamed across the contours of my body, igniting a passionate desire between us.

Conor whispered softly into my ear, "Bridget, you're so beautiful."

As we nestled back onto the bed, our lips met in a passionate kiss that lingered for a few precious moments before we slowly slipped beneath the sheets. Our bodies entwined, his warmth embraced me as his urgent kisses intensified. Tenderness flowed between us as he caressed my hair while whispering his longing for me.

"Even more than you can imagine," I whispered back into his ear, punctuating our kisses. Passion surged between us, igniting an intoxicating fire that consumed us both for the next couple of hours.

"Bridget, you're amazing," he whispered.

As we fell back, exhausted on the bed, we held each other for a few minutes, then slowly got in under the sheets again. Our bodies pressed against each other. His skin was warm, and his kisses tender. Gently, he stroked my hair and whispered how much he'd missed me.

"I'm so glad you're back in my arms," I whispered back into his ear between long kisses.

"Tell me all about Sydney. I want to know everything," I said as I sat up.

Conor laughed.

"You're very energetic after all the dancing, partying and passion. How are your eyes still open?" he asked.

"You're my opium," I replied. "I haven't seen you in days, and if you think I am going to fall asleep on you, think again, mister." I grinned. "Now, tell me, how was the trip down under?"

Conor leaned back on his elbows as he pondered the question.

"Sydney was mind-blowing. It was a whirlwind of cheering crowds, amazing stages and great music. The audience loved us. All the other bands were super friendly. Some of them want to play with us again. They were talking about the festival circuit in Germany and Croatia that we should play next."

Conor's eyes lit up as he recalled the Sydney tour. I wished I could have been a part of this experience that had so affected him. I nodded as he spoke, making sure not to miss a word.

"The city itself was beautiful. The organisers of the festival did an incredible job. From the minute we touched down at Sydney Airport, everything ran like clockwork. There was a driver standing waiting for us holding a huge sign that said Ocrás, and our schedule was organised to the T.

"Also, the hospitality was top-notch. There was even champagne waiting for us in the car. We felt like rock stars drinking it as we were driven to our accommodation, which turned out to be one of the best hotels in Sydney. We each got our own room with king-size beds and Jacuzzis. Even the shower was posh. It had one of those rainfall shower heads. The rooms also had balconies with the most incredible views of Sydney Harbour. Especially at night. And, of course, the boys had a lot of fun with room service." We both laughed.

"James?" I asked. A mischievous smile played on Conor's lips. He laughed.

"Of course. James was hilarious. He ordered lobster! And caviar. None of us had even tried caviar before, but we sat on my balcony and enjoyed it together. It was amazing!" He smiled as he recollected the food.

"The best moments were the performances, though. We weren't supposed to play on the first night. We were only booked for the closing of the festival. We spent the first day rehearsing, ensuring that our set was flawless and we were stage-fit, ready to give our best. Unexpectedly, another band pulled out at the last-minute on Friday night, and Ocrás was asked to step in. Everything was set up perfectly for us. We even had roadies sound check our instruments before going on the stage. The energy was off the charts. I've never felt an adrenaline rush like that before or played in front of such a big crowd. When they announced Orcás over the speakers, our name boomed out over thousands of people... I had goosebumps. And then we walked out under the hot, blinding lights... The crowd was amazing. They gave us a massive cheer as we walked on stage. A sea of faces, all screaming for us. It felt like I was in a movie."

Conor had a distant look in his eyes as he relived the memory. His words painted colourful images in my mind. It was easy to see how much he was inspired by his trip to Sydney and how it had affected him.

"That was the boost we needed," he continued. "Their enthusiastic cheers dissolved every drop of jet lag. Once we were on stage, the buzz was immense. The light show was amazing too. Whenever the lights would shine out over the audience, they'd turn all sorts of neon colours. It was the most amazing gig I've ever played. All of it was exhilarating. I knew, from the second I played the first note, that it was going to be my best performance yet." Conor smiled. He was deep in his imagination, still playing on the Sydney stage. The experience sounded exhilarating. "Afterwards, people were coming up to me and asking for my autograph! Mine! As if I'm famous."

"I knew it was going to be an amazing experience," I said as I hugged him tightly.

Conor was on cloud nine. As much as he wanted to appear humble and hide his excitement under an avalanche of modesty, his eyes gave it away. They sparkled with joy, and his face had the most radiant smile.

Conor had worked hard for this and deserved success more than anyone I knew. I hoped that this experience would be the start of things to come. That it would be more than just a gig. I hoped the knock-on effect would go above and beyond his expectations and put Ocrás on the map.

"The guys were simply awesome! I had never heard them play so well! They put their heart and souls into the show. Everything was top-notch." He beamed and didn't attempt to hide the pride he felt for James and Donal. I was beginning to see why they were so close. The bond, the unity, was all a recipe for success when it came to musicianship.

"I am so happy for you, Mr Musician," I said, also beaming with pride. Conor stood up and grabbed the coat he'd thrown over the lounge when we walked through the door. He fumbled around in its pocket and pulled out a rectangular box. I watched him as he walked up to me and hunched down. His eyes never left mine as he knelt down beside me. He handed me the small box and stared into my eyes.

"Don't worry, I didn't forget about you. I was thinking about you the entire time. I wished I could have kissed you after I came off stage at the end of our first set. Anyway, I saw this at The Rocks in Sydney, and I instinctively knew how beautiful it would look on you."

"What is it?" I asked excitedly.

"Open it and find out," he smiled.

I gently opened the box. Inside was a beautiful silver necklace with two delicate sycamore seeds. At the sight of the beautiful amber seeds, I gasped audibly. Conor smiled, mistaking my shock for pleasure. My head felt light, and for a moment, I thought I might faint. Gingerly, I picked the necklace out of the box to admire it and get a better look. I turned it round and round in my hands with a sheepish smile on my face. I loved it because it was beautiful. After all, it came from Conor, because he saw it and thought of me. However, there was no mistaking the sycamore seeds. They were just like the ones that had swirled around me in my dream. They were identical to the one he had put in my hand. How had he known?

He took the necklace from my hands and gently pushed my hair out of the way. Then he placed it around my neck. As he fastened the lock, he let his fingers drift along the nape of my neck. The touch made me shiver with desire but also with disquiet. The eerie coincidence sent shivers to my core.

"It looks beautiful on you," he whispered in my ear. "Mo cuishle."

Chapter Seventeen

GALWAY360

"Hey Conor, Ocrás are up next!" I shouted, my voice barely audible over the booming subwoofers backstage. Aussie rockers, Time on Earth, had just wrapped up their encore, leaving the crowd exhilarated by their high-energy guitar and drum solos. The atmosphere onstage was electric.

Conor gave me a thumbs up, nodded, and then moved into a huddle with the Ocrás lads. Though their words were inaudible, I could sense the heartfelt pep talk igniting the band's energy before their stage performance. Their undeniable chemistry as a band was truly awe-inspiring.

Conor and the boys had a few minutes for themselves before they went onstage. Out front, the festival was in full swing, as it had been for the past couple of hours. Galway360 was at full capacity. Many punters who'd turned up hoping to buy last-minute tickets at the gate had been turned away. The crowd was mesmerised by the immersive 360 stage and the way it slowly rotated. The bands seemed to love performing on it too; every rotation had been upbeat and captivated the audience. The vibrant energy of the crowd was nothing short of infectious. The lighting display was simply breathtaking, captivating the crowd as the thumping bass reverberated through the air. Cheers erupted, adding to the euphoric atmosphere. Galway360 was a feast for the eyes, showcasing the power of art and music coming together.

And amidst this vibrant festival, the ancient stone circle stood majestically in the background, adding an air of mystery and enchantment to the event. The massive stones, weathered by centuries of time, seemed to whisper tales of ancient rituals and ceremonies, becoming an integral part of the festival's identity. It was a powerful reminder that despite the passing years, the spirit of celebration, community, and artistic expression remained timeless and unending.

My hard work and many hours spent on social media campaigns had paid off. Witnessing Galway360 in its full glory was the ultimate reward. Ciara Breen was also delighted with my efforts. She'd told me several times. She had even sent me a congratulatory bouquet of flowers that morning which were just divine. I was so grateful for this gesture. There's nothing in this world that brings more joy than an unexpected bunch of flowers. I'd poured my heart and soul into Galway360, and it was all worth it.

Many hours were spent on Instagram creating posts that were branded with the festivals' colours and logo. I interviewed bands and uploaded footage of their rehearsals. The standing stones had also featured prominently in my posts.

I'd almost gone crazy combing through social media metrics to see which posts were trending the best. It was also my job to create catchy posts and increase engagement with our target audience. Occasionally, I'd fall asleep over my laptop staring at these numbers. I'd even dreamed about them. I was proud to have developed a social media strategy that successfully resonated with multiple age groups, creating a meaningful connection for all. While we may not yet rival Glastonbury, our goal was clear: to attract top talent and create an unforgettable experience. Galway360 had certainly gotten off to a great start.

It didn't hurt, either, that we'd been blessed with miraculous blue skies and warm weather all day. This was never a certainty in the West of Ireland. Drinks were flowing in all the beer tents, and the weaving queues moved quickly. Galway360 was going off.

I recalled sketching the festival scene the night I met Conor unexpectedly near the stone circle. It was as if all my thoughts and ideas had manifested themselves into the present. I was in my own world giving thanks when I heard Conor's voice echoing around the festival site. His guitar solos were breathtaking, and he had the crowd in his hand. The lads in the band had really stepped up since Sydney. Their first song was a familiar one, Cupid's Arrow. I knew the song by heart. It was one of my favourites, with a catchy, uplifting vibe.

The lyrics mirrored my elevated mood. Through my art, I was able to draw the festival before it happened. Now Conor's music brought it all to life. The cheers from the crowd were just as loud as I'd imagined. The stage made Orcás look like kings upon a slowly revolving dais. Their music was raucous and wild, as the lights dazzled and swept across upturned faces - creating an electrifying atmosphere.

Smiling, I leaned against the stage barrier. My eyes watched Conor. Mid-song, he looked down at me and winked. Even after two months, he still had the power to make my heart skip a beat.

Festival Frank appeared behind me, tapped me on the shoulder and said, "Bridget! Yer man Conor is some pup on stage. I hear you've bought all the raffle tickets!" He then laughed and winked at me. He was about to tease me more but was interrupted by his radio. "Main unit to Frank." Frank then disappeared backstage.

Ocrás performed for over forty-five minutes. During their encore, the crowd went crazy. It was the liveliest set of the day.

As I observed the crowd, their expressions spoke volumes. The pure exhilaration radiating from their faces perfectly mirrored the intense energy Conor's music evoked within them.

I was about to head backstage when suddenly my name echoed from loudspeakers. I froze on the spot.

"Ladies and gentlemen, thank you all for coming tonight!" Conor said into his microphone. His voice sounded hoarse and breathless from singing. "Galway360, are you having a good time?" he shouted.

The crowd cheered and whistled. He brushed the hair back from his face and cheered back at the crowd. Sweat glistened on his neck and forehead. He looked exactly like a rockstar.

"Happy days! So are we!" Conor trailed off, looking at his band. "So we want to thank everyone that made Galway360 happen. Ciara Breen and all her crew, our sponsor, Jameson's Irish Whiskey, made this festival possible. And let's not forget Bridget Kennedy, our social media and marketing queen! You're out there somewhere!"

I wasn't sure what Conor was doing when he came to the edge of the stage with his hand extended. In a trance, I grabbed it and allowed him to pull me up. My heart beat wildly as I stared back at thousands of people. They were all cheering as his guitar still riffed in the background. I bowed nervously, unsure of how to act before such an overwhelming number of people. How did Conor do this all the time?

"What are you doing?" I shouted. Conor was smiling, laughing at my awkwardness. His own ease on stage was effortless. He was in his element. It would have been the most captivating image on earth if I didn't feel so terrified.

"I'm showing the world how special you are," he shouted back as he pulled me closer to him. "I love you, Bridget!"

Without even giving me the chance to respond, he planted a sudden, unexpected kiss on my lips. It was a brief, yet electrifying moment that caught me completely off guard. I found myself frozen in time as he pulled away, only to kiss me once more.

"I love you too," I shouted into his ear.

Chapter Eighteen

GOING HOME

Heading home often brings back feelings of nostalgia. An overwhelming sense of happiness that warms your heart. Also, a longing for old friends, family and loving memories of those that have passed. Even though I only lived a few hours away, I hadn't been home in over five months. I felt excited about seeing Mum and Dad and being back in the place that brought back so many memories.

Conor, on the other hand, was pretty nervous about meeting my folks for the first time. I tried to get him to relax and assured him that my parents were going to love him. My mum was thrilled to hear that I was coming home with my new boyfriend, and I was sure her excitement would rub off on Dad. *Fingers crossed.*

Road signs told me we were getting closer. Ballinascreen, 10 kilometres. The town hadn't changed a bit. Exactly twenty-two weeks had passed since my last visit. I knew my mother was going to scold me for leaving it so long. Having Conor with me might soften the blow. I'd often gotten the sense that she worried about me and my lack of boyfriends. Well, she'd be pleased with Conor then. He was everything a mum could hope for and more: handsome, charming and sweet. Not to mention successful. He'd be blowing up soon in the festival circuit of Europe. Hopefully, he'd take me all over the world with him. He really was the full package.

I smiled to myself as we drove through town towards home. The colourful terraces were still the same. The red, yellow and blue facades popped against the grey cobblestone streets crisscrossed with bunting in the GAA county colours. Everything was just as I remembered it: the pharmacy, with its neon cross glowing green; Hogans Butcher's, which had somehow survived the onslaught of budget German grocery stores like Aldi and Lidl; the old stone houses with their brightly painted trims; the pubs, of course, with their large signs for Guinness accompanied by the familiar toucan, to tempt in the tourists; and of course, at the end of the main street, St. Patrick's Church, tall and imposing. How many Sundays had I spent in that church?

It was like stepping back in time. Memories came flooding back. I pulled down my window momentarily to savour the smell of the country air and the feeling of home. Fires had been lit in the homes along the street. I could tell from the smell of turf that filled the evening.

"That's my old primary school!" I yelled, pointing at a building that had fallen on bad times. Since I was there as a child, it had gone downhill so fast that it presently looked derelict. I had talked with Mum on my last visit about its decline and how fast it had closed down, but we never really got to the bottom of it.

Dad made a remark about teachers losing their jobs and a problem with rats. I never found out what he meant. Probably joking.

"The roof looks like it could cave in," Conor said, turning up his nose as he slowed the car down.

"Don't you dare turn up your nose. I've a lot of fond memories!" I said playfully as I slapped him on the shoulder. He laughed.

"What was your favourite subject at school? Art?" he asked as he overtook a tractor.

"I really loved art!" I beamed proudly.

"Your paintings are amazing, BK." He grabbed my hand and smiled. "It's such a shame the school that nurtured that talent is so dilapidated."

"I have such fond memories of it. It used to be the centre of my world," I said. "I had a great art teacher. She really believed in me and encouraged me."

Conor could detect the sadness in my voice. My eyes appraised the fallen roof, the debris-strewn exterior and the moss on the walls. Some of the windows were broken. Graffiti had been spray painted onto the side facing the road. The car sped up, and I let the thoughts of my old school slip off me like loose clothing. I then smiled at the thought of seeing my parents: my mother's expressive face and my father's warm hug.

"We're nearly home, Mr O'Neill!"

"I'm more nervous right now than any gig I've ever done," he said, letting his face fall dramatically while still maintaining his focus on the small winding road that led out of the town and up to my parent's house.

"What's there to be scared of?" I asked him, knowing the answer.

"Your dad will probably pump me full of lead shot!"

"As if he'd do that."

"What makes you so sure?" he asked.

"He's old school. He's more likely to flay your skin and hang it on the clothesline for messing with his little girl. Besides, my father doesn't own a gun." I turned my full gaze on him, holding back the laughter that threatened to erupt.

"You're so feckin' cheeky!" said Conor. My barely restrained laughter erupted.

I could see it now. Our little bungalow with its stone facade, a tall oak tree in front and well-tended hedges. I remember running around the garden as a kid, walking to primary school, and spending weekends with Laura. Mum's apple pies were always considered the best in our local community. We helped ourselves to lots of it growing up. She didn't mind; she made more. The house was always filled with the sweet cinnamon aroma of apple pies baking in the oven. The steam would fog the kitchen windows in the winter and warm the whole house. Many a cold morning, I'd wake early, run down the stairs in thick woollen socks and be greeted by a slice of apple pie and tea.

The rest of the street was lined with identical terraced stone houses. A few had *Cead Mile Failte* signs hanging in their windows or a hurling pendant or two. The same families had lived in these homes for generations. I was sure that I still knew who lived in every house, even after all these years.

I had fond memories of returning home between semesters at Trinity. The welcome was always the same, and the length of my absence was never important. Mum and Dad were always overjoyed to have me home. However, this visit felt different, as I was returning with a man. Their little girl had grown up, and I wanted them to accept my boyfriend more than anything else. Despite our playful banter, I wasn't sure what would happen when Conor met my folks, especially my dad, who was quite protective of his only daughter.

"We're here," I announced.

"Oh boy," he said. I rolled my eyes and reassured Conor he had nothing to worry about.

My parents, probably listening, came outside at the sound of the car. They stood out on the front porch, waving as the car approached.

As Conor braked, my mother, who couldn't contain herself any longer, ran up towards my window. I jumped out of the car and straight into her arms. I still thought my mum gave the best hugs. She wrapped her arms around me, holding me in an embrace that said everything that needed to be said about love. I closed my eyes and savoured the feeling of having my mum's arms around me. Like always, she smelled of cinnamon and roasted apples. She smelled like home. The scent brought tears to my eyes. Happiness and contentment spread through my body.

"Ah, Bridget," she cooed. I could see my dad hesitant between his decision to stand on the porch and wait or to be a part of the hug. The latter won, and he stepped off the porch and took giant strides that brought him to us quickly. Mother stepped aside, and I fell into his arms.

"I've missed you, Dad," I said.

"I've missed you too, Bridget," he said in his deep bass. His arms were strong around me as he held me close. I could tell by the tightness of his hug that he had missed me.

"You must be Conor!" My mother turned to Conor, who had been standing beside the car all this time. Mum hugged him. "You're very welcome, Conor, to our home. Bridget has told us lots about you."

My father shook his hand and simply said, "Welcome."

Chapter Nineteen

MEET THE PARENTS

After dinner, Dad and Conor promptly withdrew into the study. Did Dad not already interrogate him thoroughly enough at the table? I pondered. Maybe he felt a few more questions were necessary to ascertain the kind of guy his precious little girl had brought home. I liked how polite Conor had been to my parents. He was everything I had expected him to be: himself. No fussiness, no jitters. All his talk in the car about being scared had been for fun.

"He looks like a wonderful lad," whispered Mum.

"He's a keeper, Mum.".

She reached out, gently taking both of my hands, then gave me the most radiant smile. Her gaze locked onto mine, and she whispered.

"Bridget, are you in love?"

I felt myself blush as she smiled. "Don't worry, you don't have to tell your old Mum. But from the way he looks at you, I am sure he too is smitten beyond measure—and he's a cutie!" Mum teased.

I gave Mum a heartwarming hug, relieved that she felt positively about Conor. Not knowing how I would have handled any objections from her, I was grateful for her openness. While she didn't ask many questions at dinner, preferring to let Dad take the lead, it was clear that she was engaged and interested. I could see her admiration in the way she smiled whenever Conor spoke, almost as if silently confirming, "He's a good catch!" Dad, on the other hand, seemed to want more information, leading to a second round of questioning in the study. But the sound of their laughter and clinking glasses drifting out reassured me that things were going well.

"You said he's a musician?" Mum enquired as she poured me a cup of tea. I'd already told her over the phone lots about Conor but didn't go into too much detail.

I then shared with her the story of how Conor and I met at Waxies. I told her about the incredible dinner he had organised for me and the girls on the rooftop. Then, I excitedly shared with her about Conor's recent gig in Sydney.

"Oh, that must have been an amazing experience. Why didn't you go?"

"Actually, I'd love to have seen him perform in Sydney. Unfortunately, the opportunity arose unexpectedly, and it would have been impossible for me to leave work at that time."

"Musicians… you have to watch out for those!" She laughed. "They're supposed to be flaky. But he doesn't seem like that."

"Not at all!" I reassured her.

As I reached across the table for one of Mum's scones, the necklace Conor had given me slipped out of my shirt and glinted in the light.

"I've never seen you wearing that lovely piece of jewellery before," Mum commented as she examined the neckpiece.

"It was a gift from Conor. He bought it for me on his Sydney tour."

As I recalled the falling Sycamore seeds from my dream, I felt a blush spread across my cheeks.

"True love is a wonderful thing, my Bridget." as she spoke, her eyes shone with kindness.

"I am glad love found you, my girl," she said as she squeezed my hands.

"How long do you think Dad will keep interrogating him in there?"

"For as long as he wants. Don't worry your head about it, though. Conor looks like he can take care of himself." We both laughed.

"Your father is a big softie. Conor is not in any danger." Mum laughed. Conor emerged slowly from the study with Dad. They were both smiling and laughing.

"Bridget will show you around the house," Dad said, winking at me.

I felt a sense of relief wash over me.

I took him down the hall to my room. It still had the same pink wallpaper and pop culture posters that I'd had since school. I was a little embarrassed by the album art of Taylor Swift's *Red* that was taped above my headboard. However, I was proud of the 2010 Belle & Sebastian *Write About Love* UK Tour poster that I'd thumbtacked next to my dressing table. The bookshelves, too, told the story of my teenage years. The top shelf was filled with Judy Blume novels, the *Harry Potter* series, and angsty teenage girl favourites like *Angus, Thongs And Full-Frontal Snogging*. The next shelf, I was happy to see, was stacked with more impressive reads. Next to several slim poetry collections sat *Pictures of Nothing: Abstract Art Since Pollock* by Kirk Varnedoe and an oversized compendium on Hieronymus Bosch.

Conor sat next to me on my bed and looked around with a mischievous smile on his face.

"So, how many boys have slept over here and left through that window?" he asked.

"You could be the first," I replied, slapping him playfully on the arm..

"That's so not true. I bet lots of boys have been in here."

"How many is lots? Who am I?" I raised my hands in mock exasperation.

"Did your father always grill your boyfriends in this way?" he asked. "Was he too harsh on you?"

"Not really. Just protective. But if he had access to a police database, he would run a full check on me." Conor laughed, then pretended to wipe sweat from his brow.

"He is just looking out for me."

"I know," he said. "That's why I think it's so sweet."

Conor stood up and kissed me before excitedly walking around the room, his fingers tracing the outlines of old posters. Like an eager schoolboy, he couldn't help but ask me questions about the stories each item held. Suddenly, his attention was captivated by the tickets for The Script that I had saved and carefully taped to the mirror. His eyebrow raised in admiration, impressed by my choice in music. Adjacent to the mirror, a display of one of my early paintings caught his eye. It was an abstract watercolour I had titled "Virgin Summer," a pretentious nod to my hopeful aspirations as an artist back then. It was nostalgic, seeing my own creation from such a distant time when dreams seemed so attainable.

Breaking the reverie, I smiled and suggested, "Enough about my room; it's time to show you yours!"

His expression filled with confusion as he raised his hands and questioned, "My room? What do you mean?"

"Yes, silly man," I exclaimed, grabbing his hand as we made our way out of my room. Pausing at the door adjacent to mine, I swung it open to reveal a pleasantly arranged guest room. A well-made bed, donned with a clean white sheet, occupied the centre of the room. Several of my old stuffed animals sat atop the simple white bedspread, adding a touch of nostalgia. A small table stood at one end of the room, and his luggage sat neatly beside the bed. Delicate white lace curtains hung from the windows, gently swaying as a cool breeze flowed in, carrying the sweet scent of lilacs. I noticed a lilac reed diffuser placed on the bedside table, an extra touch added by my mother. The room resembled a charming bed and breakfast, showcasing my mother's pride in keeping things tidy.

"Ta-da!" I exclaimed, gesturing towards the room. Conor chuckled in response.

"Do we get adjoining rooms?" he playfully inquired.

"Not exactly adjoining, but it's close," I replied.

"Technically, it is adjoining. Only one wall separates us," he cheekily pointed out.

"There's no connecting door, mister," I countered.

He wore a rueful smile on his face. "We could communicate in Morse code with quiet taps!"

Chuckling, I replied, "I don't know Morse code, but I must warn you, the walls are quite thin."

"Sweet!" he exclaimed, a mischievous glint in his eyes. Though I had an inkling of what he had in mind, I wagged my finger at him warningly.

"My father will literally skin you alive, mister, if he catches you sneaking around at night."

Chapter Twenty

RULE BREAKER

It read 1:11 a.m. on my old digital alarm clock. The silence was interrupted by occasional creaks from wooden floorboards and random noises from hot water running through old pipes. Dim moonlight filtered through the stained glass window above the front door, creating moving shadows. Everyone was fast asleep, or so I'd hoped. I found myself unable to find rest. Exhausted from a long journey and a busy week, sleep eluded me. Despite my best efforts, my mind refused to quiet down and surrender to slumber. Thoughts swirled, and my anxieties took hold. The festival, which had caused me so much stress, haunted my thoughts even now that it was over. I worried about what people would say and how we could improve for next year. It was essential for our success that word spread, and the anticipation for future festivals grew.

Yet, it wasn't just the festival occupying my mind. The knowledge that Conor was sleeping in the room next to me drove me to distraction. The longing to be held by his warm embrace, to feel his touch on my skin, overwhelmed me. No previous boyfriend had ever spent the night in this house, which had always represented my loneliness and unfulfilled desires. Now that Conor was here, I wanted to create new and intimate memories in this space. However, guilt also plagued me. My parents trusted me, believing I would follow their rules. I was torn between honouring their trust and the newfound boldness and audacity Conor had awakened in me.

Feeling restless and conflicted, I found myself stealthily tiptoeing into the guest room where Conor slept. The old floorboards groaned beneath my weight as I ventured into the corridor. A brief, heart-stopping moment made me freeze, convinced that my parents had heard me. A soft grunt emanating from their room followed by my dad's continued snores reassured me. Relieved, I exhaled slowly, my nightie feeling unbearably loud against the silence. Determined, I pressed on and gently opened the door to Conor's room. The creek of the hinges made me squint and pause, fearing discovery.

Stepping into Conor's room felt like a teenage rebellion. Excitement coursed through me as I took in the moonlit scene. It was absurd to think that I was sneaking around my own house to meet my own boyfriend, but the thrill of the chase and the potential consequences if caught invigorated me. Maybe Conor had been onto something when he had teased me about sneaking boys into my room as a teenager. The moonlit night held a sense of adventure and a handsome reward waiting just a few feet away.

Conor's room was silent, mirroring the rest of the house. The soft sound of his deep breathing filled the air, in rhythm with the rise and fall of his chest beneath the ivory duvet. He mumbled something in his sleep, the words unintelligible, before shifting onto his side. His innocence made me smile, and I struggled to hold back a giggle that threatened to escape.

Quietly, I approached the bed, my eyes tracing the contours of Conor's face. The shadows danced across his skin, mesmerising me. With utmost care, I slipped under the duvet, revelling in the warmth it provided. Grinning, I brushed a strand of hair from Conor's face, savouring the familiar softness against my fingertips. Mindful not to disturb his slumber, I resisted the urge to wake him with a kiss. Instead, I allowed myself to simply adore his handsome form, even in sleep. The ache in my heart grew, and I marvelled at the fact that he was here, in this house, and he was mine. It still felt like a dream.

I vividly recalled the dream I had in the standing stones, where our paths intertwined. What transpired between us after that surreal encounter?

His lips were full and warm as I kissed him. The sensation was intoxicating, making me yearn for an eternity in this embrace.

With an unexpected shift, his hands firmly gripped my waist, causing a jolt of surprise to nearly escape as a scream. My eyes widened, locking with his drowsy gaze. Dilated pupils and a desire-filled expression tainted his features, while his warm breath danced upon my face, sending an exhilarating shiver down my spine.

"Bridget Kennedy, you mischievous little minx, sneaking into my room in the middle of the night," he whispered, his voice husky and deep. With a playful grin, he added, "But I was hoping you would."

Without delay, he swiftly shifted our positions, his presence overwhelming. With a firm yet gentle grip, he restrained my hands above my head. Our chests pressed together, the rhythmic thumping of his heart so strong that I could feel it.. As his lips met mine, a surge of emotions flooded my senses. I sighed, inhaling his intoxicating scent, struggling to fathom his physical presence in this very house. The realisation from my dream that I had found him seemed almost too surreal to grasp.

His full and warm lips embraced mine, igniting a desire that made time stand still. In that moment, I craved nothing more than to be forever lost in his essence.

There was nothing soft or sensible about that kiss. It was intense and seductive from the very beginning, our lips moving in sync, hungry and demanding. As I struggled to release myself from his grip, the desire between us only grew stronger. Eventually, I managed to free myself, my hands instinctively finding their way to curl in his hair. With each gentle tug of my fingers, I pulled him closer, as if longing to merge our souls in that passionate moment.

A groan vibrated through his chest as I bit his lower lip, our tongues intertwined, stepping into a dance that was far beyond what either of our bodies could take.

As his hand slipped beneath my nightie, a shiver ran down my spine in response to his touch. My back arched instinctively as his fingers delicately traced their way downwards. The anticipation heightened, and as his hand reached above my breast, his fingers tenderly cupping it, a sudden hesitation overcame me. I pulled away, locking eyes with him. In the depths of his piercing blue gaze, a wave of intense emotions surged, speaking volumes without uttering a single word.

Despite my strong desire to kiss him again and make another move, I restrained myself and suggested, "We should probably stop while we can." He seemed ready to object and draw me closer, but I pleaded in a hushed tone, "Trust me, it's harder for me." I knew deep down that this wasn't the right place for such intimacy. With a wistful sigh, I slowly withdrew and settled myself against the bed frame. We sat together in silence for a few minutes, our breathing the only audible sound in the room. Seeking to break the tension, I turned towards him and asked, "How about a hot whiskey?" "To be continued back in Galway," he replied, planting a final kiss before rising from the bed. I watched him depart longingly, my desire still pulsing through me. I wished to keep him in bed and have my way with him, but being in my parents' house meant I had to respect their rules. As Conor moved gracefully in the moonlight, he resembled a magnificent Grecian statue bathed in a milky glow.

Chapter Twenty-One

LITTLE HEATHER

"Bridget! Bridget!"

I knew that voice before I even turned around.

My little cousin Heather galloped towards me, her fiery red hair flowing in the wind.

Her arms were wrapped around me before I had even realised it. She leapt into the air, almost knocking me off my feet. Smiling, I wrapped her tightly into a hug and kissed her on the cheek, inhaling the familiar scent of strawberry shampoo in her hair. I'd often washed that hair when I babysat for my aunt and uncle. The smell of the sweet strawberries brought me back to when she was still a baby. My heart ached with love at the memory. She was so tall now, a little woman in the making. She had long eyelashes and emerald green eyes that were as big as a doll's. Add to this her ruby-red cheeks and sweet smile. I couldn't help but think that one day, she'd steal hearts effortlessly. Sooner than I cared to think.

"Hey, you!" I exclaimed with delight, finally setting her back on the ground. "Look at you! So tall, and your hair is stunning!" Her red curls cascaded luxuriously down her back. I crouched down beside her and ran my fingers through them, admiring their silky softness. "You look like a real princess!" I wrapped her in one more embrace.

Little Heather beamed with pride, her posture straightening unconsciously to prove how tall she'd grown. I'd missed my little cousin so much. When she was around, her energy lit up the place, and everything felt exciting and magical. It was an incredible thing to see the world through a child's eyes. Her wonder, awe, and childlike goodness always gave me a fresh perspective on life. As I stood up, I held onto her little hand just in time to meet another familiar face. My aunt, wearing a warm and welcoming smile, extended her arms towards me. With a tight hug, she kissed both my cheeks to welcome me back home. Her husband, Uncle Chris, was standing behind her, already deep in conversation with my dad about a special BBQ sauce he'd discovered. I was aware their discussion would meander through various nonsensical topics. So, I simply smiled and acknowledged him.

Mum entered the kitchen, gracefully placing a bottle of red wine in the centre of the table, along with groceries and a delicious chocolate cake she had purchased earlier that morning.

"And who might this handsome gentleman be?" my aunt inquired, with a mischievous glint in her eye.

Conor waited patiently beside me to be introduced. Smiling, I wrapped my arm around his and said:

"This is Conor, my boyfriend." As the words slipped from my lips, my heart raced with joy. Being able to openly share with the world that this incredible man had chosen to share his heart with me left me utterly speechless. It made me feel like the luckiest girl in existence.

"Oh, I'm Cara, her mother's favourite sister." She smiled. Conor laughed.

"Lovely to meet you," he said warmly.

My aunt, undoubtedly the epitome of coolness, had an extraordinary way of connecting with me. She would often engage me with playful quizzes about boyfriends and act more like a trusted friend than a family member. And it was on one occasion, when she graciously handed me my very first drink, that I realised she was there to guide and support me through life's pivotal moments. From experiencing the thrill of getting tipsy to countless other milestones, my aunt's role model-like presence made it evident that she hoped I would, someday, extend the same invaluable guidance to my younger cousin, Heather.

"Now, could everyone *scram* out of this kitchen and make their way to the outside table?" Mum announced.

As we walked outside, Aunt Cara turned to me and asked, "So, your mother tells me this young man is a musician?"

I proudly replied, "That's right," Aunt Cara's eyes focused on Conor, intrigued.

"Let me be honest with you, Conor. I'm her aunt, and I can assure you, Bridget has no voice. In fact, no one in our family has a musical bone in their body." She chuckled as we all sat down around the round patio table. Adjacent to it was Dad's barbecue, ensuring the steaks would go straight from the grill to our plates.

Since the last time I was home, the backyard had been beautifully decorated. Mum had strung bistro lights along the fence, creating a cosy ambiance that cast a warm, golden glow over the rose bushes and manicured grass. The table was elegantly set with bronze napkin holders, jute placemats, and silver cutlery, accompanied by floral embroidered napkins. In the centre of the table sat glass jugs filled with sangria and pink lemonade, surrounded by six wine glasses. A platter of cheeses, sliced baguette, and apples was also displayed, making everything look absolutely delectable. Mum had gone above and beyond to impress Conor, and it was evident from the admiration on his face as he surveyed the table. Her thoughtfulness had paid off;

We all sat down, and Conor began to pour everyone sangria. Then he sat back and smiled at Cara.

"Well, it's not always about being born with talent. I've taught lots of people how to sing," he said. His hand squeezed mine beneath the table.

"If only I'd known that years ago—I could have been the next Sinéad O'Connor!" Everyone laughed.

There was no harm in Aunt Cara.

"You could have been," Conor agreed. "Singing, like any other skill, is about practice. People often assume being musical is about innate talent, but I think it's about hard work."

"Hear, hear!" Cara said approvingly. My heart swelled momentarily with pride at the look of admiration on my aunt's face. Conor knew how to impress my relatives.

I sat back and observed Conor and my family together, talking and joking as if they'd known each other for years. This sight almost made my heart burst with joy. I knew from the start that they'd get along, but seeing it happen before my eyes meant more than anything I had expected.

Heather sat next to me, swinging her legs. They were too short to reach the grass. As Conor asked Cara about her work, Heather leaned towards me.

"Do you want to hear a joke?" she asked, her eyes mischievous.

"I want to hear a joke," Conor said, turning to her at once.

She blushed and suddenly looked shy. I squeezed her hand for encouragement.

"Go on then, tell us the joke," I coaxed.

Heather hesitated, then leaned in again as if telling a secret. "Why did the farmer put 239 beans on his toast?" she asked, her mouth already twitching with a pre-emptive laugh.

"Why?" Conor asked, looking amused.

"Because if he'd put one more, it would have been too farty!"

Aunt Cara, Conor, and Heather all burst into hysterical giggles while Mum clapped a hand over her mouth. I could tell she thought it was funny but was a bit surprised by Heather's language. I laughed too, although mostly from how cute it was to hear Heather say "farty".

The laughter seemed to make Heather less shy.

"Conor, do you play guitar?" she asked timidly as she looked directly at him with wide green eyes. Conor laughed and nodded.

"Yes, I sure do. Do you want to see it?"

Heather went silent and looked towards her mum for permission. She wasn't the type to immediately talk to a new person. I was delighted she'd warmed up to Conor. She then froze with all the sudden attention as she hid behind her mother.

"How about you play us something?" asked Mum.

Conor hesitated. He may have been used to large crowds, but being asked to play for his girlfriend's family on the spot surely must have felt nerve-racking. My aunt seemed to enjoy his hesitation. She intervened.

"Come on! If you don't, we'll soon have to bore you with conversations about the weather or the best BBQ sauce." She whispered the last part, gesturing towards my dad and uncle, who were still in deep conversation around the barbecue about God knows what.

I couldn't help but chuckle. Indeed, that had always been the case. The two men engaged in conversations that went nowhere every time they spoke. They would both win gold medals at the Olympics if there was a category for blathering.

Aunt Cara, with her sparkly personality and easy laughter, was anything but boring. She was twelve years younger than my mother. This age gap meant that she often felt more like my older cousin than my aunt. She was the fun aunt, the fun sister, something I think my mum resented a little bit. In her twenties, she'd travelled all over the world with a series of quirky boyfriends—she'd even lived in an Ashram in India for three months. I'd not inherited her footloose, wanderlust spirit, but I admired it. She loved hearing people's stories and always offered a shoulder to cry on.

Conor stood up. "Back in a minute. I'll go grab my guitar from the boot of the car." As he passed my chair, he leaned down and whispered, "I'm going to write a song about this weekend and your adorable family. And you'll be the villain for seducing me last night."

"You are not!" I breathed back, a little shocked.

"Hey, no secrets at the table, you two!" Cara teased. "Unless you're going to tell us what you're talking about?"

I blushed a deep crimson, which gave it all away. My mum and Cara burst into laughter.

Chapter Twenty-Two

BROODY

My eyelids were heavy with sleep, yet despite the temptation to remain in bed, I woke up feeling more recharged than I had in months. The sun's gentle rays streamed in through the window. It bathed my bedspread and skin in a luminous, golden hue. Tentatively, I stretched, feeling the release of tension in my arms and back. The past two days at home had refreshed me to the core. If I was honest with myself, I'd been exhausted—even with Conor being such a breath of fresh air, the festival had drained me of all my energy. After all the preparations, media deadlines, phone calls and dozens of meetings with Ciara, my body had yearned for some downtime. Luckily, my family gathering had come just at the right time. Returning home felt like the perfect cure to release all traces of my festival fatigue.

The inviting aroma of freshly ground coffee filled the air invigorating my senses. Smiling, I tiptoed my way to the living room, my arms wrapped around me, keeping the woollen nightgown close to my body. My feet, in their thick socks, tread lightly on the floorboards. The house was usually quiet and serene in the mornings. Today, however, the air hummed with the cheerful chatter of my loved ones. In the kitchen, my Mum and Aunt Cara animatedly exchanged stories, reminiscing about a row they'd had with a local woman in town years ago. Their laughter echoing down the hall. The absence of my father's voice indicated that he must have been up late with my uncle, leaving him to sleep in.

Another set of voices drifted from the living room in between twangs of guitar strings. I wondered what was going on. The notes were way too off-tune to be Conor's, but no one in my family played. My eyes were still sticky with sleep. Curiosity led me into the sitting room, where I was greeted by the most endearing sight.

Conor was on the couch beside my little cousin. Heather was holding his guitar and watching him with big curious eyes. Conor was teaching her to play guitar. She was staring at her fingers on the frets as she tried to absorb all of Conor's words. He offered her clear and simple instructions that she easily grasped. Heather, completely absorbed, watched her own fingers on the frets as Conor guided her, moulding them into the correct positions for different chords. With determination, she attempted to replicate his gestures, her seven-year-old fingers clumsily brushing against the guitar strings, producing rusty sounds, but nonetheless showing great promise.

The scene was absolutely heart-warming, to say the least. Watching Conor teach Heather with such patience and gentleness sparked a profound maternal instinct within me. My heart swelled, straining against my chest, overflowing with tenderness at the sight of them together. It ignited a longing deep within me to envision Conor teaching our own future children how to play guitar.

Surprisingly, the thought had never crossed my mind before. I had never imagined us having children together. Yet, in that very moment, I could clearly picture Conor as an amazing father, playing music with our kids. And I, embracing my role as a mother, teaching them to paint.

In an instant, tears welled up inside me. The emotion was so potent I had to grip the door frame to steady myself. Visions of Conor cradling our newborn child filled my mind, overwhelming me to the point where I felt lightheaded. This future became an urgent need for me. Though I had never realised I wanted it, I now found myself impatient for it. Suddenly, the desire that had been lingering on the outskirts of my consciousness the night before rushed back with a passion. I had to be with him. I felt broody.

The thought sent waves of exhilaration mixed with a touch of insanity through my being. I shook myself, desperately attempting to shake off this intrusive idea.

At my movement, they finally noticed me. Heather grinned up at me, exposing the gap where her front teeth were missing.

"Morning, sleepy head!" said Conor, flashing me a grin.

"Bridget! Bridget! Listen to what Conor's taught me!" Heather called out excitedly, her voice at a higher octave than normal.

Smiling, I walked towards them and cuddled beside Conor. He kissed my forehead as Heather struggled to balance the guitar on her lap. Conor shook his head in amusement and jumped to her aid. He draped one hand around the little girl and supported the guitar with the other. Heather looked through her long lashes at him. There was so much admiration in her gaze. Someday, I knew our child would love him that much, too.

Banishing these thoughts from my mind, I smiled and leaned back to observe them.

"There, like that," he said before wrapping his hands around me again.

Heather began to sing. She'd forgotten most of the chords, and the sequence in which she played them was far from the actual melody of the song, but I still applauded once she was done. I was proud of her motivation and enthusiasm. It was the most adorable thing I'd ever seen.

"Bridget! Did you like it?" She looked up at me hopefully.

"Of course I did." I grinned down at her and ruffled her hair.

"Conor promised me that he'll let me sing on stage with him when I grow older." A lock of hair fell across her face, and I couldn't help but brush it away. I looked between Conor and Heather and laughed.

"I am sure he will! You already got yourself two huge fans!" I exclaimed as I pulled her closer so I could kiss her cheek.

"No, Conor isn't my fan." Heather shook her head. "He said he'll marry me when I grow up!" she exclaimed as she jumped to wrap her arms around his neck.

I had to clap my hand to my mouth to keep from laughing out loud. I looked at Conor, who was also trying to muffle the sound of his laughter. Then, I turned back at Heather, who was looking at me expectantly, awaiting my reaction.

"Is that so?" I asked, nodding seriously. "Am I invited to the wedding?"

"Whose wedding?" It was my mother's voice that intervened this time.

We all turned to look towards the door. She was carrying a tray of coffee, my aunt and uncle in tow. They were all still in their pyjamas and wore the fluffy slippers I'd bought them last Christmas.

"Mine!" Heather giggled.

This time, no one was able to hold in their laughter. Uncle Chris came around the small coffee table and picked Heather up, pecking her nose before saying, "How about you finish primary school first before I walk you up the aisle?" He then sat down with his little girl and gave her a hug.

Chapter Twenty-Three

POP THAT CORK

I felt sad as we left my family home. Everyone came out onto the driveway to wave goodbye. Mum and Dad had their arms around each other. They had tears in their eyes. Chris and Cara stood smiling on either side of them. Little Heather was in her mother's arms. When the car started moving, she broke free and ran after us, waving frantically. I thought I saw a tear rolling down her cheek.

As the car slowly pulled out onto the main road, I looked back to get one last glimpse of everyone. Feelings of sadness overwhelmed me. Leaving home often reminded me that life is too short. There was no guarantee I'd ever see any of them again.

Where were these negative feelings coming from?

I rarely thought this way, but when I did it made me reflect and appreciate every moment I spent with my family.

Our drive back to Galway was breathtaking. The sun, with its vibrant hues of red and orange, painted the horizon in a mesmerising display. There were only a few clouds scattered across the sky, their delicate pink tones were enhanced by the setting sun. I gazed in awe as the soft blue sky transformed itself into a sherbet-coloured canvas as it approached the horizon. I imagined painting this. The further we travelled, the more my spirits lifted, with thoughts of our visit bringing only happiness.

My trip home had provided the solace I needed. A place where I could recharge and find respite from the whirlwind of stress that had consumed me over the past few weeks. Surrounded by the love of family makes you realise, there's no place like home. My mum, with her warm hugs and endless cups of tea, helped me release all the festival-related stress that had weighed me down.

The countryside painted a picture of tranquillity, with low stone walls and charming old farm houses, nestled against an emerald green landscape. We passed through small towns, boasting vibrant terraced houses and grand churches with heavenly steeples. As the sun began its descent over the ocean, it cast an enchanting red hue across the darkening sky. The fading light delicately kissed the tips of tall evergreens, making them appear golden. A solitary street light flickered to life, casting a warm, orange glow on the road. Time stood still, as I allowed myself to be consumed by this peaceful moment, hoping it would last forever. Aurora's haunting melody, "Runaway," played softly on the car stereo, merging with the steady hum of the engine and setting a solemn tone. Everything felt perfect.

When we arrived at Conor's apartment it was dark and empty. He fumbled with the lights and gas heater, "These feckin' heaters take ages to come on." As he spoke, I heard the clanking of old pipes. Sure enough, soon after, the acrid smell of gas wafted through the air. Old gas heaters always smelled like that when first switched on. In fact, it strangely comforted me. It reminded me of home.

While I had been to his place a couple of times before, tonight was my first time staying over. Usually, we would go back to my place because the boys often stayed at Conor's place. I realised I had a perfect opportunity to learn more about the man I was now totally besotted with.

As I shrugged off my jacket onto the couch, I took a look around the room. The place was messy in the living room area. James had left his guitar there on a stand. A blanket was draped from the edge of the couch. Around it, sheet music and a few magazines were scattered on the coffee table. Next to these were two empty bottles of champagne and a half-eaten bowl of strawberries, still fresh enough to eat. There was an empty pizza box on the edge of the dining table and two shot glasses beside it, still sticky with alcohol. Conor disappeared into the kitchen. I shivered, then walked towards the heater, slipping off my shoes.

Conor's home was clearly that of a musician. Framed posters of The Beatles and John Lennon during his solo career had been hung in the sitting room. One corner was filled with instruments of all kinds, including a bodhrán and a trumpet. I had no idea he played either of those. On the nearest bookshelf, there were framed pictures of Orcás. Next to these was a collection of old leather-bound books on Irish history. The furniture kept with this masculine theme. The chairs and couch were a similar chestnut-coloured leather, and matched the wooden coffee table. I bent down and picked up some loose paper, my eyes squinting to make out the scribbles on it. I wasn't a songwriter, but I could immediately tell it was an attempt to produce new lyrics. My house looked similar now, with discarded sketches and ideas on paper everywhere, evidence of my struggles as an artist..

"I know, it's a feckin' mess, but the boys have been here over the weekend—" Conor said suddenly as he walked towards the sofa.

With him were two glasses and a bottle of champagne. "There were three bottles in the fridge. The feckers have drunk two of them already." He'd ditched his shoes and walked in his socks across toward me.

"Where'd they come from?" Conor laughed, pointing to the strawberries. His hair was messy. His carefully styled locks had been thrown into disarray from the long drive home.

I smiled as Conor positioned the glasses and champagne on the coffee table.

"What's that for?" I inquired.

"This"—he looked at the bottle—"is to celebrate our success at Galway360. We were given three bottles after the festival from someone anonymous." I looked at the bottle and realised it was Dom Pérignon. "Wow, I like it," I teased as I reached for a glass. "Got some fans who are high rollers, eh? Conor smiled as he opened the bottle. He placed his thumb near the base and pushed the cork upwards so that it shot out with a satisfying pop. The cork hit the ceiling as bubbly froth ran down the neck of the bottle. I laughed excitedly. Conor cheered "To us," then filled both champagne flutes. We clink our glasses before taking the first sip. It was dry and delicious. The bubbles danced on my tongue making my eyes water with its crispness. I loved it. I rarely drank expensive champagne. I'd thought that I wouldn't be able to taste the difference, but I could.

As I sipped it, I closed my eyes and wondered who'd have given the lads such extravagant bottles. My first guess was a record producer, but why wouldn't they leave a note? Why be so coy? An anonymous, expensive gift reminded me of something a secret admirer might leave. But who would have a crush on Orcás... or on Conor?

As I tilted my head back and allowed the champagne's fizzy flavour to dance on my palate, I made a conscious decision to set aside my suspicion for the time being. Instead, I chose to focus on the symphony of flavours that unfolded with each sip.

Indeed, the festival was a massive success. It had turned out to be even better than I had initially planned or hoped for. Its success could soon become a calling card that could lead to exciting new opportunities.

"You know..." I moved my gaze from my glass towards Conor, "I can think of other ways we can celebrate."

I stared in Conor's direction, then blew him a kiss. I placed my empty glass on the coffee table and watched Conor's Adam's apple move slowly as he drank more champagne. His eyes lit up almost instantly. He then moved closer and gently traced the outline of my lips.

"What did you have in mind Missy?" he asked innocently, his voice sounding hoarse and heavy.

Smiling, I moved closer towards him. I reached for his hand and then gently placed it on my breast. I then took a sip from his glass and slowly placed it on the coffee table, holding eye contact.

Conor seemed to be frozen, waiting for me to make a move. I couldn't hold back any longer so I jumped up on his lap. I'd been frustrated ever since my parents' place. Now I had to have him. I thought my body would burst with desire if we didn't make love soon. I couldn't hold back these wild urges any longer. Without hesitation, I reached for him, my hands pulling him closer as our lips touched. The kiss began with a slow, tantalising rhythm, enticing my taste buds with the lingering flavour of champagne on his lips. As he groaned, a delightful pleasure rippled through me, prompting him to part his mouth, inviting our tongues to dance in harmony. Waves of exquisite sensations coursed down my spine, intensified by the gentle caress of his fingers through my hair, cascading down to my shoulders. With a firm but tender grip, Conor held me close, deepening the urgency of his kisses. Time seemed to stand still as we savoured each other, until a profound tingling sensation permeated my very being. I was on fire for him. I needed him to tear my clothes off. He sensed my eagerness as his tongue quivered along my lips, then pushed into me. He was inside of me, tasting me, devouring me. Our tongues and lips moved together in a cosmic dance that was as old as time itself. Stars seemed to be wheeling overhead, transporting us back in time. Memories began to replay before my eyes. Conor, in the grove, with the sycamore seeds.

Conor, pulling me onto the stage. Conor, kissing me between the standing stones in this life and our past life. Always Conor. The sound of the raven came to me as if I were still in the clearing. More memories rushed back. Our drive up the coast. The picnic by the standing stones; their whispers of lives past. Dancing at the restaurant. Our first kiss on the rooftop.

As our kiss grew in intensity, he suddenly picked me up and pushed me against a wall. His hands pinned my arms above my head, keeping me in place. The kiss was rough by now, leaving us breathless and gasping for air. His other hand trailed down my body, exploring its curves, his fingers lingering a bit longer over my breast then between my legs. I arched my back and gasped, then lifted one leg to curl around his waist. Groaning, he let go of my hands and secured both my legs around his torso. His fingers travelled up my thighs, pulling the hem of my dress with them. His lips had abandoned mine and moved to my neck, sending me a wave of coursing desire.

My dress was off before I knew it. My body shivered involuntarily, not because of the cool air but Conor's touch. Every cell in my body seemed to respond to him, trembling and yearning for more. I had never behaved so brazenly in my life, Conor was changing the essence of my being.

"Let's go to my room," he whispered, his voice barely audible, dripping with lust and need.

Chapter Twenty-four

UNDER THREAT?

"So, what are your plans now that the festival is over?" Conor asked as we drove slowly down Sea Road, which was congested with traffic.

I took a few moments to think about it while we waited for the traffic to clear. The truth was I wasn't really sure yet. Luckily, I'd earned enough money from Galway360, so I didn't have to rush into anything straight away. I certainly wasn't the type of person to let the grass grow under my feet or sit around and watch my savings dry up. However, I did want to focus on some other creative projects. Projects that made me happy.

"I was thinking of taking on some freelance work. That way, I could work from home and focus on passions I've been neglecting for ages."

"What kind of freelance work?"

"I'm not sure yet." I shrugged. "I haven't thought that far. Most likely what I do best, which is to promote events." I shrugged. "But if I play it smart and charge well, I can have time to do other projects while covering my bills. I have a few ideas in mind!" I said confidently.

"What about painting? Did you figure out what you'd like to paint?"

Since Galway360, I tried out new ideas and themes around the standing stones. If luck was on my side, I would complete several canvases by the end of the month. Of course, I wanted to keep this project under wraps. My confidence had been shattered, and I was still unsure of how capable I was of resurrecting my inner artist.

"Well, I'm not sure about that either," I replied.

"You know, I was thinking, how about we go somewhere for the weekend? You can take your paint and brushes, and I can take my guitar. Maybe it'll do us both a world of good!"

"Go where?" I asked curiously.

"Well, that"—he trailed off as he parked the car—"is something I don't know." He laughed.

"Well, you better figure it out, because I love the idea."

He saluted. "Yes, boss!"

I rolled my eyes, shook my head in amusement, and then leaned in to kiss him. "Good luck with the rehearsals!" I added as I opened the car door.

"Thanks for a great night, Missy. You have fun with the girls too! And ask them when they'll be free. Maybe we can all have dinner again."

I nodded, then got out of the car. After watching Conor speed off, I stood on the pavement for a few moments to acknowledge how happy I was. Last night, he had rewritten the definition of romance and passion in my life. The intensity of our lovemaking and the undeniable chemistry between us had made every minute together feel like an eternity. It was an experience unlike any other, leaving me feeling completely fulfilled and longing for more. He'd been a true gentleman and prioritised my pleasure, yet kept me begging for more. In doing so, he'd again awakened that powerful and primal need I never knew I had. In his arms, I became someone else entirely: all woman, all instinct, ready to worship and be worshipped. Last night,

Conor had certainly worshipped me, and I think I did a pretty good job of worshipping him too. Even thinking about it sent shivers down my spine. I was certainly walking on air that morning, and it was somewhat distracting! I couldn't help smiling from ear to ear.

The Galway Tea Emporium was located amidst a lively cluster of restaurants and boutiques, I couldn't help but reminisce about the memories I had made there over the years. The charming tea house had been a beloved fixture in Galway long before I had moved here. Taking a deep breath, I straightened my clothes and smoothed out my hair. I knew I couldn't let my thoughts drift to last night's passionate events in front of the girls, who were waiting for me inside. They were sure to pick up on my lack of composure, and I wasn't exactly known for being subtle. I had a feeling that if they found out, I'd never hear the end of it.

The Galway Tea Emporium was known for its vast collection of loose-leaf teas from around the world. As I stepped in, the welcoming aroma of jasmine and rose petals hit me like a warm embrace. It was a comforting and soothing scent.

Opposite these, locally-made ceramic teapots and mugs were on display for sale. The Tea House even had hookahs that could be rented by the hour. In the back, there was a mix of regular and low tables with pillows for seating. The atmosphere resembled that of a traditional Asian tea house. There was also an outside area with a covered gazebo. Flush with plants, this area was great during the warm summer months.

The girls were already inside. They were sitting at our usual spot engaged in deep conversation. Rosie was speaking animatedly with her hands while Laura listened intently. In front of both were steaming cups of tea. With a spring in my step, I made my way to the table. When Rosie and Laura spotted me, they stopped their conversation and waved. Both had mischievous grins on their faces, which made me wonder what they were talking about.

Unlike any other day, the girls were dressed casually and comfortably. They'd both ditched their usual heavy make-up and heels for clear faces and trainers. "Hey, ladies!" I said in a cheery voice as I leaned in to hug them.

"Someone's in a good mood," joked Rosie.

"Who wouldn't be? Did you forget what Conor did at the festival?" Laura announced.

I knew the girls meant the part where Conor pulled me up onstage and kissed me. But at the back of my mind, the intimate details of the last night played out.

"So, what were you girls gossiping about?"

I looked between Rosie and Laura, who exchanged a smirk. I instantly knew something was going on. I leaned over the table and squinted at them.

"Ask her!" Laura said as she winked at Rosie. A devilish grin played on Rosie's lips.

My gaze turned towards Rosie, who was practically bursting with excitement. Her eyes twinkled as she spoke, obviously searching for the right words. I thought I could guess what she was about to say. I recognised the look on her face from our countless deep, meaningful conversations over the years. Still, I waited for her to make the big reveal. Laura, on the other hand, had no patience, and loudly announced:

"Rosie and James are officially a couple!" She spat out the words as if they were burning fire. "And just so we're clear, they made sure to celebrate!" She raised one eyebrow suggestively. Rosie blushed.

I turned my attention towards Rosie. "Congratulations," I said, "he's a great guy."

"Thanks, Bridget. I only met him thanks to you." She smiled.

"What do you mean they made sure to celebrate?" I asked Laura curiously.

"You know what I mean," Laura said pointedly.

Blushing, Rosie confessed, "We had a party for two at Conor's apartment. Two bottles of champagne were delivered, courtesy of a famous Irish singer, Amanda du Prey. Little did we know that our night would escalate into a whirlwind of debauchery."

As Rosie's words hung in the air, I fell silent. Amanda du Prey, a renowned singer, had sent the champagne? The tension grew, as I pondered the implications. Why would such a prominent figure be sending champagne to Conor's apartment?

Curiosity ignited within me, and I couldn't help but ask, "How do you know it was Amanda du Prey?"

Rosie shrugged, her eyes glimmering with excitement. "James told me he got a surprise delivery and Conor had received a text from her, asking if the bottles had arrived."

It was an unexpected revelation, one that sent waves of doubt and unease through me. Why hadn't Conor mentioned anything about the sender of the champagne? The thought gnawed at me, a knot formed in my stomach. Had he intentionally left out these details?

Attempting to brush off the uneasy feeling, I forced a smile. But inside, my mind raced with questions and uncertainty. Was there something more to this story? What did Amanda du Prey's gesture really mean?

Chapter Twenty-Five

AMANDA DU PREY

I was no stranger to parties. Laura and Rosie had dragged me to countless events at a moment's notice. From product launches to promotional gigs, and even organising a few myself, I had seen it all. But this particular party was on a whole different level. A room filled to the brim with celebrities, faces I had only ever seen on social media and television. Amanda du Prey, the shining star among them, commanded attention with her massive following. From scandals to undeniable talent, she had captured the hearts of fans around the country and beyond. Despite not being my favourite musician, I couldn't deny her allure. Her songs, often scrutinised for hidden messages about her famous romances, always sparked intense debates. Tonight, I found myself amidst the glitz and glamour, feeling surprisingly out of place. As I looked around, everyone seemed flawless, dressed in expensive designer outfits and adorned with exquisite jewellery. Their impeccable hair and makeup left me feeling self-conscious. I fidgeted with my golden dress, trying to find the right posture while constantly running my fingers through my hair. If anyone knew where I was tonight and whose party I was attending, they would surely envy me. But in this moment, I couldn't help but feel like I stood out, like I didn't belong among this sea of perfection.

In the meantime, I had chosen a gold dress from Zara and hastily applied my makeup in the taxi on the way to the party. The dress was a stylish sheath mini dress with a crewneck and a cape that draped elegantly on my shoulders. When I had tried it on earlier, I had felt confident, but now I couldn't help but feel painfully under-dressed for the occasion. Conor had mentioned that the party would be fancy, yet I had assumed my Zara dress was a splurge. In hindsight, I realised I should have opted for a designer dress or something from Rent the Runway to match the glamour of the event.

It was entirely my fault. I should have known better. This wasn't just a casual night out at Busker Brownes; it was Amanda du Prey's party. I felt like such an idiot.

Conor seemed to pick up on my unease and suddenly halted, turning to face me while the rest of the group continued on and disappeared into the crowd. He took hold of my hand, his eyes filled with affection and a playful smile hinting on his lips.

"You look absolutely beautiful," he whispered softly, catching me off guard and causing a warm blush to colour my cheeks. He chuckled at my reaction and then turned to join the others, never letting go of my hand.

As we caught up with the rest of the group, they were all gazing in Amanda's direction. She looked exactly as she did on TV, if not even more stunning. With her long red hair and a shimmering blue dress that accentuated her flawless hourglass figure, I would have thought the blue clashed with her red locks, but it somehow worked effortlessly. Amanda possessed the ability to pull off any combination. As she gracefully glided through the room, exuding charisma and confidence, she appeared ravishing with her high cheekbones, captivating blue eyes, and flawless ivory skin. Her lips were painted an alluring shade of red, making her mouth look irresistibly sultry. She strode towards our group with a beaming smile, radiating power and charm. The music thumped loudly, but Amanda's clicking heels seemed to reverberate throughout the room, making a bold statement. In contrast, mine felt timid and out of place, just like I did.

"Pull yourself together, Bridget. What's wrong with you?" I silently scolded myself, determined to push away the intimidation that was creeping into my heart.

Conor was the first to greet her. She eagerly enveloped him in a hug, completely disregarding my presence. As her arms wrapped around him, I couldn't help but notice how she rested her head on his shoulder, her long red hair falling forward, emitting a captivating scent of lilacs and lavender.

"Conor!" she exclaimed when she finally released him from her tight embrace, her hand lingering on his arm just a bit too long. "I'm so glad you made it."

Conor's face lit up with joy. I couldn't help but notice a slight flush creeping across his cheeks. "Thank you for inviting us."

As I remembered the expensive bottles of champagne, doubt flickered within me, questioning Amanda's motives. I'd kept my suspicions suppressed. I scolded myself for allowing self-consciousness to cloud my thoughts, instructing myself not to project my insecurities onto others.

Conor gestured towards the rest of us, saying, "These are my band members, James and Donal. And this is Rosie, James's girlfriend."

Amanda's greeting to the others lacked the same enthusiasm she had shown towards Conor, offering them a weak handshake. Despite this, I tried to ignore it. When Conor introduced me as his girlfriend, Amanda's reaction was unmistakable. There was a sudden shift in her expression, a hint of unwelcomeness. She shook my hand limply, scrutinising me with an unimpressed look. Her friendly smile faded, replaced by an arrogant smirk, a subtle message that I wasn't welcome. Although the guys may not have noticed, any girl would have picked up on it. I could have imagined it, but my gut instinct told me otherwise. Regardless, there was nothing I could do. We were at her party, and Conor's band had been invited as guests and performers. So, I smiled back, acting oblivious to Amanda's attitude.

Without skipping a beat, Amanda refocused her attention on Conor, her radiant smile returning.

"So, shall we get that song over with? Then we can enjoy the party and leave the entertainment to the band I hired," Amanda suggested to the boys.

"Sounds like a plan. We can have a great time afterwards," Donal replied, shrugging off any signs of tension and exuding excitement. If they could have, they would have jumped on stage the moment we arrived.

"Good luck!" I whispered, planting a kiss on Conor's cheek.

"Thank you," he whispered back, before following Amanda towards the stage.

The performance was intended to test their chemistry on stage, making me feel slightly nervous. However, I had full confidence that Ocrás would excel and soon finalise their plans to go on tour. With a smile, I turned to Rosie, who was equally anxious and thrilled as she looked after James.

"Come on, let's get a closer look," I suggested, grabbing her hand and pulling her deeper into the crowd, closer to the edge of the stage.

Chapter Twenty-Six

ART SPACE

My body swayed with the music. I was lost in my own world. Loose strands of hair tickled the back of my neck with every move. My hand danced with the brush, gently guiding it against the canvas in front of me as if pulled by another force. It left jet streams of colours that curled and wrapped around each other to form an elaborate image. The colours were bright, capturing the rays of sunlight that pierced through the gap in the curtains. A kaleidoscope of sensations took hold of me. The smell of the paint was strong and pungent. The texture felt thick and wet. With each stroke, the layers became more intricate, and ridges formed where the oils overlapped and blended until my mind was lost in the shapes and patterns. I was no longer thinking. I painted by instinct, all my careful planning and sketching forgotten. It had been replaced by something inexplicable, a force like divine inspiration that took hold of me and brought my innermost desires out in a heady exploration of texture and colour. Whatever the final product would be, I knew it would be the most authentic expression of myself.

I took a step back as a green droplet fell from the tip of my wet brush. I ignored the new stain on my living room floor, much like all the other paint drops that covered my bare feet and skin from my fingers up to my elbow. I ignored everything else around me, too, like the time passing and the sun setting outside my window. The only things I focused on were the drums in the music and the sound of large raindrops hitting the window as I painted. I painted barefoot, like always. Feeling the floorboards underneath my feet helped me feel grounded. This made me feel like I was not separate from my work, but part of it. In bare feet, I could feel the rhythm of the painting and the rhythm of my body. This way, my brushstrokes didn't feel unpredictable. They flowed from the painting and into my hands, then back out from my hands to the canvas.

I stood back and stared at the canvas, checking the new layers and textures that I'd added since the early dawn. I had spent the last four days trapped between the walls of my apartment. I hadn't gone out, and no one had come in. Not even the girls dared to interrupt my sudden wave of creativity. Conor had called me a few times and occasionally texted. He'd even sent me food just to make sure I didn't forget to eat. He respected my privacy; as an artist, he knew how important peace was in the creative process.

I stood back and inspected the image that had come to life. It was nearly finished. At first, I'd been scared, uncertain of how well I'd do. Fortunately, it wasn't as bad as I'd expected. Yes, initially, it had been extremely hard. My hand felt heavy when I first dipped my brush after years away from the practice. My fingers weren't sure where to first press the brush or how to move it against the blank canvas. But with every stroke, my hand got lighter, the image in my head seemed clearer, and my vision sharpened.

I was about to resume when I was interrupted by the chime of my doorbell. Frowning, I placed the brush down and grabbed a towel, wiping my hands as I made my way to the door. When I opened it,

Conor was standing on the doorstep. He smiled excitedly as he handed me a single red rose.

"Conor!" I exclaimed, "I thought you had rehearsals!" The rose looked beautiful and had the sweetest fragrance. I'd missed contact with the outside world while I'd been locked away with my paintings.

"It got cancelled," he said. "Amanda had some 'urgent' plans." He walked past me and into the hallway, then turned and took me in his arms. "But I see your plans are still on," he joked, nodding towards my stained jumpsuit.

I laughed as Conor tucked a strand of hair that had escaped my messy bun, then kissed me. It felt good to be close to him again. Even though I'd been caught up in my art, I'd still missed him.

When I completely immersed myself in painting, the rest of the world seemed to fade away. I used to experience this back in school, which often led teachers and classmates to label me as absent-minded. The truth was, I was simply lost in my art. However, when I saw Conor holding a rose, I realised how much I'd missed him.

"Is the painting finished? Can I have a sneak peek?" Conor asked, drawing me in closer as he wrapped his hands around my waist. He didn't seem to mind the possibility of getting paint on his clothes.

I hesitated for a moment, unsure of how to respond. While I was satisfied with the progress of my painting, deep down, I wasn't ready to reveal my new work just yet. Conor had seen all my previous paintings back at my parents' house, and I had raved to him about my love for art. I didn't want to disappoint him. The thought of someone seeing my art after such a long period of concealment was terrifying, especially someone like Conor whom I admired so much. He poured his heart and soul into his art, and it had brought him immense success. Although Conor saw me as a genuine artist, I still longed for his admiration of my latest creation.

"I'll take that as a yes," he responded after a brief silence. Without warning, he was already in the living room beside my easel.

Within seconds, he stood in front of the mahogany stand, gazing down at the canvas intently. I patiently awaited his reaction. Several seconds passed, and he remained silent. I allowed him to absorb the painting without interjecting. Eventually, I couldn't handle the suspense any longer.

"Well?" I asked hesitantly, unable to discern the expression on his face, which caused my stomach to twist with nerves. After a momentous pause, Conor turned towards me, his entire face radiating with delight.

"Do you know where this painting would look absolutely perfect?" he asked excitedly.

Shaking my head, I awaited his response.

"In my new apartment," he declared. His eyes lit up as he revelled in my surprised expression. "Bridget, I love this piece, and I want it hanging in my living room, so I can admire it every day. I can't wait to show you my new place."

Chapter Twenty-Seven

A Breath of Fresh Air

Conor described his new apartment as a breath of fresh air. He was so excited to finally show me the place.

When we arrived, I couldn't have imagined such a significant upgrade. My jaw literally dropped when I walked through the front door.

Conor's old place was a typical two-bed Galway apartment with a tiny kitchen, woolly carpets, mouldy ceiling corners and creaky floorboards. There was lots of tired furniture that had seen better days. It had the familiar Galway look of having been picked out by the landlord a decade previously and never replaced. Most people would describe it as 'student digs' or even a bit of a kip. The walls were in bad need of a paint job, and the outside needed a power wash. However, the old place had character; it had a certain 'lived-in' artistic charm to it with its old Chesterfield leather couch and bright orange velvet cushions. Conor joked they had been made by a crazed fan called Vicky. I couldn't tell if he was serious or not. Loose music magazines were always piled neatly on top of one another beneath the coffee table. Several guitars, amps and pedals were arranged in one corner of the living room and beneath the kitchen bench. Song sheets and lyrics always decorated the coffee table and kitchen bar. The place might have been old, but it had Conor and Orcás written all over it.

Times had changed.

Conor's new penthouse apartment was bright and spacious, with chic furniture and a modern facade. It felt like a breath of fresh air. Wandering around it, I started to feel a little jealous.

"That piano was built in 1890 in Bieger, Switzerland," Conor said. "The landlord hasn't a clue of its value and left it behind. I think it charms the place, old versus new. We did a deal over the phone on all the furniture just before he left to go overseas."

A lot of thought and clever planning had gone into the apartment's modern design and style. It boasted a spacious living area with stylish polished concrete flooring. Light filled the living room from a large skylight and floor-to-ceiling windows . Two hand-woven Persian rugs rested on the living room floor. Both had a vast range of colours and took centre stage in the middle of the room.

The kitchen featured an island in the middle with lots of space for food prep. The floor had dark tiles that made the white cabinets along the walls pop. These were overshadowed, however, by the large range, which had six hobs. One wall was made of exposed brick that had been painted white. Every appliance was brand new and in sleek chrome-grey. It was the chicest kitchen I had ever been in. Beside the kitchen was a door leading to an outside balcony that overlooked the Galway rooftops. As I gazed straight ahead, I could spot the Spanish Arch jutting out into Galway Bay. It would be the perfect place to sit and read on cool autumn evenings or sip cocktails on summer afternoons.

I had yet to see the two bedrooms. I had a feeling they shared the same light and spacious design.

"What do you think?" Conor asked as he took off his jacket, draping it over the arm of a beautiful white couch.

"Jaysus, Conor! Wow, I'm impressed. I'm almost speechless. I'm starting to love your old landlord for making you move out." I giggled as I traced the soft velvet fabric of the matching armchair with my fingers.

I wasn't looking, but I felt Conor's gaze on me, watching my reaction as I took in every detail of his new pad. Conor seemed nervous and fidgety for some reason. He wasn't the kind to be worried about such stuff. He knew me, so he knew I didn't care about where he lived or what he drove. Such things were shallow and superficial, and insignificant to me. Still, I understood his nerves. My opinion was important to him and vice versa.

"Well, lucky for me, I'd already been looking for a new apartment. Otherwise, I would never have found this place on such short notice." Conor smiled as he grabbed my hand. "Come see the bedroom."

He took my hand then led me up a small set of stairs. I laughed with excitement then followed him through to the master bedroom. I had been right about its aesthetics. Just like the living room, it was light and airy with modern décor. It also had an ensuite. Unlike his previous bedroom, the furniture was a set. Its colour was a light brown, barely standing out under the effect of the dark grey sheets. There were silver vases on shelves. They held real eucalyptus leaves and white pampas grass, which reflected in the large mirror across from the shelves. Another skylight bathed the king-size bed in natural light and glinted off of the vases. Through the open bathroom door, I could see sparkling white tiles and a waterfall shower. The bedroom was otherwise empty, but it wasn't going to be so for long. Conor was moving in the following day.

"I love it! But this rent must be double the amount," I said.

Conor shrugged. "Well, we've been getting a lot of gigs since the festival, and the support tour has given us an advance."

Indeed, Ocrás had gained a lot of publicity in the media, and the upcoming tour was looking secure. If this new apartment was anything to go by, they were starting to do extremely well as a band.

"I am so happy for you. This place is a dream." I smiled as I approached him. My hand cupped his cheek, and I rose up on my toes, my lips pressed against his in a tender kiss. He kissed me back but pulled away quickly.

"I am so relieved you think that." He breathed out as he stepped away from me. His eyes were staring right into mine. I immediately knew there was something else going on. His eyes sparkled with excitement and anxiousness, the way they always did when he had something to tell me. He took a deep breath and parted his lips again, letting the words bothering him roll quickly off his tongue. "I'd actually been searching for an apartment long before the landlord kicked me out..." He exhaled.

"I know, you told me that." I smiled nervously, wondering what he was insinuating.

"Well, I did all this because... Bridget, I would love it if we lived here together." It took me a few seconds to realise what these words actually meant. I was in shock.

I suddenly realised why Conor had been acting so nervously. I would never have guessed that Conor wanted us to move in together. The thought that this apartment could be ours made me feel lightheaded. But more importantly, the thought of waking up next to Conor every day sent tingles down my spine. I wanted to build a home with him: to create a place that reflected our tastes and interests, where we could make memories together. Moving in together was the first step to becoming each other's family.

"I know we've only been seeing each other for a few months, and I know it's kind of fast, and I am leaving on tour, but—" He was blabbering by now, gesturing wildly with his hands. He looked cute; I'd never seen him so nervous before, not even when he was performing in front of hundreds of people.

I interrupted his rambling.

"Conor, I'd love to move in with you."

Chapter Twenty-Eight

NEW BEGINNINGS

I am not one to make spur-of-the-moment decisions. I usually make detailed plans and set clear agendas before doing anything. This is especially true for something as life-changing as moving in with a boyfriend. My lack of spontaneity can be rigid, but it also made me good at planning events. I am meticulous, organised and level-headed. But strangely, when Conor asked me to move in with him that weekend, all of my usual fastidiousness went out the window. I was ready to move in with him without a moment's notice, without any plans or timelines and without any forethought. Conor made me want to throw caution to the wind.

With the girls' help, I stashed all of my belongings in boxes and moved them over to our new apartment in the Claddagh. Meanwhile, the boys helped Conor. We both had a considerable amount of things—he had his music equipment, and I had my painting utensils, canvases, plus all of the furniture and everything else from my apartment.

Our boxes were arranged in neat piles in the living room corner between the dining table and the wall. They were all labelled in permanent marker on their sides or lids. I sighed as I dropped the last one on the top, my arms felt relieved to be free of its weight. Then I placed both hands on my waist and looked around.

The living room was packed. Rosie, Laura, and the boys were sitting around the table, all exhausted by the physical labour they'd put in that day. Moments earlier, the new place had been like an ant hill. Everyone was busy carrying boxes. They'd all gathered without a moment's notice, eager to help us celebrate this giant leap of faith in our relationship. Everyone had plans of their own that weekend. Especially Laura, who was supposed to go to Dublin. Our friends had dropped everything to help us.

It was in moments like these that I realised how lucky Conor and I were to have such loyal friends. They'd dropped everything last minute to help us. They didn't ask questions, nor did they nag; they helped us unconditionally and eagerly, happy to see that Conor and I had taken a new direction in our relationship. I had been a little surprised that Laura didn't have anything judgemental to say about the shock of us moving in together so quickly. Out of everyone, I thought that she would be the first to disapprove. She certainly wouldn't have had any trouble telling me if she did. But so far, she hadn't said a word. She seemed as happy for us as the rest of our friends. It made me feel proud, like she must have seen Conor and me as a real and lasting couple.

"God, I'm exhausted!" Rosie exclaimed as she slumped back into the living room couch. This was one of the few times Rosie wasn't all glammed up. She had ditched her weekend look for a pair of sweats and a plain white shirt. Her hair was pulled up in a messy bun, and her face hadn't any trace of makeup.

"I know, right? You guys surely own a lot of stuff!" James agreed, looking at Conor and me. I laughed and nodded. In all honesty, I never thought I owned so many things, not until I came to pack them all and realised I could barely fit them in the car.

"Bridget owns a lot less stuff than I do!" Laura said with a wink. "She doesn't have half the skincare products and makeup that I've told her she should buy. Be thankful it wasn't me you were moving in here!"

"Oh, I am very thankful," said James, with a horrified look on his face. "This move was feckin' gigantic!"

"Don't forget folks! There's still more boxes inside the other truck that'll arrive tomorrow!" Donal added.

"That's just a few lamps and things for the balcony. I told you the place didn't come with furniture for the balcony," Conor said defensively.

"Okay, boss. As you say." Donal chuckled.

I laughed out loud, then fell back onto the white sofa beside Conor. I then looked around the living room and took it all in one more time.

As we looked around the empty apartment, everything seemed unfamiliar to us. However, deep down, we were confident that once we started setting up our things around the space, it would begin to feel more like home.

With our friends there, it was already starting to feel warm and welcoming. This was our first home together. The thought made my heart swell with love and excitement. Hopefully, Conor and I would have many homes, but this was our first. We would learn each other's habits here, decorate together, and argue about which piece of furniture should go where. We would go through many firsts together in this apartment. Someday, we would look back on it and remember all the growing pains and the excitement of living together for the first time. Maybe we'd even show our kids where we used to live if the building still existed by then.

Suddenly, everyone went silent, and the guys turned their heads to Rosie and Laura. They all exchanged looks and nodded subtly. I looked at everyone's expressions and then at Conor. He just shrugged, clearly as confused as I was.

"So, you guys may kill us for what we've done," Laura warned. Donal stood up and ran out the apartment door as she continued. "We only had a few days to think of a housewarming gift, but we managed to find exactly what you guys need in your new home."

A few minutes later, Donal slowly walked backwards inside the apartment with something in his arms. At first, I couldn't quite make out what it was, but as he got closer, I gasped in shock. He was holding a small cage. My jaw nearly dropped as I stared at it, completely taken off guard.

A little bark echoed around the apartment just as James shouted, "Meet your new housemate, guys!" Donal opened the cage door, revealing the most beautiful puppy I had ever seen. He was the fluffiest little thing in the world, like a teddy bear. He had caramel-brown curly fur that reminded me of a shag rug. He was so small and adorable that I thought my heart would melt.

"We wanted to go with a cat first—less responsibility. But we remembered that a certain someone is allergic to them," James explained as he winked at Conor.

I squealed in excitement but couldn't shift my attention from the gorgeous puppy in front of me. James's words seemed far away. Donal reached into the cage, brought the puppy out, and then put him in my arms. The puppy whined slightly as he was lifted, but he snuggled close once he was in my arms. He was soft and warm against my skin. Gingerly, I reached out a hand and petted his tiny head. His fur was so soft and fluffy that my hand sank into it. Conor moved closer beside me with his hand extended to pet his soft brown fur. As he did, our eyes met. I knew he was thinking the exact same thing that I was: this was our fur baby. Surprisingly, the pup didn't seem scared by our touch; on the contrary, his little tail wagged with excitement, and his big brown eyes looked up at us from our arms. As I gazed back into his eyes, I thought I would burst into tears with love.

"And, to seal the deal!" James popped open a bottle of champagne.

Congratulations, guys!" The room erupted into cheers as the cork flew into the air and hit the ceiling, causing the puppy to let out a soft bark. The sound delighted Conor, who laughed and leaned over to kiss me. In that moment, surrounded by loved ones and celebration, I felt like I was finally ho

Chapter Twenty-nine

REVELATIONS AT BRENNAN'S

Brennan's was my favourite cafe in Galway, and it was very busy. Inside, there was a nice festive atmosphere about the place and a real Christmas tree decorated the front window. The fragrance of its pine needles filled the cafe with the most wonderful, fresh pine aroma. It mingled with the scent of freshly ground coffee beans. From its branches hung beautiful and delicate porcelain ornaments. They were painted bright blue and sparkling silver. Star lights had also been strung up around the windows. They twinkled merrily and beckoned passers-by inside.

The whole place was very cosy. In one corner, a turf fire was roaring. Stockings hung from the mantlepiece, embroidered with the names of the baristas. On the mantle, a paper advent calendar depicting kids at a skating rink counted down the days to Christmas. Jovial chatter filled the air as folks streamed through the doors. Some grabbed takeaways. Others dropped anchor to enjoy the comfy snugs.

It was freezing cold outside and I could even see my breath as I made my way through the cafe door to meet the girls. The sky was grey and cloudy, with a brisk wind blowing in off the Atlantic, and the freezing wind outside, made Brennan's feel even warmer when I arrived. Myself, Rosie and Laura were among the lucky ones to get a large corner booth all to ourselves. The girls had already taken off their coats and laid them over the corner of the snug. They both stood up excitedly when I arrived and helped me unwind my scarf, and then I removed my coat and gloves. When we hugged, I noticed that their hands and cheeks were still cold to the touch.

I settled into the comfortable booth and gazed out the window at some folks still queuing outside for a table, waiting to get in from the cold. All down the street, I could see the bright buildings and cobblestone streets that made up the West End of Galway. Frost had formed in white spiderwebs on the stones. Those who walked by were bundled up in thick jackets, hats, scarves and woollen gloves.

Brennan's was renowned in Galway for its fine teas, finger sandwiches on tiered platters and the best selection of decadent hot chocolate. Rosie had booked ahead with a new app she'd recently downloaded and raved about. She'd even placed our surprise hot chocolate orders in advance, so we didn't have long to wait.

During the Christmas season the other thing Brennan's was famous for: was its festive-flavoured homemade hot chocolate.

We had all jointly planned to skive off that afternoon and catch up. I had just finished a new proposal an hour before for an exciting new project. Maybe this would be the start of a new adventure! First, however, a second opinion was needed from the girls.

We smiled like Cheshire cats when our waiter arrived with Rosie's choice of hot chocolates. The waiter was tall and handsome, although very young, with curly brown hair, a hint of freckles on the nose and big green eyes. Laura smiled flirtatiously at him as he carefully placed the tray down in front of us. Her smile seemed to distract him. He fumbled with the mugs and spilled some hot chocolate on the table as he handed them to us.

"Oh, crumbs," he muttered, and Laura giggled.

"Did I make you nervous?" she asked, her voice low and seductive. She batted her eyelashes and pursed her lips in a pout that she evidently thought was attractive.

The boy turned scarlet. "Sorry about that, ma'am," he said, smiling shyly up at her.

"Ma'am?" Laura exclaimed, clasping a hand to her breast theatrically. "Do I look like an old lady to you?"

Rosie had to put her hand over her mouth to keep from laughing out loud as the waiter stared at Laura with uncertainty.

"N-not at all, ma'am," he stammered. Rosie and I burst out laughing. The look on Laura's face was priceless. She looked as if she'd just watched her favourite designer dress get trampled by stampeding zebras. After several moments of furious giggling, Rosie stepped in to save the poor lad.

"I haven't seen you here before," she said once her laughter subsided. "Are you new?"

"Yes, I am," he said brightly, clearly relieved that the conversation had moved on from Laura's flirting. "My aunt owns the cafe. My parents sent me to Galway as punishment during the Christmas holidays because I got into trouble at school. But I actually love it here." He smiled with a little more confidence. "It's a really lovely spot. So many nice people."

"The nicest," Laura said, a hint of suggestion in her voice. "And we tip really well."

"Thank you very much, *young man*," Rosie said with emphasis on the last two words. She shooed him away before Laura could inflict any more flirtation on the poor lad. "Good luck with *school!*" Laura shouted cheekily, staring after him dreamily.

Rosie and I looked at each other and rolled our eyes. "That waiter is far too young for you, Laura," said Rosie, poking Laura in the ribs. Sometimes that girl needed us to put her in her place.

Meanwhile, the hot chocolate aromas smelled delicious, like freshly baked Christmas cake and mulled wine. We giggled with excitement as Rosie handed us the red and white festive mugs. Mine was a salted vanilla hot chocolate, while Rosie chose a slow-cooked mint hot chocolate. Laura, posh as usual, got an earl grey hot chocolate. As the marshmallows stuck to our lips, we giggled at each other. They were soft and sticky. We each took our first sip and smiled at each other. The chocolate was creamy and delicious, and it warmed my whole body instantly. The sweetness was delicately balanced with the dark chocolate to give it a decadent flavour. This was what Christmas was all about. Hot chocolate with my girls. Cosied up in Brennan's cafe.

"So, how's the freelancing going?" Rosie asked as she reached for her mug.

"It's going better than expected," I said. "I've realised that I prefer event planning much more."

"So, are you 'planning' to get back into it?" Laura enquired with a wink.

"Haha. And yes. But I want to take a different approach," I said with a sigh. "Over the past few weeks, I've been thinking about what I really want to do. I took my time. I asked myself, what's really going to make me happy? Is there another direction I want my career to go? I know I love planning and creating events, and I really want to continue doing that, but I want to do so in a much more organised manner."

The girls were riveted by my speech. They leaned in closer as I took a deep breath.

"Girls, I want to open my own planning agency. Maybe I can hire some people. I found some potential clients while I was searching for online freelancing jobs. I just have a feeling that if I head in that direction, I can make it work."

"Well, I love the idea!" said Rosie excitedly. "You're great at what you do. Look what you did for Galway360."

"I think it's a great idea! And we support you one hundred percent, Bridget!" said Laura, who was being serious for once.

I had no doubt the girls would support me. I was lucky to have such lifelong friends like Rosie and Laura, not to mention a wonderful boyfriend who would do anything to make sure my dreams come true. I'd told Conor about my plans a few days ago, and he'd already offered to help me. But I'd refused, knowing he had his own business to deal with. The tour would be exhausting enough. The band and Amanda had been in rehearsals for days, and the time to go on tour had finally arrived: only one week remained before Conor would be on a four-week tour around the country. Amanda was throwing another party to kickstart it.

"I found an office to rent near our new apartment," I told the girls. "I'll be viewing it later today. Also, I have an interview with two other planners next week. They're both new graduates, full of energy with fresh ideas and are looking for internships."

"Bridget, this sounds amazing! Why didn't you tell us about it earlier?" Rosie exclaimed.

"Well..." I blushed. "I had the idea during Galway360, but I wasn't sure if it would work out. I wanted to get things clear in my own mind before I told anyone."

The girls nodded.

"The guys are going on tour; Bridget is opening her own planning company." Laura shook her head. "Rosie, I think we need to step up our game!" she exclaimed, making us all laugh.

"Speaking of the tour," Rosie said, "what do you think of Amanda? Is she as fabulous as all the magazines make her out to be?"

"I bet she's a stone-cold bitch," Laura posited, raising an eyebrow suggestively. "No one is *that* beautiful, *that* rich, *that* famous and *also* nice. It's just the law of attraction."

Rosie and I both laughed and rolled our eyes. I took a deep breath. After the party, I'd seen Amanda only once. She was as annoying and dismissive as she'd been at the party—which only made me certain that I hadn't imagined it. I let my breath out slowly as I stared at the table, wondering whether or not I should broach the subject in front of the girls. I was aware that I may have been stupid. Maybe my concerns were nothing more than a figment of my imagination. But still, my gut feeling told me otherwise. Part of me wanted to open up to the girls about it, but I also wanted to keep quiet. It wasn't that I felt bad gossiping about Amanda—she was a celebrity, people had said worse about her. It was more that I felt like my feelings were a poor reflection of Conor. I thought that I should keep my jealousies and insecurities to myself.

"What is it, BK?" Rosie asked gently. She could always tell when something was bothering me.

"Oh yes," Laura agreed, "hit us with all the goss!"

I took another deep breath. "Well, she has an attitude towards me."

"What do you mean?" Rosie asked as she raised a brow.

"I don't know how to explain it. It's just that at the party, she seemed all over Conor, then acted arrogantly towards me."

"Well, someone's jealous!" Laura smirked, taking a sip of her hot chocolate.

"I am not jealous!" I quickly defended myself. "I just don't like the girl!"

"First of all, yes, you are," Laura pointed out, "and second, of course she has an attitude towards you. You're dating Conor, and she's not! That's gotta sting. She's a famous musician, and you're... well, you're awesome, but you're not exactly on her level."

"Wow, be supportive, Laura!" Rosie exclaimed.

"I'm just saying!" Laura said, brushing Rosie off. "Conor is a hot commodity. A rising star in the music world. I'm sure that Amanda expects him to be all over her. Men like him probably always are. But instead, he loves you. She probably wants to figure out what your deal is and why Conor wants you."

I stared at Laura, stunned. "Are you saying *Amanda* is jealous of *me*?" The thought was laughable. Absurd. It was impossible.

Laura shrugged. "Well, she at least thinks you're someone worth being cold to. She probably wants to crush you under her giant platform stilettos."

"The truth is..." I began slowly. "I'm worried about all those things. She's a famous pop star, and I'm... what? A failed painter? An unemployed event planner?"

"You're starting your own business!" Rosie interjected. "You're a small business owner!"

"Yeah, *if* that takes off," I said with a sigh. "I believe in myself, but let's face it: Conor is moving into a whole other level. He's becoming a famous musician. Meanwhile, I'm just leading a normal twenty-something life. Finding myself, starting a career, etc. It's all good, but it's not the same as becoming a rock star." I looked around at the girls. Sympathy was creasing their brows. "I guess there is a part of me that's afraid he'll want someone on his level. It'd be one thing if I had a successful career as a painter. But I'm not even an artist anymore. Not really, anyway."

The girls were quiet for a moment, mulling over my words. As much as they wanted to support me, they couldn't argue with my logic. We'd all seen too many examples in the tabloids of famous couples who broke up when one person's career took off, and the other's didn't.

"But Conor doesn't care about status," Rosie said after a minute. "He sees through all that bullshit. It doesn't matter to him what your job is. He loves you for who you are."

"Yeah, and Amanda's attitude may be nothing," Laura added. "Even if it was something, Conor loves you. I doubt he even notices her."

I found the idea that Conor didn't notice Amanda a little far-fetched. She was stunningly gorgeous. He might not love her, but chances were, he could recognise how beautiful she was.

Still, I knew that Laura was right. I trusted Conor and believed that he wouldn't do anything to hurt me. Even still, I couldn't shake the uneasiness I felt whenever Amanda's name was brought up. Unconvinced, I just smiled and closed the subject. There was no point opening up a can of worms. The most important thing was that I trusted Conor. Whatever Amanda's agenda was, it didn't matter.

"Well, come on, let's have a hot chocolate toast," Rosie said after a few moments of silence. "To the boys' and Bridget's new business venture

Chapter Thirty

Tour d'Eire

I had absolutely no desire to attend Amanda's party; even the thought of it made my skin crawl. I'd seen it all before. Her glamorous and sophisticated decorations that planners had carefully choreographed for weeks. This lady was such a show-off. *A real phoney,* I thought with a touch of malice—or was it jealousy? Plus, I couldn't help but think of all the drama she had undoubtedly created behind the scenes with the staff. As an event manager, I'd dealt with lots of high maintenance clients before. You could always tell who would be polite and humble and who would be demanding and narcissistic. The way that Amanda spoke to me, left me in no doubt that she was the latter. She had probably stressed out every single person she'd hired to help throw this party. If my own experience with people like her was any indication, more than a few of the event staff would have had a complete nervous breakdown.

Amanda had rented Glenlo Abbey for the party. I'd never been to the abbey before, although I'd driven by it many times. In the events world, it was known as the crème de la crème of Galway events spaces.

It was a gorgeous 18th-century abbey that had been converted into a five-star hotel. Despite not wanting to see Amanda, I was secretly excited to see Glenlo.

Laura and Donal were out of town visiting their families, so just myself, Conor, James and Rosie attended the party. We took a taxi since we'd all be drinking. As we pulled into the abbey, the car passed through large iron gates and began to wend its way down the long drive. The grounds were impeccably tended with hedges and meticulous gardens. The upscale look was further exaggerated by the limousines that flanked us. This was a party for Galway's—and all of Ireland's—elite. As the car rounded a line of trees and the stone facade of the Abby came into view, I couldn't help but gasp. The building rose up in front of us, stately and serene. The large manor looked like something out of a Jane Austen novel. I half expected to see a horse-drawn carriage and Mr Darcy standing outside.

Inside was impressive. The abbey had been elegantly adorned with antique furniture, adding to its timeless charm. Crystal chandeliers, art nouveau wallpaper, crown moulding, and ornate wood panelling took my breath away. The place was designed to take visitors back in time. It was old-fashioned but beautiful, vintage but tasteful. Amanda, however, had added her own touch to the décor.

As we made our way through the lobby, we passed by an ice statue of Amanda. The white witch of Narnia sprung to mind. The statue had been excellently carved. I could tell immediately that it was Amanda. However, that didn't stop it from being the most grotesque thing I'd ever seen. Ice-Amanda towered over the entranceway, one hand lifted into the air as another held a microphone up to her lips. She looked to be about mid-way through belting one of her iconic pop ballads. She looked vain and self-centred. Whoever had carved it had put her in a tight-fitting outfit and given her far more cleavage than she really had. It was embarrassingly over-sexualised. I felt awkward just looking at it. As we passed by, James laughed out loud and then whispered,

"Amanda's ear is gonna be my ice cube later." I had to fight not to laugh. Rosie didn't try to hide her amusement. She burst into giggles and leaned closer into James affectionately.

Somehow, Amanda had convinced Glenlo Abbey to let her light real torches in the ballroom. Their flames danced and flickered romantically throughout the room. They were strategically placed around a large banquet table, which had been set with lavish silver and candelabras. Neon pink lights illuminated everything in warm, brilliant colours. There were roses everywhere. Large vases of them had been placed on the tables and around the room. Their scent filled the space, welcoming everyone into the luxurious world of Amanda.

Amanda had named her event on the invitations as:

'Tour d'Eire,'
Amanda du Prey's official launch party
for her forthcoming tour of Ireland —support act Ocrás.

As much as I hated to admit it, Amanda really did know how to throw a party. Plus, Ocrás would get a lot of exposure. This time she had invited some of her superfans in addition to celebrities: newscasters from the television, Irish actors, musicians and journalists. Along with the beautiful and perfectly manicured faces of people I recognised— including Saoirse Ronan, Barry Keoghan, Paul Mescal, and CMAT— there were plenty of people who looked more normal. People like me.

Inviting her fans hadn't just been a kind gesture on her part. I'd heard her tell Conor in the car over the loudspeaker that her manager had insisted on inviting 'groupies' for publicity shots.

As we approached the red carpet photo area, Rosie leaned back and whispered, "Where does Amanda get the energy from? She doesn't know how to slow down." Rosie then clutched James' arm as they walked towards the photographers. Amanda had secured a Step and

Repeat backdrop that featured her name in her signature handwriting. Beneath this was printed *Orcás*. Guests—both famous and not—were having their pictures taken in front of Orcás's name. These pictures would definitely be all over the internet by tomorrow. Very soon, everyone in the country was going to know the name Orcás.

I decided not to respond to Rosie. My blood boiled as I spotted Amanda being photographed at the top of the stairs. She was wearing a long red dress, the train of which fanned out behind her. The bodice hugged her sculpted body before billowing out into a wide skirt. A slit came all the way up her thigh and revealed most of her long, slender leg. As the cameras flashed, she posed and twirled. Everything she did was effortless, it seemed. Even walking down the stairs in stilettos didn't seem to bother her. On each step, she paused and pouted her lips for the cameras. The photographers were beside themselves. They kept telling her how amazing she looked and asking her to give them a smile. Their fawning was transparent and irritating.

Watching this, I knew that I couldn't possibly give Rosie an unbiased answer. I didn't want to bad-mouth Amanda based on my jealousy or insecurity, but I also didn't want to force myself to try and say anything nice. So I just smiled at Rosie and turned my attention to Conor.

His eyes scanned the room and sparkled with excitement. He took in the crowd of photographers, the flashing cameras, and the beautiful people posing naturally in front of the paparazzi. Waiters in tuxedos were moving throughout the room, passing out glasses of champagne. Celebrities in clothes that cost more than my monthly pay cheque sipped cocktails and laughed amongst themselves. The air was rich with the scent of expensive perfume and cologne. As we walked past a woman I was fairly certain was Vogue Williams, I caught the light and sensuous notes of rose mixed with a heavier and spicier jasmine. The glitz and glamour of it made me feel ill at ease. Conor, however, seemed to fit right in. His lips curled into a smile, slightly parted as mine had been, unspoken words of amazement lingering on them. He didn't look nervous at all. If I hadn't known him, I would have thought he was one of the celebrities. The ease with which he reached for a glass of champagne and then waved at Gary Lightbody made me both admire him and feel even more intimidated.

Indeed, I certainly felt dislike towards Amanda, including this extravagant Tour d'Eire party. But it was also intimidation that I felt. Maybe this was my green monster at its most potent.

I tried to keep my feelings towards Amanda bottled up. At the same time, I couldn't have been happier for Conor getting the support act. It was his talent as a musician that got him what he deserved. Groupies that wanted selfies with him, autographs and giving interviews... maybe this was his future. If so, he deserved it all. Conor had worked hard all his life. He'd shown dedication and devotion despite the lack of opportunities. Finally, his patience, determination and hard work were rewarded. Amanda had been the one to give him his big break. Unlike me, she'd been able to give him something he'd wished for his entire life. The chance to have his music heard by thousands. Maybe this was the real reason why I didn't like her. Was it sheer jealousy? Or was it the dreamy eyes she displayed whenever she was around Conor?

"Should we go find Amanda?" James asked from behind us, shouting over the loud music. It was a little hard to hear him over all the sounds in the room. The tinkling laughter, chatting celebrities, clicks of the cameras, and shouts of the photographers—who were now directing their attention towards a newly-arrived Colin Farrell—were loud and confusing.

I looked at Conor, my brows raised in an innocent, questioning look. I didn't want him to feel guilty if he left to look for Amanda. Deep down, however, I wanted him to stay with me. Conor seemed to hesitate for a moment, then shook his head. "Nah, you guys go find her first. Bridget and I are going for a drink." He smirked as he gazed towards me. "Maybe even a dance?"

I couldn't help but smile, my cheeks hot under his gaze.

"Okay!" Rosie and James then disappeared into the crowd.

"Are you sure? People came here to see you guys. You should probably—"

"Most people are here to see Amanda. They barely know us. They're either her friends or fans or people who just want to be seen at a fancy party. No one really knows us yet! Anyway, I want to hang out with you, Miss Kennedy. If they need me for anything, they can come and find me."

"For now," I added with a smile.

"For tonight. Besides, I'll be away for a couple of weeks, so I want to spend as much time with you as possible. I'm gonna miss you!"

My heart skipped a beat.

"So, can I have a dance?" Conor asked as he extended a hand.

"That would be delightful, kind sir!" I joked as I took his hand. The moment our hands touched, however, the sarcasm vanished from my lips. It was replaced by a prickling of happy tears. All my insecurities seemed to melt away as Conor led me towards the dance floor. *BK, you silly thing*, I thought to myself. There was no reason to be jealous of Amanda! Conor loved me. He didn't care about fame and money. As I felt his grip tighten on mine, I finally let go of my fears and started to enjoy the night.

Just as we approached the dance floor, the song changed. It slowed down, a slow song I had heard more times than I could count. *Imagine* by John Lennon. It was perfect timing for a dance. My body felt suddenly light and loose, ready to dance. The song's tempo washed over me like an ocean wave. My feet and hips began to move in time with it. Conor brought me to the centre of the dancing crowd. He playfully pulled me closer so suddenly that it made me squeal with laughter.

One of his hands rested on my hip while the other gently held my hand. His fingers intertwined with mine. A smile creased his lips. The sensation of his fingers cradling mine flooded my body with love. He gazed down at me, his eyes twinkling and tender. There, surrounded by some of the most famous people in the country, he had eyes only for me.

Our feet moved to the slow rhythm of the song. I felt carried away by the notes of the piano, bass and drums. My body moved in time with Conor's. Our bodies pressed tightly against each other as we swayed together. I could feel his heartbeat, calm and steady, and his breath on my hair and neck. He rested his chin on my shoulder; I'd never felt more protected and held. Then he leaned back and caught my eye. He smiled mischievously. One of his hands rose with mine into the air, and then he twirled me around. The people around me became a blur as he spun me again and again. I was light on my feet and perfectly poised. As he pulled me back in, I collided against his chest and let out another giggly shriek. We laughed together, holding each other tightly. I'd never felt so connected to him.

As he tenderly tucked a strand of hair behind my ear, he suddenly spoke, his voice sincere and earnest. "You're truly beautiful, mo cuishle," he whispered, his gaze locked with mine. In that moment, all amusement faded from his voice, replaced by a deep and meaningful connection. "You may say I'm a dreamer, but I'm not the only one." Conor softly breathed the lyrics of the song into my ear, his words conveying a message of hope and unity.

In that second, everything disappeared. The music, the chattering crowd, everything and everyone vanished, leaving us alone in a world that felt suspended in time. Memories flooded my mind, colliding with one another in a dazzling kaleidoscope of colours and shapes, painting a vivid picture of our journey together.

I saw the first time I laid eyes on Conor at Waxies, his cocky smile and those mischievous blue eyes that captured my heart. Our first kiss overlooking the rooftops of Galway, the stolen moments of pure bliss. Walking hand in hand through ancient standing stones, feeling the weight of history and the magic of our connection. The handfasting ceremony, our hands clasped together as we promised to stand by each other's side.

I remembered standing together along the rugged coast, our hearts entwined with the crashing waves, and the way he approached me on that bed, a spark of desire that ignited our passion. The sight of him on stage after his surprise return from Australia, his joy and determination shining brightly. And then, the first time he whispered those three powerful words, "I love you," and my heart swelled with an indescribable joy.

These scenes flowed through me, out of order, yet timelessly beautiful. They were the tapestry of our love, the moments that would forever define us. As Conor closed the distance between us, I could feel the anticipation building, our lips almost touching, ready to seal our love in a kiss that would transcend time and space.

"Conor! I've been searching for you everywhere,"Amanda's voice pierced through the air like a sharp blade, causing us to abruptly separate.

With an excited tone, she continued, "I have someone dying to meet you!

Oh, hi Bridget."

Chapter Thirty-One

To Us!

The first of December had finally arrived, and with it, a frigid night chill. It felt like it might freeze. Snow would cover the cobblestones by morning. Despite the chilly wind, I felt much calmer as the sound of wind eased my busy mind with gentle whispers. I stood there in the open with only a shawl wrapped around me. I was still wearing my dress from the party. I felt so exhausted and overwhelmed from the night that I hadn't even bothered to change. This quiet moment alone on the balcony was the first chance I'd had to collect my thoughts. I felt like I was coming down from an adrenaline rush. My body felt limp and shaky. I was still slightly delirious from the wealth and celebrity on display. The cold, brisk night air helped, though.

We'd just gotten back home shortly after midnight. Conor had ordered a taxi so that we could get away and be alone. He'd held my hand all the way home, but it wasn't enough to soothe my worry. Ever since Amanda had interrupted us and he'd gone off with her to meet her guests, I'd had a terrible sinking feeling. Conor was now in the shower, washing away the party. I decided to take in a few moments of silence in an effort to expel all the negative thoughts and unease that I felt in my heart. I was glad to be home. The party was in full swing when we left. A well-known DJ had started playing, and several minor celebrities disappeared into the bathroom, maybe to powder their noses! That's when we knew it was time to leave and get some alone time.

Our furry friend had sneaked outside and then sat obediently at my feet. Jimi stared up at me as his little paw tapped my leg. His big eyes reflected the lights of the city as he whimpered. It was hard to resist those eyes. I scratched him under his chin, then scooped him up into my arms and cuddled him.

Sighing, I closed my eyes and sank into silence. Ever since Amanda had interrupted us on the dance floor, I'd had an angry, metallic taste in my mouth. Resentment burned through me like wildfire, turning every good thing about the night to ash. Even my relationship with Conor was tainted by it. It was hard to think clearly with all the smoke that filled my mind and confused me. With my eyes closed, I escaped to a place of tranquillity, a space occupied only by my deepest thoughts and emotions – a pair of arms then wove themselves around me.

Conor held me close. It was just how I'd felt that night on the dance floor. His warmth seeped through my shawl. I smiled, then sank deep into his embrace.

"It's freezing! What are you two doing out here?" he asked.
"Thinking," I answered.
"About?"

I found myself at a loss for words, overwhelmed by a whirlwind of thoughts and emotions. It felt as though I was stuck in an endless loop, spinning around on a carousel of confusion. Yet, amidst the chaos, Conor's presence provided solace. His warm embrace brought a sense of calm, gradually soothing my racing mind. I wanted trust to be the foundation stone of our relationship, feeling like I could share almost anything with him. But deep down, I couldn't shake the lingering questions about our past lives and the jealousy that gnawed at my heart since Amanda showed up.

"About the tour?" asked Conor.

"About us," I said as our eyes connected.

Conor didn't say anything, and just waited for me to continue.

"I'm afraid, with all the travel, concerts, and chaos of your tour, that our time together will be scarce."

"Bridget... " Conor breathed out. He held me closer, as if to soothe my thoughts.

"Conor, I swear, I am happy for you. I thank God for finally giving you the opportunities that you deserve. It's just—" Our eyes met as Conor kissed me, his hands gently cupping my face, cradling it with both hands.

"Bridget, you're just scared of the unknown. I'm scared of it too."

I'd imagined this conversation many times. Each time, it ended with Conor dismissing or minimising my fears. I couldn't imagine a scenario where instead, he validated my anxieties and reassured me.

"I know our lives could possibly change after this tour. Or maybe they won't. Who knows?" He shrugged. "The unknown is always scary, but I trust in our love. I trust in us. We're like the stone circle. Everything may change around us, but we will remain strong."

I wanted to gasp. Conor had made the same connection that I had. My eyes filled with tears. At that moment, I wanted to confess everything—the dream, my suspicion about our past lives, everything. But before I could pluck up the courage, he spoke again.

"My point is, I know it will change, and I know a lot of it can be overwhelming. I don't know how I'll react to the aftermath of this tour. But"—he paused for a second—"I do know I will *never* let anything come between us. I dream of music, not of fame and fortune. Sure, it's nice to be paid well to do what I love, but that's not why I do it. I dream of making music that resonates with people. Music that outlasts me. Music that stands as a testament to this time and which honours our history, and our culture. Most of all, I dream of a life with you. And you know how hard I fight for my dreams."

His words made me cry. He spoke them so sincerely, from his heart.

"I promise I'll make time for us. During this tour, and after it, and wherever I am and whatever I'm doing." He smiled. "I love you."

"I love you too," I said, my voice almost breaking. Slowly I rose up and kissed him.

"Come on, let's go to bed."

Chapter Thirty-Two

CLAWS OUT

"Is he still not answering?" Laura asked as she added another dress to the already growing pile on the bed.

For once, we were over at her place. She and Rosie liked to come to my place, especially now that Conor and I had such a nice apartment. But with him gone, I wanted to get out of the house. That's how Rosie and I found ourselves in Laura's impeccably tidy bedroom. Even the pictures were framed and hung in neat, level lines on the walls. The pictures were mostly of the three of us on nights out, our arms flung around one another and our smiles wide. Looking at them, I was filled with nostalgia. We'd had some great times in Galway.

Laura's desk was equally prim and proper. Notebooks were stacked at the top in a colour-coordinated system. Coloured pens had been set neatly lined up on one side. Her laptop was perfectly clean, despite it being several years old. I knew for a fact that she cleaned the keypad regularly. Only the closet hinted at disorganisation beneath the facade of orderliness. While it wasn't messy, it was full to bursting point. Laura hadn't worn most of the shoes and dresses. Some even had their price tags still attached. Laura really loved to shop.

I shook my head. There was a faraway look in my eyes, and my mouth was a thin line of worry. I placed the phone on the table, sighed and sank deeper into the chair. It had been nearly two weeks since Conor and the band had begun their tour, and in that short period of time, their career had been thrown into a frenzy. Just as expected, touring with Amanda du Prey increased their fanbase by thousands. Screaming crowds greeted them as they disembarked from Amanda's Tour Bus. They got lots of photos taken as they made their way into luxury hotels. People posted on social media about them constantly. James winking at a fan had become a meme. They'd been listed in a recent Pitchfork article, 'Top 10 Irish Bands to Watch'. By now, people from all over Ireland and overseas knew Ocrás. Their songs were now being played on the radio. It had been the most disconcerting moment to walk into Caribou for a drink with Rosie and hear Conor's voice coming out from the speakers. Even more disorienting, one of the girls at the table next to us was singing along to the lyrics. Ocrás even had fan pages online. People were getting more curious about the band that had appeared out of nowhere, now alongside one of the most famous singers in the country.

Things were going so well on the tour that Amanda's manager was already talking about adding more shows and extending the tour by a few weeks; apparently, having a fresh band on her tour pleased Amanda's fans. This was amplified by the fact that Conor was great at getting the crowd pumped up for Amanda. He had a natural, easy charisma with any audience. When he introduced Amanda, he always made her sound like a genius, a living legend. He'd never liked her music before this tour. But from how he acted on live streams of the shows, you'd think he was her biggest fan. Their tastes were nothing alike. Orcás was soulful and authentic, whereas Amanda chased trends. She was talented at writing pop ballads, but they were still *generic* pop ballads. Conor used to change the radio when her songs came on, but now he acted like he was her cheerleader and best friend.

It didn't hurt this image that she constantly posted selfies of the two of them doing funny things together: pictures of them taking shots at parties, rehearsing together late at night and drawing moustaches on a sleeping Donal on the Tour Bus. However, as much as I didn't like it, their partnership was working. After their first performance, more and more tickets were sold, and now nearly all the concerts were totally sold out. There was lots of speculation on the forums about their relationship.

But as crazy as things were getting, Conor never missed any of my calls. Not until now. It was late afternoon, and he hadn't replied to any of my texts, not to mention my three calls. I was getting worried. Of course, I could have called one of the lads—in fact, Rosie could have easily asked James about Conor—but I refused to be that kind of girlfriend. Conor had a reason for not answering; I wasn't questioning that. I was just worried about his well-being. I constantly reassured myself that if something was really wrong, then the others would have let me know by now.

"Don't worry, Bridget. I'm sure he's fine. Maybe he forgot his phone or something," Rosie said as she walked towards Laura's closet, her hand reaching for one of the blue dresses in the corner. "How about this one?"

"Isn't it a bit too much for an interview?" Laura asked.

Laura had finally released her first self-help book, and she was planning to meet with a local television station that had shown interest in her and agreed to take part in her marketing campaign. We'd been at her place for hours now and gone through her closet twice, mixing pieces of clothes and jewellery in hopes of finding the perfect outfit. The clothes thrown on the bed were the rejected items. The ones hanging on the armchair had potential, and those in the closet were still to be touched. Of course, Laura wanted to go out and buy something new, but we'd said no. She had enough clothes already.

"Of course not! We've got to show those people that a writer can be sexy too!" Rosie winked as she threw the blue dress at Laura.

"Besides, you can wear it with a pair of runners, and you'll break the over-classy look." I shrugged.

"Ugh, okay." Laura sighed.

"There! Finally!" Rosie exhaled loudly, rolling her eyes at me.

"Wait, I'll get the white runners," Laura said, turning back to the closet and rifling through her shoes.

"I'll go and open a bottle of wine!" I suggested. I jumped up and made my way towards the kitchen. I needed a glass to calm my anxious mind.

"Yes, please, BK!" Laura shouted after me.

I chuckled at her enthusiasm. Laura was always up for a drink, especially when I needed it most.

The two bottles of red wine we had purchased on our way over were still sitting on the kitchen table. I located a corkscrew and filled a glass, taking a long gulp and emptying half of it. The surge of confidence motivated me to dial Conor's number once more. Considering it was already 5 p.m., he more than likely had completed the sound check by now.

I bit down on my lower lip as I listened to the rings, counting them anxiously. When the sixth still echoed in my ear, someone answered on the other end. However, it wasn't Conor's voice. Instead, I heard a bored, feminine drawl. Immediately, I felt a wave of nausea, which I was pretty sure had nothing to do with the wine I'd just downed. I knew exactly who had answered Conor's phone.

"Hey, Bridget," she said sarcastically. "It's Amanda."

I went silent. What was I supposed to say? It was late, my boyfriend didn't answer my calls or texts all day, and when I finally got through, it was Amanda du Prey—who constantly drooled over Conor. I thought I was going to be sick. I wanted to sound cool and nonchalant, like I didn't consider her a threat. Instead, words failed me. I had nothing witty to say, not even an angry jab. My lips hung open, but nothing came out.

"Conor can't talk right now," she continued in a sugary-sweet purr. "He's in the shower. But I'll tell him to call you when he's out. Thanks for calling!" Without another word, she hung up.

My jaw dropped at the same time that my phone clattered to the floor. I wasn't even aware of letting go of the phone; I was in shock. What had just happened? I could barely believe my own ears, yet I'd just heard Amanda, as clear as day.

Logically, I knew that Conor would never betray me. But why would Amanda be answering Conor's phone when he was in the shower? There weren't any logical explanations for that, except ones that pointed to infidelity.

My stomach roiled with nausea. I was half furious, half numb. I thought Conor would never do anything to hurt me. But if that were true, he wouldn't have let Amanda into his room while he showered. Was he just clueless? Or was something more devious at play? A horrible realisation hit me: was it possible that I didn't know Conor at all?

"Bridget, do you need help?" Laura's voice echoed through the hallway.

Her voice released me from the sudden state of shock I'd fallen into. I shook my head in disbelief and downed the rest of my wine. Tears welled up inside me, but I pushed them aside.

"No, I'm coming!" I shouted back quickly. There was a lump in my throat that I was sure the girls would be able to detect, so I tried to sound as calm as possible. Then I grabbed the bottle of wine and headed back into the bedroom. I wasn't going to tell the girls what had just happened. There was no point in ruining the night with speculation. At least, not until I talked to Conor myself. This could all be a misunderstanding. It *had* to be a misunderstanding...

Otherwise, what the *hell* was Amanda du Prey doing in Conor's room?

Chapter Thirty-Three

CONFRONTING THE ISSUE

I should have been feeling overjoyed as I stood in the elevator, waiting for it to reach the top floor. Instead, I felt only anger and fear. In my hand, I was holding the signed lease to my first office as a business owner. I'd worked so hard for this moment, and it had finally arrived. Under different circumstances, I would be buzzing with excitement and pride. But ever since the phone call with Amanda, a sickening dread and cold fury had numbed every other emotion.

Conor called back an hour after Amanda had picked up, which made me rather curious as to why he was 'in the shower' so long. I was too angry to answer his call. Since then, I hadn't heard anything from him, apart from one text asking if I'd slept well. Over twelve hours had passed since I'd ghosted his message, and he still hadn't called or texted.

I couldn't believe that he hadn't tried to call me back. He must have sensed something was wrong. Worst of all, he knew today was an important day for me. He knew it was the date for signing the lease for my new office space in town. Family and friends had sent texts to congratulate me—even Laura, who was preparing for an interview herself. Yet Conor, from him, crickets.

Images of Amanda and Conor together in the shower fucking consumed me. In my head, she laughed triumphantly as she dug her claw-like fingernails into his back. Steam floated up around her perfect body, making her look even sexier. I felt sick. I knew I was being paranoid, but that didn't make the image of the two of them together go away.

I should have felt excited and motivated to finally be starting my own business. Instead, all I could think about was Conor's betrayal.

"I'll give him one more hour," I said out loud as the elevator came to a stop. "That's all he gets before I really give him a piece of my mind."

I rarely talked to myself out loud, but when I did, it usually meant I was furious. With a deep sigh, I took out my keys and unlocked the front door, preparing to face another night alone in the apartment. Jimi was normally at the door, but I couldn't hear him. The moment I took a step inside, I felt something was off. I couldn't tell exactly. I just felt it. It was like the emptiness had been filled. I didn't even take my time to kick my shoes off. I just threw my bag on the floor and placed the stash of papers on one of the shelves on the opposite wall.

As I put my paperwork down, I felt the hairs on the back of my neck prickle. I knew suddenly that someone else was in the apartment. Whirling around, I was shocked to find Conor standing in the middle of the living room, holding a large bouquet of flowers. He was cradling Jimi with his other hand. There was a huge banner on the wall behind him that read *Congratulations*. My jaw dropped. Conor was *here*?! I almost ran to hug him and then stopped myself. A flurry of emotions whirled inside of me like a hurricane tearing me apart.

"Surprise!" he shouted, grinning at me. His face looked so happy. Triumphant, even. He was clearly proud of himself for my surprised reaction. Instead of making me feel special, though, it made my blood boil. Conor approached me, moving closer ready to kiss me. However, I unconsciously took a step back, feeling my anger directed towards him.

"What are you doing here?" I asked fiercely.

"What do you mean?" I could tell the coldness in my voice surprised him. "It's a big day for you! I wanted to be here to celebrate."

For a moment, I wavered, and then I took a deep breath.

"Conor, we need to talk."

The words hung heavy between us. Conor continued to smile, but the look started to appear as if it had been plastered to his face. "Okay...?" he said cautiously. He sounded confused, and then he took a step towards me with a concerned look on his face.

I stood my ground.

"You can't just show up like this without any explanation," I began. "You can't just win me back with flowers and a banner."

Conor's face fell. "Explanation? Win you back? What are you talking about, Bridget?"

"Amanda answered your phone when you were in the shower!"

This time, it was his turn to look shocked.

"What do you mean?" he stammered. His arms fell limply by his sides, the bouquet of flowers spilling petals onto the floor.

I crossed my arms and planted my feet firmly on the floor. It made me feel strong and ready to take the bull by the horns.

"I called you last night, and Amanda answered. She was in your hotel room. She told me you couldn't talk because you were in the shower. Does any of this ring a bell?" I said calmly, raising my eyebrows.

"That's not possible," Conor said at once. "She doesn't have access to my room. I never had her over while I was showering. I wouldn't do that, Bridget." There was a hint of a plea in his voice, but I couldn't let myself believe him. Not yet.

"Then what was she talking about?" I asked.

Conor thought for a moment. "Well... there's a shower in the dressing room of the venue we were just at," he said slowly. "I did shower there once, and I do remember not having my phone on me. But Amanda never mentioned anything about a call. She wouldn't hide that from me."

"Wouldn't she?" I could barely conceal my anger. Honestly, Conor was being so naive.

"What time was this? I can check my call history."

I told him the time, and then watched him scroll through his incoming call history. Hesitantly, he looked up at me.

"There's no call from you," he said. He sounded more than a little freaked out, so I got my phone out as well.

"There, look," I said, showing him my phone screen. Sure enough, in my outgoing calls was an answered call to Conor at the time I'd specified. When I clicked on it, we both saw that it had lasted 33 seconds.

"I was on the phone with her in shock," I said, "and now there's no record of it on your phone."

Conor stared at my phone, then at his. He looked confused and uncertain.

"Are you saying she deleted the call from my phone?" he said, looking up at me. His eyes were wide, but the thin line of his mouth told me he was starting to work it out.

"I'm not saying anything!" I snapped. "I'm just pointing out the facts. I don't know if Amanda did that, but it certainly seems suspicious."

"Sure, it seems suspicious, but there could be another explanation!"

I felt my anger rise. "Like what?"

"Like..." Conor cast around. "I don't know, but technology fails all the time. There could be something wrong with my phone."

"You are being so naive right now," I said, rolling my eyes.

Conor's eyes narrowed. "Don't call me naive," he said, anger lacing his voice. "I know quite a lot about how the world works, thanks."

Immediately I was furious. "And yet you fail to see how Amanda is *clearly* trying to drive a wedge between us!" I cried.

"Well then, she's doing a very good job!" he snapped. "Because this is ridiculous!"

"She answered your phone!" I shouted. "She told me you were in the shower! She was trying to make me believe you were having an affair! And all you can do is tell me that it's a misunderstanding? Wake up, Conor! Even if she didn't delete the call, she was completely out of line."

Conor took a deep breath. "You're right," he said at last. "She was out of line."

I let out my own sigh of relief. "So you believe me?" I asked.

"Of course I believe you!" Conor said at once. "But you seem really mad at me for something I didn't do."

I considered his words carefully for a few moments. "I don't think you cheated on me," I said finally, "but I do think you've ignored how cold and rude she's been to me again and again. I understand that she's employed Orcás to support her on her tour, but it really pains me when she disregards our relationship in front of you, and you do nothing."

Conor and I stared at each other for a few moments. I could tell that these last words resonated with him. There was pain and hurt in his eyes.

"Bridget, I didn't know you felt this way," he began quietly. "I promise you, I would never have another woman over to my hotel room while I showered. I would *never* betray you like that. And I promise you, I will get to the bottom of this. If Amanda did this, I'll make her apologise. I'll ensure she never touches my phone again. Okay? Also, I promise I'll never let her disrespect you in front of me again."

My heart was in my throat. Part of me wanted to yell at him, to kick him out of the apartment. Another part of me knew it was true. Conor didn't have a poker face. He couldn't lie. As my anger subsided, I knew deep down that I trusted him.

Slowly, I nodded. He then took me in his arms, folding me into a tight embrace.

"I love you so much," he whispered.

I stared up at him, my arms around his neck. There was a smile on his lips as he leaned down towards me. It was funny how I couldn't stay mad at him for very long. Yes, he was going to pay for worrying me, but for now, I was just happy to have him there. I inhaled his scent with closed eyes, welcoming the warmth that radiated from his body.

"Well, I've missed you so much! I can't believe that happened. I wish you'd have told me." Conor hugged me again. His arms pressed tightly against my back, pulling me closer to him. I felt a huge sense of relief and hugged him tightly.

"You're lucky! I was plotting your murder in the elevator!" I exclaimed as I pulled away. My eyes narrowed as I tried to look threatening. "I'm glad you didn't!" he said in amusement. Around our feet, Jimi was yapping happily, his tail wagging. I could tell that he liked seeing his family back together.

"How did you get away? You have a concert tomorrow!"

"We do. I told the boys that I needed to get back to Galway to surprise you on your big day!" he said.

"So that's what all this is about?" I asked as I pointed at the banner.

"Bridget Kennedy is finally a business owner!" he exclaimed. I rolled my eyes and laughed.

"Okay, I guess it might call for a celebration," I said as I tucked a strand of hair behind my ear.

"Of course it does! Look what I have in the fridge to celebrate. Champagne and strawberries." He reached for a strawberry and hesitantly popped it into my mouth.

"When are you officially opening?"

"Well, I've hired two interns already," I said. "I've also done a deal on the existing office furniture, so all that's left is to get office supplies and other accessories to brighten up the place. If everything goes according to plan, we'll start working on Monday."

"I am so happy for you Bridget !"

As he said this, he opened the champagne. We both laughed as he filled two champagne flutes. He handed one to me, then raised his glass in the air.

"To Bridget Kennedy, the most reliable, responsible, and capable—not to mention most beautiful—event planner in Galway!" he proclaimed. I can't wait to see all the amazing things you'll do as an event planner."

I struggled to keep my face composed as tears of joy and relief welled in my eyes. "Sláinte," I said, raising my glass to his. "And thank you, Conor. This means more than I can say."

"BK, I've missed you so much." The words left his lips in a whisper, and his sincerity left me breathless. The need in his eyes mirrored my own. My whole body yearned for him. I needed to feel him holding me after everything that had happened. I could tell he felt the same.

We kissed passionately then Conor picked me up and carried me into the bedroom. Conor gently laid me down on the bed, his eyes filled with desire and love.

As he lowered himself beside me, his fingers traced delicately along my jawline, sending shivers of anticipation down my spine. His touch ignited a fire within me, fueling my desire for him. Our lips met again, the intensity of our connection growing with every passing second. Lost in the intoxication of our embrace, time seemed to stand still. We explored every inch of each other's bodies, lavishing in the ecstasy that it brought. The room filled with the symphony of our whispered moans, signalling the depth of our shared pleasure.

Conor's touch was both gentle and fervent, his hands memorising every curve and contour of my body. Every caress, every kiss, sparked a wildfire within me, consuming me in its passionate embrace. Our bodies moved in perfect synchronisation, each movement a harmonious symphony of desire.

As the waves of pleasure washed over us, I couldn't help but marvel at the unbreakable bond we shared. It was as if our souls were entangled, dancing together in a realm where only love and passion existed. In those moments, nothing else mattered but the overwhelming power of our love.

Hours turned into an eternity as we explored the depths of our desires. The outside world faded away, leaving only the two of us in a cocoon of love and ecstasy. Time seemed irrelevant, for in that moment, nothing else mattered but the electric connection between us.

Finally, as the night drew to a close, we held each other tightly, our bodies entwined, exhausted but completely fulfilled. Our hearts beat in sync, the rhythm of our love echoing throughout the room. Sweat glistened on our skin, evidence of the intensity of our shared encounter.

With gentle whispers and tender kisses, we drifted into a peaceful slumber, knowing that the love we shared was limitless and transcendent. In the warmth of each other's arms, we found solace and contentment, grateful for the exquisite journey we had embarked on together.

Chapter Thirty-Four

TIME CAPSULE

As I gazed at Conor and the scattered papers, a wave of curiosity came over me. They had appeared next to my coffee mug as I woke up, but until then, my mind had been preoccupied with the aroma of the coffee. I gracefully stretched, folded my legs beneath me, fixing my gaze on the envelopes.

"Could you repeat that one more time?" I inquired, reaching for the coffee mug.

Conor laughed and shook his head. "Basically, I couldn't stop thinking about what you said before I left on tour, about your concerns that our relationship might suffer from the distance."

I attempted to correct him once more, feeling guilty for ever doubting our love. "I told you that I have faith in us. It was just that—"

"I know what you meant," he interjected. "It wasn't an irrational fear. Relationships require effort, and you reminded me of that truth.

So, I came up with a fun idea: why don't we write down all the things we love about each other, seal them in envelopes, and bury them in a secret location? If we ever encounter challenging times, we can dig them up and remember everything that is special between us."

"Like a time capsule?" I questioned. Conor's idea was heartwarming.

"Yes, exactly. The letters serve as our personal time capsule. It will be our secret," Conor responded. I always admired how easily he came up with romantic ideas, which never failed to steal my heart. Unlike me, he never hesitated to surprise me or to be vulnerable and wear his heart on his sleeve. I had a softer side as well, but I struggled to express it.

"Okay, I love it! It's a great idea." I finally exclaimed with a smile. "Shall we each write down a specific number of things or have the freedom to choose?"

"What if we each write down ten things? I know I'll be better at this. Words are my forte, after all." he teased, laughing softly.

"Very funny," I retorted, rolling my eyes playfully. "How about we go to the park to write them?"

"Fantastic idea! We can bury the letters in a small tin box that I used to keep guitar picks in," Conor smiled, his eyes brightening with excitement.

"Come on! It'll be fun! Even though it's cold outside, we can warm up with coffee afterwards. Besides, you're leaving tonight, and I don't want to waste the day indoors,"

An hour later, hand in hand, we strolled through Father Burke Park with Jimi, searching for a bench. To our luck, it wasn't as cold as expected. The park was bustling with activity. The sound of children's laughter filled the air as they played. The joyful atmosphere brought a smile to my face and filled my heart with happiness. The sun shone brightly above us, despite the dark clouds looming in the distance, threatening to dampen our spirits.

"Over there!" Conor exclaimed, as he pointed towards an empty bench beneath an oak tree.

"Perfect! Let's go," I responded, my grin widening in anticipation.

Conor, retrieved a stack of paper, two books, and the tin box from his bag. Meanwhile, Jimi happily chewed on a small stick beneath our feet.

"Okay! No peeking!" Conor playfully warned, leaning against the iron armrest of the bench.

Conor went straight to work, his attention completely consumed by the words flowing from his pen. I gazed up at the oak tree and thought about the multitude of things I adored about him. Conor was right; he was truly a words person, effortlessly crafting song lyrics and now, a future love note for me. As a painter, my skill lay in observing the world and the people around me.

As I witnessed him at that moment, the right words came effortlessly to me. I began to write them down:

1. In your presence, I am a goddess, cherished and adored by a man who understands the power of true intimacy. Each passionate encounter with you is an enchanting journey, where our bodies become vessels of pleasure, and our hearts find solace in the fire of our connection.

2. Your passion in bed matches the intensity of your physicality. With each touch, each stroke, you awaken a primal side of me I never knew existed.

3. Your hunger for success and your unwavering determination to conquer any challenge is intoxicating, and it only makes me crave you more.

4. In bed your touch and affectionate whispers make me feel cherished, appreciated, and desired like no other.

5. Your ability to embrace my family as your own, warms my heart. The way you effortlessly blend into our lives shows me that you are not just my lover but also the missing puzzle piece in the tapestry of our love.

6. The way you effortlessly weave laughter into our lives is bewitching, turning the dullest moments into moments of bliss.

7. Your passion for music is an aphrodisiac that seeps into my veins and stirs the deepest parts of me. The way your fingers effortlessly dance across the strings, creating enchanting melodies, showcases your sensual prowess, leaving me breathless and yearning for more.

8. The way you surprise me with the most delicious breakfasts, ignites a fire within me. Each bite is an erotic symphony of flavour, a reminder that you are not only the master of my heart but also the master of my desires.

9. Your ability to surprise me in the most unexpected of ways has turned my world upside down. Each surprise gesture is a playful tease, leaving me craving your touch.

10. I confess my belief that we have been together before, bound by an unbreakable thread that intertwines our souls. I hope you'll join me on this journey of rediscovering a love that has spanned lifetimes.

A wave of relief washed over me as I realised that my confession of our past lives would remain hidden, buried beneath the oak tree.

Chapter Thirty-Five

DONEGAL

It's incredible how time flies when you're enjoying yourself. I still remember the day I met Conor like it was yesterday. We were both at Waxies, standing by the bar, bathed in the warm glow of the stage lights. That night, his charming smile and mesmerising blue eyes stole my heart.

As soon as I locked eyes with him, I was captivated. His gaze held me in a trance, rendering me speechless. I was drawn to his smile, so full of mischief, and his words were expertly selected to ensnare my interest. It was that very night, I fell under his spell.

"I hope our performance doesn't make you run for the hills."

I couldn't help but think that Conor's words had come true as we embarked on our journey to Donegal.

We had planned to get away for a couple of nights by ourselves before heading to my parents' home for Christmas Day. I couldn't wait to see Mum and Dad, little Heather too. But first, we needed a change of scenery.

Before we left, Rosie and James kindly offered to dog-sit Jimi in our apartment, to which we graciously accepted. Seeing Jimi sitting comfortably between them on our couch warmed our hearts. Not only were Rosie and James taking great care of him, but it was clear that they were also strengthening their own bond as a couple.

Conor surprised me by renting a holiday cottage in Donegal.

"It's snowy and secluded there at this time of year—the perfect place for us to snuggle up for a few days and forget about the outside world."

I looked forward to sitting in front of a roaring fire, watching the snow fall outside the windows.

During the drive, we'd discussed how we'd take advantage of our time away, recharge our batteries and have fun in the snow. The place even advertised a snow sledge. Our car was filled with an excited vibe, radiating festive cheer, as we embarked on our journey to Donegal. Christmas songs played on the radio, as we laughed and sang along with immense enthusiasm. Every stoplight became an opportunity to steal a quick kiss, enhancing the romance that enveloped us. We indulged in spicy curry chips at our one-stop in Sligo, this added a tasty touch of magic to our adventure. It truly felt like we were on holidays, venturing into the wilds of Ireland, creating lifelong memories together. Fairytale of New York played on the radio. We sang our hearts out and promised that it would be our forever Christmas song. Our hearts were brimming with an intoxicating mix of festive spirit and love, making every moment unforgettable.

Our cottage, nestled at the base of Mount Errigal near Gweedore in County Donegal, offered a picturesque escape. Known for its towering presence among the Derryveagh Mountains, Errigal claimed the title of Donegal's highest peak. Despite being just a four-hour drive north from Galway, the temperature dropped significantly, and a blanket of fresh snow covered the landscape during our journey. As we ventured closer, the snowfall intensified, transforming the surrounding hills into a winter wonderland. Upon arrival, we were mesmerised by the untouched beauty that greeted us, leaving us in awe as we looked up at Mount Errigal.

"This place is beautiful." I said as we got out of the car. My words danced before me, in delicate wisps of mist.

"I know, it's stunning." Conor smiled. "I came here with my family once, back when my mother was alive. My sister and I would play in the snow while my parents cooked together and waltzed to old Irish songs in the kitchen," he reminisced, and smiled at the memory. Then his face became more sombre. He gazed into the distance as if the shadows of the past were dancing gracefully between the dark gaps in the trees. "After she died, none of us returned. It was far too painful to face the memories."

I reached for his hand, wrapping my fingers tightly with his. "So why now?" I asked gently.

"Now I want to create happy memories here with you, Bridget," he said, his voice low and sultry. He brushed his hand gently across my cheek. "You make me stronger. When I'm with you, I can face anything. Even the cruel fate that decided to take my mother away. With you, the sad memories become bittersweet. Even joyful." I kissed Conor and gave him a long hug.

"Come on, let's go inside. I wonder if they have a Christmas tree," I said excitedly. We raced up the rest of the steps towards the front door of the cottage. Our breaths danced in front of us as we ran. Our cheeks turned red and rosy in the freezing air. I couldn't wait to see inside the cottage. This would be our home away from home. Conor had travelled extensively without me. Now I yearned for him to join me on adventures—especially somewhere other than my parents' house. Here, we didn't have to worry about being assigned separate bedrooms.

"Of course they've a feckin' tree! I double checked. I know how excited you get about Christmas. Even Rudolf is waiting out the back with a sleigh." Conor laughed and teased me as he unlocked the front door.

Conor was right: the stone cottage exuded Christmas spirit. It had a quaint and inviting atmosphere, with its stone floors and rustic wooden beams. A grand fireplace was already prepared with kindling, logs and turf, ready to ignite a warm and cosy fire. On the mantelpiece, a delicate nativity scene sat, below this hung festive red and white stockings. Snow globes, candles, and holiday-themed cushions on the sofa. The centre of attention was a magnificent Christmas tree, decorated with glistening lights that added a touch of enchantment to the space, as the sun began to set.

"Wow," I whispered, "I could live here forever."
"We don't have forever, but we do have two nights!"

"Well then, let's not waste a single moment," I said excitedly. "How about we open a bottle of red wine and make a fire?" I suggested as I threw my coat on the hanger by the door.

"Talk about impatience," Conor remarked. "You open the wine while I get the fire going. There should be wine glasses in the kitchen." I smiled warmly at him and returned his hug with a long kiss.

As I uncorked the wine, I felt waves of excitement rush through me. Everything seemed perfect. We'd never been somewhere so remote. The mere thought of being in such a captivating and romantic place with Conor sent my senses into overdrive. I couldn't help but imagine the taste of passion that awaited us.

To steady myself, I poured two glasses of wine, then took a rather large drink from mine. Before heading back into the sitting area, I went into the bedroom to touch up my makeup and fix my hair in the mirror. I wanted him to find me irresistible in this romantic cottage. I quickly grabbed my bag and pulled out a small, delicate package from the bottom. Inside was a beautiful set of lacy black lingerie, with intricate floral patterns and a seductive cut that emphasised all the right curves. I knew this would surprise him. As I felt the soft material against my skin, I felt instantly more confident and alluring. As I admired myself in the bedroom mirror, I slipped on my warm nightgown that I planned to wear. I couldn't wait to surprise Conor.

Each passing minute only heightened my yearning to be closer to him, to feel his touch igniting sparks on my skin. As I stood there, the wine glass gently cupped in my hand, I could feel my heartbeat quickening, matching the rhythm of my desires. With every breath I took, I could almost taste the passion and tenderness that awaited me, a promise of an unforgettable night infused with love and pure bliss.

As I stepped into the room, the crackling fire filled the winter cottage with a mesmerising warmth. His handsome features were illuminated by its flickering glow. With a mischievous smile, I made my way towards Conor, while he stared into the flames. The candles he'd lit added an extra touch of romance to the ambiance. As I approached him, he turned around, his eyes widened with surprise, his gaze fixated on my every move. I could see the desire in his eyes as they traced the contours of my body, the soft fabric hugging my curves in all the right places. I felt a surge of excitement and confidence as our eyes locked. Lost in the moment, I drew closer to him, my heart racing with desire. Time stood still as we silently stared into each other's eyes.

In that instant, I knew our night would be etched in our memories forever. My surprise had ignited a fire within us, effortlessly amplifying the magic of our intimate getaway, transforming the cottage weekend into something truly extraordinary.

Chapter Thirty-Six

Good News

The sledge looked like it hadn't been used in ages. However, the runners were still smooth and glided easily through the snow, as we pulled it up the steep hill behind the cottage.

As we reached the top, I felt nervous. It looked very steep. I hadn't ridden a sledge since I was a kid. The thought of hurtling down the slope was both terrifying and exhilarating. I knew I'd be clinging to Conor for dear life, the whole way down,

Conor lugged the sledge over the last crest of the slope. Then he angled it so that it rested on the edge, teetering downwards.

"Are you ready Bridget? Get on!" he teased, grinning gleefully at me. His excitement was infectious.

"I'm feckin' terrified, you crazy man!" I laughed then jumped up and down, trying to psych myself up.

"Don't worry, I'll keep you safe."
"You better!" I squealed. "Or it'll be your head."

He reached out a hand and I jumped onboard. In the brilliant sunlight, his blue eyes sparkled with mischief.

"Come on!" he shouted. "Let's feckin' fly!"

We roared with laughter as we raced down the slope. It only lasted a few seconds but it was exhilarating. At the bottom, we tumbled and rolled together, into a joyful heap, narrowly missing some pine trees.

The sun was high in the sky, its rays mirrored on the snowdrifts, creating a beautiful and perfect illusion of a white paradise. The views around us were breathtaking. Untouched snow glistened from every surrounding hilltop. The sun glinted off crystals of ice, creating rainbows everywhere we looked. All around us, the trees looked as if they had been dusted in layers of icing sugar. All alone, surrounded by bright and snowy fields, we could see for miles in every direction, with only a few stone farmhouses visible in the distance. Curling smoke rose slowly from their chimneys. I loved the sensation of being completely alone together, removed from the rest of the world, cocooned in our own little love bubble.

Conor laughed as a snowball hit me right on the forehead, momentarily blurring my vision. I then fell head-first into a pile of snow. Concerned, he ran over to check if I was alright. Rubbing my eyes, I squinted up at him, pretending to be injured. But my revenge was already brewing as I swiftly gathered snow in both hands.

As Conor leaned over me, his laughter slowly fading into concern, I couldn't resist the mischievous grin spreading across my face. As he reached out to help me up, I suddenly lunged forward, smashing the cold snowball into his face. He stumbled backward, shocked by my unexpected retaliation.

Laughter erupted between us, as Conor scooped up handfuls of snow. With a mischievous smirk, he launched it towards me, missing by inches but covering me in a powdery spray.

Determined not to be outdone, I swiftly crafted my own snowball. With a swift throw, I watched as it sailed through the air, finding its mark. It hit Conor square on the forehead, sending a burst of snow cascading down his coat.

Our snowball fight continued, our laughter and shouts echoing across the winter landscape. We ducked behind trees, used snow banks as makeshift forts, and dove into the fluffy white powder to escape the oncoming onslaught.

Each throw became more daring, more challenging, as we sought to outdo one another. We danced around each other, weaving through the snow-covered landscape, our steps leaving imprints of joy and icy delight.

As the flurry of snowballs flew through the air, time seemed to stand still. The world around us faded into the background, leaving just the two of us locked in this friendly battle. With every hit and miss, both of us were filled with a sense of exhilaration and connection. I loved every second of it.

"Okay, okay!" I screamed between fits of giggles. "You win!"

"Finally!" Conor shouted.

Exhausted, we both fell backwards into a deep snow drift. Gazing up at the blue sky. I found a comfortable place on his chest and rested my head. In those quiet moments, everything felt perfect.

Breaking the silence after a few minutes, Conor spoke. "Ocrás has been offered a record deal."

"Conor, that's incredible! I... I don't even know what to say. When do they want you to sign?"

"Well, the tour ends in two weeks, so probably around that time. I guess they still want to see how the rest of the tour goes," he replied.

"I'm so happy for you!" I exclaimed, wrapped my arms around him. "Congratulations!"

"Thank you, Bridget," he said, as I rested my head back on his chest. "And what about you? How is your new venture going?"

"We only just officially opened a few days ago, but... I'll be signing a contract before New Year's. We're organising a fundraiser for the children's hospital in town."

"So, I'm not the only one with good news!" Conor smiled.

"This year has been amazing, hasn't it?" I said as I gazed up at the sky.

"Yes, indeed, a beautiful lady has come into my life," Conor said, as he hugged me. "And what about your art? We haven't talked about that lately."

"It's still a work in progress. But I'll get there."

"When can I see some paintings?"

"Not for a long time, pal. I want people to see something perfect."

"Art can't be perfect. It's a reflection of our souls, our hearts, and our minds. And no human mind is perfect."

Lying there in the snow with Conor felt so peaceful and wonderful.

"Mo cuishle, you're so beautiful," Conor whispered, his eyes searching mine. After a long moment, he leaned in and kissed me.

"I'm freezing. Let's head inside and warm up by the fire," I suggested.

Laughing, we helped each other up, then shook off the snow. Arm in arm, we walked slowly towards the cottage, our footprints blending together.

We took off our coats, boots and gloves as we entered the cottage, a wave of warmth and the comforting sound of wood crackling in the fireplace embraced us. The flickering flames illuminated our faces. I gently pulled Conor close, feeling the heat of the fire radiating between us as we warmed our hands up.

We gazed into each other's eyes, our cheeks flushed from the chilly winter air. Without a word, our lips met in a tender loving kiss.

"There's a song I've written I'd like to play for you," he whispered.

"I'd love to hear it."

Conor grabbed his guitar from its case and sat across from me.

"I've been keeping this for Christmas, but today feels just right. It's called 'Hear my Whisper'," He closed his eyes and began to play.

Hold my hand
Hold my hand
My love

Come close
Come close
To hear my whisper

You are never alone, never alone
So don't be afraid, don't be afraid

I'll be waiting
Waiting for you
Waiting for you
Til the end, til the end
The end of time
The end of time
Forever
Forever
Forever my love
Forever my love

"Bridget, these lyrics came to me in a dream, as a fierce battle raged all around," his words sent shivers down my spine. The hairs on the back of my neck stood on end, as if I had stepped into the very dream he described. It was as if an ancient presence had awakened within me, connecting us through time.

Chapter Thirty-Seven

GIRLS COLLIDE

"So, did you sign the new client?" Rosie asked excitedly.

"Of course she did. Look at that big goofy grin!" Laura exclaimed as she hugged me. I smiled from ear to ear as she squeezed me tight. Not only had the trip to Donegal been magical, but I'd also just signed a one-year contract with Galway children's hospital. I felt like I was on top of the world.

The three of us were at Laura's place again. It was just as neat and fastidious as usual, although I noticed she'd added a few more pairs of shoes to her closet. She'd invited us over before going shopping together for some final preparations for New Year's Eve. Numerous local shops had promoted an exclusive sale on New Year's Eve party dresses.

"So, tell us in detail. How did it go? When is the fundraiser? Was the hospital's manager cute?" Laura questioned.

I rolled my eyes and laughed just as I threw my bag on the living room chair. I loved my girls. They were the perfect balance of not giving a fuck and being overly excited. Okay, maybe they tended to lean towards the latter half, but they quickly regained their balance. The bond between us was unbreakable. It didn't matter that sometimes Laura drove me crazy or that Rosie gave out to me for my lack of interest in fashion and cosmetics. In fact, it was a sign of our closeness that we could argue without falling out. We girls were like family; we loved each other unconditionally, warts and all.

"She'll tell us on the way!" Rosie exclaimed, then whined, "we have to go shopping! Or all the best dresses will be gone." She stared at herself in the mirror appraisingly. Laura and I sent each other meaningful glances. Rosie was obsessed with looking great on New Year's Eve. for James. She hadn't had someone to kiss at midnight in several years. She was dying to be kissed just as Auld Lang Syne filled the room, and fireworks exploded in the night sky.

It was true. She'd been pleading with us to go shopping for a New Year's Eve dress for days. But, with the new office and Laura's book campaign, we barely got the time to even grab a coffee together, let alone indulge in one of our crazy shopping sprees. Of course, it was usually Laura who bossed us around and led our shopping trips. I could tell she didn't like Rosie taking charge. It was a role she wasn't ready to relinquish. Laura pulled a funny face only I was meant to see, just as I grabbed my bag.

"Fine, let's go! We wouldn't want James to miss out on a perfectly dressed girlfriend," I teased, knowing full well why Rosie was putting extra effort into this year's holiday outfits. It wasn't just a kiss Rosie was after. Every time James's name was mentioned, she got a starry-eyed, faraway look in her eyes. I could tell she was really smitten. She and James really bonded when they house-sat for us. Even Jimi had fallen in love with James. He'd whined pitifully when James left after we got back.

"Oh, please. As if you two are any better," she accused.

"Don't look at me!" Laura exclaimed, raising both hands in defence. "I'm as single as a snowflake in summer!"

"Which is why you're putting in the extra effort." Rosie joked with a wink.

An hour later, we were going through our second shop. Groups of girls were clustered around dress racks or else sifting through half-price bins. Others were trying on strappy sandals. A few were even practising walking in stilettos.

"It'll be even harder when you're pissed," I distinctly heard one girl say to her friend, who was staggering around in a pair of gold platform heels. They all burst into hysterical giggles.

Even though this day was all about Rosie, once we got to the shops, I started to get excited too. There was no reason why I couldn't buy myself a new dress for New Year's Eve. I justified it by telling myself I would wear it again. I'd soon be organising galas and fundraisers where I'd have to wear more formal dresses. With a particularly lovely blue velvet dress hanging on my arm, I walked around the shop, my gaze lingering on all the different colours and designs. Most of the dresses were adorned with shimmering sequins, while others were embroidered with pearls and crystals.

Whispers filled the air as shoppers noticed a familiar face. Amanda du Prey had just walked into the store, and I found myself frozen in place.

Should I say hello or pretend I hadn't seen her? Despite knowing that our feelings for each other were nonexistent, I couldn't bear the thought of standing there awkwardly.

Striding towards her, I exclaimed, "Amanda, hi!" The effort was evident in my voice, but I didn't let it deter me.

She wore large square sunglasses, the rest of her ensemble oozing with chicness. A black leather jumpsuit clung to her curves, accentuated by a shaggy white fur coat draped over her shoulders. Adorned with silver rings and chain necklaces, she completed the look with bold red lips. Upon spotting me, she removed her sunglasses, revealing a bored smile that left no doubt of her indifference.

"Bridget! I didn't expect to see you here," she said coolly, her eyes scanning my outfit critically. "This is such a nice place." Sarcasm dripped from her words, suggesting that she viewed me as inferior.

"Well, here I am! I wasn't expecting to see you here either!" I retorted, trying not to let my voice betray any annoyance. Her extravagant shopping sprees were well-known, after all.

"I was going to go to the Maldives, but we'll have to go on tour in a few days," she explained, emphasising the last part.

Curiosity got the better of me as I asked, "Have you decided on what you're going for New Year's Eve?"

She sighed, the dismissive wave of her glasses conveying her annoyance. "Oh, well, I'm still deciding. I might go to a party in London. What about you?"

"Conor and I are going out with some friends," I smiled, holding the ace card in this exchange. We both knew it.

Amanda's artificial smile faltered briefly, only to be replaced by a glossy, strained version. "Well, try to enjoy yourself," she said. "I know it's rare for you to get time alone with Conor, what with me taking him away on tour all the time." Her smug smile made my stomach churn, but she wasn't done. Before walking away, she turned back with sickening sweetness. "Oh, and some advice? With your frame, velvet will add several pounds. Better to go for something lighter."

Chapter Thirty-Eight

THE BATTLE OF CLONTARF 1014

The crowd gathered in the centre of Róisín Dubh's dance floor, bathed in cascading pink and blue lights, anticipating a deluge of colourful confetti. The transformed room boasted beaded crystal curtains that shimmered under strobe lights, casting rainbows over the excited faces in the crowd. A large banner reading "Happy New Year Galway" adorned the back wall.

As the live band paused, all eyes turned to the large countdown clock strategically placed on the stage. An excited crowd was ready to welcome in the new year.

At a cosy booth near the stage, Orcás, the girls, and I sat together. Conor, by my side, held a champagne bottle, while the rest of us held glasses for the upcoming toast. Rosie sat on Jame's knee and held hands, Laura chatted animatedly with her date - a guy she'd recently met on a dating app. Everyone shimmered in their finest attire.

Throughout the evening, fans approached our table, seeking autographs and selfies from the band. It was thrilling yet surreal to witness. However, the lads remained humble, making time for everyone.

Surrounded by my closest friends, a wave of gratitude washed over me for the incredible year that had passed. The year had brought us achievements to be proud of and moments to cherish.

Suddenly, a clock appeared on the big screen, capturing everyone's attention. Adrenaline coursed through my veins as the final countdown commenced.

On a night filled with love and joy, I celebrated the arrival of the new year with a man I truly loved by my side. He squeezed my hand firmly, matching the excitement radiating from him. Meanwhile, Rosie, brimming with excitement, let out a joyful squeal as James enveloped her in a warm and tender embrace. Determined to seize the moment, Laura readied her shot glass, determined to take a celebratory shot at the stroke of midnight. And as the clock approached midnight, the entire party joined in a lively chorus, chanting the brilliant golden numerals that danced across the screen.

"Ten! Nine! Eight!"

The exhilaration of the moment sent shivers down my spine.

"Seven! Six! Five! Four!"

Conor shook the champagne bottle vigorously while the last three digits lingered before us.

"Three! Two! One!"

At long last, the eagerly awaited moment arrived – the cork popped, soaring across the dancefloor as foamy bubbles erupted from the bottle. James and Rosie melted into a kiss. Conor kissed me passionately as the clock struck midnight, then eagerly filled everyone's glasses.

"Here's to us! May this year surpass all our successes from the last one!" he announced, and we all clinked our glasses together.

As the confetti filled the air, cheers and applause erupted throughout the venue. The familiar melody of "Auld Lang Syne" played, prompting everyone to stand and link arms. Amidst the jubilant atmosphere, a slow song softly started, and Conor turned to me, extending his hand invitingly.

"Missy, may I have the first dance of the year?"

"Of course!" I replied, reaching out to take his hand.

Conor guided me onto the dance floor. We kissed passionately as our arms wrapped around each other. Our feet clumsily found their rhythm, but it didn't matter. Perhaps it was the champagne's effect. Deepest thoughts tied us together in a stare. And then, he whispered those magic words,

"I love you Bridget. Happy New Year."

"I love you too. This night has been perfect."

Our kiss spoke volumes, a declaration of pure love from soul to soul.

There were ten Norsemen on horseback, of that I was certain. The rest were difficult to count. Maybe another dozen, maybe more, stood beside them, their brown tunics fluttered in the wind. Over this coarse fabric, some wore chainmail, others armour. Rings of metal clinked together as the breeze blew over the dead bodies in the field behind them. Each gust of wind brought with it the putrid smells of battle.

The mounted Norsemen had their swords drawn and axes ready, except for one, who stood holding the reins of his horse. This man was taller than the others. He had a mane of red hair that cascaded down his back in oiled dreadlocks. The beads braided into the hair clattered against one another as the man tossed his head. He was their leader—it was evident from the way he shouted at them. He spoke in a strange, foreign tongue, the sounds erupted from his mouth like spit. I didn't understand the words, but I recognised the rage behind them. The man's eyes held madness and a fury that twisted his face. As he yelled, he pointed to a large tent on a hill, about five hundred metres away.

Behind him, several thousand bodies lay dead in the mud. All around was confusion. The Kingsmen had the advantage. Men were strewn up on the ground in every direction, their faces permanently frozen in pain and shock. Some were missing limbs, others decapitated. Those who were still alive wouldn't be for long. Their cries and screams could barely be heard over the stampede of horses' hooves and the deafening clash of steel.

The sun set low in the sky, partly obscured by dark grey clouds that threatened to unleash torrential rain. Through the fading light, it was possible to make out a mass of men farther down the hill, struggling against one another. As a fork of lightning cracked open the sky, the flash of light illuminated these men. Norsemen and Kingsmen hacked at each other, their faces streaked with blood. Those who were disarmed fought for their lives with whatever weapons they could scavenge. Somehow, banners were still held aloft. One had the gold stitching of a harp.

I'd seen this place before, I realised, in Irish history books. This was Clontarf. Which meant —from the banners and dress of the soldiers around me—that I was at the Battle of Clontarf in the year 1014. This was the battle that made Brian Boru a hero, also the battle that claimed his life.

In the fading light, it was difficult to tell who was who, let alone who was winning. Down the hill, there seemed to be a swell of men fighting against Norse foot soldiers. The mounted Norsemen above remained intensely focused on the King's tent. They faced three shielded walls, surrounded by ranks of guards on all sides. It was unclear what they were waiting for, until a resounding horn echoed across the battlefield. I realised that it was a victory call. Those chosen to defend the King's tent lowered their shields and cheered. This was exactly what the mounted Norsemen had been waiting for.

The Norse leader let out a ferocious war cry that sent chills down my spine. His men raised their swords into the air and responded with a thunderous roar. Then they began to advance, slowly at first, then faster and faster into a charge. Somehow, I was taken with them. I could feel the power and strength of their horses as mud flew up from their hooves.

Completely taken off guard, the Kingsmen hastily regrouped, quickly raising their shields. However, the sheer speed and pure strength of the horses was unstoppable, as they crashed through their defences, sending men sprawling to the ground. The Norse riders struck down swiftly with their swords, cutting through the first rank of guards. These soldiers, who moments ago had thought victory was theirs, died, still shocked at the sudden attack. Many had been trampled underneath the horses. When Norse foot soldiers arrived they butchered anyone who had survived the surprise attack.

The second line of defence scrambled to regroup. This time, the guards had time to release a volley of arrows. Around me, men began to fall. But it wasn't enough. Their momentum was too great, and the guards were not powerful enough to take them down. The second line of defence took longer, but the slaughter was no less bloody.

Now the third line of defence was all that was left before the tent. Even though these guards had more time to prepare, they looked scared and insignificant as the horses thundered towards them. The battle that took place next was ferocious. The clash of swords rang out over the hills, echoing from one to the next. The ground was slippery. Men lost their footing, pulling each other down as they fell into the mud. One man lost his sword on the ground but found a rock, which he used to smash open the head of his adversary. Horses were sliding, crushing their riders underneath them. Confusion reigned. Everywhere I looked, Norsemen and Kingsmen alike were being impaled on swords and lances. The leader of the Norsemen reared his steed, bringing its front hooves down upon a man's head crushing his skull.

As darkness enveloped the world, the Norsemen emerged from the rabble, slowly but determined. Despite their few numbers, their matted hair caked with mud, they stood tall and unyielding. Eerie wisps from their breath lingered in the air. The leader, his beard stained with blood, summoned the remaining Norsemen to rise. With cautious steps, they advanced toward the tent's entrance, drawn to the flickering glow of candlelight within. Steadily, the leader pulled back the flap and entered.

Inside, the tent was richly furnished. It was hung with sumptuous sable furs and set with elegant furniture, including a large war table. Maps and figurines, somewhat like chess pieces, were scattered across it. In the centre of the tent, an elaborately embroidered tapestry had been laid on the ground. Around it stood three bodyguards, their swords drawn. They showed no fear as the Norsemen stepped towards them. Their armour was clean and undented; they had not yet seen battle. But their faces were resolute. All three stood to attention, ready to sacrifice their lives for the High King of Ireland.

The King knelt behind them on the tapestry, deep in prayer. He wore a red tunic fashioned from the finest materials. The front was embroidered with an intricate gold harp. Around his neck was fastened a fur cape, which haloed out around his kneeling body. The King, with his long grey hair and full beard, wore a thick band of gold upon his head.

Beside the King stood a younger man, modestly dressed in a simple grey tunic, clutching a beautiful harp with delicate strings. Upon entering the tent, it seemed as though the bard was preparing to play. However, his eyes widened in shock upon seeing the intruders, causing the colour to drain from his face. With a panicked gesture, he extended a hand to shield the King from view. As he reached for his sword, the harp slipped from his grasp and crashed to the ground, its neck cracking and several strings breaking.

The Norsemen charged at the King's bodyguards, their swords raised and with them a new maniacal savagery in their eyes. The bodyguards rushed forward to meet them. Where their swords clashed, sparks flew. The first bodyguard fell to the leader, who parried his blow easily and drove his sword between the man's ribs. He laughed out loud as he twisted the sword in and watched the bodyguard fall. Next to him, his soldiers were making quick work of the other two bodyguards. As they died, their screams filled the air.

A moment of silence fell through the tent. Then, at last, Brian Boru opened his eyes, and got to his feet. He and the bard looked at each other, then at the men who'd come to kill him. The bard valiantly stepped in front of the King. They both drew their swords. The leader of the Norsemen laughed again, the cruel sound filling the tent. The bard lunged at the Norsemen. The three quickly surrounded him. One of them cut him on the thigh; another nicked him on the left elbow. He was outnumbered and outskilled.

The bard, however, was quick. He whirled expertly on his feet, slashing and parrying, dodging under the blades that cut through the air. Then the leader of the Norsemen stepped forward and met the bard's sword with so much force that it rang like a bell. The bard cried out in pain and threw himself towards his King, to protect him with his body. The leader brought his blade down, tip first, into the left side of the bard's neck, piercing him all the way through to the ground on the other side. The bard had no time to scream, no time even to gasp before he fell. The point of the sword, which protruded out of his neck, sank into the soft earth.

The High King of Ireland, blessed himself one last time, then looked up at the Norse leader with sombre eyes as they bore down on him.

I awoke suddenly, my screams echoing around the room as I sat bolt upright in bed. The dream had been so vivid that I stared wildly around, half-expecting to see Conor's lifeless body next to me. Shapes loomed out of the darkness, evoking another scream from me until I realised they were just objects like the dresser and chair. The smells of the battlefield still lingered, the cries of dying men still echoed in my head. Tears streamed down my face as I desperately reached out for Conor, needing to ensure his safety. But the early light of dawn revealed an empty space on his side of the bed. Agonising sobs escaped me as I grappled with his absence. He had left for Dublin earlier, careful not to disturb my sleep. My trembling hands scanned his side of the bed, hoping to find some trace of him. And there, my fingers closed over a small piece of paper. My hands shook as I held it up to the light, taking in the heartfelt words: "Forever, mo cuishle xx."

Chapter Thirty-nine

OCRÁS

Conor painted a vivid image in my mind of cheering crowds and packed concert venues. The way he described fans pushing in for autographs while the vibrant stage lights illuminated their faces got me excited too. It made me wonder what it would feel like to be at the epicentre of all that media attention and adoration from fans. The energy and frenzy of touring sounded absolutely thrilling.

Their days were jam-packed, overflowing with rehearsals, sound checks, interviews, and meetings with sound technicians all arranged by their unyielding tour manager. For Ocrás, it was a dream come true to have every detail taken care of for them. They could simply check out of their hotel rooms, plug in their instruments and play. It was a refreshing change from the days of lugging gear up countless flights of stairs and managing everything on their own. I followed their jam-packed tour schedule and social posts online. This made me feel like I was a part of the show. Fueled by the constant flow of fan footage and live streams my excitement escalated as Ocrás approached their final performance.

My mind wandered as I sat in the reserved section of Olympia Theatre, Dublin. I thought back to the excitement of the Galway360 festival. So much had happened since then, yet I remembered all of it like it was yesterday. Memories of our picnic beside the stone circle came flooding back to me. This was followed by even sweeter memories of our drive up the coast. Then when Conor lifted me up on stage, his first *I love you...* as the crowd went wild at the end of the Orcás set.

The crowds' excitement and energy grew as we waited for Ocrás to walk onstage. Conor had initially suggested I sit backstage with Rosie and Laura, but we'd all agreed we would rather watch the show out front with the audience in order to get the full experience. We definitely made the right choice. Conor had reserved a private area right in front of the stage. We felt spoiled. It had red velvet seats and a small table with bottle service, but it still felt like we were part of the mosh pit. Women squealed a few feet from us. A few of them were wearing Orcás t-shirts. The energy in our area was intense.

As soon as the lads walked on stage, everyone cheered, some whistled, and applause erupted all around us. The lads waved to their audience, then their eyes focused on us, the three girls in the front row. We waved back. I blew a cheeky kiss to Conor. He caught it, threw it back with a smile, then grabbed his microphone.

"Hello Dublin!" Thanks a million for coming tonight!" The crowd cheered in response as Conor's voice echoed through the venue. "This will be our final concert supporting Amanda du Prey," he continued as he pointed backstage, where Amanda was probably watching. "It has been an honour to perform beside such a brilliant and respected artist. She's taught us a lot, and we hope that in the near future, we can pass on that knowledge to other young artists who are willing to take a step into the musical world."

Everyone started to chant Amanda's name and raised their posters and banners in the air. Cameras moved above them, filming the spectacle. Others held signs for Orcás. The girls closest to us were holding a rather clever one that said, "I'm Orcás4Orcás." I noticed that a few posters were addressed specifically to Conor. One read, "Conor: Marry Me?" This made me laugh out loud.

"Here's a brand new song of ours, something we saved for our last show.

Dublin! Are you ready for a good night? Are you ready for Orcás?" The crowd cheered. Conor then shouted. "There's a rumour going 'round that you Dublin folks are gonna be our best crowd ever! Dublin, are you ready for a great night? Get your hands going, folks. Here we go!" The cheering crowd was so loud that I was sure they could hear us back in Galway. Conor really knew how to whip up the crowd.

Ocrás kicked off their new song, an upbeat love song called 'Cupid's Arrow'. As I listened, I felt every tender word, every passionate embrace come alive in the lyrics. It was like a time capsule of our relationship, telling our journey together.

On the day Conor wrote the song, Jimi couldn't resist his mischievous attempts at stealing Conor's notebook. Leaping onto Conor's lap, he playfully took small bites out of the paper. At one moment, he managed to grab the notebook and swiftly dashed off into our bedroom, seeking refuge underneath our bed. Conor, determined to retrieve his precious work, embarked on a comical chase around the apartment. The sight of Conor in pursuit of Jimi was utterly hilarious. Eventually, Conor successfully wrestled the notebook from Jimi's tiny jaws. Our little rascal, undeterred, ecstatically jumped up and down, eagerly anticipating another round of this exhilarating game.

Conor, completely engrossed in his creative process, escaped onto the outside balcony. With his guitar in hand, he effortlessly composed Cupid's Arrow, the cords and lyrics flowing through him seamlessly. From the comfort of the living room, I found myself captivated by the melodies echoing from the balcony. Conor was in his own world, completely immersed in the song. Not wanting to disrupt his creative flow, I silently observed, in awe of his unwavering focus.

From the moment Cupid's Arrow started playing, the energy in the room was electrifying. Song after song, we sang, danced, and let the music consume us. The boys gave everything they had, and by the end of their performance, even the audience was breathless from the excitement. But the night wasn't over yet; we still had Amanda's performance to get through. Although talented, her music didn't compare to the connection we felt with Ocrás.

Just when we thought the show was about to end, the boys came back on stage for an encore. Tears of joy filled my eyes as Rosie grabbed my hand and confessed she was deeply in love with James. It was an incredible moment, and I couldn't be happier for them. The lads played their final song, and it felt like a bittersweet ending to an unforgettable night. The tour had brought so much meaning to our lives, and now it was coming to an end.

As the crowd shouted for more, we joined in, clapping and cheering. The boys laughed and promised to play faster if we clapped harder. And then they started playing "Galway Girl," our song. Joy and love flooded my heart as we screamed the lyrics along with the rest of the audience. In that moment, I felt an overwhelming sense of love for Conor, my friends, and our city. We were the Galway girls who had found our dreams in the men on that stage. Our journey with Ocrás had taken us to unimaginable heights, and there was no doubt that their adventure was far from over.

With a final bow and a shout of gratitude, Ocrás bid their farewell. The crowd erupted in applause, their energy matching the electric atmosphere of the night.

Chapter Forty

HAPPY BIRTHDAY

"So basically, these are the only suggestions the client had. They want it to be colourful, kid-friendly and have enough room for activities and lots of games." I shrugged as I summarised the long presentation I had just delivered. "Oh, and they want a guest appearance from what's his name...? Hip-Hop the kangaroo," I added with a snap of my fingers as I recalled his name. Everyone in the office laughed.

"Do you mean that giant pink kangaroo?" Sami, my intern designer, asked. "The one with the annoying song that takes you days to forget?" He then laughed as he hummed the song.

"I don't know," I said with a frown, "the one you see in Galway city centre hopping with kids during school holidays. I didn't know his name until this morning. We'll figure out how to get a hold of him and see if he'll agree to entertain the kids' charity event."

"He's all the rage right now," Sami explained. "Ever since he went viral on TikTok, Millennials have been booking him left and right for their kids' birthdays. Kids love him too. He hops around like crazy and teaches them about exercise, kangaerobics or something."

"Wait," Mark, our publicist, interjected. "Is he the one with the catchphrase? 'Well Done Me?' And then he pats himself on the shoulders and says, 'Well Done You?'"

"Yeah! That's him!"

Mark laughed. "He was at my niece's birthday party. It was pretty crazy. He's the next Barney."

"Bridget, how did you manage all this by yourself?" Karen, our social media manager and photographer, asked from beside me. She was the youngest intern in the office. When she'd shown me her portfolio at her first interview, I'd hired her on the spot. She was brilliant at graphics, punchy slogans and catchphrases. She also had a sharp eye for artistic details that looked great on camera.

"Well, I basically did everything myself, but now I have a wonderful team." I smiled and gestured at everyone at the table. "I used to run all over the city and search for people to work with for different events."

My legs started hurting just thinking about those hectic days. The way I used to run from meeting to meeting, searching for designers, photographers and venues. Though I'd never said as much, I'd felt like a pack mule. I didn't want to complain. Anyway, I was happy to work hard for my dreams. Now, my workload has really been cut in half. Everything I needed for my business was under one roof. The interns I'd hired were brilliant. They were creative and hungry, always willing to learn and try new things. I felt incredibly lucky to have them. Best of all, I could trust them and discuss ideas like a real team should.

They'd all been at Galway360, so I knew they shared my passion for inspirational events that brought people together. More than one had mentioned in their interview that Galway360 was the best festival they'd been to. They were blown away when they found out I had run the social media and marketing for it. I hated to have notions, but it felt really gratifying to feel their admiration. I'd worked hard for it.

"Is there anything else?" Mark asked. Mark was one of my best finds. He was a sweet kid just out of Trinity, where he'd studied English and Film. He was very nice and very geeky. This was evident in his attire, which usually consisted of a t-shirt for some RPG game. Karen had to explain to me what *Zelda: Breath of the Wild* was after Mark wore a different Zelda shirt three days in a row. On top of this, Mark was funny. He didn't speak much, but when he did, it was to make us laugh. Plus, his writing was brilliant. The written word just flowed out of him. I'd never seen a person write a publicity release with such eloquence or ease.

"Nope. We're free to play with design and colours, and ideas. Our first event at the kids' hospital will be fun. The concept is really open," I said enthusiastically as I sat down. The projected image of my presentation faded away as I pressed the off button on my laptop.

"Well done, team. This is our biggest project to date, plus they've signed a contract to run all their events and social media campaigns with us for twelve months, so let's work hard!" I clapped, and everyone cheered.

Although everyone on the team had different roles, we all helped each other. If any of us had new suggestions or wanted to pitch an idea, the others would immediately welcome it. And while I was the official owner, everyone knew we were on the same footing. We were equal. Everyone had loyalty shares that went towards a Christmas bonus. This motivated the team to put in their best efforts.

In short, everything was just as I envisioned. A fun place where we worked hard to make people's visions a reality.

Looking around, I felt a swell of pride. Everyone, not just me, had worked hard for this. The team had been instrumental in pitching the client. The interns liked to be hands-on and learn as much as they could, so I'd let them take the reins a bit. It had paid off. Now, we would be running our client's social media on all platforms, putting together media releases, making videos and promoting them on RTE and TG4. It was the most comprehensive project I'd ever taken on. I couldn't have done it alone, though. This win belonged to us all.

They started congratulating each other. My team was a bubbly bunch, bursting with excitement. Someone called for a bottle of champagne, which elicited a few laughs. If I'd had one, I would have opened it. The feeling of enthusiasm was infectious. We were ready for this challenge. We were ready to show the world that we could do it, that we could play a bigger part in the event planning and social media world. This was an exciting time, and we'd only just started.

"Now that we've got that out of our way…" Karen said mysteriously as she stood up, sending a meaningful look around the room. Everyone went silent. Their wide smiles turned into mischievous grins—the kind that seemed to hint at a shared secret. I felt everyone stare at me subtly from the corners of their eyes. My face blushed red with embarrassment. What was going on?

Then their heads turned expectantly towards the door through which Karen had just exited. I sat in confusion, staring at the door as well. The whole room seemed to be holding its breath. Then the door was flung open, and Karen reappeared. She was carrying a birthday cake, on top of which were rows of delicate gold candles. It was a beautiful, two-tiered semi-naked white cake. Around the flickering candles had been carefully placed peach-coloured roses and sprigs of pine. Sculpted drips of frosting cascaded down the sides, adding to its extravagant and decadent look. Around the base were gold and peach-coloured macarons. It was the most stunning cake I'd ever seen. In unison, everyone shouted, "Happy birthday, Bridget!" Then they pulled party poppers from their pockets, filling the air with bangs and confetti.

Tears filled my eyes as my gaze travelled from the cake to my team singing around me. They all clapped and congratulated me, pleased by the emotional reaction they were getting. To be honest, I had no idea they even knew it was my birthday. I'd only known them a short time, so receiving so much love made me feel so grateful.

"It's from Brennan's! Your favourite hot chocolate place!" Karen said delightedly as she brought the cake over to me.

"Come on," Sami said as Karen placed the cake in front of me. "Make a wish."

I looked around for a second and then out the window, where I imagined all my friends and loved ones to be. I tried thinking of something better than what I already had, but nothing crossed my mind. I had been blessed with so much; what else could I possibly wish for? So I closed my eyes and wished for everything to stay as it was. I wished that everyone would stay with me because as long as they were in my life, everything else would work out on its own. I then blew out the candles, extinguishing the lit tips in a single puff. Everyone clapped and cheered.

"Happy birthday!" everyone said in a chorus.

"Thank you, guys!" I said breathlessly. "I really don't know what to say."

"You can tell us what you'll be doing tonight," Sami said curiously.

"I'm spending it with Conor. I thought that maybe this weekend, we could all get together for some drinks?" I asked, looking around the room.

I wasn't used to celebrating my birthday twice; usually, the girls barely dragged me out once. But my birthday turned out to be in the middle of the week this year, and Laura was outside the city, and Rosie had a work-related meeting, so having everyone get together during the weekend seemed like the best idea. Besides, having a private birthday party with Conor was more than enough for me. This was my first birthday celebration with Conor, and I couldn't wait. He made everything in my life so much better. There was no way this birthday wouldn't be better than all the rest, even if we did nothing other than stay home and watch TV. Just being with him made me feel safe and complete.

"Oh, I bet he has something amazing planned!" said Karen. I blushed and laughed. I wasn't sure what he'd planned. He hadn't told me anything aside from the dress code and hour.

"Well, speaking of that..." I said as I hurriedly gathered up my stuff. "I should probably go and get ready. He said he'll pick me up at six."

"Have fun!" Everyone shouted from behind me as I exited the room.

I made a getaway before thoughts of work could pull me back.

When you're running your own business, it seems there's always more work to do and leaving the office late becomes the norm. However, tonight I decided to give myself a break and take the night off.

Just before departing, I opted to leave the rest of the cake for my team to enjoy. After all, they had put in a great deal of effort and deserved a treat. As I walked towards the exit, I could hear the sounds of laughter and chatter coming from the conference room. It was evident that a lighthearted and jovial atmosphere had taken over. Turning back, I caught a glimpse of my team sitting around the table, each with their slice of cake in front of them. In that moment, I realised how fortunate I was to have such an incredible team by my side.

Chapter Forty-One

SUSPICIOUS MINDS

"I vote for the red dress!" Laura's voice echoed from beside the mirror. Rosie and Laura's faces filled up the screen of my phone, which I'd placed on the vanity. This corner of the apartment was all mine. Conor had his music studio in the far corner of the living room; I had the vanity in our bedroom. Conor called it my goddess corner because it was here that I transformed into, in his words, "a Celtic goddess." He said it was the way I pulled my hair up high with hair combs, letting soft ringlets fall, and made up my eyes, so their green sparkled like emeralds on a wild stormy night. Conor had shared his endearing description of me a few weeks back, causing me to blush uncontrollably. I couldn't help but send him a grateful smile through the mirror that reflected his admiration.

The retro aesthetic, complete with a magnificent marble top and LED-lit mirror, exuded personality and character. It made me feel like a leading lady, every time I took a seat in front of it. Accompanied by my delightful rose gold earring tree and a jewellery box that perfectly matched its allure, my vanity was truly a sight to behold. But it wasn't just about looks, it was also about functionality. To keep my makeup perfectly organised, I had designated colourful cosmetic bags for each category. Lipsticks found their home in one bag, eye makeup nestled in another, and my blushes, foundations, and concealers were neatly stationed in a third bag.

As I sat down to prepare for my birthday night out, I couldn't help but feel a strong sense of self-worth and confidence.

The girls were eager to assist me in preparing for my special birthday night with Conor, even though they were all busy with their own lives. We all hopped on a video call, with Laura joining in from her hotel in Dublin, where she claimed to be for work. However, there was something about her demeanour that made me feel like she was keeping secrets, especially when she mentioned that she was staying at The Shelbourne Hotel. It seemed unlikely that her publisher would cover such a luxurious expense. Furthermore, Laura's modesty was uncharacteristic, and she refrained from bragging about the high-end accommodations.

Rosie was getting ready to meet James, but my outfit, rather than her own, was the subject of her attention. It really hit me during the call just how busy our lives had become. When we were younger, we moved as one unit through life. Now, new responsibilities and commitments demanded our attention. We were going to miss things in one another's lives. It was just inevitable. That's why it was so special that they'd taken the time to video call on my birthday.

"No, no," Rosie said, her voice echoed due to a poor connection. "Red is so expected on a night out." She leaned into her camera. "Wear the gold one. It's sexy, and he won't see it coming." She smirked as she lifted a shoulder in a suggestive pose.

"But I wore it for New Year," I said with uncertainty, eyeing the dress.

"That's why it's unexpected! It'll stand out, trust me."

"I totally agree," said Laura. "Nice thinking."

"Thank you, thank you. You can all stop applauding now," Rosie said as she bowed to the camera and resumed her hairstyling routine.

"I was expecting more push-back from you, Laura," I said with a laugh. "You always have an opinion on what I should wear."

"They're both nice," she said with a slight smile. It was unlike her to be so diplomatic and easy-going. This only added to my suspicions. "But if you asked me, you can never go wrong with an LBD."

"I'd be surprised if Bridget even had a Little Black Dress!" Rosie giggled. "She's too much of a Charlotte."

I winked sarcastically. "Oh, I have one, but only Conor gets to see it."

The joyful laughter of the girls echoed on the video call. As I looked at them, I couldn't help but feel grateful for their presence in my life. These ladies were the definition of true friends - always there for me whenever I needed them. Not only did they help me look my best, but they also kept me grounded and humble. I knew that no matter what life threw my way, they would always have my back.

I looked at the two dresses, contemplating the choice. In the end, I went with the gold one. Rosie was very persuasive. She always had facts and solid arguments to back up all her opinions, making it hard not to listen to her.

"What about your hair and makeup?"

As Laura asked her question, I struggled to pull the back zipper of my dress up. It was far more difficult than what we see in movies, and I had to resort to using the end of a wire hanger to reach it. It made me wonder whether the dress was to blame or my own clumsiness was the true culprit.

"Waves, green shimmer eyeshadow, and nude lipstick?" Laura suggested as she wagged a finger in mid-air, her eyes glistening as if she could imagine it all. "That way, the gold of the dress will pop."

"No, red lips!" Rosie shouted as she headed to her closet. "You have to go with a red lipstick when you're wearing gold. Think Taylor Swift at the VMAs."

"Red lips," I repeated as I sat down in front of my vanity, positioning the phone in front of me. She was right. It had to be red.

"Okay, girls, I think I need to go," Laura said. Behind her, we heard her hotel room door open and close, then the deep sound of a man's voice. Laura quickly waved a hand at whoever had entered to silence him, but Rosie and I had heard enough. We both squealed with delight. Laura? With a secret man?! I wanted to ask a million questions, but I didn't want to embarrass her if he was still in the room. Rosie was similarly tactful.

"Me too! I'm running late," Rosie added, her voice a bit muffled due to the distance from her phone.

"Okay! Thank you for helping me!" I said as I waved at them.

"Happy birthday, Bridget. We love you!" both girls said in unison. Then, spontaneously, they burst into song. Their voices sounded tinny through the phone, but the song still flooded my heart with love. As they sang, "Happy birthday, dear Bridget," my eyes started to grow misty. Suddenly it seemed incredibly sad that we couldn't be all together on my birthday. This was the first birthday that we hadn't celebrated the three of us. I knew that I'd see them over the weekend, but my heart still ached.

"I love you, girls," I said, wiping a tear away. "Thank you so much for this. And I can't wait to see you both on Saturday!"

"We're going to have so much fun!" Rosie squealed as she grabbed the phone, blowing us both a kiss.

"Bye!" And then all lines went dead. In the sudden silence that followed, I felt the ache in my heart grow sharper. The silence in my apartment made my ears ring. I tried not to let myself feel sad, but the quick departure of the girls exacerbated how hard it was to be alone on my birthday. A feeling of loneliness pressed down on me. Also, Conor was running late.

Despite my attempts to calm myself down with logical reasoning, I couldn't shake off the feeling of unease that came with waiting for

Conor. I reminded myself that being alone wasn't so bad and decided to focus on getting ready for my birthday. Nevertheless, my mind kept circling back to the dream, and the more I thought about it, the more unsettling it became. It was hard to ignore the nagging worry that maybe, just maybe, there was more to the dream than just a figment of my imagination. But how could I explain these thoughts to Conor without sounding crazy?

It was a dilemma that left me feeling frustrated and anxious, wondering if I was losing my grip on reality, or worse, my relationship with Conor.

So, with a sigh, I grabbed my foundation and the nearest brush and tried to ignore my worry. My makeup routine was usually very simple, but I had decided to add a little extra effort for the occasion. I took my time to prep my skin, following all the steps carefully, the way those beauty gurus do. Of course, with my poor skills, I had to start over a few times, but in the end, I had two sharp wings to contour my eyes and some red lips to dramatise the look. Then I styled my hair in loose waves, just as I had promised the girls. I was rarely very pleased with the way I looked, but I had to admit that I'd done a pretty good job.

Always impatient, I decided to call Conor and see if he was on the way. The last time I'd talked to him, he had just finished a meeting with a sponsor and was about to head home. He answered after just one ring.

"Hey, Bridget. I was just about to call you."

As soon as he spoke, a sense of unease overcame me. After all the time we'd spent together, it was easy for me to pick up from his voice if something was wrong.. Unfortunately, this time, something just felt off.

"A friend just called me—" He paused for a second. "He got into a car accident and asked me to take him home. I think I'll be a bit late. Not too late. Like, around an hour."

"Don't worry about it! Make sure your friend gets home safe," I urged. "I'll call my parents in the meantime."

"Sorry," Conor whispered.

"Don't worry! He's your friend. You should take care of him first," I said with a smile. "Go on now. I love you. Oh. Which friend is it?" But my final question was cut off as Conor ended the call. As I stared at the screen, I felt a vague flicker of something that I couldn't quite identify. Was it anger? Suspicion? It wasn't like Conor to hang up on me like that—or to not answer my question.

I shook my head, trying to brush the strange feeling away. His friend was in a car accident—he was probably just worried! At least Conor was safe and sound, even if I was alone.

A few moments later, my parents video called. When I answered, they immediately began to sing "Happy Birthday". I smiled, but it was difficult to hide my disappointment from them.

As my parents finished singing, my mum noticed a change in my demeanour and asked, "Honey, what's wrong? You seem upset."

"Nothing," I said quickly. "Just some birthday blues. You know how it is. Getting older... the girls being out of town."

"I'm sorry, sweetie," she said as my dad nodded along. "At least you have Conor. I'm sure he's going to spoil you tonight."

"Yeah!" My dad chimed in. "What's Conor got planned? I bet he's taking you somewhere nice."

I didn't have the heart to tell them that he was delayed, so I smiled and tried to convince both them—and myself—that everything was going to be alright.

Chapter Forty-Two

TICK TOCK BOOM

Three hours. That's how much time had passed since Conor's "one-hour" delay. Staring at the clock, I realised it was time to give up, so I pulled up my hair and changed out of my party dress. I went into the kitchen and poured a large glass of wine, then watched three episodes of some lame reality show that was playing on Netflix. None of this was as bad as the fact that Conor's phone had been switched off. The last time I called, it went straight to voicemail. Before that, I'd sent a series of unanswered text messages. At first, panic had set in. Now, worry was giving way to shame, followed by anger. I felt foolish. for expecting Conor to make my birthday special. I'd been so sure that he would go above and beyond for me that I hadn't made other plans. Even though I knew he had a good excuse, annoyance still twisted my stomach. Sure, it was only a birthday. I'd have many more. But to leave me alone like this—to not even answer my texts and calls—felt uncharacteristically cruel.

I found myself tucked under a blanket on the living room couch. My dress lay abandoned on our bed, its once smooth fabric now wrinkled - much like the excitement that had gradually faded away within me.

With a sense of emptiness, my eyes remained fixed on my phone. The background was a picture of Conor and me at Galway360. We captured the moment perfectly with a selfie taken on stage after Conor's performance. We were laughing and hugging each other. He still clutched his guitar, having just uttered those three little words for the very first time: "I love you."

As I took another gulp of wine, I tried to suppress the feeling of bitter disappointment rising inside of me. Normally, I would have just brushed it off as anxiety. However, this time, I couldn't shake the sense that something else was going on with Conor. I couldn't put my finger on it exactly, but I knew he wasn't being entirely truthful with me. It bothered me to be left in the dark like this. After all, I trusted him with my life, yet he couldn't even confide in me? Another hour passed. I could feel my annoyance growing into a simmering fury in the pit of my stomach.

The thought had crossed my mind that maybe this was another one of Conor's elaborate surprises, like when he had returned from Australia unexpectedly. However, if this was the case, we needed to have a serious conversation about why he kept hurting me for the sake of a big surprise. It was no longer okay and needed to stop.

If it weren't a surprise, though... if he were abandoning me on my birthday without even getting in touch, well... We were also going to have to have a serious conversation about that.

My hand shook with suppressed anger as I reached for my glass of wine. Some of it spilt onto the couch. I swore loudly, then shrugged. I'd clean it up later. Instead, I took another mouthful to calm my nerves.

I then stared back at my phone, ready to dial Conor's number again. Not that it would do any good if his phone were dead. Suddenly, a text popped on the screen from an unknown number. My heart leapt. Surely this was Conor, texting me from his friend's phone when he realised his battery was flat! My heart sank as I opened it.

The message was short, and the words clear. But even so, I struggled to understand their meaning. I read it over and over again, then placed the glass of wine on the small coffee table before me with a shaky hand. I straightened up and slid to the edge of the couch, the indistinct mumbles of the TV echoed behind me.

Sorry I kept him busy on your birthday!
– Love Amanda XOXO

Just when things couldn't get more confusing, another message popped on my screen from another number—Amanda's number. It had a link. Trembling, I pressed my finger against it. I tried to breathe normally, but in those few short seconds, it felt as if I were choking on the suddenly-thin air. My eyes strained in anticipation. But as soon as the link opened, I wished it hadn't.

AMANDA'S MYSTERY MAN!

The title of the article flashed in bold letters, clear and plain, leaving no room for doubt. There was no need to read the article: the time it had been posted and the accompanying photo was enough to give me a clear insight into what Amanda's previous text had meant. The article didn't mention Conor's name. The picture had been taken from a weird angle, shielding his face. But I recognised him. Many of his fans, I knew, would also recognise him.

I felt my blood boil. Jealousy and anger swept through me with the force of a tsunami. I was on my feet before I realised it, my fists balled up in rage. Had he really been out with Amanda tonight? Did that mean he had lied to me? It was hard to believe that Conor would do that to me. I had never been lied to like that. My world suddenly felt like it had dropped from under my feet. The floor seemed rickety, like the rolling deck of a ship during a storm. I wanted to be sick and scream at the same time.

The front door flung open just as I was about to scream. Its heavy chain echoed through the room. I whirled around, positive for half a moment that I was about to see Amanda and Conor enter together, their arms and lips wrapped around each other. What had happened to me? I felt like I was going insane.

Instead, Conor appeared in the living room doorway, his cheeks red from the cold, his hair dishevelled, and his dark waves in a tangle. It looked as if he had run his hands through it one too many times. My heart missed a beat when I saw him, and I stared at him with tearful eyes, my lips parted. I was lost for words. Blood pounded in my head, obscuring any noise. Conor seemed to move towards me in slow motion. I was so angry and disoriented that I thought I might faint.

"Bridget, I'm sorry I'm late. My phone died, and my friend—"

"Stop it." I choked on the whispered words. I shook my hands to interrupt him and walked past him, handing him the phone on my way towards the bedroom. Conor didn't say anything. Even though my back was to him, I knew he must have been reading Amanda's messages.

Meanwhile, I entered the bedroom and tore open my closet door. Between tears, I reached for whatever coat I could grab and threw it over my clothes. My boots followed, but before I could pull them both on, Conor was speaking from the doorway.

"Bridget, I can explain." His voice was low, filled with exasperation. However, I couldn't help but make note of the guilty look in his eyes.

"I know you can!" I yelled in anger. "You always have an excuse. For everything!"

Conor folded his arms. "What's that supposed to mean?"

"It means you always say the right thing, but then nothing changes," I snarled. "I've been telling you for *weeks* that something is up with Amanda, and you've brushed me off every time."

"I've tried to tell you—you're overreacting about her!"

"And I've tried to tell you, Conor, that you're either naive or hiding something."

"I'm not hiding anything!" Conor was starting to look angry now too.

I laughed maniacally at this. I knew I sounded crazy, but for once, so did he. "Oh yeah?" I raged. "Then why did you lie to me tonight? Where were you, Conor? And don't you *dare* say your friend was in a car accident."

"That's not what..." Conor trailed off. "Will you stop? Where are you going?" he asked, his voice a bit louder. His hand wrapped around my arm, trying to get me to stand still. I had finished lacing up my boots and now was moving towards the door.

"Let go of me!" I shouted, tearing his hand off of my arm. "Don't you dare touch me! I'm going home."

"What do you mean? You *are* home. You're not making any sense!"

"*I'm* not making sense?" I was so angry I could barely speak. I felt out of control with rage and humiliation. "You're the one who can't get your story straight!"

"Please listen," he insisted. "You can't leave. We need to talk about... this." He frowned as he threw my phone on the bed. I reached for it and shoved it in my back pocket.

"Okay. Talk." I faced him now. This was his last chance. He was staring at me, a slight smile on his face. It was the kind of smile that people only get when they have been caught doing something embarrassing. "Not that it will make a difference," I added maliciously.

My foot tapped against the floor as I folded my arms over my chest, a clear sign of my impatience. Conor took a deep breath and slowly ran his fingers through his hair. He contemplated what to say next. I stared at him. I was shaking with rage and disappointment. A few seconds later, he said in a calm voice, "I'll talk with you when you cool down." Conor grabbed his jacket and walked out the door.

As the door slammed shut, I was left standing in stunned silence. My mind was reeling with confusion and disbelief. Conor's abrupt departure had taken me completely by surprise and I couldn't even bring myself to scream or cry. This was not the man I thought I knew and the sudden dismissal on my birthday left me feeling abandoned.

Chapter Forty-Three

MAD AS HELL

My connection with Conor was unique. My feelings for him had no comparison to any of my previous relationships. Our chemistry had been instantaneous and profound. I'd never fully understood it. It was a mystery why I had been so immediately drawn to him. The mystery of it was also why it was intoxicating. All I knew was that when we were together, I felt as if my soul was complete. In fact, everything about us had been special from the very beginning: how we met, how we got to know each other, and the things we went through together. However, one thing remained the same when it came to heartache, even when it came to Conor: the cure was ice cream, good company and a weepy movie—the kind where the guy always gets the girl, usually after running through an airport to declare his love. Rosie knew exactly what I needed. That's why she finished her date with James early and rushed over to see me.

She arrived at my apartment about an hour after my text. Rosie was out of breath and sweating like she'd run a marathon. She arrived with a brown carrier bag filled with essentials: red wine, choc chip cookies, and tubs of Rocky Road and mint chocolate chip ice cream. Also, a large box of tissues, clearly, not for her.

From the moment I opened the door, we silently agreed not to talk about it, at least not until I was high on sugar and crying my eyes out at the movie's sappy yet gut-wrenching dialogue. Rosie already knew what to do. She was such a supportive friend and always had the remedy. She did nothing but tuck me into a fluffy blanket and then handed me a tub of mint ice cream with a large spoon in it.

This time, however, the cheesy movie failed to make me cry. As I watched the bland, Tom Hanks-type man trick the girl next door into another shady scheme I knew she'd eventually forgive him for, I felt myself growing angry. These movies were all the same. The man did something terrible—like pretend to be someone he wasn't—in order to find something out about the woman. When he was eventually exposed, she was rightfully mad. But of course, after a grand, romantic gesture in a public place, she forgave him. I used to find this scenario romantic, but today I found it infuriating.

How did all these men get away with being such scumbags? I thought bitterly. *Why are beautiful women always settling for these losers?*

Even so, I might have been able to forgive the horrible plot if the acting wasn't also atrocious.

"Okay, turn that shit off!" I yelled halfway through the movie. "I've had enough of this. How can these Hollywood actors get paid for such rubbish acting?" I let out an angry breath as I threw the fluffy blanket to the floor. Rosie was cuddled next to me and also lost the blanket when I tossed it off. She just chuckled and shrugged as she sipped her wine.

After she switched off the movie, she eyed me cautiously. I knew she was afraid to say anything, as if I was a ticking bomb—and frankly, I was. However, only Conor had the power to set me off. Rosie would see my full wrath if he were foolish enough to show up here before my anger had cooled.

"So, are you ready to talk? Or should I feed you some of those chocolate chip cookies?" Rosie asked from the corner of the couch. I contemplated for a second, wondering if I'd had enough sugar to get me through the conversation. I sighed and nodded.

"As you know, Conor and I were supposed to go out," I began, earning a nod from Rosie. "So, at around six, I call him, and he says he's helping a friend that got into some sort of car accident." Blood boiled inside me as I remembered the lies; how easily he'd thrown them in my face, as if I was some kind of gullible fool. I took a deep breath, trying to keep my cool while I was talking to Rosie. "Of course I said he should take care of his friend because I'm a reasonable person. And honestly, it had me worried. He said he'd only be an hour late, which was fine. But then he showed up four hours later after having his phone off. He didn't even check in to say he was going to be later than expected."

"Well, Bridget... What if he ran out of battery? His friend needed help. You can't blame him for that," Rosie said fairly, her voice low.

"That's what I said at first. But—" I thrust my finger vigorously towards her, as harshly as I would point towards a criminal I was indicting. The force of the gesture seemed to say, "Just you wait." With my other hand, I retrieved my phone from the small coffee table. "Before he came back, I got this message."

Rosie turned the phone towards her face. It washed her skin in an eerie blue. She frowned, her eyebrows knitting together in growing astonishment as she read the words—more than once. A cloud of confusion and anger passed over her face. Then she stared up at me, her mouth gaping open. Just like me, she was at a loss for words and clearly hoped that she was reading it wrong.

"Apparently, Amanda was that friend," I explained. "He took her home, did God knows what for four hours, and then came back."

"Bridget, I don't think Conor would do anything to hurt you. I know how this looks, but..."

"Even if nothing happened, what does it matter? He betrayed me by lying to me!"

"There could be a good explanation," Rosie said in a pleading voice.

I shook my head. Rosie's inability to grasp the severity of Conor's actions made me want to grab her by the shoulders and shake her. Instead, I said as calmly as I could, hoping that someone would finally get me, "You trust him. So did I. That's why I'm madder about the fact that he lied than the fact that he helped her out. He lied, so he must know he did something wrong. Rosie, you know me better than anyone. If Amanda were in an accident, I would have never kept him from helping her!"

"I know." Rosie sighed. "Maybe you should talk with him... once you calm down." She added the last part as a subtle reference to the anger oozing off of me.

"Do *not* tell me to calm down!" Suddenly I was furious, even more furious than I had been when Conor had left. "Conor said the same thing, but I will not calm down just to spare your—and his—feelings! He abandoned me, lied to me and made a fool of me *on my birthday*. Then, when I confronted him, instead of explaining, he just left!" I burst into tears.

"Maybe he didn't think you'd listen to him when you were mad?"

"He doesn't get to decide that!" I yelled. I was on my feet now. Anger coursed through me. "I'm allowed to be mad! He did something terrible, and now he has to face the consequences of that! If he doesn't want me to be mad, then he shouldn't have lied to me to begin with. But to *leave* just because he doesn't want to deal with my anger? It's cowardly, Rosie!"

Abruptly, all the anger inside of me erupted in violent sobs that wracked my whole body. I collapsed on the sofa, tears flowed freely down my face. I felt suddenly exhausted. I took a deep, shuddering breath and put my head in my hands.

Gingerly, Rosie reached out and began to rub my back.

"I'm sorry, BK," she murmured, "you're right. You get to be as angry as you need to be."

"What does it say about him that instead of working this out with me, he just left?" I turned a tear-stained face up to her. "I want a man who is totally honest. I want a man who doesn't walk away when things get hard."

"It was wrong. Hopefully when you talk to him, he'll explain."

"I don't want to talk to him."

"Bridget, you know you guys have to talk it through."

I knew it, but that didn't mean I was ready to admit it.

I shrugged. "No, we don't. It's his problem. He did it. He should solve it alone."

"I guess it's time I open the other bottle of wine." Rosie sighed, then stood up and vanished into the kitchen. "I have a feeling that it's going to be a long night."

Chapter Forty-Four

MEA CULPA

I'd lost track of time. It was well past midnight by the time I convinced Rosie to head back to her place. She'd insisted on sleeping over; at one point refused to leave the couch, adamant that she should stay over to keep an eye on me. Even though she'd assured me it was no bother to stay, I didn't want to be a nuisance. As much as I loved Rosie's company, I also wanted some time alone. I'd talked things through with her, and she'd given me her opinion and suggestions. Now I just needed time to think.

The TV was still on in the background, its blue rays flickered across my sleepy eyes. Now that I was alone, it was harder to sit with my own thoughts than I'd anticipated. The worry about what was going to happen with Conor was overwhelming. I felt sad and alone as I looked around our apartment. Truth be told, it had been the worst birthday on record. I felt numb inside.

Where was Conor? What was he doing? When he'd first left, it had been a relief to have some space from him. Now that I no longer wanted to scream at him, I felt resentful that he hadn't come back yet. This apartment was supposed to be our home, our safe haven. I especially hated to think of him blowing off steam with the lads, telling them how crazy I was. I didn't think Conor would say that to his band members, but I couldn't be sure anymore. I also hadn't thought he was the kind of person who would lie to me.

Thinking about Conor's lies started to make me angry again. I was still wrapped in a blanket, firmly holding onto a half-empty box of tissues.

With a deliberate pace, I drew in a long deep breath and slowly released it while counting to ten with a steady rhythm. As I exhaled fully, I could feel my nerves settling, and my anxiety easing just in time for me to inhale a fresh breath. The sensation of calmness washed over me, instilling a sense of tranquillity.

I stood up, stretched, and then sat down. Restlessness plagued me. I needed something to distract me from checking my phone every thirty seconds. I contemplated cleaning the apartment just to have something to do with my hands and mind. Cleaning probably wasn't the answer, though; I was too tired, and my neighbours would complain about the noise.

Just then, Jimi came out of the bedroom. He had been asleep under our bed. When he spotted me, he wagged his tail and came over to sit at my feet. I reached down to scratch under his chin. He yawned lazily.

That was an idea. I could take Jimi for a walk. A brisk walk might be the only thing that would clear my head. It would also be good for Jimi. He was probably traumatised from listening to Conor and me fight. If dogs even noticed that kind of thing. I took a deep breath and pushed myself off of the couch. Suddenly, the doorbell rang just as I reached for my coat and Jimi's leash.

I froze. Immediately, a nervous lump formed in my throat. Nervous butterflies flitted through my stomach. I knew, without checking the peephole, that it was Conor. The image of the man I'd come to love so much flashed before my eyes. I could easily imagine how dishevelled he looked: dressed in the same jeans, loose white shirt and leather jacket; his hair a mess, pointing in all directions from the numerous times he'd pulled and tugged at the strands. I don't know how long I stood there motionless, picturing the man I wanted so desperately to forgive, but it must have been a while. The doorbell turned into knocking, joined by Conor's familiar voice.

"Bridget, I know you're there! Please open the door. The deadbolt is on." His voice was loud enough to wake the neighbours. It also served to break me out of my reverie. A vindictive part of me felt proud that I had remembered to lock the deadbolt. *That'll show him*, I thought. It was childish, but I couldn't help it. Even so, I didn't want Conor to wake the neighbours. I also really wanted to see him, although I would never have admitted that to him. I took a deep breath and hurried to the door.

There, standing in the corridor, a miserable look on his face, was the same Conor I'd pictured in my mind. His hand was mid-air, ready to knock again. He smiled the minute he saw me, and his entire body relaxed. Despite myself, the smile made my heart surge with love. This feeling was immediately followed by anger.

"You opened," he breathed out. Relief flooded his face.

"I did," I said, folding my arms across my chest. "But I'm still not talking to you." Without another word, I headed back inside the living room. I could feel Conor's presence as he followed me into the apartment. I turned off the TV, welcoming the silence. Then I sat down on the couch. Conor sat down across from me. Neither of us spoke for several long moments.

He was the first to break the uncomfortable silence.

"Can we talk this through?" he asked quietly. There was a note of desperation in his voice. His eyes struggled to meet mine. When they did, I saw that they were misty.

Stiffly, I nodded. I didn't trust myself to speak. Part of me wanted to yell, but a larger part wanted to cry. The room felt heavy with all our sadness and anger. I knew that whatever was said now could change our relationship forever. It made me realise how much I wanted that relationship to last, no matter how angry I was.

"I don't know what to say," Conor began haltingly. To my surprise, he looked somewhat embarrassed. "I rehearsed an entire speech on my way back, but Bridget, you already know what happened. There is no excuse for what I did or for lying about whom I was going to help." He trailed off, his hands vividly flying in wild gestures. "I can just tell you that I wasn't thinking straight at that moment in time. Maybe you can understand."

I doubt it, I wanted to say. But as mad as I was, I didn't want to get into another fight. I wanted to hear his explanation.

"When Amanda called, I didn't want to go, but I was scared that something serious had happened. She'd been in a car accident! If something happened to her and I ignored it, I couldn't forgive myself."

"Conor," I interrupted, "I told you, this is not about going there! She asked for your help, and any decent human being would have helped her. Even I would have helped. And I hate her!"

"I know. I know. But I also knew it was your birthday. I thought I could be back in an hour. My phone also died. I'm sorry I lied and didn't tell you whom I was going to help. I didn't want to upset you on your birthday. I know how little respect that woman has for you, and I can't ever allow someone to disrespect you."

"You've allowed it again and again," I said hotly, my fury rising again.

"I know." Conor looked stricken. "I thought she held the key to Orcás's success. I didn't know how to stand up to her. But after today, I couldn't let it go on any longer. So... that's why I've refused to support her on another tour."

"She asked you to support her on another tour?" My jaw dropped.

Conor nodded. "I know what her intentions are now. I don't want to associate with someone who doesn't respect our relationship."

"But Orcás..." I began. I didn't know why I was arguing. There was no part of me that wanted Conor to continue to tour with Amanda. But I also didn't want him to give up his best opportunity.

"Orcás doesn't need her," Conor said forcefully. "We're good enough without her. But that's not why I said no. I did it for you. For us." I was breathless. He'd literally given up an opportunity to go on tour with one of the most famous pop stars in Europe. For me. For us.

"Anyway," he continued, "that's why I lied. I didn't even want to mention Amanda's name on your birthday. I thought I could help her really quickly, it would only take an hour, and then I would be back and ready to celebrate with you. When it started to take longer, I panicked. I knew I had dug myself too deep into the lie. I'm so sorry, Bridget. There's no excuse. I don't expect you to forgive me. It was such a colossal fuck-up, and you have every right to be mad at me. But I hope you know that I never meant to hurt you. And I would never, ever betray you."

He looked up at me, tears shining in his eyes. "Do you forgive me?"

Chapter Forty-Five

FAREWELL, MO CUISHLE

I stood alone in a field that overlooked a small village. Wind rustled through the leaves of the Sycamore trees that towered above me. I recognised the village and knew instinctively that I had once lived there. The dwellings were clustered within circular stone walls; smoke was rising from the thatched roofs. The smell of turf fires filled the air. Livestock roamed freely in some of the farm yards; others were fenced in behind stone walls. Villagers moved among the houses, carrying woven baskets. Their clothes were drab, brown and loose-fitting.

It had been a week since I had heard from my beloved bard. All news of the battle that had reached us had been horrific. The King's army had been victorious at Clontarf, but thousands had lost their lives. Many women in our village would never see their husbands again. King Brian Boru himself had been slain at Clontarf. The last messenger had carried this terrible news. He'd told us that the King's body had been taken in procession by his army to Armagh Cathedral for burial.

I knew that if my love had survived the battle, he would be at Armagh with his beloved King.

But then, why had he not sent word to me? He would never keep me waiting like this, fearing the worst. Even if he were badly injured, he would have sent a message with someone. Perhaps his grief for his King was so ardent that he'd lost all sense of himself. Or perhaps...

I closed my eyes and breathed in the smoky, turf-filled air. The wind caressed my face, brushing away my tears. I couldn't let myself think the worst had happened. He deserved my hope and faith. He would return to me soon; Armagh was not far away. He would soon be back in my arms.

I had never made love with my husband-to-be. If I had to spend a lifetime without him, I knew I would never let another into my bed.

At that moment, as if my own thoughts had conjured him, a rider appeared on the horizon. The rider was moving at a quick pace, heading straight for our village from the direction of Armagh. Even from a distance, I could tell that the rider was a man wearing the colours of Brian Boru. My heart leapt with wild joy at the sight. It had to be my beloved! He had found a way home to me, just as I knew he would.

When he entered the village, the rider slowed to a stop beside several clustered villagers. To my astonishment and joy, the villagers turned and pointed up the hill to where I stood. The rider was looking for me. It really was him. I had been going to this spot every day to watch the road and wait for him to return; everyone in the village knew that this was where I would be. As the rider turned the horse in my direction, I thought my heart would burst from my chest. I couldn't wait a moment longer. Picking up my skirts, I started to run down the hill to meet him; tears began to stream from my eyes.

But the man who rode up the hill towards me was not my betrothed. This man, taller and broader than my love, was a stranger and decidedly more savage-looking than my beloved. He was dressed in a worn tunic that was covered in chainmail. To my horror, this metal was still red with blood, as if he hadn't had a chance to wash it since the battle. If he had not worn the livery of the King, I might have mistaken him for a Norse raider. His hair was wild and long, and his beard tangled. His face was hard. A long sword was strapped to the side of his horse. On the other side was an axe. This man was no harp player; he was a warrior.

Yet there, strapped below the axe, was an instrument I recognised. It was cracked and broken, the strings flailing against the side of the horse, but I still knew it.

Something was wrong. Something was terribly, terribly wrong. A feeling of despair sank deep into me, like a sword plunging through my heart. My body went cold as if my bones were turning to ice inside of me. I wanted to escape, to run as quickly as possible away from this man, but I couldn't move. My feet were frozen to the ground. I wasn't afraid of what he'd do to me, but I knew—I was beyond certain—that the news he was bringing would cause greater pain than any physical injury ever could.

The horse came to a halt several paces in front of me. The rider met my gaze. Despite his wild look, his eyes were gentle. Around his mouth, he wore an expression of deep grief. I could see the heaviness in his heart, even in the way he sat atop the horse; he was stooped and haggard. A great weight was bearing down upon him.

We stared at each other for a few moments. He did not speak, but I already knew what he would say. I couldn't move; I could barely breathe. I felt faint. Sound was far too loud, then muffled. My vision blurred, then sharpened. Only my heart continued to beat. Its strength and regularity seemed to mock me. You live, it sneered, while he... does not.

At last, the man dismounted from the horse. He carefully untied the broken harp from the saddle. Then he turned slowly towards me. My eyes were fixed on the harp. My breathing felt sharp in my lungs, as if I were being stabbed with each breath.

The man took a step towards me and held out the harp. Somehow, I managed to lift my arms and take it from him. The instrument was surprisingly light. Some of it was missing. I wondered vaguely how it had broken. Had my betrothed had to watch them destroy his precious instrument before they also took his life? Or had they killed him first?

"He fell defending the King," the man said hoarsely. "A hero's death."

I wanted to nod or acknowledge the loss of the King, but my mind went blank. It echoed only with those last words: A hero's death.

"He would have wanted you to have this," the man continued. His voice was choked with emotion. "He spoke of you often. Before the battle, he bid me find you, should the fight go ill for him."

When I did not respond, the man said my name several times. I must have fallen to my knees because he tried to grab me and lift me up, but my body had become as heavy as stone.

A long time passed. At some point, although I wasn't aware of it, the man left. I only knew that by the time consciousness returned to me, I was lying on the ground holding the broken harp. It was raining softly. A few women stood around me, whispering amongst themselves, pointing at the harp. The messenger and his horse were gone. The world, I knew, had ended, and the scream that tore out of me could have brought down mountains.

Somehow I returned home. Someone must have carried me. My father, perhaps. He had never approved of our match; well, now he would have his wish. Scenes faded in and out. My mother bent over me, applying a cool cloth to my forehead. My father, raging over the death of the King. Several times, my mother tried to feed me. She raised bowls of broth and barley to my lips. I tried to eat, but hunger evaded me. After the first few sips, I could stomach no more. When she tried again the next day, the smell of the food made me violently ill. I pushed the bowl away without a bite.

In my dreams, he died again and again. Even though I had forgotten to ask the messenger for details of his death, I knew how it had happened. I saw it every time I closed my eyes: the Norse leader, with his oiled braids of red hair, stabbing him through the back as he turned to defend his King. I couldn't say how I knew that these dreams were real; I just knew. Each time, I woke covered in sweat, clumps of bloody hair surrounding me. My mother said I ripped it out while I screamed in my sleep.

Days, maybe weeks, passed. My body grew thin. My lips cracked from lack of water, and my skin became puckered and translucent. Whispers filled my head; my mother and father, wondering if they should take me to the healer woman who lived in the forest—the one who knew the berries and herbs that could revive even the illest.

But there was no cure for what I suffered.

One day, after days of rain, the sun shone brightly against a blue sky. The seasons had changed; Bealtaine had come to the land. The sun gave me the first strength I'd felt in weeks. Strength enough to rouse myself. I walked barefoot out of our home. A light breeze whispered through the trees. I closed my eyes and let the wind curl through my hair. It was matted and greasy, what was left of it, anyway.

Two women were walking down the path outside the stone wall of our rath, carrying baskets of rushes. As they came towards me, their words floated towards me on the breeze.

"His soldiers sat in mourning for twelve days," one of the women was saying. "Can you imagine? He was our own Cuchulainn, taken from us before his time."

"We'll never see such a leader again," her friend agreed, shaking her head.

"Nor was he alone," the first woman said. "He was interred in Armagh with his son, nephew, and King Mothla mac Domnaill of the Déisi Muman."

"Such heroes—all!" wailed another woman.

"What of his bard?" My words sliced through the air with all the force of a sword. The two women stopped in their tracks. They looked around before their eyes settled on me. One took a step back while the other clasped a hand over her mouth. I knew what I must have looked like: hair missing, a bloodied scalp, wild and unkempt. But I didn't care.

"The great Kings of Munster were mourned for twelve days and nights; their bodies interred at the Cathedral of Armagh. But what of the other fallen heroes?" I was screaming now. "What of the King's bard?" My whole body was shaking. I thought that I might faint both from the effort of speaking after so long in my bed and from the rage that had overtaken my body. "Does he not deserve an

honourable burial as well?" Spit flew from my mouth as my ears filled with the sound of rushing water. "Where is the body of the bard?" Sobs broke in my throat. Suddenly the ground was rushing up to meet me. The day was too hot, too bright. Everything was bad. Nothing would ever, ever be good again.

Several days later, as the full moon revealed her pearly cheek above the village, I rose from my bed. As quietly as possible, I opened the box where I kept my valuables and took the emerald ring from it. Since he'd left, I had kept it hidden so that my parents would not know we had pledged ourselves to one another. Silently, I slipped through the house and out into the night.

I travelled by moonlight to the stone circle. In the milky glow, the stones looked even taller than I remembered. They towered above me as I approached on bare feet. The night was cool, and I wore only a thin white night dress. It didn't matter. The memory of the last time I was here filled me with radiant warmth. He and I had taken a solemn vow underneath these immortal stones. They were the witnesses to our love.

They would also be its tomb.

I would sit in front of them and mourn him—not for twelve days, as Brian Boru's soldiers had sat in mourning for their King—but for as long as I could. My betrothed may not have been a king, but he deserved a king's burial.

The moment I stepped into the circle, I could feel its energy. Although the night was still and silent, inside the stones, there was a faint humming. A breeze, like the breath of spirits, passed through my hair. I knelt at the foot of the tallest stone and whispered a short prayer. With the small trowel I'd smuggled from my father's shed, I began to dig into the soil. It was soft and wet from the spring rains and came away easily until I'd made a hole about as deep as my elbow. The emerald ring was still glittering on my finger. I removed it and held it up to the moonlight. In the silvery light, the green blinked like a distant star. The gold shone lustrously. I raised the ring to my lips with trembling hands and kissed it.

"Farewell, mo cuishle," I whispered. The tears streamed down my cheeks like rivers through a valley. Inside, the pain was so strong I thought it would

split me in two. He was gone, forever and ever, and I would never again be able to hold him in my arms. Never again laugh with him. Never kiss his lips or smooth back his hair. Death made no sense. How could a person be there one day and gone the next? Especially someone like him, whose essence I could still feel vibrating through these stones?

I lowered the ring into the hole and covered it with wet dirt. I didn't want an animal to come by, see the fresh dirt, and think there was food buried, so I packed the dirt down as tightly as I could. Then I crossed my legs and sat in front of the large stone. I would not move again until I had sat vigil for my beloved.

Hours slipped away. The full, ripe moon traversed the sky above me as slowly as my own heartbeat. My body was already so weak. After the first hour, I could no longer sit. I had to lie on the ground as I watched over the grave. By the third hour, my eyes had closed. My heartbeat slowed. My hand stayed on top of the emerald grave, protecting it. The wind whispered through the long grass. Owls hooted softly to one another. At one point, I thought I heard someone calling my name—perhaps my father, looking for me. Perhaps some ancient ancestor was trying to convince me to leave my vigil. I didn't open my eyes or even look up. Words had left me.

At one point, I seemed to leave my body and float up through the stones to stare at myself from above. My body was skin and bones, but I looked peaceful.

At last, the dawn came. I managed to open my eyes, although the effort cost me what little strength I had left. The sunrise pierced the top of the hills, sending warm red light cascading through the stone circle. The sunshine glittered on the grey stones, washing them in orange and pink. It was one of the most beautiful sights I had ever seen, and I thanked God that I had lived to see it. The world was beautiful and still as it held its breath. It wouldn't be long now. It wouldn't be long. Soon, we would be reunited.

In the earth below me, the ring was safe. It lay with the dead bodies, another skeleton to tell the story of our brief time on this earth and the love we once shared.

As my mind slipped towards the darkness, strange but profound thoughts flashed through my mind.

Maybe death wasn't the end. Perhaps I was not my own, individual self, but a part of something larger. The energy of existence. And when I died, I would return back into the energy, like a drop of rain falling back into the ocean. I'd never understood what the priests meant when they spoke of everlasting life. They'd gotten it all wrong: God wasn't a singular deity ruling above us all; God is the energy of which we all comprised. God was Us. We are one. We are everyone. We are Everything.

That Everything was the truth of existence. This mortal life I led was the dream; the Everything spinning itself a yarn while it slumbered. I'd forget the dream upon waking, but the love I'd experienced here would stay with me. Like echoes gliding upon a lake. Until it pulled me back into the dream. My beloved was dead, but the love I'd given him would stay with his immortal soul. It would pull him back into the dream as well. He would not be able to resist my call. No more than I could his. Until we meet again my love, for another brief sojourn through the dreamscape.

Slowly, my eyes blinked open.

I took a deep breath as my mind gently disentangled itself from the dream. Unlike the previous dreams that had shown me my strange and mysterious past, this dream did not wake me abruptly. Instead, I slipped easily from the dream world to reality. I blinked, trying to recall the last moments of the dream. Their details evaporated with every passing second. The last thing I remembered, I had been so weak and faint that I could barely raise my head. My heartbeat had been so slow. A shiver went through my body as I recalled the feeling of drifting in and out of consciousness. There had been a beautiful sunrise. A burial. A ring.

I'd been dying, I realised. A cold wave of nausea gripped my stomach. I must have woken from the dream just as I died. There was no more memory for me to relive.

As the nausea subsided, so did more of the dream's details. I rolled over and felt the warm sunlight on my face. In the light of day, the dream didn't seem so scary. I hugged the soft duvet, breathing in the familiar scent of Conor's cologne. I allowed myself a smile as it washed over me.

Whatever had happened years—centuries—before, I was alive now. Conor was alive. I couldn't let the past control me anymore.

I reached for the other side of the bed, seeking the shape of the body that I knew so well. But I didn't find it.

Our bed felt cold, a sign that Conor had been gone for a while. I sighed and turned to rest on my back; my eyes closed for one more second before I opened them again for good. I wasn't sure how late it was, but judging by the sun, it was probably nearly noon. Slowly, I became more aware of the things going on around me. Birds called to one another from outside the window. The sounds of people having lunch at outdoor cafés filled my ears. Galway was wide awake.

I stared up at the ceiling of our bedroom. More than anything, I wished Conor was lying next to me. The dream had disturbed me more than any of the previous ones. I'd witnessed my own death. It would be an understatement to say I was freaked out. I needed Conor by my side to hold me and tell me that everything would be all right.

But how could everything be alright if the terrible things I dreamt had happened a millennia ago? It hadn't been all right. Conor had died violently, alone and scared. I had died young and broken-hearted.

Instinctively, I reached for my left ring finger. I don't know what I was expecting to find. In the dream, the ring had felt so real. I half expected to feel its indent on my finger. There was nothing. Of course there was nothing.

Except...

With a jolt, I sat bolt upright in bed. An idea had come to me that was insane, beyond anything I had ever done before. I would be mad to attempt it. And yet... The woman in the dream had left behind a record of her and her beloved. Proof that they had existed.

That *we* had existed.

I knew exactly where she had buried that ring. It was impossible, absolutely impossible, that it was there. It would be crazy to go to the stone circle and try to dig up something placed there in a dream. Yet I knew, without a shadow of a doubt, that that was exactly what I was going to do. I had to know, once and for all, if my dreams were true.

Chapter Forty-Six

RESURRECTION

"Bridget, have you heard from Conor?" James asked as he adjusted the red strap of his guitar. He was slouched on the leather couch, impatiently tapping his foot on the floor. The atmosphere in the recording studio was tense; everyone was getting impatient with the delay.

My own anxiety was somewhat softened by the warm LED glow that emanated from lights along the ceiling. They created a cool, relaxed ambience. In fact, the whole recording studio was more sophisticated than any studio I'd been inside. Orcas had come a long way from studios filled with empty pizza boxes, bongs and ripped foam sofas that smelled like stale beer and wet dog. Now, we were surrounded by atmospheric gold and red lighting, sleek white leather couches and leafy tropical potted plants. Framed photographs of famous artists that had been recorded in the studio lined the walls. Some of them were signed.

Rosie and I were sitting on the comfy leather armchairs. We both giggled as we sank into them. The white leather felt smooth to the touch. I was afraid to drink anything while sitting on it. There was a well stocked bar along one wall filled with different spirits. We'd been told we could help ourselves, but it was a bit early in the day for us. We both left work at lunchtime to be with the lads as they recorded a new song. Everyone had been there since noon, right on time—everyone except Conor.

"His phone's still going to voicemail," I told James.

That morning, I had seen him briefly. We had both woken up early, but because I had to rush out to attend an 8 a.m. meeting, I couldn't spend much time with him. He had sent me a message informing me that he had somewhere to be and wouldn't be able to pick me up. Instead, he said he would meet me at the studio. Unfortunately, those were the only details I got. I had no idea where he was or what he was doing. I can't deny that I was feeling a bit concerned.

"Did he tell you where he was going?" I asked the lads. They shook their heads, then gave each other a loyal look that told me otherwise. I was just about to question them further when Conor burst into the room. He was breathless as if he'd been running. There were beads of sweat on his forehead, and his hair was a little dishevelled.

"Sorry I'm late, guys!" he panted as he opened his guitar case.

"Finally. I thought you'd been abducted by aliens," James said as he stood up. "I'll go and round up the troops. They're having coffee and discussing your punishment."

I stood up and walked towards Conor. He smiled and reached to grab my hand.

"Where were you, mister?" I whispered. "I called you, but your phone was off."

Conor hesitated before answering. He looked at James and Donal, then winked. He smiled—not his usual smile, but the one he used to hide something.

"I had to get new strings for my guitar. I then got caught up in traffic on my way over here," he said without looking me in the eyes. I knew something was up, I just didn't know what. I wasn't about to find out, either. James walked back into the room with the producer and the sound engineer. They started talking about the new track, layering, vibe and rhythm. The jargon they used was too technical for me to understand. Typical musicians.

"Sorry I'm late," Conor apologised as he shook hands with Andy, the producer and owner of the record label. The guys talked for a few more minutes while I resumed my seat next to Rosie. We both watched silently as the guys talked over the details of the song and what they expected from it. More technical terms followed that neither Rosie nor myself understood. A few minutes later, they walked into the recording room behind the glass and started to play.

"They're planning something," Rosie said suspiciously as she pointed towards the guys.

"I know." I nodded as I crossed my arms over my chest. "And I have a feeling that Conor's in charge of whatever they're doing. I hate surprises."

"You'd think Conor would have figured that out by now!"

I laughed. "Oh, he knows. But he thinks they're good for me."

"Feck, these lads always keep us guessing." Rosie exhaled as she leaned back on the leather couch, her eyes now focused on James behind the glass window in the recording room.

"I know. That's why we love them, though. They keep things fun," I said with a smile.

We went silent after that as we fell under the trance cast by the guys. My mind focused on Conor and blocked out everything else. Whenever I watched him play music, I was transported back to the first time I saw him perform at Waxies. The feeling of awe and desire that it had aroused in me had never gone away. I was as mesmerised by him now as I had been that first night. Now, I watched him as he sang, studying his expressions. They were joyous, euphoric and focused. He was completely unselfconscious as to how he looked. He just let the music take him where he needed to go.

As I gazed at him, a strange image flashed through my mind. All at once, I saw Conor sitting in a forest, holding a harp. This was followed by an image of him dropping the harp to the ground as a Norse leader approached. I reached for the sofa's arm to steady myself. My heart was racing. My face felt flushed. Next to me, Rosie sent me an odd, questioning look.

I glanced back up at Conor, hoping that the flashback would go away, but it came to me again. The look on Conor's face was the same as the one he had worn in the first dream when he'd serenaded me. The feeling it brought to my heart was identical to what I'd felt then.

"Are you okay?" Rosie whispered. She didn't need to whisper; nothing we said on our side of the wall could be heard in the recording studio. However, she must have sensed that I didn't want anyone to overhear. I nodded and tried to return my attention to the lads' recording behind the glass.

They hadn't given us any headphones, so I wasn't able to hear the song, but I didn't need to. I could feel it. I'd heard it before, and the memory of it played like it had been downloaded in my mind. As I watched Conor's lips form the words, the soundtrack in my head accompanied him.

I loved watching him sing and play guitar. It was like he was baring his soul to the world. He threw away all the masks and all the rules imposed by society and was just Conor. Every emotion that the song evoked in him was reflected in his eyes. When he sang, it was like he was alone, unconscious of everything else around him. I understood that space; it was exactly how I felt while I painted. It was a feeling that couldn't be described. If I were to try, I would say it felt like emptying my soul of all its earthly burdens and freeing it into a world of abstracts and colours.

As I watched him, I felt myself fall into a transcendental state. It reminded me of the way Buddhist monks talked about meditation, when you moved outside of your body and became one with the universe. All my worries about Amanda and our fight seemed to melt away. Even my fears about the dreams took a backseat. This was the Conor I knew, the one who would never lie to me again or make me worry. No matter what happened with the dreams, Conor would never think I was crazy. He would understand.

"It's amazing how much they've grown," Rosie whispered. "I'm so glad we got to witness them blooming."

"Me too," I whispered back.

Rosie, of course, was talking about how far Orcás had come since we met them. But I couldn't help but think about Conor the bard, playing simple melodies in the stone circle. If my gut feeling was right, then he truly had come very, very far.

I leaned towards Rosie so that I could whisper into her ear. "Do you believe in reincarnation?" I asked quietly.

Rosie looked thoughtful. "Hmm, not really," she said after a pause. "I feel like if reincarnation were true, then why didn't the dinosaurs reincarnate? Or are we them? It raises more questions than it answers."

"Yeah, you're probably right," I said heavily.

She cocked her head to one side. "Why do you ask?"

I hesitated, but I'd brought it up. I couldn't back out now. "Sometimes I just wonder..." I began slowly. "I get this feeling, like Conor and I have met before."

"You might have run into each other in Galway before," Rosie said with a wink.

"No." I shook my head. "Like in a past life." I felt foolish saying it out loud. Rosie smiled, but thankfully she didn't laugh at me. She was a good enough friend not to make fun of me.

"I think love always feels that way," she said wisely. "It's so rare to find someone who gets you so completely; it's easy to feel like they got a head start in a previous life."

"Yeah, maybe..." For a moment, I thought about telling Rosie about the dreams, but I stopped myself. I needed proof first. If I could find it...

"Don't let yourself get pulled into all that new-age, off-with-the-fairies shite," Rosie advised as the boys finished their song. "Conor is real and here right now. What does it matter what came before?"

It may not have mattered to Rosie, but as Conor smiled at me through the glass window, his grin seeming to light up the whole room, I knew that I couldn't wait any longer for the truth.

#

In the midst of a storm, the sheer terror can be overwhelming. I found myself, surrounded by flashes of lightning as I walked up the hill towards the stone circle. The atmosphere was filled with an intense, crackling energy that prickled at the hairs on the back of my neck. With each step I took across the wet grass, the darkness yielded, as though a black velvet curtain were parting for my arrival. Overhead, sheet lightning illuminated the sky, while thunder rumbled ominously. The dark clouds themselves seemed to flicker and spark, as if poised to burst into flames at any second. In that fleeting instant, their eerie glow transformed my surroundings into a surreal, fluorescent spectacle.

I hadn't told Conor the truth about where I was going. I'd said I was staying at Rosie's for a girls' night so as not to arouse suspicion. I couldn't risk him disturbing me or discovering what I was up to. I couldn't turn back now.

When I reached the top of the next hill, I looked up. A full moon was rising. It moved from behind the clouds and flooded the earth with an eerie, silvery glow. The sight sent shivers down my spine. Below me, the light illuminated a circle of towering monoliths. They looked black against the light-filled sky and cast long shadows, like giant fingers clawing their way above ground. My thoughts turned to another full moon, which had also bathed these stones with its luminescence many centuries before. The night before I died in my dream. *Was it really a dream?*

By the time I reached the stone circle I felt exhausted and a stitch had formed in my side. Clutching it, I leaned over to catch my breath. Then I checked nervously over my shoulder. The field below, which had once been filled with thousands of festival goers at Galway360, was deserted. I stood in front of the tallest of the standing stones. It towered above me. Its powerful presence sent shivers down my spine. The last time I'd seen this stone wasn't at Galway360 or even when we'd picnicked here. It was in my dream—the dream that felt as real as any of my waking thoughts.

I shook with fear as I knelt beneath it. The grass was soaked from the lashing rain. Near me, a puddle had formed in the ground. I caught sight of my reflection between each flash of lightning. My hands felt the coarse grass; then, my fingers dug deep into the wet soil below, ready to dig.

"*I stir, summon and call thee back to this world, back to this life. I stir, summon and call thee to help me put things right,*" voices whispered and echoed these words in every direction. They didn't come from the ground or the stones but from all around me—as if the night itself was speaking in tongues. I turned around quickly and looked in every direction, but there was no one there. A metallic taste of fear flooded my senses.

Shaking, I reached into my bag and pulled out a small trowel. It had a metal spade and plastic handle but otherwise looked very similar to the one I had used in my dream to bury the emerald ring. Carefully, I pushed it into the dirt. As I did so, I muttered a small prayer of thanks. This monument was protected by the Office of Public Works—and who knew what spirits. I didn't take its yielding to my trowel lightly.

The soil gave way easily. The overpowering scent of damp earth filled the air. I breathed in deeply, letting both fear and hope wash over me. Any minute now I would know the truth.

I heard chanting behind me. In between flashes of lightning, I saw clearly an ancient tribe of people standing between each stone. Their skin was painted with ancient blue symbols, and their arms were raised up to the heavens as if in prayer. I gasped and dropped the trowel. I froze with fear as a cold sweat swept throughout my body. A few seconds later these ancient people were gone. I was alone in the stone circle; my heart was racing.

What had I just witnessed? I wanted to scream, but my throat and lungs felt paralysed. Were they really gone? I was afraid to move or to turn around in case they were standing right behind me.

A few seconds later, another flash of lightning brought the apparition of two children with long, braided hair. It was a boy and a girl, no older than eleven or twelve. They were laughing and shouting in a strange language as they chased a rabbit through the stones. The tunics they wore were similar to the one Conor had worn in the first dream, and the looks on their faces were ones of pure and innocent devotion. They were holding hands. Before I'd had time to register this fully, the children were gone, replaced by another vision. This time, a woman in a corseted gown with a billowing skirt was sitting against one of the stones as a man lay with his head in her lap. She was playing with his hair while he read a book. This was followed by the mirage of a soldier in a crisp red uniform, leaning with one hand on a stone as he pissed on it. In the next moment, another soldier appeared, dressed in a green uniform strapped with a leather bandolier and a rifle. He was kneeling before the stones; his hands clasped around a set of rosary beads.

The pace and intensity of the images filled me with nausea. It was as if I had been on a merry-go-round. I shut my eyes tight, hoping to ease the sickness. Part of me also hoped that whatever was happening would go away if I simply refused to acknowledge it.

When I opened my eyes, I was alone again amongst the stones. All the apparitions were gone. The silence was unnerving. I breathed a sigh of relief and picked up the trowel. As I turned back to the tallest stone, I felt a strange and powerful presence beside me. It was as if everyone I had seen was still sitting among the stones, watching. The hairs on the back of my neck prickled as I began to dig.

Every fibre of me longed to run away as fast as I could. But first, I had to find it. The top layer of soil would be very deep by now. I'd have to dig further down than when I had buried it. Had I buried the emerald ring? Or was I going crazy?

The dream I had couldn't possibly be real; it defied all logic and reason. Nonetheless, I persisted in my digging, driven by an unknown force, unsure of what awaited me beneath the earth's surface. With each passing minute, exhaustion took its toll, and I contemplated giving up. But just as I was about to abandon my search, a sharp hit from the trowel sent a wave of anticipation through me. I reached down, my hands trembling with a mix of excitement and trepidation, to see what I had uncovered.

In the darkness, with only the moon's occasional glow piercing the clouded sky, it was difficult to make out any details. My fingers fumbled through the mud and tangled roots, until they finally found what the trowel had struck. I closed my eyes in anticipation as my fingers curled around the mysterious object. Part of me hoped it was the long-lost talisman I had been desperately searching for, while another part feared it was something entirely different, something I wasn't prepared to uncover.

With a deep breath, I opened my eyes and stared in utter disbelief. The object was covered in layers of mud, obscuring its true form. I hurriedly dipped it into a nearby puddle, using my fingers to wash away the grime, eager to reveal its secrets. As the water cascaded over it, my eyes widened in awe. The moonlight shimmered off an emerald, its vibrant green hue capturing my gaze and taking my breath away. The gem was nestled on a golden band, creating a mesmerising combination that held a magical allure. It was as if the universe had orchestrated our reunion, right before the towering stone that had guided my quest.

Chapter Forty-Seven

I Hate Surprises

"Are you still not going to feckin' tell me where we're going?" I asked as I popped another jelly bean into my mouth. When Conor didn't answer, I pouted. "You know I hate surprises!"

It was a miserable afternoon in Galway. The grey sky hung low with heavy rain. All the trees were bare, and the cafés had pulled their outdoor dining chairs and tables back in off the street. The result was that the whole city felt empty and devoid of colour. Still, Conor was taking me somewhere, so I barely noticed the bad weather. It was another one of his elaborate surprises. After the last few, I was on the edge of my seat. He'd given me no hints, just told me to dress up nice and not to ask any questions. Now that I was all ready and in the car, the anticipation was killing me.

Conor smiled, obviously enjoying the slow torture he was inflicting on me. His eyes twinkled with mischief.

"I know. That's what makes them so much fun!" he finally said.

"*I* think it's more fun to know what's coming so that I can look forward to it," I said haughtily. "Looking forward to something is half the enjoyment."

"I disagree," Conor said sagely. "I think being surprised and kept in the dark is what's enjoyable."

"Well, it would be, if your surprises impressed me."

"Okay, that was just low." He laughed. "And I know you don't mean it. Can I have a jelly bean?"

"No, you certainly can't have a jelly bean, Conor O'Neill! Can you please give me a clue?" I pretended to care as I teasingly popped two more into my mouth. Conor seemed amused by my childish antics. His smirk was getting wider and wider, cracking into a cheeky grin.

"You know," he said, "I think they got that saying wrong. Curiosity didn't kill the cat; I think it died from eating all the jelly beans."

I nearly erupted with laughter but managed to stay in character with a sulky expression.

"Well, you're going to be the proof of that," I tried to say in a scary voice, but it was hard to hide my amusement. Luckily Conor was driving, so he didn't see how my lips twitched with a suppressed smile. "You're lucky our families are meeting next week. I'm just keeping you alive because I don't want them to make a trip to Galway for nothing."

"They're so lucky I met someone so thoughtful!" Conor said sarcastically as he shook his head. "Since you've decided not to kill me, can you feed me some jelly beans too?"

"You should have bought your own bag!" I exclaimed as I squeezed mine protectively.

"I didn't expect you to devour the lot! That bag was huge!"

"Never come between a woman and her confectionery," I reprimanded. "We go through so much already. We deserve occasional sweet treats."

"Oh, is this the 'self-care' I hear so much about?"

"It certainly is."

"What about us lads? Don't we deserve some self-care too?"

"Oh, all right—I'll sacrifice one! Just because I love you," I said dramatically as I reached for a red one. Conor opened his mouth for me to feed him like a baby bird; however, little did I know of the evil plan inside his head. Before I could retreat my hand, his teeth closed on my fingers, and he bit down for a split second.

"What was that for?!" I exclaimed as I pulled back, laughing.

"For being selfish when it comes to sharing!" Conor joked as he pulled into a car park. "Sharing is caring, didn't you know?"

"And you say *I'm* childish," I twittered under my breath.

I took a look around and saw that we were in front of a huge building. The area was right near Shop Street, where most of the fancy shops were located. We'd parked in front of a gallery, but I doubted that was where he was bringing me. There weren't any exhibitions booked for that day. My guess was that he was taking me to one of the cafés that had recently opened in that area. It was the only thing I could think of. We both got out of the car. Conor still wasn't saying anything and continued to wear his poker face, not revealing any clues.

It was a cold, windy day. All afternoon, there'd been nothing but grey clouds in the sky. But as we got out of the car, the clouds shifted to reveal a patch of blue. A beam of sunshine filtered through, bathing us in golden light. I felt giddy with excitement and curiosity.

"Let's go," Conor said excitedly as he grabbed my hand. Silently, I walked by his side, growing even more confused. My previous guess seemed to be completely wrong. He wasn't leading me to a cafe but towards the entrance of the glass building. I'd been to this gallery many times before, but I wasn't used to seeing it closed and empty. It was usually filled with alternative artsy types and wealthy collectors. Today, with no exhibition on, there was no one about. Our car was one of the few in the car park.

"Where are we going, mister?" I asked when Conor stopped in front of the door. "It's closed."

Conor reached into his back pocket and pulled out a key. He grinned at me and winked.

"Where did you get that?" He didn't answer. My excitement and curiosity were becoming difficult to contain. Within seconds the door was open, and Conor was smiling cheekily.

"Now it's open," he said with a grand bow.

I barely heard him. As I walked slowly inside, I felt as if I were in a trance. My head swirled with questions. I still had no idea what was going on, but whatever it was, Conor had clearly gone above and beyond.

Automatically, my feet guided me through the hallway that led to the large exhibition room. The place was familiar but foreign at the same time. I'd seen it numerous times before, but never when it was so bare and empty.

"I give up," I said, turning back to Conor, who had followed me into the room. "What's going on?"

Conor smirked and took in a deep breath. "This is where you're going to hold your first exhibition," he announced, his voice overwhelmed with excitement.

"My what?"

"I saw your paintings, Bridget. You've done such a great job. It would be a pity not to have other people see them, too," Conor explained. "It was hard, but I managed to pull some strings and book the place for you. I showed the curator some photos of your work, and he was very impressed."

I stared at Conor and understood every word he said, but it still felt surreal. My brain couldn't properly register any of it.

"You're kidding, right?" I asked breathlessly. Conor just shook his head and then smiled. "Conor, I... I don't know what to say!"

"Well, you kind of have to say something," he said as he took a step towards me. "Say that you'll do it."

"I'll do it." My voice broke as I spoke. I had never felt more grateful for anything in my entire life. Conor was right: his surprises *did* impress me. He never disappointed.

"Phew!" He sighed before he chuckled. "Now have I earned a jelly bean?" he joked.

"No way!" I exclaimed, poking him in the chest. "Those are mine! But you did earn this," I finished in a softer voice as I rose on my tiptoes to kiss his lips.

When I pulled away, I asked, "So, when is this exhibition?"

"Well, that's the other surprise," he said. "It's in one month."

"One month?!" My jaw dropped. "Conor, I'm a professional event planner. I know it takes longer than one month to pull something like this off."

"In that case," he said, grinning, "you better get going."

Chapter Forty-Eight

READY, SET

"How could you not like the idea of a wall filled with white roses?" asked Sami dramatically.

"I don't know, because it's a bit cliché?" I teased. "We can have a flower wall, but not just white roses. Plus, it doesn't fit the theme I'm after."

Sami took a few seconds to think about what I'd said, then impatiently tapped his pencil against the sketchpad he held in his left hand and glanced around. His expression was serious, the way it always looked when he was concentrating hard. Karen was also busy deciding on the best corner to host her photo booth. My entire team was at the art gallery, happy to chip in. They'd dropped everything and headed over, willing to volunteer. They were all as excited as I was, although, unlike me, their enthusiasm wasn't masked by an awful feeling of anxiousness and urgency. Their presence helped to ease some of the stress. When I'd hired them, I'd chosen a trustworthy team. I'd never expected them to become like a family to me. It surprised me how necessary they were for my own peace of mind. They'd all become work colleagues—and friends—that I couldn't live without. And from their enthusiasm, I knew they all felt the same towards me.

"Okay, I agree, Bridget!" Sami finally snapped. "How about we have wildflowers, moss and purple heather on the wall? It'll be a subtle nod to Connemara and your Galway roots. We can also create matching displays in vases and have these featured around the gallery!" His hand hovered excitedly over the sketchpad; then, his pencil dipped to draw his idea. "We can also have some thin ivory or cream pieces of veils draping from the ceiling. With fairy lights, of course. They'll light the way to your masterpiece. You know, I think we can really create a kind of forest or faerie aesthetic. I want people to walk in and *feel* like they're walking through an ancient Irish forest. Your paintings will be the scenery."

Sami didn't need to go on; I could already imagine it all. I liked Sami's idea of making the attendees feel as if they were in nature as they walked through the exhibition. It fit the theme of my paintings, all of which depicted the natural and ancient world. The forest aesthetic would also give the gallery a mythical vibe. After all, my pièce de résistance was the painting of the stone circle. This was the masterpiece that fairy lights and hanging veils would guide viewers towards. I wanted people to feel as if they had been transported to this magical monument as they stood in front of my painting of the tallest stone.

I smiled and nodded, much to Sami's pleasure.

"Great! I'll head into the city and get some quotes for the plants," he announced as he finished sketching ideas.

"Wait, you don't have to go now!" I called after him.

"What are you talking about, boss? The exhibition is in less than five days. We need to do everything now!" he shouted back dramatically.

"Wait, I'll go with you!" Karen shouted from a few feet away. "You know how much I love choosing flowers!" She was already draping her camera across her arm and zipping up her jacket.

"I'm coming too!" Mark shouted.

Together, all three of them hurried towards the main door. Their enthusiasm filled my eyes with tears of joy.

"Thank you, guys. Really." Emotion flooded me, filling my heart up with gratitude and love. It wasn't just my incredible team or the amazing gallery space; it was more about the energy of the people getting involved in my vision. At first, I'd been sceptical about whether or not I'd be able to pull this exhibition off. I still wasn't sure that my art was good enough for an exhibition. But with such positive friends around me and their infectious enthusiasm – surely we could make it a success.

"Friends don't thank each other," Sami said with a stern look, but I could see he was as emotional as I was. "Come on, guys, let's move it!"

As my incredible team exited the building, Conor and the boys arrived through the main door, followed by Laura and Rosie. They were all carrying canvases packed protectively with white foam padding. They'd been at our apartment to collect my paintings. I'd been up late the night before, wrapping my paintings with foam and packing them into crates. It had been a stressful experience—made even more so by Jimi, who kept eating the foam. Now, the guys were holding two each while the girls were carrying the smaller canvases—my earlier versions. I'd painted them as part of a series. "Are there any more?" Donal asked after gently placing his canvas on the floor next to a pillar.

"Just a dozen more, big boy, from the looks of it," Laura said flirtatiously with a giggle. "I'll come help you," she offered as the pair walked out the door again.

I smiled as I walked towards the newcomers. Conor met me halfway. His hand wrapped around my waist while his lips pressed against my forehead.

"Did you guys settle on the design details?" he asked.

"Yeah. I just have to organise some flower installations and talk to the catering company. So, we're almost good to go." My voice was breathless, overwhelmed by the busyness and excitement.

"You're doing such a great job!" Conor beamed. "I know it's stressful."

"It is, but it's a good kind of stress. I've been looking forward to having my own exhibition for so long. Every time I feel anxious, I just remind myself how lucky I am to even be doing this."

Conor shook his head admiringly. "You have such an amazing attitude," he said.

"We're done!" Laura exclaimed from behind Conor. I looked over his shoulder and saw that she and Donal had brought the last of the canvases in.

"Good, now let's go," Rosie said impatiently as Conor and I approached the group.

"Where are we going?" I asked in confusion.

"We're going shopping, BK!" she replied as if it was the most obvious thing in the world. "This place isn't the only thing that needs to look impeccable!"

"Rosie, we can't go. There's so much to be done!" I answered back.

"No, no, there isn't. We'll have plenty of time to do it all over the next few days. Now, it's shopping time."

"You girls go ahead. We'll catch up—" James gestured between the three guys.

"You're going nowhere, Mr Guitarist," Rosie interrupted mockingly as she grabbed onto his hand. "The shopping spree is for everyone. I won't allow you to show up in those worn-out jeans and a tired looking shirt. I know that works for Orcás, but this isn't a grungy trad-fusion concert. This is an important opening at a posh gallery." Looking at each of the guys, she said seriously, "It applies to all of you."

Laura and I said nothing, as we were barely holding in the laughter that threatened to explode.

"Yes, boss, that's fine," James sighed.

The three guys looked like scolded children, vulnerable and cornered.

They had no idea what they were in for.

Chapter Forty-nine

Go, Yes, Go

My exhibition was at its peak. All three rooms were packed with well dressed Galway folks. This was the art crowd, so they were in dark colours, the women wore low heels, long dresses, elaborate earrings and silk scarves. The men wore fashionable dark-rimmed glasses and suit jackets. Other than my friends, most people were over forty, with salt-and-pepper hair and looked wealthy. I recognised many of them from events I'd managed.

My career as an event manager had introduced me to most of the well-to-do Galwegians: the ones that dined every weekend at Michelin-starred restaurants like Loam and Aniar, who owned property in Dublin and vacationed at their summer homes in Connemara or Kerry. Whenever I interacted with these people in the past, they were the ones hosting the fancy events while I was working at them. Now, it was *I* who was hosting the event they were attending. I couldn't quite believe it as I shook hands with one of Galway's most famous local chefs—who owned a string of five-star restaurants—and then chatted amiably with Charlie Byrne—who might be getting on in years but who still ran things at the iconic Galway bookstore that bore his name.

These Galway elites—and the other guests of their ilk—were all admiring my paintings and sipping on wine or champagne, which Laura had insisted we get from Thomas Woodberry's. ("Only the best wine in Galway for your party," she'd trilled.) I walked between the guests, stopping every once in a while to chat with old acquaintances. They asked me about my paintings, what inspired me and what drove me to paint a particular piece. It wasn't easy to answer these questions, partially because the answers were so personal and intimate. But, in the end, that's what gave each painting life; a piece of art without a story is inanimate, a lifeless decoration that is as worthless as a pebble.

Rosie was walking from corner to corner, ensuring everyone had their glasses filled and that they weren't too shy to reach for the canapes being passed around on silver trays. Laura was chatting with guests as well. She was using her inner writer to give even more meaning to the colourful canvases. Her descriptions of my works were amazing. She was like my own mini PR team. I knew for a fact that she'd already convinced the creative director of the Druid Theatre to buy one.

My team members were doing their parts, too, making sure everything went according to plan. Sami had truly delivered on the floral decorations. The gallery had been transformed into a magical forest full of twinkling lights and whimsical botanicals. Moss crept down the walls as if they were boulders while heather added a blaze of red to the greenery. Wildflowers had been braided into wrought iron archways that led from one gallery room to the next. Sami had curated everything perfectly, beyond my wildest dreams. He wouldn't allow a single petal to fall on his watch. Meanwhile, Mark and Karen took pictures of the guests.

The boys from Orcás were with my parents, keeping them company. Conor had introduced them earlier that day, and my parents immediately grew fond of the two band members. Even still, James didn't escape my dad's threats—he promised to hurt him in more ways than one if James ever hurt Rosie.

"Hey." Conor suddenly sneaked up behind me. His low voice brushed against my neck as his hands wrapped around my waist. His chin came to rest on my shoulder. "How is our lovely artist doing?" he whispered.

I smiled and placed a hand over his. "Overwhelmed." I chuckled. "But so good."

It was the truth. I couldn't exactly explain what I was feeling, but I could safely sum it up as happiness. I was completely filled with joy and fulfilment, and it was all thanks to Conor.

"Thank you," I whispered. I didn't turn around; he didn't need to see my face to know how genuine my words were. My voice said it all: it was breaking with tears, hoarse and dripping with the emotions swirling inside me.

"For what?" Conor asked.

Conor's humility never failed to amaze me. He had made this happen, in more ways than one.

"Thank you for everything," I murmured. "Without you, I would have never found the inspiration to start painting again. The artist inside me would have withered and died. And even if I did find the inspiration I'd been searching for, I would never have had the courage to show it to the world."

Conor turned me around gently so that his eyes bored into mine. He brushed his thumb over my cheek and smiled.

"I have no merit to it. You did it on your own. I just encouraged you. I want to…" He trailed off for a second. "I have more to say, but let's go over there." He jerked his head towards the main room.

"Why?" I asked.

He shrugged. "I want to make a toast." He spoke the words with ease, but I could tell something was off. His eyes told a different story than his voice; they were coated with an emotion I couldn't exactly pinpoint.

I followed him nonetheless. He guided me through the small crowd and to the centre of the main room. I expected him to grab a glass of champagne, something to toast with, but to my surprise, he came to stand in the middle of the room empty-handed. My parents and our friends were standing around us, not too close but close enough to hear us speak. There was tension in the room, as if everyone were waiting with bated breath. I couldn't tell whom it was coming from. It seemed to be all around me in the air. Everyone was eying us in a way that made my heart skip a beat. I knew something big was up; they'd given away that much.

"Conor, what's going on?" I asked breathlessly. But he ignored me and turned toward the room at large.

He cleared his throat and called, "Ladies and Gentlemen! May I have your attention?" He repeated himself once more and waited for everyone to gather around. The crowd grew silent. "I won't take too long. I know you're all in a hurry to go back and admire the wonderful paintings." He chuckled. Conor was incredible when it came to talking to a crowd, but at that precise moment, he didn't seem too confident. I could feel the nerves rolling off him. "Wow, this is harder than I imagined," he mumbled to himself.

He let go of my hand and reached for the pocket inside his jacket. My heart stopped.

"I interrupted you all because I have something important to say to—or rather ask—our gifted artist." Conor laughed nervously. He then turned to face me and lowered himself to one knee.

I felt like my knees would buckle under my weight. The world was suddenly spinning, my hands were shaking, and my lungs were craving air. Conor seemed to move in slow motion as he looked up at me, his smile hopeful and eager.

"Bridget, I've been rehearsing this for a long time, but I still don't know what to say." He smiled. "So, I'll keep it simple. If this were to be a song, it would probably be easier for me to say it all, to bare my soul to you. Bridget, I love you. I don't have the fancy words to wrap it all together neatly. But no matter how I say it, it will always mean the same thing. It means I am yours, my body, my soul and my heart. They are all yours. You said I inspired you. Well, Bridget, you don't just inspire me; you are the entire reason and motivation for my existence," Conor breathed out. Tears were streaming down my face.

"Conor, you're making me cry," I whispered unconsciously.

"Don't. I don't ever want to see you cry. I just want to see you smiling and laughing. The world is bright only when you smile," he said seriously, intensely. Desire and love coursed through me and made my heart sing. "Anyway, I'll just say it before everyone gets tired of me." He seemed like he was encouraging himself more than anything else. "Bridget Kennedy, will you marry me?"

The words were like a lightning strike. They pierced through my heart, making it stop for half a second. It felt like I hadn't taken a breath since he'd started talking. I realised tears were somehow still trickling down my face. I didn't look around; I couldn't take my eyes off of the man kneeling in front of me, but I did feel everyone's gaze on me.

"Bridget, please answer. I'm having a heart attack here," Conor whispered nervously.

"Yes. A thousand times, yes!"

Chapter Fifty

MOLDAVITE

Scheduling a wedding three months out was a crazy idea—even when the bride-to-be owned her own event planning company. Of course, I'd organised weddings before, so I knew the trade inside out. But as I soon discovered, planning your own wedding is a very different kettle of fish. The stakes are suddenly much higher, and you're no longer managing bridezilla; you are Bridezilla. Or, in our case, engaged to Groomzilla.

But did a challenge or an impossible schedule ever stop Conor and me from making a decision? Of course not. Just like always, we both got overly excited and decided we wanted our wedding as soon as possible. The idea of a long engagement sounded horrible to both of us; we just wanted to be married. Not even a week after our engagement, we booked Mount Druid, an alternative venue nestled in the hills of Meath that had an unconsecrated temple, a boathouse bar, and a hedge maze, and started organising everything for the big day. The wedding itself would be a small affair with just family and close friends. But in the end, we decided to invite everyone we loved to the evening reception.

For the last couple of weeks, I'd been running around, trying to sort everything out. Luckily, I had lots of help. My team organised most of it, from the flowers and the band to the lighting and the picture booth. Rosie and Laura were taking care of the invitations, table settings and signage, the gowns, my hen party and other minor details. They were both by my side, twenty-four-seven, especially while Conor was out of the country, busy with a concert that had been scheduled in New York long before we decided to indulge in the wedding frenzy.

The toughest part had passed, however, now that the wedding was only two days away. Conor was back, and almost everything was going according to plan. I was currently at my last wedding gown fitting, and if that went well, I had nothing more to ask for.

My heart was beating so fast that I feared it was going to burst. The seamstress and Rosie were walking towards me, each holding a side of the dress, ready to help me slip into it. My palms were sweaty, and my eyes were as tearful as my mum's, who was quietly crying in the corner. I swear she hadn't stopped crying since the engagement at the gallery.

"Okay, extend your arms," the seamstress said, and I instinctively followed her instructions.

The moment the dress glided over my body, it felt like I'd stepped into another world. The feeling of the satin material against my skin made everything feel so real. It was my third fitting, but I still couldn't get used to seeing myself in my wedding dress.

I wasn't facing a mirror, but from the way it fit, I already knew the dress was finally perfect. The minute Rosie buttoned it up, the material hugged my body just the way I imagined it would. The seamstress moved around me, tucking and pulling on the fabric until everything was perfectly in place.

She was an odd-looking woman, middle-aged, with long, thick red hair that she piled on top of her head in a beehive-like bun. From the top of it protruded knitting needles. At every one of my fittings, she wore elaborate floor-length linen dresses. Most eye-catching of all was a pendant she wore around her neck with a strange and alluring stone at its centre. I'd never seen anything like it. It was a raw, uncut gem, translucent and mossy green in colour. Gold wires held it in its setting, which hung from a gold chain. As the seamstress adjusted the fit of the bodice, my eyes were drawn to the necklace. My gaze was interrupted by my mother.

"You look so beautiful!" she cried as she hurried to put on my veil. Rosie quickly pinned my hair into a messy bun while Laura joined us with the tiara that she and Rosie had bought as a gift.

It was strange being the centre of attention and everyone fussing over me. Not only that, it was overwhelming to invite so many friends and family to see me finally marry the man of my dreams. Rosie and Laura were like the sisters I never had, and they had proved that time and time again, especially now with the wedding. They'd been my shadows over the last few weeks. They'd cried and laughed with me about it, and I believed they almost felt the same amount of happiness I did. I could never thank them enough for loving me so sincerely. I could only wish I could do the same for them someday when they got married.

"Okay, you can look now," Laura said as she stepped back. My heart stopped. I wasn't sure if I was ready to look in the mirror. But ready or not, I had to. The girls pushed me from the back and towards the mirror. It was a miracle I didn't trip on my own two feet.

I could ask the best poets and writers in the world, but I am certain I would never be able to find the right words to explain how I felt when I saw myself in my wedding dress.

The dress was perfect. It was made of pure white satin and hugged my body perfectly, falling smoothly down my hips and to the floor. It was held in place by two thin straps on each shoulder. The veil was much longer than the dress. It had a lot of volume and draped down my back and onto the floor. The tiara was small and resembled intertwined twigs. It had a few pearls delicately arranged, fitting my taste to perfection.

"It's okay; cry now! We can't afford to let you cry on your wedding day," Rosie joked as she wiped one of my tears. "You look so beautiful, BK!"

As I was about to express my satisfaction with the gown, my phone suddenly began to ring. The faint sound reverberated from within my purse, which was carelessly thrown on the couch. Swiftly, Laura darted towards it and successfully retrieved the phone just before the call slipped through her fingers.

"You just missed a call from Prince Charming!" she cried out.

At the same time, Rosie's cell phone also began to ring.

"It's the bakery," she said, frowning at it. "Will you excuse me for a minute?" She stepped outside to take the call. Thankfully, my mother soon followed the girls, probably in need of some fresh air after all the tears.

I turned back to the mirror, admiring the dress. I was overcome by how beautiful the dress looked and how happy I felt. The joy seemed to radiate through me. I was positively glowing.

"So you're happy with this fit?" the seamstress asked as she fluffed the skirt around me.

"Very," I smiled, smoothing down the skirt of the dress. As I did so, the woman's necklace once again caught my eye. There was something entrancing about it; I could have stared at it for hours. The seamstress followed my gaze. She smiled as she touched her pendant.

"I see you're drawn to the moldavite," she said, in a somewhat softer and—unless I imagined it—knowing tone.

"It's beautiful," I murmured. "What's it called? Maldo...?"

"Moldavite," she said with a nod. "A very rare glass and greatly prized in psychic circles. It was formed 15 million years ago when a meteor collided with earth."

I started. "Wait—really? It's from space?"

The woman laughed. "Not *from* space exactly, but formed from the heat and pressure of the meteor hitting the earth." She paused for a moment and looked deeply into my eyes. I held my breath, not daring to blink or look away. There was something spooky about this woman, whose eyes, I now noticed, were flecked with the same forest green as the moldavite. "Because of this, however, it does have a cosmic oversoul," she continued in a strange, somewhat ethereal voice. At her words, I felt tingles creep up my arms, and I had to suppress a shudder.

"What does that mean?" I asked. My mouth felt very dry. Even though I didn't believe in crystals' healing properties, I couldn't rule anything out anymore—not after finding the ring.

"It means it can be used to commune with the ascended masters," she said, her eyes staring into mine. The hairs on the back of my neck were standing up. "It's a powerful crystal. It awakens your third eye and increases the vibrational resonances of other stones. Not all can feel its magic just by looking at it. But I wasn't surprised when you could."

"You weren't?" I asked, taken aback.

The seamstress smiled.

"You should get a moldavite crystal," she said after a long moment. "Your energy speaks to your ability to *see*. And it will go with your ring."

At first, I wasn't sure I had heard her correctly. I stared at her in the mirror. Her eyes, however, were back on my dress.

"Wha—what did you say?" I managed to gasp.

"Your ring," the seamstress repeated, her eyes met mine. As they did, a cloud must have passed over the sun, because the fitting room was suddenly thrown into shadow. Through the gloom, the woman's eerie green eyes glittered ominously.

"My ring?" I clutched my engagement ring. This one was sterling silver and set with a regular diamond. The moldavite wouldn't go with it at all. She had to mean the emerald ring, but she couldn't possibly know about that ring. There was no way...

"What do you mean?" I insisted. My voice was more aggressive than I intended, but I didn't care.

The woman smiled cryptically. I couldn't tell if I was imagining it or not, but the smile seemed otherworldly. "It's lucky you found it," she said quietly. "Sometimes we have to dig deep to find what it is we are really looking for."

Goosebumps erupted down my arms, and I shivered violently. I opened my mouth to speak, to demand that she explain herself at once, but just then, Rosie burst back into the fitting room. As she did, the sun moved from behind the clouds and warmth and sunshine once more flooded the space.

"The bakery just wanted to confirm that we'll be picking up the cake," Rosie said brightly, completely unaware of the strange mood that had lifted so abruptly. "They don't deliver to Meath—in case we'd forgotten!" She laughed. I tried to laugh too. I watched the seamstress in the mirror as she moved away to tidy up from my fitting. She didn't look at me again until she put the gown into the bag we would carry home. By then, the mysterious look in her eyes was gone. Her words would be engraved in my mind forever.

Chapter Fifty-One

Ditto

Mount Druid was a rare find in Ireland. Most of the weddings that Conor and I had attended took place in traditional churches. We wanted something different: a place that felt as sacred to us as the standing stones. When we'd first watched the videos of Mount Druid online, we knew instantly that it was the perfect place for us to get married.

Nestled on over 100 acres of parkland in Co. Westmeath, Mount Druid was an idyllic setting. The event manager in me would have described it as "where retro-chic meets pagan cottagecore." The beautiful barn where we would host dinner had two rooms: a dining room and an atrium. The atrium was light, airy, and the perfect place for greeting guests. It had tall ceilings, a baby grand piano and a Jacobean library furnished with Victorian sofas, ornamental carpets and antique books. It opened up into the dining room, which was set with long wooden tables adorned with brass candleholders with tall blue taper candles.

The whole place felt like a fairy tale. Our drinks reception would be held in the boathouse. This had a bright blue bar, quaint nautical paintings, and a wall of vintage women's high heels. Best of all was the unconsecrated chapel in which we would say our vows.

The tin chapel resonated with reverence. The first time Conor and I entered it (on a quick trip to Westmeath to see the venue), we both gasped. The space was small and intimate, with dark wooden pews on either side of a candle-lined aisle. At the end of the aisle, a thousand origami cranes fluttered above an altar. In the light that spilt in through a small window, their many-coloured wings appeared to be soaring. The sight was so beautiful it made my heart leap. It was exactly the place where I wanted to get married. Underneath the cranes, two antique blue sofa chairs had been placed. We would sit on these as the celebrant led us through the ceremony.

Not only did the tin chapel captivate us, but the on-site accommodation sealed the deal. Westmeath was a two-hour drive from Galway, so we wanted a place for our loved ones to stay the night. Mount Druid had that and more. There was a historic stone home where the girls and I would stay, numerous shepherd's huts, tin huts with double beds and traditional stove heating and four beautiful tigins, or cottages. For more adventurous guests, a number of yurts were available. Coolest of all was the converted double-decker bus. The graffiti-clad bus maintained many of its original features but also had a living area, an ensuite bedroom, and a kitchen. It also had breathtaking views all over the parkland.

Conor and the boys would be staying on the bus. Everyone had insisted that the bride and groom shouldn't stay under the same roof the night before the wedding. It was a superstition that neither of us believed in, but we caved into the army of loved ones who did believe in it. Rosie had even threatened James that if he let Conor out of his sight, he would be sleeping on her couch for a week. Since they were practically living together, he promised not to take the risk.

As much as I would have liked to have stayed with Conor, I was also glad to be with the girls at the house. It was a bright, spacious home, eclectically decorated with quirky furnishings. Rosie was the most excited about being able to spend the night there and refused to waste any time on the road. She firmly announced that she needed at least four hours to prepare my makeup. I still wasn't sure what she planned to do to me for four hours, but how could I hold her back from fussing over me on my wedding day? A night out in Galway was enough to put her into a makeover frenzy, so I was rather nervous about what a wedding would do to her. She'd packed an entire suitcase full of hair and makeup products that she would need. Peering into the bag before we left, I thought some of the instruments looked more like torture devices than cosmetics. Rosie, however, assured me that she knew what she was doing.

"We'll start with makeup and eyes tomorrow since the mink lashes will take a while," she said on the car ride to Mount Druid. "You'll have to keep your eyes closed while the glue sets. Meanwhile, I can get started on your hair."

"Glue?" I asked nervously. "Around my eyes?"

"Don't worry, it's perfectly safe. And it won't hurt."

I could only nod. It didn't sound safe.

"I wish you'd given me more time to come up with a hairstyle." She sighed fretfully. "I still am not sure if you really prefer the Grace Kelly look or if you were just sick of me pestering you."

"It's just hair, Rosie!" I laughed. "The most important thing is that I'm marrying Conor. My hair doesn't matter."

Rosie shook her head. "You say that now," she lectured, "but when the big day comes, and you turn into Bridezilla, you'll be glad I thought through everything."

Rosie had been showing me potential hairstyles for weeks. She'd gone through photos of every famous celebrity's wedding for inspiration. Unfortunately, she'd also made me look at all of these. We'd spent more time picking out the makeup and trying out hairstyles than we had on picking out the dress. Laura had backed up Rosie during the entire process. They both wanted me to be the most beautiful bride in Ireland. Even though it was exhausting, I was grateful to them. I didn't have an eye—or an interest—in hair and makeup. I wanted to look beautiful, but I would never have known where to start without the girls. Laura, of course, had found my wedding dress designer. She said the designer fit my "alternative painter meets girl boss vibes." With Rosie's skills and Laura's vision, all my dreams were coming true.

When we pulled into Mount Druid, I was delighted to see the girls' jaws drop. Miraculously, it was a beautiful evening. There wasn't a cloud in the sky. The late evening sun was sparkling off the lush green grass, swaying gently in the breeze. Tall evergreens and willows surrounded the expansive fields, giving the place an open yet secluded feel. We decided to go for a drink at the boathouse bar, where we found all the guests who would be staying the night at Mount Druid. My relatives, childhood friends and colleagues from Galway were gathered around there, sipping drinks from delicate cocktail glasses or pints of Guinness, and talking loudly. As soon as Laura, Rosie and I walked in, everyone started to cheer.

"There she is!" someone shouted.

"Here comes the bride!" Sami yelled, raising a glass to toast me. Mark and Karen flanked Sami on either side. Karen let out a loud "Whoop!" when she saw me.

Behind them was Ciara Breen. She was beaming at me as she held out her arms for a hug.

"Congratulations, my dear," she whispered into my ear as she wrapped me in a tight embrace. "Conor's a one-of-a-kind guy."

"Hear, hear!" A large hand clapped me on the shoulder, and I broke away from Ciara. It was Festival Frank. Dressed in an impeccable white shirt, slacks, and shiny shoes, he was more cleaned up than I'd ever seen him.

"Congrats, kiddo," he said. Frank's face was flushed, and he was holding a pint of Guinness in one hand. He seemed a little tipsy but very happy. "I was so chuffed to get the invite," he continued.

"Conor and I *had* to have you here!" I said with a laugh. "You were there from the start!"

"Well, it was very good of you, Bridget."

Just then, I felt Conor's presence behind me. I didn't even have to look to know he was there. I felt it like a ray of sunshine on my back. Slowly, I turned. Conor was standing at the window across from me. He was holding a glass of red wine and looking at me with eyes that radiated love. Several groups of people separated us, but it didn't matter. He was by my side in a few short strides, slipping his hand into mine and planting a light kiss on my cheek.

"I'm so happy to see you," he whispered. "I missed you so much."

"It's only been a few hours!" I laughed.

"A few hours too long," he said with a grin. Conor's eyes then rested on Ciara.

"Ms Breen!" he exclaimed, delighted. "It's so wonderful of you to make it!"

"Oh, of course, Conor! I wouldn't miss it for the world."

As Conor engaged Ciara in conversation, my eyes wandered the room. Everyone I knew and loved was there. Everyone except mine and Conor's parents, who were grabbing dinner down at the local pub. The girls I'd gone to school with were laughing animatedly in one corner, a bottle of prosecco between them. I hadn't seen many of them in years, but here they were, supporting me on my wedding day. Next to them, I recognised the lads who worked at Waxies. They were admiring a cabinet of Irish Whiskey bottles and making eyes at my old school friends. In another corner, several of my university friends were engaged in a spirited debate about politics with James and Donal. My Uncle Chris and Aunt Cara were chatting by the door while my little niece Heather scampered around them. She looked adorable in a floral dress and pink ribbons in her hair. When she saw me, she screamed and ran over. She leapt into my arms, and I planted a kiss on her cheek.

They were all here. Friends old and new. Family. Conor's loved ones. I had never been surrounded by so many loved ones in my entire life. I felt so much gratitude.

#

Much later, Rosie, Laura and I made our way to our stone house. The girls would be sharing the second bedroom while my parents were staying in the third. When we got in, they still hadn't arrived home, so we set out to explore the house. Laura loved the squashy leather armchairs in the sitting room, while Rosie couldn't get over the French country kitchen with its stone walls and teal-coloured presses. At last, just as darkness crept over the grounds, Rosie popped some champagne, and we flopped down on the bed in the master bedroom. The room had hardwood floors, a wireframe bed and stone walls. It was particularly atmospheric and romantic; the girls joked that I was like an olden-day princess in a tower, awaiting my prince. We sipped our champagne and giggled over what a ridiculously luxurious experience this was. "You guys should sleep in here!" I said to the girls as I stood up from the double bed.

"No way! If we stay here, we're going to chat until morning. The bride needs to rest," Laura insisted.

We wore matching nightgowns with pink robes on top. We bought them while we were shopping for the dress. We even had enough time to personalise them and write *BK's Wedding* on the back. They were cliché but fun nonetheless.

"Oh, and don't you forget about that face mask," Rosie warned. "I want to see a smooth face in the morning."

"Yes, yes!" I said in a bored voice as I ushered both of them out. Rosie's skincare regimen for me was very strict and confusing. She didn't need to know that I wouldn't be following every step precisely.

A moment later, both of the girls were out the door, and I was left alone. I turned around, took a deep breath, and bit down my lower lip. I felt an awful wave of nausea and anxiousness pass through me. I was now prey to all my thoughts and worries about the day. It was all so surreal, like a piece from a broken dream. I wasn't sure if I was ever going to wake up from it, but frankly, I didn't want to. Suddenly, loud tapping at my window interrupted my train of thought. I frowned in fear, and my heart skipped a beat. I contemplated calling the girls back but decided against it. I had a feeling I knew who my mysterious, late-night visitor might be.

I walked towards the window and opened the curtains in one swift move, revealing Conor's eager face. His features were dimmed by the dark shadows of the night. But the glint of mischievousness in his eyes was unmistakable. I looked at the door and then back at him before my hands hurried to open the window.

"Finally!" he exclaimed as he hoisted himself inside the room. "I thought they'd never leave." He grabbed me by the waist and pulled me into a kiss. I was shocked to see him there, but even in my state of shock, my body responded instantly to the feeling of his lips on mine. The scene felt like it was from a romantic movie. I had to pinch myself.

"What are you doing here?" I asked when we finally pulled apart.

"I was too restless. I can't spend a night away from you," he confessed.

"But how did you get away from the boys?" I asked anxiously. "They were supposed to be on strict Conor Watch."

Conor laughed. "Let's just say the boys know how to take advantage of an open bar. They passed out pretty early. Not that I didn't encourage them a little..." He winked. "I just missed you so much." I couldn't help but laugh. Affectionately, my thumb brushed over his cheek.

"I missed you too," I said softly. "But they will call off the wedding if Rosie or Laura see you here."

"Don't I know that?" Conor sighed. "How about you lock the door? I can leave before sunrise."

I considered his proposal, then slowly pulled away from his embrace to lock the door.

#

It was after 2 a.m., and we still couldn't sleep. The nervous excitement and anticipation of our wedding felt like a drug coursing through our veins, making sleep impossible. Instead, we watched the full moon traverse the skies through the skylight above the bed.

"Maybe we should go for a walk," Conor whispered. "There's a hedge maze on the property that we could try to navigate."

I propped myself up on one shoulder so I could see him better. The mischievous look was back in his eyes.

"Aren't you afraid we'd get lost in there?" I asked. "Imagine if we missed our own wedding because we got lost in a hedge maze."

"I'd never be lost. Not as long as I'm with you, Miss Kennedy."

I grabbed a pair of runners from my bag and a long overcoat, which I threw over my nightie. This way, if the girls saw me leaving, I could claim I was just going outside for a breath of fresh air. Once we were both a safe distance from the house, we began to move decisively in the direction of the maze. We'd seen it on the website and in the brochures. On our tour, the owner had also pointed it out from a distance. It was just a few minutes' walk from the house, down by the lake. Finding our way there in the dark wasn't too difficult. We had the silvery light of the moon to guide us.

After several minutes of walking, we heard a splash and a rustle of wings as some bird took off from a body of water.

"We're close," Conor whispered.

Sure enough, within moments, we were standing in front of a large field and its neighbouring lake. In the middle of the field were rows of tall hedges. I knew that if we were to look at them from above, they would be arranged in an intricate pattern.

"Come on," Conor whispered, taking my hand. "Let's go."

As we slowly entered the maze, the sounds of the night became muffled by the thick hedges. The lights from the main house disappeared. Shadows surrounded us. Conor turned on his phone's torch to light our way. The place had an eerie feel to it, as though it were filled with magic. Only the stars and moonlight penetrated into its inner depths. Conor and I kept our hands clenched together. Instinctively, we moved slowly, following the bends and turns. To my surprise, it wasn't as hard to navigate as I had thought it would be. Whenever we went the wrong way, we immediately met a dead end and were able to turn back. As we walked further and further into the maze, the paths became wider. By the time we finally stumbled out into the centre, a large clearing awaited us. To our surprise, there was a stone statue standing in the middle of it.

Slowly, we approached the statue. Carved into it was the face of someone ancient and powerful. A Celtic god or goddess, perhaps. Maybe a wise Druid. Or a king. Whoever it was, when I looked at its face, I felt the same tingling sensation as when I stood in the stone circle. When I closed my eyes and listened, I heard the same ancient whispers.

Fear welled up inside of me. Had Conor been able to look into my heart, he would have seen a mountain of worry. I had to tell him what I knew; the coincidences were becoming too numerous. They were trying to tell me something. I had to listen. Conor needed to know what I knew. If I didn't tell him now, then when he did find out, he might never forgive me for keeping it from him. Of course, if I did tell him, it was very possible he would think I was crazy. Maybe he really would run for the hills. But I couldn't marry him without telling him what I knew now with utter certainty; that we had walked this earth together in a past life.

Conor was gazing at the statue with rapt attention when I turned to him. He noticed my glance and turned towards me, smiling.

"This place is so cool—" he began, but I cut him off.

"Conor, there's something I need to tell you."

"Okay." His eyebrows knit together as he took in my concern. "What is it?"

"I'm scared to tell you," I murmured. To my embarrassment, I realised that a few tears had rolled down my cheeks.

"You should never be scared to tell me anything," he said gently, resting his hand on my shoulder. "Whatever it is, we will work it out together."

The fear felt sickening. I stared into his eyes, sure that he could hear the racing of my heart. There was no way he wouldn't think I had lost my mind. And yet... if I didn't tell him, it would always feel like I was keeping something from him.

I took a deep breath. It was now or never. "There's something I've suspected for a while now," I began. "Dreams I've been having. I knew when I met you that something was different. The way we were so instantly drawn to one another was unlike anything I have experienced before or since."

"It was surreal," Conor agreed, nodding. "But what do you mean about your dreams?" He looked suddenly as nervous as I felt.

"I don't even know if they are dreams," I whispered. "They feel more like... memories."

With this last word, our eyes met. Conor stared at me. There was a look of both disbelief and recognition on his face. I wasn't sure what it meant.

"What kind of memories?" he asked softly.

"Memories of us," I whispered. "Memories of us from hundreds of years ago. I think—I *know*—that we have met before. In another life. Not just met. We were in love. We were engaged."

The silence that filled the air around us was thick with tension. I could have sliced through it with a knife. Conor and I gazed at each other. His face looked shocked. At any moment, I knew he would realise the gravity of my confession. Then he would start to back away.

His expression might be replaced by one of disgust. He would call me crazy. He would call off the wedding. He'd tell everyone I had lost my mind. He would leave me just like he had left me for Clontarf, and just like before, I would die again of a broken heart. I had to speak. I had to say something. Anything. Before I lost the love of my life. Again.

Desperation clawed at my insides. Why had I told him this? Was I really such an idiot that I would risk losing him over some dreams? I thought I would vomit. I started to shake violently. The scariest question of all loomed in front of me: was I destined to lose Conor in another lifetime?

He reached forward gently to steady me. His hands were warm and comforting. Then he spoke. His voice was very soft. I could hardly hear him, but he never took his eyes from mine. "And in these dreams—memories, was I killed at the Battle of Clontarf?"

I gasped. "How do you know that? Have I been talking in my sleep?" I wracked my memories, trying to remember if I had ever written down my suspicions in a place he might have accidentally found and read them.

Conor shook his head. "No, Bridget," he said, and his hands came to rest on my arms as he pulled me closer. "I know because I've had them too."

The relief that flooded through me felt like freedom. As I wrapped my arms around him, he took me in one of the deepest embraces of our entire relationship. In this kiss, I could see through time and space, to the edge of the cosmos and the outer limits of the beginning and end of the universe; in his arms, I was no longer afraid of the past, the present or the future. I was sure that no matter how long humans lived on this earth, he and I would find each other.

At long last, we pulled apart. Conor was crying. His tears lingered on my cheeks and mingled with my own.

"I wasn't sure what to tell you," he whispered. "The dreams have always been so hazy for me. I knew what they meant, but I wasn't always certain of the details."

"They were very clear to me. I can still see them when I close my eyes."

Conor laughed in wonder. "I can't tell you how relieved I am. I thought I was going insane!"

"So did I! I never believed in this kind of thing before. But from the first dream, I knew it was real."

"I knew from the moment we met," Conor said. He was smiling even as the tears fell down his cheeks. "When I met you, I felt as if my soul had met its other half. It was as if I had been going through the world with only part of myself. I didn't even know it was missing until I saw you in Waxies. But I didn't know what it meant. People talk about soulmates, but it felt deeper than that. Afterwards, I knew I had to see you again and understand what it was exactly that connected us. It was at the picnic at the standing stones that I knew for certain: we had shared a love before—before this lifetime." He traced my jawline with his thumb. "There is one thing I want to know, though," he said. "My memories... They end with the battle. With... with my death." He swallowed. "I was so scared at that moment, Bridget. Not of the Norsemen, or even for my King, but for you. I didn't want to leave you alone for the rest of your life. The fear of abandoning you was the strongest emotion, right before he killed me. So tell me... what happened to you?"

For half a moment, I wanted to lie to him; to tell him that I had lived long and well, that I had mourned him properly and told the stories of his great deeds to all who would listen. Instead, I lowered my eyes.

"I died too, Conor," I confessed. "I couldn't go on living without you. I watched myself slowly die of a broken heart shortly after you. Just before I died, I buried the emerald ring in the ground below the tallest of the standing stones."

Conor's eyes grew wide. "The ring I gave you before I left for Clontarf?"

"Yeah. And Conor... just before you surprised me with the gallery, I went back to the stones and dug it up."

From my pocket, I produced the emerald ring. As I held it up to Conor, the emerald glinted in the moonlight. Reverently, Conor reached for it and held it up to the light, his face awash in awe. After a long moment, he looked back down at me.

"This must be our secret," he said softly. "No one else needs to know. They won't understand."

"They won't," I agreed. "I won't tell anyone—not even the girls."

Conor raised an eyebrow with scepticism. I laughed.

"Some things are meant just for us," I teased. "For husband and wife."

Conor laughed, and then a solemn look came over his face.

"I need you to make a pledge to me, BK." His voice was suddenly intense. "And when you do, we will seal it with this ring. Okay?"

"Okay."

Conor took my hand in his. The moonlight spilt over our interlocked fingers as if blessing our ritual. "Bridget," he began, "I need you to pledge to me that should I ever be taken from you too soon, you will honour our love by living the happiest and fullest life possible. Even if, by some terrible act of fate, I die young again, my soul won't travel light knowing you are unhappy. I want you to have a happy life. Our connection goes across and beyond time. Will you promise me this?

Love, fear, grief and hope welled up inside of me until I thought I would burst. Then all the pain of both our lifetimes seemed to wash out of me as I felt his promise envelop me. It was like a warm blanket being draped over my shoulders. With tears rushing down my cheeks, I nodded.

"I promise, Conor. I promise."

Reverently, he slipped the emerald ring onto my ring finger. It fit snugly next to my engagement ring.

"And I promise you," he said. "It will be us forever. Until the end of time."

Chapter Fifty-Two

SEALED KNOT

As I stood outside the chapel door, the sweet and delicate strains of music began to play. The harp's tinkling notes danced through the air like the sound of summer rain drops dancing on crystal chimes. The beautiful melody resonated through the entire chapel and outside to where I stood. In a few moments, the harpist would begin to play 'Tabhair Dom Do Lámh - Give Me Your Hand'. This would be our signal to proceed into the chapel. And so, with anticipation and joy in my heart, I would walk down the aisle towards Conor.

Around me, tall pines swayed as if whispering amongst themselves. The branches swished softly against each other. Their needles looked vibrant green against the soft blue sky. The wind felt calm and gentle. It coaxed a strand of hair out of place that tickled my cheek. I tucked it slowly behind my ear.

The day was glorious. I couldn't have asked for better weather. Warm sunlight glinted off droplets of morning dew from the chapel roof, creating showers of light and tiny rainbows. I watched the colours spiral and pirouette in the air. They seemed to twirl and sway in perfect harmony with the melodious notes of the harp. In this enchanting moment the serenity of the scene enveloped me, calming my anxious heart as an overwhelming stillness settled upon me.

Outside the chapel, we waited in a line. Rosie, Laura, little Heather, and Jimi, anxiously awaiting for the harpist to begin playing our chosen song. The tin chapel, adorned with bistro lights, emanated a warm glow even in the daylight. Whispers could be heard from within, as guests took their seats and rustled their clothing. All eyes would soon be on me as I entered. Thoughts of Conor provided the strength to keep me from fainting. He was my rock, ensuring my safety. The sight of him would make all my nerves vanish. I wondered if he, too, felt the same nervousness. With my veil covering my face, I hoped it concealed the tears in my eyes. My hands trembled, and my heart raced, thumping against my chest. Nervousness consumed me, making it difficult to even breathe. Yet, I remained focused on standing tall, knowing I wouldn't be upright without the support of my father. He stood steadfastly beside me, overwhelmed and silent as I was.

"Are you nervous?" he asked as he squeezed my hand gently.

"Are you joking?" I said. "I can't even breathe."

My dad laughed, but I could tell that he wasn't as relaxed as he let on. "You never did like to be the centre of attention. That man of yours, though, he's used to being in the spotlight."

"Maybe that's why we fit together so well," I said with a small smile. "We balance each other out."

"I reckon you do," he said with another laugh. "Never seen two people so perfectly suited, if truth be told. You shouldn't be nervous. The guy waiting for you on the other end of the aisle loves you. I hate to admit it, but he is worthy of my Bridget."

"I know he is. Sometimes I wonder if I'm worthy of him."

My dad was about to answer, but he never got to; before his lips even managed to part, the harp echoed through the air. The music stirred something deep inside me. It wasn't that my nervousness went away, but at the first wavering notes, a more powerful feeling emerged. I was overjoyed. This was happening. I was about to marry the love of my life.

I was standing at the back of the procession. At the very front was little Heather. She looked adorable in her cream-coloured dress and a beautiful emerald tiara. Her red ringlets bobbed up and down every time she moved her head, shimmering in the light. In one hand, she held a basket of rose petals. In the other, she gripped Jimi's leash. For once, our puppy was behaving perfectly. It was as if he knew what a momentous occasion this was and was on his best behaviour. On our special day, Jimi had an important role to play as our ring bearer. We had attached a pillow to his collar and sewn our wedding bands onto the pillow. Once we were up at the altar, Rosie had a small pair of scissors in her handbag that she would use to cut them loose.

The girls turned to look at me, and I smiled, silently encouraging them to go on. Rosie was already in a flood of tears. Fortunately, she'd thought ahead and had put all three of us in waterproof makeup. Even as tears streamed freely down her cheeks, her mascara, eyeshadow and eyeliner remained perfectly in place. There wasn't even a smudge of black beneath her eyes. Rosie gave me a watery smile and nodded. Then she turned to little Heather and gave her shoulder a squeeze.

"You're up, girlie," she said, and Heather beamed at her. Slowly, Heather started walking, Jimi leading the way. Rosie and Laura followed after her. One after the other, they walked up the aisle. Every step I took felt right. I didn't hesitate for even one moment. Every cell and every fibre in my body knew that walking towards Conor was the best thing that I would ever do.

When my dad and I entered the chapel, everyone turned to look at us. Just like I had imagined, the moment made me feel temporarily weak-kneed. Dad squeezed my hand and stood up a little straighter. It was a subtle movement, but I knew it was his way of telling me that he was supporting me; he wouldn't let me stumble. Together, we began to move down the aisle. It was lined with rose petals from little Heather's basket. At the front of the aisle, I saw her throw her last handful of petals. Then she led Jimi to the front row, where she sat next to her mum.

There were rows of guests on each side of me, mostly family members I hadn't seen in ages and friends who had been there for us since day one. I caught sight of Ciara Breen and Festival Frank near the back, grinning broadly. Further up, my staff were all together, smiling from ear to ear. Halfway down the aisle, Michael caught my eye. My heart jumped with joy. He hadn't been sure he could make it home from New York to the wedding, and to see him there filled me with happiness. Michael was standing arm-in-arm with a man I had never met before. The stranger was wearing a flamboyant velvet suit, a bow tie and cat eyeglasses. He smiled sweetly as Michael widened his eyes at me and then nodded towards the man. I almost laughed. Even at my wedding, as I was walking down the aisle, Michael was making this about himself. But I didn't care. Michael had brought a man to my wedding; after so many years of hiding, he wasn't afraid anymore. If this is how he wanted to introduce us—well, that was exactly what I would expect. I sent him a big smile back, and he shot me a thumbs-up. Suppressing a laugh, I turned my attention back towards the task at hand. There, right up front, my mum was sitting next to Conor's family. She was wearing a large, elegant fascinator and clutching a hankie. Tears rolled down her cheeks as she shed more tears of joy for both her daughter and herself. I smiled at her and then looked away before I started crying myself.

Finally, my gaze settled on Conor, and tears welled up inside me. He stood in front of the altar beneath the origami cranes, his expression was filled with an indescribable intensity. My heart skipped a beat as I absorbed the emotions etched across his face. When our eyes met,

Conor smiled, and the cranes above danced in the sunlight, their wings fluttering and beaks lifted as if in song. In that moment, I realised they were a tangible representation of our love, infusing the room with vibrant colours and radiant light. Love has a profound impact, not only making our lives more joyful but also influencing everyone around us. It exemplified our partnership that was nurturing, caring, and giving. Conor's love provided me with confidence and acceptance, enabling me to be a better friend, artist, businesswoman, boss, and daughter. By selflessly caring for those I loved, I was able to help them become better individuals in their own relationships. The more love we give, whether to our partners, friends, or family, the more love we spread throughout the world.

Next to Conor stood the lads. They looked transported with joy. James' eyes were shining, and I saw them rest for a long time on Rosie. Conor and his groomsmen were in well-tailored navy suits that made them look particularly sharp. There was no one I'd rather see next to Conor than the boys from Ocrás, who had stood by him through thick and thin, who loved him like a brother. As my dad and I approached, Donal slapped a hand on Conor's shoulder. James wiped away a tear.

A moment later, my dad and I came to a stop in front of Conor. They shook hands. My dad whispered something in my groom's ear, something that was surely a threat, and then he gave him my hand.

That is the moment I will never forget, for nothing was as meaningful as my father entrusting me to Conor. He kissed my cheek, and I could swear I felt a tear run down his face. I then turned away from the man who had raised me and towards the one who would be by my side for the rest of my life.

When Conor lifted my veil, all my nervousness melted away. The brief touch of his fingers on my face made my heart melt. He leaned in and kissed my forehead. His lips lingered there for a second, and then he pulled away, but not before he whispered:

"Mo cuishle! You look so beautiful!"

As he said this, the harpist played the final, wavering notes. Together, we turned to face the celebrant. He smiled, then lifted his arms in welcome.

"Please be seated," he boomed out to the congregation. The celebrant was someone we'd found through the Humanist Association of Ireland. We didn't want a priest. Although we were raised Catholic, we both felt more connected to the spirituality of the people who had built the standing stones. My mum hadn't been pleased when we told her we weren't using a priest, but she'd accepted it.

"Welcome, friends and family, loved ones from near and far," the celebrant, Daniel, began, "to the wedding of Conor O'Neill and Bridget Kennedy. We have all gathered here today to witness the commitment that these two young people have made to one another. Some of us have travelled vast distances. Many have known the couple from before they even knew each other. What unites us all is their love and their promise to live faithfully and truly for one another."

The tears had already begun. One rolled down my cheek, thankfully away from the onlookers. I looked up at Conor and saw that his eyes were gleaming as well. Daniel looked kindly at us before resuming his speech.

"Conor and Bridget met just twelve months ago, but their bond was immediate and profound. They knew, from the moment that they set eyes on one another, that they were destined for each other. As a celebrant, I often hear about love at first sight, but when I sat down with Bridget and Conor to discuss this ceremony, I was struck by the intensity of their first meeting. Both spoke eloquently and passionately about the mysterious force that drew them to one another. Both used the word 'fate'. After half an hour talking to this young couple, I was left in no doubt that their love really was written in the stars." Several people in the wedding party, including Laura, giggled.

Everyone who knew us knew the intensity of our first attraction. Many were probably remembering now how obsessive those early days had felt. It was true, too, that Daniel had been surprised when we told him the way we felt after our first meeting. It hadn't taken long to convince him of our sincerity. He was a romantic, after all, and a mystic. He wore lots of Celtic jewellery and played the bodhrán. He'd been in bands all his life and had toured all over the world, just like Conor. After living in Australia for many years, he returned to Ireland to do a Research PhD at Trinity in Irish and Celtic Studies. Studying his pagan ancestry inspired him to become a celebrant for alternative Irish weddings.

"These two are meant for each other," Daniel continued now. "Their care, respect, and devotion to one another is an example to all those around them. As they go forward in their relationship, they will meet many difficulties, as most couples do. But they will weather these storms with the kindness, understanding, and humility with which they always treat each other."

Conor squeezed my hand. When I looked at him, he gave me a bittersweet smile. I knew he was thinking about Amanda and all the trouble she had caused. I squeezed his hand back. Daniel was right. We could weather any storm as long as we had each other.

As Daniel continued to tell the story of how we met, I found myself thinking about our past life. It was funny to listen to Daniel describe our meeting at Waxies as if it were our first. Conor and I both knew better. My mind drifted to 1014 and our handfasting ceremony inside the standing stones. Suddenly, it struck me that the details of how we met in that life remained elusive. The dreams had failed to unveil that crucial piece of the puzzle. Perhaps, the premonition of the children chasing after the rabbit on that fateful night when I found the ring, held some significance. It would have to become my mission, over the next few years, to track down as much information as I could about who we'd been in the 11th century. Maybe then, we could start to piece together the whole of our love story. We could write it down; ensure that our children and their children knew the full story. Maybe, when we met in the next life, we could find this manuscript and continue to add to it. I looked at Conor, and he smiled back. His hand traced over the spot on my finger where he had slipped the emerald ring the night before. I knew he was also thinking about our past and future.

"Bridget, are you ready to read your vows?" Daniel asked. He was looking at me expectantly. I hadn't realised we had gotten so far into the ceremony. I laughed, nodded, and turned to Rosie. She snapped open her handbag and pulled out the piece of paper on which I'd written my vows. I unfolded it. My vows were mostly memorised, but I'd brought along a copy just in case. Conor and I faced each other. He grasped one of my hands tightly. Daniel then brought out a braided green ribbon, the colour of the emerald ring. He wound the ribbon around our hands, binding us together like in an ancient Celtic handfasting ritual. It was the one thing Conor and I had both insisted on.

"Conor," I began. Immediately, a lump came to my throat. I took a deep breath and tried to calm myself. Clearing my throat, I began again. "Conor. I never believed in soulmates until I met you. How crazy is it that there's only one person for you in the world, and if you don't find them, you're out of luck?" Behind me, some of the guests laughed. Conor grinned as well, and I felt my confidence surge. "It didn't seem real. Then I met you, and I knew at once that we were meant to be. I can't describe what it felt like to find you. I'm not a wordsmith like you, but I'll try. With you, I feel as if a part of me that was missing has been found. I didn't even know it was lost. But now that I've found you, I could never be without you. You complete me. There's a lot I want to promise you. Some promises I've already made." Conor grinned, and I knew we were both thinking about the hedge maze last night. "But in front of everyone we love, I want to make you this promise: I will cherish you throughout all the versions of us. We may change, even to the point where we feel like different people." Conor raised an eyebrow, probably wondering if I was going to give anything away, and I smiled coyly. "But no matter who we become, where we go, and what awaits us, I will love you with my heart. I promise this. You are the one I have always searched for, and I will never stop loving you."

My vows were like my own confession booth. They were my opportunity to declare my love in all its aspects, not just to Conor but to everyone present who mattered and cared. It had been difficult to write about the way I felt. I wasn't sure I had succeeded until I looked back up at Conor. Tears were flowing freely down his cheeks. In the pews, I heard several sniffles and someone blowing their nose. I knew if I looked at the girls, I'd see them crying. Through his tears, Conor took out his own vows. James leaned forward and passed him a handkerchief, which he used to dry his eyes. Then he smiled at me, kissed my hand, and began to read:

"Bridget, before you, my songs were empty vessels. They were my perception of love from stories, poetry and Irish legends. I didn't know how love really felt. After you walked into my life, it all started to make sense. My lyrics became my story; my music became my feelings."

Conor took in a deep breath and thought for a moment. His hands were shaky, much like his voice.

"The love I hold for you is so great that it is often so overwhelming. I have to get it out, to express it, to tell it to the world. I know that you're the reason why Orcás has taken off recently, because, at last, I have my soulmate. My love for you is so big that it will last an eternity. No matter where life takes us, you better find me because I can't even breathe when you're not around." He laughed. "Bridget, I promise I'll be there for you. I swear, that as long as you want me, I'll be your shadow, your air, and your water. I will smile and laugh and cry and scream with you until this world ceases to exist."

I was crying now. There was no point holding it in; his words pierced right through my heart. Through the blurry tears, I saw our celebrant Daniel smiling. He raised his hands into the air as if calling down a blessing from above.

"I now pronounce you husband and wife," Daniel declared. "You may kiss the bride."

At these words, the uilleann pipes kicked in. We'd hired a piper called Andrew that Conor knew and trusted just for this moment. As Conor pulled me closer, the bright, happy sound of the pipes filled the chapel. Conor's eyes shined with happiness as he leaned down to kiss me. My eyelids closed as he brought his lips to my ear.

"My wife," he whispered so that only I could hear. Then he kissed me in a tender embrace. It was a gentle kiss, sweet and full of love, a kiss that told me he would cherish and protect me for all our days. As we broke apart, people cheered and clapped. James whooped loudly.

"My husband," I whispered back, tracing his cheek with my fingertips. His smile was radiant as he gazed into my eyes. We were husband and wife now, for all time. I couldn't have imagined a more perfect moment.

#

The wedding reception was a night to remember. First, we gathered in the boathouse, where Conor and I stood in the receiving line. We got to greet and hug everyone who had made the journey for our wedding. It was particularly heart-warming to hug Michael and be introduced to his boyfriend, Jason. Last in the line were my parents. They hugged Conor tightly and then me. My mum was still crying, but my dad had a pint in hand already and looked ready to party.

We'd planned an epic night. Conor and I had settled on a 1920s Gatsby theme. We wanted people to dance and have fun. I'd chosen the canapes that waiters passed around on silver trays while Conor had picked the music. He'd chosen a large swing band for the night that would give the celebration a roaring twenties feel. Conor had worked with them to craft a timeless setlist, incorporating classics and more modern hits. As the last of the guests moved from the receiving line to the bar, the band trooped in. All the members were dressed elegantly in black suits. The female singer looked magnificent in a glittering black flapper dress, bright pink lipstick, and '20s-style coiffed hair.

Before dancing, I changed into the white flapper dress that I had bought for the occasion. It had thin spaghetti straps and delicate beading that cascaded down its front. The pristine white colour let everyone know that while I might not be in my wedding dress, I was still the bride.

When I came out from the changing rooms, Rosie and Laura screamed with delight at my dress.

"You look exactly like a flapper!" Laura screeched.

"That's the idea!" I laughed. "Did you see the drinks menu?"

We'd picked out a custom cocktail menu that reflected the Gatsby-style party we wanted. The drinks had names like The Bootlegged Martini, The Gatsby, the Speakeasy Sazerac, Daisy's Daiquiri, and the Old (Boy) Fashioned. There were also such 1920s classics as the Tom Collins, Clover Club, and French 75.

"It's adorable!" Rosie gushed. "I love the art deco design on the menus!"

"That's thanks to us!" Sami had materialised at my side holding two Speakeasy Sazeracs. She placed one into my hand. "For the bride!" she squealed.

"You put this together?" Rosie asked.

"Bridget said Gatsby, so we made it happen!" Sami beamed. "We are professional event planners, after all."

"Well, it looks great!" Laura smiled.

The band started to play a slower song. Then the singer spoke into the microphone.

"Ladies and gentlemen," she began, "for their first dance together as a married couple, please put your hands together for Conor and Bridget O'Neill!"

A spotlight came on and washed me in light. I turned to stare in the direction of the second light and saw Conor. He had added a fedora, a cane and two-toned spectators to his ensemble. They gave him the perfect roaring twenties look. He was standing in the middle of the dancefloor; his hand held out towards me.

"My beautiful wife," he said gallantly. "Would you do me the honour of accepting this dance?"

We practised this moment many times. In one swift movement, I threw back the sazerac. Then I set it on the bar and strode across the dance floor. Delicately, I set my hand into his. For a moment, we swayed on the spot, staring into each other's eyes. Then Conor dipped me low. A mischievous look glinted in his eyes. As he lifted me out of the dip, the music suddenly became fast and raucous. Conor and I sprang to action. We'd worked with a swing instructor called Ian to choreograph this dance perfectly. As the horns of the band blared, we flawlessly executed the spins and turns. Everyone was clapping and cheering. Those who dared to try swing stepped out onto the dancefloor to join us. Suddenly it was full of people. Conor laughed and twirled me closer, then grabbed me up under my arms to lift me into the air. With apparent ease, he lifted me high up off the dance floor. Then he brought me down around his waist, my legs on either side, just like we'd rehearsed. I heard "oohs" and "aahs" from the crowd around us. We'd worked hard at this, and I was delighted that we'd pulled it off. Pink-faced from the exertion, I spun away from him and then back into his arms. Finally, the last notes sounded from the trumpets, and Conor kissed me.

Around us, everyone burst into applause. Conor lifted my hand up into the air in triumph. I was laughing. Sweat streamed down my back. It was the most fun I'd ever had.

Fortunately, a slower song came on next. Conor pulled me close and wrapped his arms around my waist. Our foreheads came together, and both our eyelids closed as we swayed gently on the spot. The music was lush and romantic. My head felt dizzy, and my heart full of love. I couldn't believe that this was my wedding day, that I was married to

Conor. We would grow old together, raise a family, perhaps. We had our whole future stretching ahead of us. Knowing we'd be together forever made me feel calm and unafraid. I could face anything as long as I had Conor by my side.

The feeling of love overwhelmed us as we kissed. He opened his eyes and smiled.

"What are you thinking about, Bridget?" he whispered in my ear.

"I'm thinking, is this all a dream?" I gently traced my hand along his face. "And if it is, can I never wake up?"

Conor laughed. "Maybe you are dreaming." He kissed me passionately, then hooked his finger around the thin chain that I was wearing around my neck. The emerald ring hung from the end of it, hidden under the front of my dress. Conor kissed the ring delicately before tucking it back. "Maybe we both are." I laughed softly and curled my fingers through his hair. Conor looked serious and thoughtful. He stared into my eyes and said, "We are nothing but stardust, mo cuishle. The dreams of the slumbering universe. Our lives are outside of time. Both endless and still. A recurring cycle into infinity. That's how I know we will always find each other."

ACKNOWLEDGMENTS

Writing a novel is never a solitary endeavour; it is the result of countless individuals who offer their support, opinions, encouragement, and expertise along the way. I would like to express my heartfelt gratitude to the following people:

I am indebted to my close circle of friends, Richard Sapsford, Anikiko, Mark Browne, Dave Wilks and Sharon Kelly, for their unwavering support, understanding, and countless hours of brainstorming sessions. Your creative input and constructive feedback have been invaluable.

I would also like to acknowledge the assistance and encouragement of Indira Hnatiuk, Sine Santamaría-Falls, Niko Nikolas, Patrice McCauley, Peter Nawn, Tracy Kerr, Katie Kelly, Emma-Rose Kelly, Chris McCrombie, Andrew Beattie, Frank McKenna, Anne McKenna, James McKendry, Marcus Holden, Siobhán Mackey, Guyy Lilleyman and Rowan Diamond, who provided valuable insights and inspired me to push beyond my limits.

Also a special shout out to Jimi, my furry friend.

Thank you for your camaraderie and for the countless hours spent workshopping and refining together.

Last but not least, I am grateful to my readers. Your kind words, enthusiasm, and unwavering support have provided me with the motivation to keep writing throughout this journey.

Thank you, each and every one of you, for being a part of Diary of a Galway Girl. I am forever grateful for your love, support, and contributions.

Kevin Kelly

Hailing from the stunning landscapes of Ballinascreen County Derry in Ireland, Kevin Kelly, has a deep connection to the land's enchanting beauty, folklore, music and rich history. This connection serves as a constant source of inspiration for his writing, and in Diary of a Galway Girl, Kelly transports his readers on a mystical journey through the serene and magical beauty of the Emerald Isle.

Throughout this vivid and romantic tale about handsome singer – Conor – and the pretty, yet reserved event manager and artist – Bridget – Kelly's vivid descriptions of their passionate love affair and surroundings brings the story to life. You can touch the stone circles they visit, you can smell the sweet scent of flowers they pick and taste the delicious food they enjoy. With a pacey storytelling style, Kelly captures the true essence of Irish charm, effortlessly blending the ancient and modern aspects of this captivating land.

However, Kelly is not just a writer; he is also a talented musician with over three decades of performances, also playing and teaching the Bodhrán, Ireland's traditional drum. His deep love for Irish music and songwriting shines through his work, and it was his heartfelt love song, Cupid's Arrow, that inspired the creation of Diary of a Galway Girl. Alongside his creative endeavours, Kelly is the founder of www. BodhranWorld.com, a platform dedicated to sharing his passion for the Bodhrán and connecting with fellow enthusiasts.

www.ingramcontent.com/pod-product-compliance
Lightning Source LLC
Chambersburg PA
CBHW072351030726
47505CB00014B/1460